HOW DARE SHE COME TO HIS BED?

A cool, logical part of his mind warned that a clever woman in Jehanne's situation would make swift moves to reestablish herself with her husband.

Galeran seemed to be split into three separate parts, though, and the cool, logical part was only one.

The second part was the man who loved Jehanne of Heywood too deeply for prudence.

The third part was an animal, consumed by scarce-contained lust for this woman.

She slid down to join him in the bed, stripping off her kirtle at the last moment. She would have covered herself, but he held the sheet away.

So she surrendered to his eyes.

THE SHATTERED ROSE

Jo Beverley

ZEBRA BOOKS
KENSINGTON PUBLISHING CORP.

ZEBRA BOOKS are published by

Kensington Publishing Corp.
850 Third Avenue
New York, NY 10022

First Printing: May, 1996
10 9 8 7 6 5 4 3 2 1

Printed in the United States of America

One

Northumbria, England, July 1100

The troop of armed men rode steadily along the rough, wooded road, each heavy hoof-fall spraying mud over already muddy beasts. Travel-worn and weary, they pressed on as inexorably as a river heading for the sea.

Motley patches scattered blowing cloaks, and wind whipped through ragged holes that had not been patched at all. Under dirt and mud, little could distinguish man from master, but three things set two men apart.

They rode better horses.

They wore chain mail beneath the cloaks.

And while their men carried bow or spear, each of these two bore a well-used sword at his side and a shield on his saddle.

The lighter-built of the two men raised a hand and reined in. Without further word, the other eight swung down toward the nearby river to rest and water the horses.

As they dismounted, it could be seen that some limped, and one man had only a stump where his right hand used to be. The leader's haggard face bore a puckered burn mark on the forehead and a blade scar along the jaw, made obvious because the stubble did not grow well around it.

These were men just back from war, and the darkness of their skin suggested they had fought in lands far hotter than this northern corner of England. In fact, faded and obscured by dirt, a red cross remained on some of the cloaks.

These men had been upon the Enterprise of God. They were crusaders.

Perhaps they had seen the Jordan, where Christ was baptized, and Jerusalem, where he suffered and died. They had likely waded through the rivers of blood that flowed through the streets of the Holy City when the Christian forces finally claimed it.

The leader dismounted, stretched, then pushed back his chain mail coif to shake loose damp, shaggy brown hair. It was clear nature had never intended him to be a big man, but now he was fined down to muscle and sinew, his dark eyes sunk deep beneath dark brows.

Galeran of Heywood shivered under the chill of the North Sea breeze on his sweaty nape, but it was a pleasant chill— an English chill. He was in England, and before sunset he would be home.

After more than two long years, he would be home.

The previous day they'd landed at Stockton in a mizzling rain that had set Galeran's companion, Raoul de Jouray, shuddering and wondering that anyone could call such weather summer. Galeran, however, had welcomed it. There'd been many times these past two years when he'd feared he would never feel damp again, never ride through an English morning mist, never touch ice or see the vibrant green growth fostered by the rainy English climate.

He had thought he would die in the searing heat of Outremer.

They could have spent the night in Stockton. In fact, they could have lingered there a twelvemonth, and never paid for board or lodging except with stories of their holy adventures. For Galeran's haste to be home meant they were the first crusaders to be seen in the area.

Galeran, however, had stopped in the port just long

enough to buy horses, then had pushed on, heading, like a hart to water, home.

To Jehanne, his beloved wife.

And to his son—a son he had never seen, born nine months after he left for Jerusalem. A son who was both reason for taking the cross, and reason to regret it. And reason to stay even when the bloodshed sickened him. For Galeran had gone on crusade to beg God for a child, and God in His love had been kind.

Jehanne had called the child Galeran, but said in her first letter after the birth that he would be called Gallot, at least while he was little. Gallot had surely been conceived on their last night together, after Galeran had taken the cross and made his vow to free Jerusalem from the heathen or to die in the attempt.

Gallot, his firstborn son, now eighteen months old and doubtless walking, but without any knowledge of his father. That was a bitter sacrifice, but necessary. Christ had never said that his yoke would be easy. . . .

It was only when John Redbeard, his sergeant, took Galeran's restive mount to walk it that he realized he'd been daydreaming instead of taking proper care of the beast. It was part tiredness, for they'd ridden through most of the last night, but it was also the grip of his need to be home with his wife and child.

He'd joined the crusade for one reason only, to break the curse of their childlessness, but he'd never dreamed that Christ's reward would be so prompt. That generosity, however, had bound Galeran as if with iron chains. How could he flinch from the task of liberating the Holy City when God had granted his boon so quickly and so perfectly?

Through all the hardship and disillusion, sickened by what he saw around him and longing to be home, Galeran had held to his vow. Because of that miracle—a child for Jehanne—he had fought on till the bitter, triumphant end, till the forces of Christendom had entered Jerusalem.

As always, that memory seized him, froze him with a vision of blood, rivers of blood, and the screaming mouths of men, women, and children. . . .

He shook his head. That was long past and over, and soon he would have his reward—his son in his arms, and his wife content at last.

He wished he'd had more news, so he would have a better picture in his mind of the child. The last letter to reach him had been written when the babe was three months old. Jehanne had recounted a screed of description and clever doings, but that chubby babe was gone now, and presumably smiling was no longer a matter of pride. The bald head Jehanne had lamented would be covered with hair. Dark like his own? Or pale, silky blond like his mother's?

Which?

It seemed a father should know.

That letter had arrived just as Galeran was riding off to help liberate Bethlehem, and when he had knelt on the ground of Christ's birthplace he had been guiltily aware that his joy at being there was largely because they were close to Jerusalem. Within days they would see the walls of the Holy City. With God's help they would quickly take it, and Galeran's vow would be satisfied.

He could return home.

From the moment of taking sail, all he had wanted was to be home.

Gallot had Galeran's brown eyes. That had been fixed at three months. With luck, he'd inherited his father's darker skin as well or he'd never be able to take the cross. Jehanne's delicate pallor would have blistered to a crisp in Outremer, as many northern complexions had.

Gallot wouldn't be big unless he threw back to the grandparents. Jehanne's father had been a tall man, and Galeran's father was a great bear of a man, a fearsome warrior in his day. All his sons had taken after him except Galeran.

A light build was a disadvantage in a fighting man, but

training could compensate, as Galeran had proved. Anyway, smaller men were often more agile, and big, fleshy men had perished more quickly in the heat and privation of the crusade than the sinewy ones. . . .

"You can't live on dreams, you know."

Galeran turned to see Raoul offering a mutton pie. "Eat. Your lovely wife won't welcome a scarecrow." Raoul was one of the big men, but hard with muscle and seemingly able to survive anything, appetites and good humor intact.

"She'll welcome me in any form," Galeran said, but when he bit into the cold pie he realized he was hungry. And he might need his strength.

He hoped he would need his strength.

Tonight.

At the thought of the night and a bed and Jehanne, a ripple of painful desire shot through him to land predictably in his cock and harden it.

"How close are we?" Raoul shot a long stream of wine into his mouth from a wineskin, then passed it over.

Galeran tilted the skin and drank, subduing his lust, as he had done a thousand times before. "Less than ten leagues. With God's blessing we should arrive before dark."

Raoul grinned. "With your impatience, we'll push on even if darkness falls. Not that I blame you. If I'd taken a vow of fidelity and was within sniffing distance of my wife, nothing would stop me either."

"The very thought of you taking a vow of fidelity makes my head ache, my friend. Perhaps interest in carnal matters fades after time."

"Does it?"

Galeran laughed. "No."

"Didn't think so. So, let's press on. We don't want you to explode." He bellowed to the men to prepare the horses.

Still smiling, Galeran took time to finish the pie, grateful to have Raoul by his side. His friend was by no means stupid, but he had an uncomplicated view of life. He fought fiercely when he had to, but then put it out of his head. Galeran fought fiercely when he had to, but he agonized over each death, particularly over the deaths of innocents.

In Jerusalem, even the children had fought. And died. . . .

Again he pushed such thoughts out of his head. They did no good, no good at all.

Raoul ate when he was hungry, drank when he was thirsty, and used women when he felt the need. He reminded Galeran to eat and drink, and teased him about his celibacy. "Everyone knows it's harmful for a man to store his seed," he had argued.

"Monks survive."

"God gives them a special blessing."

"Then I'd think God would give the same blessing to crusaders."

"But we're not pledged to celibacy. God knows it would weaken us."

"Are you saying I'm weak?"

Raoul had laughed, for, shorter and lighter, Galeran could often beat him in armed combat. At wrestling Raoul had the edge, but Galeran could still hold his own.

Raoul was another of God's blessings. They'd met in the service of Duke Robert and, despite their different natures, instantly taken to each other. The unlikely friendship had saved Galeran's sanity, and probably his life.

Born and raised in the balmy lands of southern France, Raoul had taken the cross for adventure, not blessings. As far as Galeran could tell, he'd found no spiritual meaning in visiting the land where Christ once walked. When they'd liberated Bethlehem, Raoul had not knelt on the ground, but looked around at the small houses cluttered with poultry, goats, and grubby children and remarked that he'd expected the Lord's birthplace to be somewhat grander.

Having seen that Jerusalem, too, was just a city, Raoul had been happy enough to return to Europe. It was clear, however, that his main purpose in returning so quickly was to take care of his friend.

Perhaps out of guilt.

At the end of the taking of Jerusalem, finally revolted by the slaughter, Galeran had tried to defend a bunch of boys from a group of German knights. The children had been armed only with sticks and slingshots, but they'd been dangerous nevertheless, fighting with the same ferocity as their fathers. It was sensible to kill them, insane to get involved, but Galeran had been ready to die there by their side.

Raoul had stopped him, knocking him senseless and dragging him away. It had taken days for him to get his wits back, so it wasn't surprising that Raoul had been concerned. Sometimes Galeran thought that he'd not wanted to get his wits back and remember those children. . . .

Any ill effects of the blow had worn off long since, but Raoul was being proved right about the lust. If the horses could go without rest, Galeran would never stop, and he never ate without prompting. He shook his head and instructed himself to be sensible. Getting lost in heated daydreams was more likely to delay his arrival than speed it.

He tightened his horse's girth and checked the dun gelding. He'd not taken time to seek out ideal horses, but this one seemed to be fair enough.

Satisfied, he mounted and pulled up his coif.

Raoul rode over to his side, tawny hair still uncovered. "Do you expect trouble here? There's been no sign of unrest."

Galeran shrugged and pushed the chain hood back again. "I suppose not, though King William does not keep an orderly realm, and we're close to the Scottish lands."

Raoul scanned the area. Here by the river, trees softened the landscape, but to the west and north lay sweeping moorland made sullen by the cloudy day. "It's hard to imagine anyone wanting this place. You warned me, my friend, but I didn't expect something quite so . . . bleak."

"I gather it was somewhat less bleak before it was fought over in 'sixty-eight."

Raoul grimaced. "I don't think fighting caused the climate."

Galeran laughed. "I suppose not. The sun does shine sometimes, I promise." He urged his horse up the slope to the road. "And you're right. We're safe enough. If the Scots were bold enough to raid hereabouts, my father and brothers would drive them back with their tails between their legs."

Raoul joined him, and they went forward at a walk to ease the horses. "Your father's castle is close by our road?"

"Yes."

"That's good. We can get a proper meal."

"Do you think of nothing but food?"

"Someone has to."

"Well, hungry or not, we ride by."

Raoul stared at him. "After two years abroad?"

"I can hardly stop, gobble a hunk of beef, and leave, can I? And I intend to be home today. I'll do the happy family reunion another time."

After a moment, Raoul said, "Have you thought that it might be a shock, you just showing up at your gate?"

Galeran looked sideways. "Oh, is that it? You want me to stop at Brome and send a polite message to warn Jehanne to air the mattress?"

"It might be a—"

"No."

Raoul shrugged with a rattle of mail. "So be it, but if your wife falls into a dead faint at your feet, don't blame me."

"Jehanne never faints."

"The Lady Jehanne has probably never had a husband turn up from nowhere before. You should have written from Bruges."

"What point, when a letter would travel no faster than I?"

"When *did* you last write? Will she have any idea to expect you?"

"Before Jerusalem." And Galeran kicked the dun up to speed before his startled friend could ask more questions.

He'd written regularly on the way out, sending letters from Rome, Cyprus, and Antioch. After the horrors of Jerusalem, however, he'd not been able to write anything to anyone. He'd concentrated blindly on getting home. Without Raoul's help he might not have made it, and in order to keep going he had blocked out all thought except his goal.

Heywood, Jehanne, and his son.

It hadn't occurred to him until now that for Jehanne there would have been a silence of over a year. In a way, he'd expected her to know where he was and what he was doing without being told.

But Jehanne wouldn't faint. She hadn't fainted when told she had to marry him. She hadn't fainted when they'd been attacked by brigands and one of her attendants had died before her eyes. Those were probably the two most shocking events in her life.

Then he remembered the boar.

But she hadn't fainted then, either.

They'd been in the woods making love. Yes, making love—for in those early days it had seemed to him that each joyous coupling had added love to the world.

Jehanne had liked to make love in the open. She found the idea of someone interrupting them exciting rather than embarrassing. A boar, however, was rather more than either of them had counted on, and it came upon them at a miserable time.

Jehanne was on top and Galeran was close to release. Then she was gone, and when Galeran gathered together the scraps of his shattered mind, he found her straddled over him, his heavy sword in her small hands. "Hell's flames, Galeran. Get your brain out of your cock and kill the beast! Or do I have to do it myself?"

There'd been many a time when he'd wished he'd said "Go ahead" and watched her have to beg.

She wouldn't have begged, though.

Jehanne never begged.

She'd have tried. She might even have succeeded. Jehanne was tall for a woman, which had not best pleased him as a youth. Though slender, she was strong. Of course, she wouldn't have been able to kill a boar with a sword—that was a difficult feat for a skillful man—but she would have tried.

Perhaps the boar knew it. Unusually for that animal, it had backed away and fled, perhaps dismayed by the tall, white-skinned, pale-haired woman snarling at it, sword in hand.

Galeran had dissolved into laughter, and the next he knew, Jehanne was back, driving him into another, more wonderful dissolution.

A form of dissolution he longed to experience once again.

No. Not just once . . .

He urged his mount to greater speed, wondering if their marriage would be as if he had never left.

Or better?

He knew he'd changed while away. He'd been twenty-two when he'd taken the cross, and had generally led a pleasant life. Now, at twenty-five, he was leaner, harder, and callused on body and soul. He'd seen marvels to strengthen his faith, and horrors to sour it.

Jehanne must have changed too.

Perhaps she would have plumped up after having a child. He'd always admired her slender elegance, but bigger breasts and a cozy armful might be good too.

Jehanne in any form would be good.

Raoul was right; he should have sent warning from Bruges. He should stop and send warning today.

He wouldn't, though.

With an anticipatory grin, Galeran realized he *wanted* to surprise her. He wanted to catch his cool wife in her working clothes, skirt kirtled up, her fine hair escaping its braids as it always did. He wanted her to look up and gape with shock, then flush with joy.

Jehanne didn't like to be caught unawares, so every now and then he liked to do it. Like when he gave her the rose . . .

He wasn't a man for giving fancy gifts, and up north they didn't see many, but on a trip to York he'd spotted the rose on a merchant's stall, wonderfully carved out of ivory, each petal edge fine as a real one. It was an impractical thing, too small to decorate a room and too big for jewelry, but he'd bought it anyway because its sharp-edged beauty made him think of Jehanne, and after just a few days away he missed her.

When he'd given it to her, her cheeks had flushed and her eyes had shone, perhaps even with a hint of tears. Jehanne rarely cried.

She'd cried, though, when she broke it. He smiled ruefully at the memory of her grief over the accident. Other losses had been met with fierce composure, but the rose— sent flying off its shelf in a careless moment—had melted her to tears. They'd stuck the broken petals back with wax, but one was chipped and another cracked and it had never been as perfect as it was.

Ah, well. He'd brought her gifts from the Holy Land. Perhaps one of them would be the equal of the rose.

He thought he might have some bed tricks, too, that would catch her unawares. He'd kept his vow, but other men had explored the Eastern women and brought back stories. Jehanne would be interested. She liked to experiment, and now that there was no anxiety about barrenness she would be happy to play again.

Tonight.

Jehanne.

Jehanne in bed.

Or on the bed so he could feast on the sight of her—pale blond hair spilling loose over the mattress, supple body his again to touch, to taste, to finally, finally enter . . .

Such thoughts were not wise.

He was hard as a rock, bulging, throbbing, as if he might prove Raoul's words true and explode.

He'd controlled lust and frustration for over two years, so he should be able to do so for a few more hours, but he had to adjust carefully in the saddle to find a tolerable position as he rode.

He realized then that he was into familiar land at last— his own valley land, the strip fields rich with summer, the fells dotted with plump sheep. The sun was setting and the dun was beginning to tire, but now was no time to stop. He kicked him on, galloping through familiar villages, scattering geese, chickens, and people. The cries of "It's Lord Galeran! Lord Galeran!" fell quickly behind like the cries of the startled birds.

Then he saw the square stone keep of Heywood Castle beyond some trees and reined in sharply. He'd dreamed of this so many times that it almost felt like another dream. He needed a moment to convince himself that it was finally, blessedly, real.

It looked no different. It was as if he'd ridden away yesterday.

Raoul reined up beside him, his horse foaming with effort. "So, we made it, though your men are straggled out behind for a league. Do we wait for them to gather and ride down quietly, as if there had been no hurry at all?"

The thought had crossed Galeran's mind. Trust Raoul to read him so well. "No," he said, and kicked into a canter to ride around the curve of the road and into full view of his home. . . .

He hauled the dun to a rearing stop.

An army seethed around Heywood.

His castle was under siege!

"By the five wounds, who?"

Raoul shaded his eyes from the flare of the setting sun. "The pennant shows red and green."

Raoul's eyesight had always been remarkable, but Galeran could scarcely believe it. "That's my father's pennant."

"Then your father is besieging your castle."

Two

Galeran couldn't deny Raoul's words. By now he, too, could make out the familiar banner of William of Brome fixed by the handsome main tent. He even recognized the tent. It was his father's pride and joy.

All joy dissolved into dread. He stared at Heywood, at the simple square keep, and at the solid curtain wall, newly completed just before he left. They bore no marks.

Heywood was one of the strongest castles in the north. Who had taken it without a battle? And what had happened to his wife and child?

Ice on his heart, he surged down the slope into the camp, ignoring cries and attempts to bar his way. He was aware of the sword in his hand only when he almost used it on a man.

He halted the action just as the guard stopped his attack, shock on his face. "My Lord Galeran!"

"It's Lord Galeran."

"It's the lord of Heywood."

The words whispered about him strangely.

Shocked.

Disbelieving.

Horrified.

Then his father pushed through the crowd, still massive and ruddy-faced, but grayer than Galeran remembered. "Galeran! Is it you? Christ be praised! We thought you dead."

A groom had run to hold Galeran's bridle. His father almost dragged him from the horse into a rib-crushing, back-pounding hug. "Welcome home! Welcome home! We thought you dead! Praise be to God. Praise be to God!"

Galeran tore from the embrace. "Who holds my castle?"

Silence fell.

Joy drained from Lord William's heavy features. "You'd best come in the tent, lad."

Galeran realized then that he was surrounded by brothers and uncles, and that none of them was truly meeting his eyes.

Jehanne.

She was dead.

The conviction grew in him like a sickness, dizzying him, making him want to vomit. He let himself be steered into the tent, aware of his family cramming in behind, but with eyes only for his father. "Jehanne?"

Lord William poured wine into a goblet and held it out. "Drink."

Galeran almost dashed it from his hand. *Where is she?*

His father placed the goblet on a small table between them. "In the castle."

Galeran almost collapsed with relief. A prisoner only. Thank God, thank God. "Who holds her?"

There was something like a snort from his uncle Thomas. "That's a good question."

Galeran stared around, alerted by tone more than words. It was only when his younger brother, Gilbert, stepped back, hands raised, that he realized he still had his sword in his hand. He lowered it slowly and just as slowly sheathed it. "What is going on?"

"I'm sorry," said his father. "It's not good. Your wife has installed Raymond of Lowick as master of Heywood. Since she refused to send him away, we've come to insist on it."

Just then the tent flap was swept back and another big

man entered—Galeran's oldest brother, Will. His whole bloody family was here.

"Little brother! You're a sight for my eyes, though this is a hell of a situation to come home to."

Since he couldn't avoid the fierce hug, Galeran endured it. It gave him time to think anyway, to have things settle about him.

Jehanne and Raymond of Lowick.

No. He couldn't believe it. Certainly Lowick had been her father's squire, and she'd fancied herself in love with the handsome young knight he'd become, but that had been years ago. . . .

When he was free of Will's hug, he turned to his father. "I thought Lowick married in Nottinghamshire."

"His wife died childless and he ended up with little of her property. Around that time your seneschal took a fever and died. Next I knew, your wife had taken him on here."

The air was like gall, but Galeran had to keep breathing. "That is her right. I left her with control of Heywood. Lowick was always a sound knight."

Lord William's jaw worked side to side as it always did when he didn't want to say something. The silence stretched until blunt Will revealed the truth. "Just over a month ago, your wife bore him a child."

Lord William picked up the goblet and pressed it into Galeran's hands. "Drink."

Galeran drained the cup in a haze of disbelief. Had he fallen from his horse and lost his wits? Was he, God forbid, still lying raving by the walls of Jerusalem?

"We heard you were dead." Lord William's voice seemed far away. "Near a year ago word came that you'd fallen in the taking of Jerusalem. It wasn't much to go on, and none of us took it as a settled thing, but it did set off a fine debate about Jehanne's future. Who would hold Heywood. Who would have guardianship of the babe. . . ."

Another silence fell, and Galeran stared at the solid tent

pole. One thing at a time. Don't think about Jehanne with another man. Don't think about her squandering her hard-won fertility to produce a bastard.

"By what right does she refuse you admittance?"

"By no right," growled his father. "She just knows—they both know—that it will go hard with them when I'm in there."

One thing at a time.

Galeran placed the goblet back on the table. "It will go with them as I say."

He turned and walked out of the tent, aware of his father and brothers following, of the eyes of all the camp on him. He didn't even try to look at Raoul.

All his rapturous praise of Jehanne was ashes, and yet . . . And yet.

She'd thought him dead. There was a grain of comfort in that.

He took his reins from the groom and mounted his weary horse. His father grabbed the bridle close by the bit. "What are you doing? If you want to lead an assault, we'll do it tomorrow."

Galeran didn't try to force the horse forward. "Let us first see if they'll open to their rightful lord."

"By Peter's toe, lad, they'll shoot you on sight! It would suit them fine to kill you."

"If my wife wants me dead, I would be better off so." He met his father's angry eyes, and after a moment Lord William released the horse.

Galeran rode toward his castle bareheaded. He had no pennant, but enough people should be able to recognize him when he was close. There were guards on the walls.

Heywood was built on a natural rise of heath-covered rock, which was kept clear of all larger growth so the watchman at the top of the keep always had a clear view of anyone approaching. As Galeran rode up the long, sloping road at a walk, he heard the man blow his horn. In moments, new people hurried onto the ramparts over the gate.

One was Jehanne, accompanied by a tall man in armor. Presumably Raymond of Lowick, though it was impossible to tell.

Lowick had always been a handsome man, and Galeran could see no reason why that would have changed now that he was close to thirty. He'd always been a skilled warrior too, both in battle and personal combat.

Galeran could tell nothing of how Jehanne looked, or how the two people looked together. In fact, he thought dispassionately, the figures could be another blond woman and another tall knight, and he would be none the wiser yet.

Would an arrow fly? He was wearing mail, so the chance of it killing him was small, but it could take him in the eye. For that matter, if they had the brutal crossbow, a bolt could pierce his mail. He found he didn't care. At this moment, living or dying seemed immaterial.

Unopposed, he rode near to the closed gates. By then there could be no doubt that the woman was his wife.

She had not changed. She was still slender, and her fine blond hair escaped as usual to blow in unruly wisps. She looked pale, but that was to be expected. She met his eyes steadily, but he expected that.

Jehanne would stare down Satan at the gates of hell.

A flare of rage almost shattered his control.

Why?

He wanted to bellow it at her here and now, for he knew there had to be reasons. He knew his wife. He still loved his wife, but his image of her was like the fragments of that shattered rose. Did the wax exist to cobble his life together again?

He looked away to scan the armed men on the walls. They, too, looked pale, but the pallor could have been from the rapidly failing light. "I am Lord Galeran of Heywood," he announced in a voice loud enough to be heard by all, "rightful lord of this castle. At first light tomorrow I will approach with my men and my family's men and expect admittance. Deny me at your peril."

He waited a moment in case there would be a response, but there was none, not even defiance. The only movement was Jehanne's blue scarf blowing in the chilly wind.

Galeran swung away and rode back down to the camp. There he dismounted and turned his weary horse over to John.

"Why tomorrow?" his father demanded. "If they'll let you in then, they'll let you in now!"

"Perhaps I need time to think before meeting my wife."

With that, Galeran walked away, away from the camp, away from everyone.

And, thanks be to God, they let him go.

He stopped after a while because there wasn't any point in pushing onward unless he wanted to walk all the way back to Jerusalem—which was strangely appealing. He leaned against a tree, slid wearily down to sit, then rested his head on his knees.

Dear Lord in heaven, what was he supposed to do now?

He knew what he was *supposed* to do. Kill Lowick, banish Jehanne to a convent, probably after beating her black and blue, put her aside, and find a more virtuous wife.

Or perhaps even give her to the courts to be executed.

He fought down the need to vomit up that cold mutton pie.

What about the children? Gallot and the bastard. Perhaps they were young enough to come to love another woman as their mother, but Jehanne would never recover from losing them.

He'd been surprised when his cool-headed, quick-witted wife had revealed a passionate maternal longing, but once established, it had become the ruling force in their lives.

Her desire for a child had eroded their sexual pleasure and made her silently miserable every month of the year. That misery had driven him to do the one thing he had no wish to do—leave her and take the cross.

Their childlessness had not mattered at first. Betrothed at sixteen, married at seventeen, life stretched before them like an open road, and the tangled pleasures of fighting and bed play absorbed all their attention. After a year or so, however, the questions started—well-meaning questions about when Jehanne would quicken. Galeran was even taken aside by his embarrassed father to check that the young couple were actually doing all that was necessary.

They certainly were, and enjoying it so much that they were in no great hurry to have the fun interrupted by pregnancy and birth. The concern of all around began to affect them, however, so they took measures.

Herbs were recommended, and dutifully used. Prayers were offered. Jehanne even agreed to wear an amulet to keep away the evil spirits that could eat a woman's children before they started to grow.

Still, it was all more a matter for amusement than concern. At eighteen they lived in youthful optimism that everything would come in time, and in the meantime they had much to absorb them.

Jehanne had already perfected her skills as chatelaine and was an industrious, efficient manager. Galeran was continuing to develop fighting skills as well as the administrative abilities he would need to run the barony when Jehanne's father died. He was entranced by the power and prestige of Heywood. After all, as a younger son, he had never expected to become a landed lord so easily.

The unexpected marriage had come about because Jehanne's brothers had died, leaving her heir to her ailing father's estates. Fulk of Heywood decided to marry her off quickly to a suitable young man, one old enough for responsibility but young enough to be trained by him.

He naturally looked to the large family of his neighbor, William of Brome. Will, the eldest son, was already married. Eustace, the second son, was nineteen and all a man could want in a son-by-marriage.

The betrothal negotiations were well advanced, when Eustace threw everything into disorder by announcing that he felt called to become a priest, a fighting priest opposing the Moors in Iberia. Fulk howled, Lord William raged, but Eustace held his ground as firmly as one would expect of a holy warrior.

Thus Galeran found himself the focus of dynastic plans. Just sixteen and more interested in horses and hounds than women, he was not consulted. He was summoned from Lancashire, where he served as squire to Lord Andrew of Forth, stuffed into unusually fine clothes, and taken to Heywood to be betrothed to a frosty girl a few months older and a few inches taller than he. Scarce over that shock, he was told he would live at Heywood and complete his training in arms under Lord Fulk, while learning how to manage property.

Despite the shock, Galeran recognized his good fortune. He was being handed a castle and estates of his own and was likely to have them soon, since Lord Fulk was ailing. The only mold in this tasty loaf was his betrothed wife.

The Lady Jehanne made no secret of the fact that she would prefer to marry another, Raymond of Lowick. Tall, handsome Raymond had been her father's squire, and was now known throughout the north for his skill with arms. At her father's command, she had accepted that she was to marry Eustace of Brome, who was equally tall and handsome in a rough-cut way, and who had also proved himself in battle.

She had not expected to marry a slightly built boy.

"I'm a full two months older than you" was virtually the first thing she said to him.

He had sisters and knew how to handle that. "Then you'll doubtless die sooner." But his voice had cracked on it, and he would have given his right hand that it not, because she wasn't his sister. She was that frightening creature, the woman who would one day be his wife.

They'd already made the vows and signed the documents, witnessed by thirty or so men of standing in the north. Now they'd been sent to sit together at the opposite end of the hall while the contented men drank their health. They were both dressed in the finest silks and bullion, but Jehanne wore hers as if accustomed, and Galeran had never had such fine clothes in his life.

His dark hair was neatly trimmed. Hers had clearly never been cut. It rippled in a shimmering fall of pale gold silk down to her slender hips. Coming from a dark-haired family, it seemed a marvel to him, but a marvel like lightning, or dragon-fire, or flood.

Dangerous rather than desirable.

His skin was dusky, for his family came not long ago from southern France, where the sun was hot. Jehanne's bloodlines were more northern. Her translucent skin, smooth as fine, polished horn, lay neatly over delicate bones. Her red lips promised warmth, but her clear blue eyes were winter-cold.

She tossed her head, causing the golden silk to undulate like a live thing. "I wanted to marry a *man*. Even your brother would be better than you."

"My brother preferred the Church." He hoped she caught the silent rider that it was now clear why.

Her lips tightened and she looked him over. "I'd think the Church would appeal to you too. You don't have the build of a fighting man."

That remark was enough to double Galeran's devotion to his military training. He knew he was small, but he had every faith that he would grow. Perhaps he would never be as big as his father or older brothers, but he would grow. Surely he would soon be bigger than his wife. Despite his size, he already had considerable skill in swordplay and riding, and though scarcely acknowledging it, he set out to show Jehanne that she was not marrying a priest.

He enjoyed such exercise too, except when his bride-to-be came to observe.

She watched his sword work one day, then commented, "Your left arm is weaker than your right."

He turned, shaking sweat from his hair. "Everyone's is, including yours."

She smirked. "No, it isn't. I'm left-handed."

"Cursed, you mean," he retorted, referring to a common superstition.

She tossed her head. "Only by you, sirrah."

But as she walked away he turned back to his work, satisfied that he'd scored in that bout.

Perhaps that was why she changed tactics and waylayed him in the quiet of the stables. "Since we're to be married, Galeran, you had better kiss me."

He moved uneasily away. "I don't want to kiss you."

"Of course you do." She cocked her head and studied him with a slight smile. "Or is it that you don't know how to kiss?"

He felt the red rise in his face. "*I* know, but you shouldn't."

She laughed. "You'd like that, wouldn't you? Then I'd never know if you did it right." Chameleonlike, she turned sultry and moved forward to lay a hand on his chest. "If you learn to kiss properly, Galeran, I might let you do more. . . . Or is that what you're afraid of?"

She'd used perfume—something flowery, but spicy too—and it rose off her like a warning.

This new territory terrified him so much, he dodged away from her. "You speak wickedness. One day, Jehanne, I will beat you."

She laughed. "You'll have to grow a bit first."

When he lunged for her, she danced away, still laughing at him. He could have caught her, but he came to his senses.

He might be her promised husband, but that didn't mean he had a husband's rights.

Yet.

The thought of husbandly rights led him to thoughts of husbandly duties. The wedding was but four months away and Jehanne was right—he didn't know what to do. At least, he knew the facts, and had seen his brothers with a maid now and then, but he had no practical knowledge. He hadn't been much interested in women before his betrothal, and since then he'd been at Heywood. It didn't seem right, somehow, to dally with the maids in his wife's home.

But he did need some practice, and so he overcame his scruples and started to kiss the wenches who appealed to him. He found the business pleasant enough. It also introduced him to other joys—the soft feel of a woman's body, especially her breasts; the warm glow in her eyes when she was pleased; the sultry smell of a woman—so different from that of a sweaty man; the feelings in his own body, demanding more.

He didn't act on those demands—that still didn't seem right—but he often thought of visiting Brome, where he knew the names of some willing women.

Then, one day, Jehanne came upon him with his favorite dairy maid in his lap. Though stung by guilt, he was heartened by the naked fury in his betrothed wife's eyes. He knew then that he had wanted Jehanne to catch him, wanted to see her angry over it. He pushed the maid off his knees and gave her a playful swat on the rear to send her on her way.

Jehanne, of course, swiftly controlled herself. "I suppose you're practicing," she said with a dismissive air. "Are you hoping to get it right before we're wed?"

"Why would I care as long as I broach you and get you with child?"

She virtually snarled at him. "So I won't laugh at you."

"If you don't laugh at me, I won't laugh at you."

And he scored that time too, for she stormed off with angry color in her cheeks.

But perhaps, after all, she won that bout, for he found he didn't like to upset her and gave up his games with the maids. More than ever, though, he wanted to visit Brome so he could truly practice for his wedding night.

Broaching was all very well in theory, for he knew what bit went where, but many things that seemed simple in theory proved to be quite difficult when arrived at—like aiming a ballista so that the rock it threw actually did some damage. He remembered his first attempt at that exercise, and the way his rock had thumped into the ground far short of the target.

He certainly didn't want to fall short in the marriage bed.

Did she know any more than he, though? Surely not. She was a high-spirited girl, for her mother had died years before and her father had been somewhat neglectful in her rearing, but Fulk was not the sort of man to tolerate a wanton daughter. She couldn't have dallied with other men. Could she?

He did wonder uneasily about Raymond of Lowick, who visited Heywood too often for Galeran's comfort. Ostensibly, he came to pay respects to his old master, but he flirted with Jehanne. She did not appear to encourage him, but she didn't reject him either.

In fact, to Galeran Jehanne was a tangled mystery.

She didn't walk delicately, but strode about, skirts swinging. Yet she looked as graceful as other women. She didn't bend her neck and lower her gaze, but looked men straight in the eye, whether it was her father, Galeran, or Lowick. Yet it was not unbecoming. She rode out to the hunt as fast and fierce as any man, and liked to be in at the kill. Galeran had quickly learned that any impression of delicacy was an illusion. She was a dead shot with her bow, could wield a light sword with skill, and lift a sack of grain without difficulty.

He found he didn't mind this at all since she was just as

skillful in women's matters. She could spin fine thread and weave sound cloth, and her embroidery was a marvel to him. More important, she could organize others to spin and weave and embroider, so Heywood prospered under her rule. She knew just how everything should be done, and seemed to have her eye everywhere. Swift with punishment for those who failed in their duties, she was never cruel, but simply drew the best work out of everyone.

The people of Heywood were proud of their lady, and so was Galeran. He admired her, sharp tongue and all, and though she still made him nervous, he learned how to handle her. He learned military matters from the master-at-arms, and more personal fighting from Jehanne.

And he enjoyed both.

And at last he was growing. One day he realized he was taller than she, and in the next little while he put on even more height and weight, so that by two months before the wedding he topped her by half a head. Perhaps in response to this, Jehanne taunted less. Now she watched him with a different light in her eyes and she never accosted him alone.

But then, when their wedding day was but a month ahead, she trapped him in a deserted corridor. "Are you ready to kiss me yet, husband-to-be?" She had to look up at him.

Yes, he was ready, and more than ready. He immediately caught her wrist, then trapped her waist with his other arm. She stiffened, blue eyes wide. With shock? Anger? Excitement? He still couldn't read her, and at that moment he didn't much care.

He put his lips against hers, then stopped, wondering what she would do. She did nothing, but disconcertingly, still stared at him, unblinking.

"Don't you know what to do?" he taunted against her lips.

"I'm waiting to see if you do." But the words moved her lips against his, and brought a hint of her warm breath to play. His body reacted instantly and he froze, frightened of himself.

He saw the glint in her eye, and the next moment she stuck out her tongue and licked at his lips.

He pushed her away, but not far. "Who's taught you tricks like that?"

She smiled in the way that infuriated him. "Who's taught you to recognize them?"

"It's different for men and women."

"Is it?"

Infuriated, he dragged her back and kissed her, hard and rough, not caring if she was impressed or not, just intent on showing her who was master. She stayed stiff in his arms for a moment, but then suddenly relaxed and kissed him back, tongue playing, body curving in closer to his.

He enjoyed it thoroughly until he realized what was happening. Then he jerked back with shock and let her go. "You *have* kissed before!"

She cocked her hip. "Have I?"

"Who?"

"Wouldn't you like to know?"

"Yes, so I could kill him."

She laughed. *"You?"*

He hit her.

She cried out, hand to her red cheek. Then she hissed with rage and went for him with her fists, her nails, with every part of her slender, strong body. He tried to control her and found it impossible, so they ended up in an all-out fight, a tangled wrestling match, scraped, scratched, bruised, and with fine clothing torn to rags. They had to be pulled apart, snarling like wild dogs, and he'd been sent home to face his father's wrath.

Three

"Heywood's talking of annulling the betrothal, you dumbskull!"

"She drives me mad!"

"So you hit her?" Lord William's hand cracked against Galeran's face with the full force of his mighty arm behind it, knocking Galeran to his knees and loosening a couple of teeth. "Can't you think of another way of handling a delicate maid?"

"Delicate? That she-wolf?"

That got him hauled to his feet and slammed on the other side of his face. For all his gruff manner, Lord William hated to see a woman hurt. His father whipped him, and when he'd finished said, "Keep out of my way, and when you're healed, get back to Heywood and put it right."

It had taken three weeks for the sores to heal and the bruises to fade, three weeks of wishing the torments of hell on Jehanne of Heywood but strangely, of missing her too. It had never occurred to him to complete his sexual education.

When Galeran returned to Heywood he had been very uncertain of his welcome from Fulk or his daughter, but certain that he wanted forgiveness. The thought of losing Jehanne was like acid.

Anyway, he reasoned, his father was right. It should not be necessary for a man to hit a woman to control her, even a woman like Jehanne. He was prepared to apologize to her, though he hoped she didn't gloat or his tolerance would be stretched thin.

To his surprise, Fulk made no difficulty over the matter at all, merely remarking that he hoped that the next time Jehanne displeased him, Galeran would beat her properly instead of getting into a brawl over it.

The mere idea was daunting unless six strong men tied her up first, but Galeran said all the right things and went in search of his wife-to-be.

He found her in the garden, subdued and radiating grievance rather than satisfaction. She listened to his carefully phrased apology, then said, "You got me whipped."

"*I* got *you* whipped!"

Her eyes brightened. "If you were punished, you deserved it."

"If you were punished, so did you."

"I did nothing!"

"You dedicate your life to spoiling mine!"

"I, my Lord Galeran, have better things to do with my life than plan misfortunes for you."

"Then apply yourself to them as a proper maiden should."

But even as they squabbled, their eyes tangled in a new kind of awareness.

"Did he really whip you?" Galeran asked.

Her lids hid her eyes. "He had me whipped."

"Ah, is that the secret of it?"

Her lids rose, revealing fire. "Whip me or have me whipped, Galeran, and you'll rue it."

As he retreated to the relative safety of swords and horses and grappling irons, Galeran knew it was true. He could enforce his will, yes. He was a man with strength, power, and the weight of the law on his side. But if he ever pushed matters that far, Jehanne would die before submitting.

On the other hand, she was still a thorn in his flesh and had to be handled somehow. The way he'd most like to handle her was not yet blessed, and so he did his best to avoid her for the remaining week.

It wasn't easy when he was heated by the mere sight of her, and maddened by the brush of her arm against his at dinner, or the trace of her subtle perfume in the air.

Perhaps she had no idea of the effect she was having, or the power of lust in a young, healthy male. If she had, surely she wouldn't keep teasing him.

He tried to stay out of her way, but she became diabolically good at turning up wherever he was. He grew clever at evading her touch, but she seemed to be always trying to touch him. Then she found ways to dress and move that made him not want to evade her at all.

But by prayer and will he held out.

Until he awoke one morning two days before the wedding to find her sitting cross-legged on his bed.

"Hell's flames, Jehanne. What are you doing here?"

"You've been avoiding me, Galeran." Her hair hung loose, and she wore only a light kirtle in a bewitching shade of pink.

Galeran fought the need to drag her beneath the sheets. "That means I don't want to see you. Go away."

"No."

"Then I'll leave."

As he pushed back the covers, she said, "I've thrown all your clothes out the window."

"What?" He saw his chest standing open and empty, and laughed at her. "Do you think I'm shy, you silly girl?" He leaped out of bed and faced her naked.

Then froze.

What in the name of the Savior did he think he was doing? Now she'd shriek and they'd have the whole castle down on them.

He should have known better. She showed no alarm, but looked him over, eyes a little wide, cheeks as pink as her kirtle, but otherwise composed. "Not bad. You're growing."

And he was stuck there, exposed to her scrutiny. He couldn't lose face by dashing back beneath the covers, but he had no clothes to put on. So he did the only thing he could and looked her over in turn. "I suppose you're growing too, but it's hard to tell when you're covered."

Her eyes widened a little more, then she began to pull up her skirt.

He lunged forward and grabbed her hand. "No!"

"No? You dared me."

"I did not."

"It sounded like a dare to me. I won't refuse a dare."

"Then, by the Cross, I dare you to jump out of the window after my clothes!"

She met his eyes. "Only if you do too. Hand in hand into eternity, Galeran . . ."

And he'd known, terrifyingly, that she would do it.

He was still gripping her, and she turned his hand in hers, shifting it so he brushed her breast, her small, high breast, with the nipple clearly felt through the fine cloth. "You see. I am growing." Then she looked down and smiled. "And so are you."

He knew he was. For the first time, lust was hitting him hard and with immediate purpose. He'd lusted before, but never with a woman—a special woman—so close, so available, so hot beneath his hand.

He began to tremble. "We can't . . ."

"Of course we can't. But we can kiss. You owe me a kiss."

"Jehanne, no. I can't . . ." He couldn't find the words to explain the danger, the danger that he would lose control of this ravening beast.

But perhaps she understood. She sucked in a breath and slid swiftly away. "If you can't, you can't," she said, as if nothing had happened. "I'll send your clothes up." She slipped out of the room, leaving only a trace of perfume and a raging erection to torment him.

Though she didn't tease him again, her presence was enough to stretch him to the limit. By their wedding day, he was ready to ignite like a dead tree at the first touch of flame, and the long hours of ceremony and feasting were endless torment.

When they were finally left alone in the marriage bed, however, Galeran found himself frozen—frozen a little by fear that she knew more of this than he and would laugh, but frozen mainly by the terror of unleashing the force that raged through him—a force he neither understood nor controlled—and hurting her.

After a while, she touched his chest. "Galeran . . . ?"

He shuddered quite involuntarily, fighting to control everything even though he was terrified that if he succeeded in controlling things well enough, he'd never actually claim his bride at all.

"You were right," he whispered. "You should have married someone older."

"Why?" She sounded amused. "He'd only have died the sooner."

Galeran stared at the ceiling, fists clenched. "He'd have known what to do. I don't, Jehanne. I've never done this before."

Her fingers made a small, nervously reassuring movement against his tight chest. "Nor have I, but I know what bit goes where."

"So do I." But he didn't know when, or how. . . .

Her hand moved down like a trickle of fire and found the source of his anguish and hopes.

He gasped.

So did she.

"I didn't expect it to be quite so hard," she said. But instead of shrinking away in maidenly modesty, she pushed the covers back to look, fingers testing him. He had to drag her hand away before he exploded. They made a little fight of it and ended up face-to-face, looking at each other—it seemed—for the first time.

"Don't, Jehanne."

"Does it hurt?"

"Yes. But it's not that—"

"Then use it."

Naked beneath him, veins visible beneath her fine skin, she seemed impossibly fragile. "I'm afraid I'll hurt you."

"You're supposed to."

"I don't want to hurt you." He tried to move away, but she held him with hands and legs, reminding him that she wasn't fragile at all.

"Don't be afraid. My nurse told me"—she began to pinken in a way he found both fascinating and immensely desirable—"she said it would go easier if I was ready, and if I was ready I'd be creamy. . . ." Her voice dropped to a whisper and her cheeks turned full red. "I've been ready for weeks, Galeran, and I'm . . . I'm ready now."

She took his hand and guided it between her legs to creamy, hot folds, proving the truth of her words, opening herself, easing under him. . . .

His suddenly mindless body followed his hand like a plow after the team, finding her, broaching her, filling her, using her.

He had never expected it to be like that—connected to his gropings with the maids as an inferno is connected to a candle flame; connected even to the times he'd relieved himself as a hearth fire is to wildfire.

He collapsed over her when he was done, and she pushed at him, gasping, "Galeran, I can't breathe!"

He moved away hastily. "I'm sorry. Did I hurt you?" Then, seeing the answer in her face, he added, "If I did, it was your fault."

"My fault?"

"I could have waited if you hadn't been so bold."

"It wouldn't have mattered how long you waited," she

snapped. "It is the nature of men to rut, and the fate of women to bleed."

He tried awkwardly to comfort her. "Now that you're a virgin no longer, it won't hurt again."

"How would you know?" With that, she turned away.

So, despite the fact that he would have liked to repeat the wonderful exercise, he turned the other way and eventually went to sleep.

The next day the sheet was displayed to confirm their act. Galeran was congratulated as if he had defeated a dragon, and Jehanne was fussed over as if she'd been injured.

Which he supposed she had been.

Despite male approval, he felt rather miserable. Presumably none of the men, especially Fulk, knew how violently he had taken Jehanne and that she was unhappy about it.

The only thing to do was refrain from repeating the act until she was healed. But when would that be?

When they retired to bed the next night, he asked if she still hurt. "Only a little," she said in a resigned tone that killed any desire he felt.

On the other hand, he was highly frustrated. He didn't want to inflict himself upon an unwilling and wounded wife, but having tasted sex, he wanted more. He briefly thought of the obliging maids, but that wouldn't do.

The next night he asked again if she still hurt, and she said, "No." With a sigh of relief he entered her and found the pleasure he longed for, remembering this time to support his weight himself. But even in his climax he was more aware and knew that Jehanne was unhappy.

Afterward, he gathered her into his arms. "What is it, sweeting? What do you want?"

He thought she wouldn't answer, but then she said, "I want what you have."

"A cock?" he asked in genuine bewilderment.

She thumped his shoulder with her fist. "No, you dolt.

The pleasure! Women do have it, I know they do. I can feel it, but it doesn't . . ." And there were tears in her eyes, the first he'd ever seen there.

He rocked her helplessly. "I'm sorry, love. We'll find it. . . ."

Perhaps it was instinct, or perhaps snippets of half-understood gossip, or perhaps even his times with the maids, but he put his hand to her left breast and immediately felt her response. "This might help?"

"It might. . . ."

He stroked and played with it, finding pleasure for himself in the doing, and in the tightening of her small pink nipple. Then he lowered his head and kissed it.

"Yes," she whispered, so he kept on kissing and licking. After a little while, she said, "Perhaps if you sucked on it . . ."

So he did, with great willingness, finding that her pleasuring became submerged in his greedy own. She didn't seem to mind that his gentle sucking became more thorough, and though she frowned more than she smiled, he sensed that he was doing something right.

His control could not last forever, but when he had to enter her he could tell she was more attuned to him. Because it was the second time that night he was in no hurry, and was able to try to act as she wanted, continuing the pleasuring of her breasts between deep kisses.

Afterward she appeared happy, but he didn't think she'd found what he found. He secretly wondered whether women did experience the same release, but he certainly had no problem with trying.

Since neither of them knew precisely what they sought, it took them some weeks and a great deal of enjoyable exploration to find it, but when they did, there had been no mistaking it.

Jehanne left teeth and nail marks on his skin, and her

noises made him think she was dying—until he tried to stop and she threatened him with hell if he did.

Afterward, she lay there as stunned as he had been his first time. "Galeran . . ."

"Hmmm?" He smugly stroked her now very familiar body.

"I liked that."

"Strange. I never would have guessed."

Despite their harmony in bed, life hadn't been completely peaceful. Jehanne had strong opinions on every subject and expressed them, whereas Galeran, in his youthful arrogance, believed that his was the ultimate word after Fulk's. They always ended their quarrels in laughter and in lovemaking, however, happily exploring the depth and breadth of their bodies' pleasures.

Until eventually the shadow of barrenness fell over them.

Fulk was dead by then, and they were lord and lady of their domain. Clever planning, efficiency, and hard work were making Heywood into a prosperous estate. Galeran had completed Fulk's project of building a stone wall around the bailey to replace the wooden palisade. The keep was painted white outside and hung with rich woolen cloths inside, all woven and dyed by Jehanne and her women.

The days were pleasantly full of productive work, and in the evenings the household enjoyed music, storytelling, and the occasional wandering entertainer.

Everything was perfect, except that there was no heir to all this, and people were beginning to whisper that there never would be.

Worse, people were beginning to whisper that there was no heir because the Lady Jehanne did not behave as a proper lady should. She was too bold, too active. That was why no child could hold inside her womb.

Galeran told her it was nonsense, that serf women worked

morn till night and carried one babe after another—but Jehanne began to change. She rested every day, she never lifted anything heavy, and she refused to ride at more than a walk.

The next old wives' tale was that sour moods and anger could kill a babe, so she did her best to control her temper. Galeran found her struggle to change her nature agonizing, and sometimes teased her just to raise the spirit he so loved.

After the quarrel, however, there would be no laughter or lovemaking. Instead, Jehanne would weep and accuse him of not wanting a child at all so he, too, tried to create an environment of honey-sweetness.

Then, because of yet more advice, she refused to make love except lying underneath him.

When a rumor started that Jehanne was using evil tricks to prevent conception, all Galeran's frustrated rage erupted and he whipped one woman he heard gossiping about it. It wasn't wise, for it just turned everyone's attention to the problem.

Night after night he told Jehanne that he didn't care if she was barren, and it was the truth. He wanted children, yes, particularly a son, but not above all else. More than any child, he wanted his bold, strong, clever wife back.

And every month, she wept.

He held her close one day when her bleeding had started, rocking her. "It doesn't matter, dearling. It doesn't matter. Will already has two sons. Little Gil can have Heywood."

"*I* want a child." It was said fiercely, not piteously.

"Then we can find a child for you to raise. A daughter."

She pushed away from him. "I want a child *in* me, you stupid man! It's a hunger. I can't bear it!"

"It's God's will, Jehanne."

"Then God's will must be changed."

And being Jehanne, she assaulted heaven as if it were a fortress, firing endowments and gold crucifixes, dispatching battalions of litanies and masses. And every month the bleeding announced failure and she huddled alone in her misery.

Or hit out. The castle people learned to walk carefully around her, and it was at such a time that she'd broken the rose. He'd not asked whether it had been a complete accident or a blind act of rage, just comforted her, then done his best to put the pieces together again.

But the pieces of their life wouldn't go back together. In fact, matters just grew worse.

A priest told her that a woman's sexual excitement killed the seed, and so the only lovemaking she would accept was brief and without attention to her needs. At his slightest caress she would seize his hand and say, "No. Not until there is a child."

Since he did not believe there ever would be a child, it seemed they were trapped like flies in a spiderweb of frustration.

The first call to liberate the shrines of the Holy Land had come and gone before matters reached this dire state. Galeran hardly noticed, for the venture hadn't found much favor in King William Rufus's England. Rufus dismissed most priestly matters out of hand and had no intention of encouraging his best fighting men to travel to Outremer.

Late the next year, however, news began to trickle back of successes. It seemed the Christian armies would actually reach the Holy City and liberate it, and some men planned to take ship direct to Palestine. They could be there in a few months and with luck take part in the great battle.

Galeran was too involved with personal matters to be entranced by that adventure until Jehanne urged it. Yet another helpful priest—this time a wandering preacher trying to stir interest in the crusade—had suggested that such noble service might be the weapon to breach the walls.

"It hardly seems the way to get with child," Galeran pointed out, "for us to separate for years."

Instead of arguing, Jehanne turned away. "I thought you might be relieved to go."

"Why would you think that?"

"I know I've become a misery, that I've been demanding—"

"You can't imagine that I mind your demands."

She turned to look him straight in the eye. "Can't I?"

He sighed. "It's not the frequency I mind, Jehanne, but the desperation. When did we last laugh as we loved?"

"I think I've forgotten how."

He wanted to suggest that she relearn, that they forget about children, but he might as well suggest she forget to breathe. "So you think God wants my sword in Jerusalem."

He couldn't make himself sound enthusiastic, for though he enjoyed martial exercises, he'd never found pleasure in killing. He'd often given thanks for living in quite peaceful times.

She touched him then, lightly on his arm. "I don't like the thought either. Asking you to leave, Galeran, is like cutting off my hand."

And thus it showed the depth of her need. He took her in his arms. "It surely is a noble service to make the holy places safe for pilgrims. All Christians should lend their strength. But we cannot assume that God will repay us as we wish."

"He should, for it will be a horrible sacrifice." She looked up at him, and it was almost like the old Jehanne again, the one who had picked up his sword to face a boar. "If this doesn't work, Galeran, I'm going to convert to Mahomet's religion!"

He laughed, but he suspected it wasn't far from the truth. If the God of the Infidels promised Jehanne a child, she would kneel to Him.

They traveled to London to join the other Crusaders, escorted by Lord William and Jehanne's uncle, Hubert of Burstock. Hubert's second son, Hugh, also intended to take the cross, but solely out of ambition for glory and land.

The vow was the same, though, no matter what the motive—to take the Holy City of Jerusalem or die in the attempt, and not to turn back before that goal was reached.

Galeran made an additional silent vow—that he would stay faithful to his wife. He didn't think it would be hard, for he'd never lain with a woman other than Jehanne, and never wanted to. In view of their cause, though, for him to waste his seed on whores would surely be wicked.

As was ordered by the Pope, Jehanne stepped forward to attest that she agreed to her husband going so far away for so long. Galeran left all his affairs in his wife's capable hands, subject only to the advice of a disapproving Lord William.

Then they spent one last night together, a night much closer to their early joyous ones than any they had experienced recently.

A night that had resulted in a son.

God truly was good.

Despite present circumstances, Galeran still believed that, and sitting in the dark woods, he lowered his head to pray.

It was Raoul who woke him.

In the still, gray dawn, Galeran stretched painfully, chilled through and almost set into the awkward position he'd slept in. Sleeping in mail hadn't helped. His flesh was probably permanently indented.

"Trying to kill yourself?" Raoul asked rather testily, offering a flagon of hot spiced cider.

Galeran wrapped his cold hands around it gratefully and sipped. "I don't want to die."

"Good." Raoul had brought freshly cooked pork and warm bread, and passed some over. "I must say, your family eats well on campaign."

"My father always liked his comforts."

They ate in silence for a while, then Raoul tossed a bone into the misty bushes. "The castle's still shut tight, and it'll be first light soon. What are you going to do when she defies you?"

"First light is hard to define. Jehanne will open at the last moment."

"Why would she let you in? She must know it'll go hard with her, and your castle could hold for a long time. That's a fine wall around it. What's more, they might expect outside help. I gather this Raymond of Lowick has the ear of the local bishop, who's a man in favor with the king."

Galeran looked up at that. "That certainly makes the situation interesting."

Raoul snorted. "Interesting! It's hardly lacking in interest without it. God's breath, Galeran, can't you see the danger here? Your personal affairs might become entangled with those of royalty. Your father's a worried man."

Galeran pushed to his feet and brushed crumbs off his braies. It was a relief to debate a simple political tangle. "I doubt the king will get involved. We're too far north. It's always dangerous for a king of England to leave the south untended. Look what happened to Harold—"

"The bishop could act on his own," Raoul interrupted. "Apparently this Ranulph Flambard—"

"Flambard!" Now Galeran's attention was caught. "What's he doing as Bishop of Durham? When I left England, he wasn't even a priest!"

"He's clearly risen with great speed. Perhaps as a reward for running the country for the last decade or so—ruthlessly, but profitably. So, what if this powerful and ruthless churchman, who seems to have the king in his pocket, decides your wife's lover is in the right?"

Galeran controlled the urge to make Raoul choke on the word *lover*. "My father's been a power in the north for thirty years, and he's faithfully served this king and his father before him. Why would Flambard or Rufus tangle with Brome over this kind of matter?"

"If you have to take the castle by force . . ."

"I won't have to."

Even in the misty grayness, Galeran could see his friend frown. "You really think she'll open the gates?"

"Yes."

"Why, in the name of the Cross?"

"Because it's right."

Raoul let out a snort of disbelief. "Women don't think of right and wrong."

"Jehanne does." Galeran fervently hoped it was still true. "But if you don't like that argument, what about this? If Jehanne doesn't see it that way, the garrison will. They are local men who know me. Most have sworn their oath to me."

Raoul thought about that, then nodded. "Well, that makes sense at least. I suppose with word of your death passing by, your men had little choice other than to obey your lady since you left her in control. Even if she brought in another man, and—" Raoul looked at Galeran and then occupied his mouth in draining the last of his cider instead of talking.

"Very wise."

"Christ's crown," Raoul exclaimed, "you can't pretend she's innocent! Not with a babe at the breast."

"No, I don't suppose I can."

Raoul opened his mouth, then shut it. "What are you going to do?"

"Want more pork?"

Raoul shook his head, both to the offer and at the situation. Suddenly, into the silence, a bird began to trill—the herald of the dawn chorus. Would Jehanne hear it and take it as the sign of first light?

Galeran threw the remains of the meat into the brush and led the way back to the camp.

Four

His father's men were fed and armed, and the horses saddled. A battering ram stood ready beside a ballista that could hurl huge rocks at the walls. All was ready to batter his home to rubble. Galeran went into the tent, where his relatives waited, mailed and ready. His arrival caused a sudden silence.

"I assume Lowick has few men of his own there," Galeran said.

"Aye." His father eyed him as he would an unpredictable and possibly ungovernable new war-horse. "Only five, I think. But we don't know how the allegiance of the others stands. They're mostly Heywood men and could count their allegiance toward old Fulk and his daughter rather than you."

"Nevertheless, I'm going in with just my men."

"God's breath, Galeran—"

Galeran cut his father off with a look. "I want this to be my rightful homecoming, not an armed invasion. If they cut me down, then do your worst."

His younger brother, Gilbert, was turning red in the face. "If they so much as scrape you, Galeran, I'll roast Lowick over a slow fire. That I vow! And as for that bitch—"

Galeran stopped him with a look too. "No one will touch Jehanne except me. No one."

"Fine," said Gilbert with a snarl, "but I want to watch!"

Before Galeran could respond to that, a man burst in. "My lords, the gates are opening!"

Thank God.

Galeran fought the need to collapse with relief and turned on his heel to sweep out like the vengeful lord and master he was supposed to be.

The woods clamored with bird song now, and the sun pinkened the rim of the sky, shooting the first bright rays up into the gloom. It was the first dawn chorus Galeran had heard since coming home, and despite everything, his heart swelled.

He looked toward Heywood, and even through the morning mist the sun touched the white walls gold, showing clearly the open castle gate and the uncertain dark beyond.

Today the walls were bare of people—soldiers or women.

He gestured for his horse, the simple gelding he'd bought in Stockton. Raoul brought him over, along with his own mount.

"This is no business of yours," Galeran said. "My family is staying here to see if I'm spitted on sight. You could stay with them."

"Oh, I wouldn't miss this for a whole beam of the True Cross."

"I'm glad we're providing you with entertainment."

Galeran mounted and turned to his men, the small group who had returned with him from the Holy Land. "Remember, this is my castle, held by my wife. I expect to be welcomed. But we do not know for certain who holds the power in Heywood. If there's trouble, I want no heroics. Break free and return to the camp to serve under my father. He will avenge me."

There was a muttering of discontent, but Galeran said, "On your oaths, obey me."

Then he turned his horse toward his home.

Nothing moved. The castle appeared deserted—almost magically so in the dawn light and mist—but it couldn't be. With the encircling army drawn back, it was possible that a few people had slipped away, but not the whole garrison and population. Heywood normally held some fifty people.

He hoped that Lowick had gone. That was a good part of the reason for the delay in surrender. Having to kill the man would just complicate a complex situation.

Galeran's greatest fear was that Jehanne and his son had left with him.

He rode forward bareheaded again, so that no one could have any doubt that he was in truth Galeran of Heywood, lord of this demesne. So that no one could claim they fired on him by mistake.

No arrow hummed out of a narrow slit. No cross-bow bolt streaked to pierce him. Then he was before the walls, too close for that kind of attack.

His skin prickled as he clattered through the open gate and into the shadow of the thick stone walls. There was a murder hole in the arch here that could pour down pitch or scorching sand. . . .

But nothing fell, and beyond in the bailey the garrison stood in two rigid lines, awaiting him.

They looked scared to death.

As well they might.

Some of the weight slid from Galeran's shoulders. This part, at least, was going to be all right.

He rode into their midst, halted, and dismounted, the jingle of harness and rattle of his mail the only sounds. Signaling to his men to stay on their horses just in case, he slowly, silently, looked around.

Beyond the rigid, pale-faced soldiers, the castle folk hovered nervously, women clutching wide-eyed children, old people staring with predictions of suffering in their weary eyes.

Where was Jehanne?

She wouldn't be with the peasantry. If this were a normal

homecoming, she would be on the keep steps waiting to give him a formal welcome. She might even be running down into the bailey to greet him with a smile and an edged comment denied by glowing eyes.

She was nowhere to be seen.

If she had fled with her lover, should he let her go?

Not if she'd taken his son.

The dense silence pressed on him, almost strangling speech, but he swallowed and raised his voice. "Does anyone here not accept me as his liege, as lord of this demesne?"

Silence answered him, but silence lightened by hope.

Galeran wanted only to ask about Jehanne, to race into the castle and search for her, but he had a part to play here. He moved with dignity to the steps and mounted to the second.

Before he could speak again, a man came forward and knelt at his feet, bare head bent. Walter of Matlock, captain of the garrison. "Lord Galeran, be merciful. We were left in your lady's command, and had word you were dead. We served as we thought right."

"Rise, Walter. No man will suffer for having obeyed my lady as he was bid."

The sergeant-at-arms rose and Galeran saw tears of relief in his eyes. In wanting to give Lowick time to escape, he'd inflicted a night of fear on these men and on their families.

He went quickly down the steps and kissed Walter lightly on the cheek, the kiss of peace. "It is as it was, Walter. There is no need even for a renewal of oaths." He spoke loud enough to be heard, and relief rippled through the bailey like a breeze. People started to mutter, and as if released from constraint, a child cried.

"I assume none of Lowick's men are here," Galeran said quietly.

"They left in the night, my lord." Walter flashed him a look. "We didn't try to stop them."

Galeran even found a smile for that. "Wise man."

He didn't want to ask, but had to in the end. "And the Lady Jehanne?"

The man's face went carefully blank. "Awaits you in the hall, I believe, my lord."

Another weight slid from Galeran's shoulders, leaving him light, almost too light. It was hard to think, hard even to feel in solid contact with the ground beneath his feet.

But Lowick was gone, and Jehanne was here. Perhaps something could be done to put the pieces together again.

He turned to Raoul and his men. "Stay here, care for the horses, settle in. Oh, and send word back to my father that all is well and he may enter when it pleases him."

Then, as the sun burst up to bring a new day, Galeran climbed the wooden stairs to the entrance of his keep.

To walk into the hall was to walk back into chill and gloom, though the first shafts of golden light criss-crossed from the narrow windows. For a moment he was blind, and when his dogs fawned around him, he had not seen them coming.

He greeted them, for that at least was a simple matter and gave him a little time.

Then he looked up and saw a bunch of women in one corner—Jehanne's women. His wife, however, stood apart in the center of the large chamber, her own two black hunting dogs by her side. She wore her favorite colors—blue and cream—and her long hair was disciplined into thick, neat plaits bound with blue ribbons to match her eyes. She stood there calmly, as if waiting to greet a stranger with neither excitement nor fear.

But then, Jehanne never gave away more than she intended.

A lump lodged at the top of Galeran's throat, and he wanted quite desperately to crush her to him.

He might have done it were it not for the tiny baby in her arms.

Her bastard child.

Trust Jehanne to face him with her sin proclaimed.

Where was Gallot? Galeran glanced around but saw only her wide-eyed, frightened women. Wise, he thought, to keep an older, more aware child out of this.

So, how had his clever, wise wife put them in this situation?

He walked forward, unusually aware of the rattle and clink of his mail and the fact that it hadn't been off his body in days. He must stink. What was Jehanne seeing? Perhaps he did appear a stranger. His stubble had almost attained the status of a beard, and there were new scars to mar him.

His dogs had known him on the instant. Her hounds, too well-behaved to leave their mistress without permission, still thumped their tails in welcome.

Only she seemed indifferent.

But she wasn't indifferent. As he drew closer, her control cracked a little and her eyes widened and grew intent. He couldn't tell, however, if she was terrified or merely surprised by his appearance.

He stopped in front of her, marveling at how little she had changed. She matched almost perfectly the image of his dreams.

Two pregnancies had not rounded her, though her breasts were bigger at the moment, doubtless full of the bastard's milk. Apart from that, she was perhaps a little thinner and paler than he remembered, but just as beautiful. Her skin still had the pearly translucence that had always fascinated him, her eyes were still a clear blue. Her hair still made him think of gold and silver threads spun by fairies, and tendrils still escaped to curl around her face as they had always done.

Why, Jehanne? Why?

If she heard the silent question, she did not answer. She simply met his eyes in silence. He supposed there wasn't much to say unless she fell on her knees like Walter to beg for mercy.

He knew she'd rather die.

What would she do, though, if he threatened her brat? Would that break her?

He was immediately ashamed of that vicious thought.

"Lowick?" he asked.

"Has left." Unlike her familiar clear voice, it came out huskily and he saw her swallow to clear her throat.

"Did he want you to leave with him?"

"Yes. But I am no use to him without Heywood."

Then why? Why give yourself to a man who valued you so little? Did he lie to you? I thought you were impossible to lie to.

"Did you want to go?"

She held the child a little closer. "I was afraid to stay," she whispered.

"But you did stay."

With quiet composure she added, "I am your wife and this is my home."

Galeran looked away at the anxious women, grasping a moment to think. One face scowled rather than trembled. Jehanne's sturdy young cousin, Aline, was there. He'd forgotten she'd left St. Radegund's convent to bear Jehanne company during his absence. What had the almost-nun made of all this, and why was she frowning at *him?* But then, she had eyebrows that generally gave a severe impression.

His favorite and most intelligent hound, Grua, picked up the mood and whimpered, pressing close. Stroking the smooth head, Galeran wished Aline and Grua could instantly tell him all they knew.

Why had he imagined that his first moments with Jehanne would provide answers? Or any he wanted to hear. She hadn't denied wanting to leave with Lowick, and she'd as good as said that it was only duty that kept her in their home.

Jehanne had always held to duty, guarding her honor as fiercely as any man.

So why had she done what she had done?

Was it simply that she'd thought him dead? Duty would surely demand more evidence than a rumor, and more mourning time as well.

And if she'd truly thought him dead, why had she not married her lover?

Distant noises told him his father was arriving in the bailey, already blistering the castle people in the way Galeran had not. The bellowing voice grew louder as Lord William began to mount the stairs to the hall, still berating any and all for this affront on his family's honor.

Lord William, who blustered and raged but could not stand to see a woman hurt.

Galeran walked back to Jehanne. "Give the babe to his nurse."

Jehanne's eyes widened slightly, but after a noticeable hesitation she obeyed and passed the sleeping child over.

"Fall," he said quietly, and timing it to coincide with his father's entrance, he hit his wife.

It was no playful tap, but Jehanne could have stayed on her feet. For a moment instinct kept her there, bringing a flash of outrage into her eyes, but then she crumpled, hand to reddened cheek.

Her dogs leaped to defend her, but Galeran grabbed her arm anyway. He was mailed. The dogs could do their worst. Perhaps that's why she snapped, "Sit!"

Galeran began to haul her up, but was stopped from further violence by Lord William's iron grip. "Hey, now, lad, we don't want you killing her, for all she's done."

He broke Galeran's hold on Jehanne and thrust him into the restraining custody of Will and Gilbert. Then he went forward to raise his erring daughter-in-law, berating her, but assuring her that she'd be safe in his protection.

Gilbert growled, "You should have beaten her before Father arrived. You know how soft-hearted he is about women!"

Will said, "For once I agree with Gil. Now that he's promised her his protection, he'll not let you touch her."

"You can get a Church court to impose a penance," mused Gilbert. "Father can't interfere with that. Or when you send her to a convent, order her a daily whipping for a year. . . ."

Galeran let it wash over him. He'd planned on being stopped by his father, knowing the best way to melt his father's anger and get Lord William on Jehanne's side was to hit her. What sickened him was that he'd found it satisfying to hit her; his move to follow, to grab her and hit her harder, had not been acting.

He sent up a fervent prayer for strength and control.

He shrugged out of his brothers' loosening hold and went over to where his father was scolding Jehanne as if she'd just spent too much at the midsummer fair. He made peace with her confused hounds, then said, "Enough of that, Father. I want to talk to my wife in private. I promise not to hit her again. Today at least."

At his tone her dogs weaved between them, as if trying to separate them. Jehanne reassured them and sent them to the far side of the hall, away from their dilemma.

Lord William seemed just as concerned as the dogs, as if he, too, would like to get between them, but he stepped back. "Away with you, then."

Galeran seized Jehanne's arm and steered her toward the solar. He knew his grip was too tight, but his fury seemed to have traveled to his hand and he couldn't control it. The last time he remembered being so unable to control himself was on his wedding night.

It was like his wedding night in other ways too. Pent-up desire simmered in him, threatening to overwhelm at any moment. He was again like a dead tree ready to burst into flame at a spark.

He had every right, too. Every right to throw Jehanne down and enjoy her body. Every right. Even if he were about to cast her off.

He dragged her into the solar, kicked the door shut, and released her with a violence that staggered her. He saw that her face was red and would bruise. Despite his promise to his father, she looked as if she expected more of the same.

He turned abruptly to put the width of the room between them, to rest his head on his arms against the hanging that covered the rough stone wall. "I'm sorry. I seem to be violent today."

"I don't think you need reproach yourself for that." She spoke softly, but every word was clear.

"Such violence serves no purpose."

"That blow did."

He pushed away and turned, leaning against the wall, arms folded. "I wanted to hit you, Jehanne."

"If our situations were reversed, I'd want to *kill* you."

He looked at her, testing the implications of her words. "Would you indeed?"

Now it was she who turned away, moving to fuss with the hangings around the bed. Their bed. Where she and Lowick had . . . ?

"No," she said. "I wouldn't want you dead. But I'd want you punished. I'd find a way to make you suffer." She turned stiffly. "What punishment, Galeran? Don't play with me."

"What would hurt you most? Beating? No." He *was* playing with her and wasn't proud of it, but didn't seem able to stop. "To take the babes away, I suppose . . ."

She stared, turning sheet-white. "Galeran!"

Ashamed, he pushed away from the wall to go to her. "Don't, Jehanne. I didn't mean it—"

"Didn't they tell you?"

"Tell me what?"

She whirled and raced into the hall. Without a pause she

picked up a pitcher of ale and hurled it full in Lord William's face, flinging the stone jug after. Fortunately he was still agile enough to duck, and the pot smashed on the wall.

Even over his father's bellow Galeran could hear Jehanne screaming, "Why didn't you *tell* him? *How could you not have told him?*"

He grabbed her before his father overcame a lifetime's scruples and beat a woman. "Told me what?"

She was rigid in his arms. Rigid as stone, or a corpse.

The dogs were all around them again, whining.

Lord William wiped his red face with a cloth hurriedly presented to him. "I thought you'd had enough blows for one day, lad. . . ."

"Told me what?"

"Gallot's dead, Galeran," said Jehanne icily. "It was all for nothing. He's dead."

Into the silence Gilbert said, "Don't forget the rest, you frozen-hearted bitch. You killed him to make way for your lover's bastard."

In the end Galeran ordered his wife into guarded confinement in the small nursing chamber next to the solar, more to protect her from others than to punish her. He couldn't even begin to comprehend what had happened in his absence and wasn't ready to try. Days of hard traveling had left him unfit for this crisis, and his poor rest the night before was just masking exhaustion.

He took refuge alone in the solar, looking sightlessly out of the narrow window.

His firstborn son was dead before he'd ever held him, and some people suspected that Jehanne had in some way caused the death. He'd gathered that much from the cacophony of information before he'd shut it off.

Later.

He'd handle it later.

His tired eyes followed the road away from the castle, into the nearby woods. It drew him, but running away once was enough for any grown man.

He needed sleep but knew his tormented mind would not permit it yet, and anyway, it was only morning. There was a day to get through.

His precious first day home.

With a bitter laugh, he pushed away from the window. He'd have to put his insane, purposeless energy to use, and hope activity would drown out half-formed images of a child he had never seen. A child all the people here could tell him of if he asked—

Tears swelled in his chest, more agonizing than a wound. . . .

No. Not yet.

He would not weep yet, for if he began, he was not sure he could stop.

He headed for the door, but halted, looking at an ivory rose in its accustomed place on a small table against the wall. He had to believe it had some meaning for her. Had it sat there throughout his absence, even when she . . . ?

He picked it up, and the cracked petal tilted then fell off. Muttering a curse, he fumbled to push it back into the soft wax that held it in place. Then he froze, holding it in his hand, fighting the urge to crush it, even though the sharp edges would lacerate his hand.

With a deep breath he put it down, even though the petal was crooked. The risks were too great.

He went out to his great chair in the hall and summoned his officers to report on their management of his property during his absence. He didn't make much sense of it, but could tell Heywood had been well cared for.

He couldn't help noticing the way they all looked at him, though. On the faces of some he detected a sneer that said they didn't think he had the balls to handle his sinful woman, that he'd forgive her without a twitch of protest.

Some eyed him warily, however, as if expecting him to burst into berserker rage at any moment.

Either could be right, which is why he'd hit her, to get someone on her side. Galeran's father had sent Will back to camp and Gilbert back to Brome, but he stayed in the keep, watching from a distance in case Galeran turned to violence again.

And Galeran was glad there was someone to make sure he didn't.

Five

If he tried hard, a man could take a long time reviewing a two-year absence. What's more, the exercise could cram his mind so full of petty details, there was no space for other things.

Like a dead child . . .

Like an unfaithful wife . . .

Galeran tried very hard.

Once his senior officers had been interviewed, he went, trailed by his dogs, to inspect all parts of the castle.

He knew that no matter what had happened, Jehanne would have run the estate perfectly, but he went over all the records and discussed matters with every person in the castle of any importance.

When he found himself discussing bluing with the head laundry woman, however, he knew he'd gone mad. He handled it well enough, until he saw the line of white baby-cloths hanging out to dry. Then he left the woman in mid-speech.

He couldn't escape it, though. Now reminders of babies seemed to be everywhere.

He came across the record of the cradle made for Gallot by the carpenter. He couldn't bring himself to ask whether the cuckoo was in that same lovingly crafted nest.

A small pony chewed hay in the stable, the animal bought by Jehanne within weeks of Gallot's birth to be trained ready for him. If he'd lived, he might have been ready to sit on its back.

In one ledger he saw the price of a small pair of shoes of soft leather, suitable for a child taking its first wavering steps.

These things almost broke through Galeran's control, but he pushed them away and concentrated on practical matters—new pens for the animals, supplies of arrows, last year's corn yield.

Not long after noon, Raoul, bearing bread, chicken, and wine, found him outside the walls near the pasture observing the mares in foal. "Your household is eating in the hall."

"I'm not hungry."

"Eat!" Raoul thrust a chicken leg into his hand. "Fainting won't solve any problems."

Without appetite, Galeran pulled meat from the bone with his teeth. "Are you my official nursemaid?" But he was feeling all the silliness of his impulse to escape.

"Just your friend."

Galeran turned to lean on the fence, watching the healthy horses. One of his best mares was in foal to his father's newest and finest war-horse, or so he'd been told. The product could be exciting, but excitement seemed beyond him. "As a friend, then, what would you do in my situation?"

Raoul gave a wry grin. "Go *very* slowly and keep out of the way of my wife. I think egg-laying must be fascinating."

Galeran surprised himself by laughing. He returned to the castle with Raoul and went to investigate the welfare of the poultry.

By evening he had achieved a certain balance. The sharp core of pain in his chest had not disappeared, but it had crusted over, possibly just because of the deadening effect of exhaustion.

As he'd expected, everything in Heywood was in order. Even Lowick's labors had been efficient, probably because he thought he was looking after his own property. He'd not been much liked, though, and the joy at Galeran's return seemed genuine. That helped.

Galeran had not asked anyone about Jehanne, but her presence had been unavoidable throughout the day, conveyed in casual but concerned comments. That told him the people here still cared about her, and he wanted that. He wanted her loved and cherished as she had always been.

He wanted her protected against himself.

He gained the impression that she had not been happy this past year, and welcomed that too. He could not have endured a picture of her glowing with radiance.

When the sun began to move toward the horizon, Galeran decided he could at last allow himself rest and headed for the keep. He stopped dead in the middle of the bailey when it occurred to him that a thorough bath was necessary if he wasn't to foul any bed he slept in.

Which brought the thought that Jehanne always bathed and shaved him.

Without trying to analyze his motives, he sent the order that she prepare to do so.

He then realized he was still in his mail. He must have looked ridiculous checking domestic matters in full mail, but he supposed he was going to look ridiculous no matter what he did. He went to the armory and had the smith help him out of the metal and quilted leather.

It felt remarkably good to be free of the weight.

When the hauberk was off and he was just in his filthy linen shirt and woolen braies, he stretched freely for the first time in days. "My skin is probably marked for life."

"Skin recovers, Lord," said the smith, "which is more than can be said of mail." He looked the armor over with a grimace. "I fear you'll need new."

"Probably. But cherish that. It's been to Jerusalem."

The man's disgusted expression gave way to one of reverence, and he handled the rusty mail tenderly. "Aye, Lord,

I will." He looked up almost shyly. "Does it glow, Lord? The Holy City?"

Galeran sighed. "It's just a city, Cuthbert, with houses, inns, markets, and whores. It reminds us all that God came to earth and lived as a man, just like other men. I was in Bethlehem too, and it's just a village, not much different from Hey Hamlet."

It was clear that Cuthbert didn't believe him, and even had doubts that Galeran had been to the Holy Land at all.

People's beliefs were chancy things and hard to change. Some people believed Jehanne had killed her baby. . . .

Galeran took a deep breath and headed back toward the keep. He met Raoul at the base of the steps, and noticed his friend had clearly already availed himself of a bath.

"Took your mail off at last, I see," Raoul remarked.

"Believe it or not, nursemaid, I'd have taken it off hours ago if someone had suggested it. It had become like a second skin."

"I assumed you were doing penance."

"Why would I need to do penance?"

"I never said you *needed* to. Your father ordered me to make sure you didn't murder your wife, and then went back to spend the night in his tent. Do you fancy a game of chess?"

"No. I'm going to have a bath."

Raoul wrinkled his nose. "You certainly need one."

"And my wife is going to bathe me."

"Oh-ho!"

Galeran gave him a look, and Raoul assumed an innocent expression. "In that case, do I have your word you won't drown her?"

"Yes. Go explore the maids here. I'm sure one will be to your taste. But don't interfere with Jehanne's women."

"Sets strict standards, does she?" Then Raoul immediately threw up his hands. "Don't gut me. I apologize."

"Jehanne is my wife and will be treated with respect. Complete respect."

Raoul grimaced. "Galeran, at risk of my head, I have to say you can't just ignore what's happened. Even the people here, who seem to admire her all in all, expect her to suffer some retribution."

"By the Cross and Nails, what do they want? That I tie her to a post in the bailey and flog her?"

Raoul shrugged. "A good beating might clear the air. Then if you get rid of the bastard——"

Galeran just walked by him and climbed the steps.

God knows, but there was a part of him that thirsted for that beating just as much as the castle people and his brothers did. Probably most of Northumbria was waiting to hear Jehanne scream.

But he couldn't do it.

He could never do it.

Nor could he imagine snatching Jehanne's child from her arms.

As he reached the door to the hall, he suddenly realized that he didn't know whether it was a boy or a girl.

He entered the large chamber and found it just as it had been most evenings of his life. Two of Jehanne's women sat in the window-light spinning and gossiping. They flashed him a look and spoke more quietly. Servants busied themselves putting up trestle tables for the evening meal, and a couple of men-at-arms sat at one dicing. Each person slid him a look, then concentrated on their own business.

Each person expected violence.

They'd be disappointed.

He hoped.

Would Jehanne have obeyed him and be prepared to bathe him? He thought she would. It was her *duty*, after all.

Raoul's plans for the evening prompted other thoughts, thoughts of sex with Jehanne. Galeran searched his mind, wondering if that was his intent.

Despite exhaustion, he was thinking of having sex with someone, or his body was. Approaching Heywood the previous day, he'd begun to release the tight control he'd kept on his desire, and like a stream undammed, it didn't seem possible to reverse the process.

He realized that his body had been smoldering in desire all day, and the flames were now licking higher and hotter. A plump, saucy maid slid him a sly glance, and seeing she had his attention, rolled her hips in subtle invitation, wetting her lips with her tongue.

Surely his vow no longer bound him. If one party broke a contract, the contract was void.

But he did not burn for *a* woman.

He burned for Jehanne.

He turned away from the wench and crossed the hall toward the solar. Jehanne was his wife and still had a duty to serve his needs. More to the point, he had never truly desired any other woman and still didn't.

He stopped dead when he saw the guard at the door to the solar. That could mean only that Jehanne was there and that his orders to guard her were being taken literally. But, he suddenly realized, he was going to present himself to her in a state of rampant erection.

A moment's effort convinced him that willpower could not change anything, so he went to a nearby garde-robe and changed things physically. With images of Jehanne burning in his mind, and her but a few steps away, it was both satisfying and bitterly frustrating.

He was, however, able to appear quite calm when he entered the solar.

It was all painfully familiar.

The large oak tub lined with thick linen cloths was half full of steaming, herb-scented water. Additional jugs of water, both hot and cold, stood ready. Drying cloths hung pristine white on a nearby rack, close enough to the brazier to be pleasantly warm when used.

In other words, everything was perfectly in order, just as it always had been with Jehanne in command.

She was awaiting him, dressed plainly now, her sleeves rolled up, and her hair bound under a scarf so it wouldn't get in the way. That was a shame. He'd quite like it to get in the way. . . .

Dissatisfied lust was glowing again in the cinders.

How would she react if he said "Get on the bed. I want to fuck you." He'd never said anything so crude to her in his life.

How could he say "Come to bed. I want to make love to you?"

How could he make love to a woman who loved another?

Like a blow, he faced the question he'd hidden from all day. Did Jehanne love Lowick? Had she always, and merely made do with the husband forced on her?

Did she wish Galeran dead so she could be with Lowick for all time? Lowick, after all, was taller, broader, more handsome. . . .

But how could a strong, clever woman love a man who wanted just her property?

He realized he'd been standing in silence for an embarrassingly long time, and moved to strip off his stinking garments. He was not so far gone, anyway, as to attempt carnal intimacy in this foul state. Jehanne had always been very fastidious.

For that reason, he didn't ask her to help him undress, and when he'd stripped, he opened the door and threw the clothes out into the hall. "Get someone to burn that lot," he told the guard.

Then he turned back and caught Jehanne looking him over intently. It reminded him too sharply of that time in his chamber before they were married—the time she'd thrown his clothes out the window. There was no embarrassment in her face now, though, just a rather objective concern.

"A few extra scars," he said.

"And many extra bites. You must be infested. Get into the water." Her brisk tone was impersonal, but her eyes were not. He could not read them, though. Did she wish him dead?

If she did, he thought he would rather be.

As he eased into the tub, the sensation of hot, herb-scented water on his skin drew an involuntary sigh of delight from him. For the moment, other desires were suppressed and other pains forgotten.

She began with his feet. "How long since you've had a bath?"

He leaned his head back and closed his eyes. "Months. Though until the last week, I changed my underclothes regularly." He didn't say that he'd refused to stop for such comforts in Bruges because he was so eager to reach her. Perhaps she guessed, for she didn't pursue it.

She scrubbed at his feet and pared the toenails, then worked up his legs. At times her fierce scrubbing bordered on pain, but he didn't complain. He knew she was just trying to make sure there were no unwanted inhabitants on his skin.

She stopped at his thighs, though, and moved around to start on his arms.

Galeran could almost fall asleep. Almost but not quite. This interlude was too precious to miss. If he let himself, he could imagine he was in the past and Jehanne was bathing him after a hard day's hunting.

She had always been clean when she came to bathe him, for bathing had always been followed by lovemaking and she believed clean should go with clean. Was she clean now? If he'd thought, he would have asked the guard whether the Lady Jehanne had bathed today.

Now his chest. "Thank goodness you don't have much hair here," she muttered. "I've picked off a dozen lice."

He almost smiled. It was good to hear her scolding. But

amusement faded. These pleasant moments weren't going to solve anything.

Did he want to keep Jehanne as his wife?

Oh, yes.

Even if she loved Lowick?

Yes.

Was it *wise* to keep Jehanne as his wife?

He didn't know.

Was it *possible* to keep Jehanne as his wife after her open adultery, and suspicion of murder? The latter was surely untrue, but her unfaithfulness could not be ignored.

Was he going to have to beat her to redeem her?

If so, she was likely to go unredeemed. Of all the trials he had ever imagined facing in life, that one he shrank from. If he'd known how much he'd hate hitting her, he'd never have found the will to do it.

She cleaned down his torso, but again stopped just short of his genitals.

"Lean forward."

When he obeyed so she could get at his back, he saw the filthy scum on the water. "I'm sorry. I don't think you've ever had to deal with me in such a state."

"If I mind, I can think of any number of reasons why I should be inflicted."

Trust Jehanne. Sometimes life would be more comfortable if she would avoid a confrontation or allow herself a polite lie.

After a moment, she added. "Is any of this dirt from the Holy Land? If it is, we should preserve it and build a shrine."

He couldn't tell if she was serious or not. "No. I did have a thorough bath in Constantinople. They take bathing seriously there. You'd like it." Head resting on his knees, he went on to describe the beautiful city, the ornate baths, and the sensual bathing rituals, realizing only when it was too late that this was talk for the Jehanne of his dreams, not for his adulterous wife.

She stopped her cleansing and went to get the smaller bowl to wash his hair. "Shall I cut it?"

"I'm sure it will make it easier."

She used the sharp knife with skill to cut his hair quite short, shorter than was fashionable. The working of her fingers against his scalp was almost unbearably arousing. Then she soaped and washed it three times before combing it carefully and squashing some nits. "It's not too bad," she said. "A pennyroyal rinse should keep it free of pests. Shall I shave you, or do you want one of the men to do it?"

He looked up at her. "If you were going to cut my throat, you'd have already done it."

"They burn women who kill their husbands."

He stared at her, trying to read meaning into the flat words, but then sighed and closed his eyes. "Yes. Shave me."

As she used the sharp edge of the blade to scrape away his rough beard, he wondered how long he could live in this wasteland without cutting his own throat.

At one point he thought he felt her fingers trace the scar down his chin, but she said nothing. Then she was wiping the soap away. "Stand up, and I'll get the rinse water."

He stood, finally irritated by her calm. "You've forgotten some bits of me."

She turned sharply, almost at bay, and he knew she wasn't calm. But being Jehanne, she didn't back down. "The water's too dirty now. I'll rinse you first."

She sluiced him with clean water. Then, without noticeable hesitation, soaped her cloth and began to wash his genitals. At the first touch he caught his breath, and in moments he was hard.

Her hands faltered. "Galeran?"

The rising edge of it revealed the true state of her nerves. It asked for guidance, but carried with it a note of submission, an agreement to do whatever he commanded. If he said, "Take me in your mouth. Clean me with your tongue," she would do it.

Was this all that was left between them—fear and penance?

"I'll do it." He took the cloth and completed the cleaning, then stepped out of the bath, rinsing each scummy foot.

She was composed again and ready with the cloths, but he noticed she kept her eyes lowered. Jehanne, who never lowered her eyes except in church. He rubbed himself dry, then wrapped a clean cloth loosely about his hips and sat on a bench.

Finally he said the words he had avoided all day. "Tell me about Gallot."

She was folding a cloth and her hands froze. "He's dead."

"I know that. When did he die?"

"Ten and a half months ago."

He had the feeling she could record it in days, hours, heartbeats even.

"How did he die?"

She finished folding the cloth with untypically clumsy movements. "He just died."

"Children don't just die, Jehanne. Was it a fever? Gripe?"

She turned to face him. "He just died. He was happy and healthy. He slept with me. We played together before he slept. . . ."

He thought she wouldn't go on, and in the face of her pain, he wasn't sure he wanted her to.

"Perhaps he was a little more fractious than usual. I don't know. . . . I tended some accounts and joined him in the bed and went to sleep too. When I awoke," she whispered, "he was dead."

Galeran stared at her as if her frozen face could provide answers. "Of what?"

"I don't know."

"Don't be foolish! You must know. Did you overlay him?"

"No." But she wouldn't look at him.

"Jehanne. It can happen. . . ."

She turned on him. "I did *not* overlay him! Drunken women do that. I was not drunk. I'm even a light sleeper and he was eight months old. If I'd begun to smother him, he'd have struggled. . . ." Her lips trembled and she pressed them together. "He did nothing. . . ."

"Was he sick?"

"No. No. . . . He had some marks about him, but nothing to kill. . . . Don't you think this hasn't been gone over?"

"Then how, in God's name, did my son die?"

She turned icy eyes on him. "Perhaps I killed him. Is that what you're thinking, like Gil? You were dead, or so that passing monk said. Lowick was here, wanting to replace you, but not wanting your son replacing his. Easy enough to get rid of a small child. A hand covering mouth and nose . . ."

"Easy enough for him."

Her face changed and he knew it wasn't a novel idea. "I was sleeping with Gallot," she said shakily. "It isn't possible."

"Perhaps you were sleeping with both of them. Rutting with Lowick beside my son's body."

"No!"

He lunged to his feet. "By the Holy Nails and Spear, Jehanne, I'll have the truth!"

An unsteady hand covered her mouth. "Oh, Galeran, no more vows . . ."

The squawk of a babe pierced the moment, the demanding squawk of a hungry young babe. Jehanne put her arm over her breasts and Galeran saw a damp patch begin to spread there. Those breasts had poured fourth milk on demand for his son once, and now they gushed for the child of Raymond of Lowick.

"Go feed it," he snarled, and she left almost at a run.

Galeran fisted the wall hard enough to bruise. So much for any idea of bodily ease. He could summon her back later, but he knew he wouldn't. No matter what had happened, he couldn't use Jehanne like a privy for his relief. There had to be something between them, something more than this.

He collapsed back on the bench and sank his head in his hands. Was it possible that she had killed the child?

No. Never. He would never believe that.

Was it possible that she had connived at Lowick killing the child?

He didn't think so, but love could do strange things. Look what it was doing to him.

He couldn't deny that there was something very strange about Jehanne now, and the events as he knew them made no sense. She had clearly conceived the bastard at about the time of Gallot's death, and soon after the news of his own supposed death.

Was it possible Lowick had raped her?

He shook his head. Jehanne would have cut off his balls and choked him with them.

Instead, she had kept Lowick here, and when Galeran had approached, had let him leave. He could see no sign of enmity.

He'd have to find out what had really happened before he could have any chance of peace. What was he going to do, however, if Jehanne and Lowick *had* caused his son's death in any way, even if only by neglect?

Kill them both.

He would have no choice.

He rose to pace the room, seeking desperately for some explanation that he liked and finding none.

He'd intended to sleep after the bath, but now nervous energy fought with exhaustion so that he could neither think straight nor sit still. He might as well get dressed.

If he had anything to wear.

Yet again he was painfully reminded of the time Jehanne had thrown his clothes out the window, for if she'd thought him dead she would surely have given his clothes away. If Lowick had left anything behind, it would be too large.

He threw open a wooden chest and stopped in surprise at the sight of his belongings neatly stored.

Everything was in excellent condition, well interspersed with herbs to ward off moths and other pests. He found clean braies and shirt—a new shirt finely made by Jehanne's own hand—and his favorite red wool tunic with marten fur trim. His shoes were even in excellent condition, kept oiled and supple.

He turned a shoe thoughtfully in his hand. If Jehanne had believed word of his supposed death nearly a year ago, why this careful care of his belongings?

Servants came, presumably sent by Jehanne, to clear away the bath. Galeran dressed and went out into the hall, head humming with weariness and tangled thoughts. He gestured and a servant brought ale. It had been foolish to avoid the midday meal, which was a time for the castle community to come together, so now he walked around and talked to some of the people.

There was no sign of Raoul. He, no doubt, was sensibly in bed with a cheerful, uncomplicated serving maid, one who'd be delighted to bear his child if God gave them one, since either the castle would pay her to raise it, or a good marriage would be arranged, or both.

Matters were somewhat simpler among the servant body.

But even there, adultery was not condoned. A man might accept a lord's child in the hope of favors, but he didn't want his fellow's cuckoos.

Galeran caught some strange looks. Doubtless everyone was wishing they'd been witness to the events in the solar. Doubtless they'd all kept their ears peeled back for sounds of a deserved beating being well delivered.

How dull they must all find this, and how puzzling.

They weren't the only ones to find it a puzzle.

Trailed by his dogs, Galeran went in search of his steward, Matthew, who was most likely to have answers to some questions.

The man was at home in his small cottage within the bailey, but on demand he willingly accompanied Galeran to the walls, where they could talk in privacy.

"Yes, my lord?"

"How did Lowick come to be seneschal here?"

The solid, middle-aged man hitched his belt uneasily over his belly. "He came to visit, my lord. He was well known to all here, of course, so we had no hesitation about letting him in. Sir Gregory had died of that cough he had—truth to tell, he'd not flourished much after you left—and Lady Jehanne had been considering with your father whom to take on in his place. It seems that when she heard Sir Raymond was available, she gave him the post."

Galeran was trying to remember whether his seneschal, Sir Gregory, had been particularly ill when he'd last seen him. He had been the kind of man who always seemed to be coughing and spitting. Surely it wasn't possible, though, that he had been disposed of to make room for Raymond.

That was too deep a plot.

But like a blow it came to him that it had been Jehanne who had urged him to go on the Crusade. The plot, if it existed, could go back years, back even to the time of their betrothal.

No, not that far, for Lowick had married elsewhere. But his wife had died.

Another convenient death.

"Do you know when Lord Raymond's wife died, Matthew?"

The man flashed him an astute glance. Did everyone have these suspicions? More to the point, was there anything in them?

" 'Round about the time you left for the Holy Land, my lord."

"And what did she die of?"

"Some fever, my lord. According to Sir Raymond's men, who accompanied him here, she was never strong. She miscarried of four babes in the marriage. Rich, though. She brought some sturdy land with her, as I understand it, at a place called Beeston, but by the contract, if she had no children, the land reverted to her family. Sir Raymond did his best to get a child of her."

"He always was ambitious. . . ." Galeran had never had much to do with Lowick, but he knew his nature. He was brave and honorable, but also ambitious. Lowick was sure that his looks and warlike skills gave him a right to a high place in life, such as that of husband to Jehanne of Heywood.

When Lowick had flirted with Jehanne during his visits, Galeran had judged it was more to annoy him than to seduce her. He'd never made an issue of it. That would have sullied Jehanne's name, annoyed his father-in-law, and possibly brought it to a matter of arms. Which he probably would have lost, since in those days he'd been no match for a larger man.

He'd wondered sometimes if that had been Lowick's plan—to force a fight and kill him. Crude, but possibly effective.

Jehanne had never objected to Lowick's behavior, but Galeran had always assumed that her reasons had been similar to his own—a desire not to cause discord in the house. Having been her father's squire, Lowick was in many ways like a brother to her.

Galeran had once asked Fulk why he'd not offered Lowick the chance to marry Jehanne. The old man had never been one to explain himself, but he'd said he wanted someone with better connections for his heiress.

Raymond's father had been a friend of Fulk's, both of them coming over with the Conqueror, but he'd not prospered. Fulk had taken Raymond into his household as a kindness, but kindness stopped at making him a son. No advantage in it, he'd said.

Had it all been a façade? Had Jehanne really loved Lowick all the time?

Six

Galeran realized that the steward was standing by patiently. This wasn't what he'd wanted to talk to Matthew about anyway.

It was hard to even speak the words, though. "And what of my son, Matthew? What do you know of how he died?"

The man cleared his throat and looked away. "As to that, my lord, it was a great mystery. A fine lad making his first steps . . ." The steward coughed, perhaps to hide a genuine lump in his throat. "There wasn't even any screaming, if you know what I mean. Lady Jehanne walked into the hall with the child in her arms and just said, 'He won't wake.' Quite a few of us were in the hall, and we didn't know what to make of it at first, her being so calm. Then she looked down at the little one again and said, 'I think he's dead,' in that same ordinary voice. But then she said it louder. And then she started shaking. . . ."

The man cleared his throat again. "Her women gathered and took the babe, but he was already cold. There was nothing to be done."

Galeran had his eyes closed and a pain in his chest that was likely to choke him. That simple telling revealed to him the depth of Jehanne's anguish.

And he had been so far away.

He had not even known.

If there was sense in the universe, he should have *known*. He sent his mind hunting back. Gallot had died while

Galeran had been on the way home, perhaps while he had been allowing the bath attendants of Constantinople to pamper his weary body. He remembered being restless then. He'd arranged to return home in the party of the Duke of Normandy, but the duke traveled slowly, so slowly.

He remembered still having nightmares about Jerusalem, but try as he might, he could not remember any other shadow. He'd had no flash of awareness that thousands of miles away he had suffered a terrible loss.

His voice was husky when he said, "Did anyone decide what caused the death?"

"No one could, my lord." Hesitantly, Matthew added, "Of course, there were whispers of evil spells and such. You know the way folks are. And after that one outburst she . . . Lady Jehanne . . . became so calm. Just carried on as if nothing had happened."

"It was always her way, you know that, Matthew."

"Aye, my lord, but when a woman's lost her only child, it looks funny. And when there's been news that she's lost her husband too, it looks even worse. . . ."

Galeran looked out over his land, fading to invisibility as darkness settled, but scattered with the fires of his father's army. Desperately, he wished he'd known his son, that he'd been here when all this had happened.

But if he'd been here, it might never have happened.

Could a woman's love—obsession—with a man cause her to connive at the murder of her child?

He turned his mind from torment to puzzles. "So, Gregory died and Lowick came here. That would be—what?— about two months after I left."

"Aye, lord."

"About the time Lady Jehanne found herself with child . . ."

He caught his breath.

Whose child?

All those years of trying and no babe, then miraculously,

a babe. And later, another babe without great difficulty. Had Jehanne gone to Lowick as soon as she'd left Galeran in London? Or had she, even, been with child when she urged him to take the Cross?

No, he gathered his flailing mind. Gallot had been born almost an exact nine-month after that last night.

Hadn't he?

"Gallot's birthday was St. Stephen's Day, yes?" That was what Jehanne had told him in her letter.

"Yes, my lord, and a day we all remember. A right happy one."

Thank God for that. He could check later to see if Jehanne had come straight back to Heywood. She'd been with Lord William, her uncle Hubert, and ten men-at-arms, however, and accompanied by three women. It would have been a remarkable feat to arrange an assignation in that company.

"Sir Raymond was always a competent knight," Galeran said. "I assume he ran the castle affairs well."

"Aye, lord." But it was said grudgingly.

"Why the scowl?"

"He was a proud man and acted as if it were all his."

"Had he reason to?"

Matthew knew what Galeran was asking, and shook his head. "I don't think so, my lord."

A fragment of good news. "So, the next thing that happened was word of my supposed death."

"Aye, lord. A monk it was who'd heard news from Rome of deaths against the infidels, and counted you one of them. It was a night for tears, my lord." The man cleared his throat and looked away.

It was nice, Galeran supposed, to be mourned. "And within days Gallot was dead."

"Aye, lord."

Galeran was beginning to feel uneasy about the questions he was asking and the interpretation that could be put on them. He trusted Matthew, however. He was an honest, shrewd man who could hold his tongue.

"How did my wife react to the news of my death?"

The older man took his time in replying. "You know the Lady Jehanne, Lord. She's never done what anyone expected. The news hit her, that's for certain. She asked the monk a great many questions and was clearly upset. But then she regained her spirits and said she'd not believe it unless she had proof. After that she seemed to put the matter out of her mind, apart from the fact that she prayed more than usual. I remember Sir Raymond talking to her, trying to make her accept the news, but she shrugged it off. Turned quite sharpish with him, in fact. He did persuade her to go to your father about it, but I don't know what happened there. She came back as if nothing were amiss, so we all took her lead. None of us wanted to think you dead, my lord."

"Thank you."

"But after that," added Matthew, "Sir Raymond grew bolder. I think he truly thought the place was his for the taking."

"And then Gallot died."

"Aye, Lord. And the lady changed."

"So I would hope."

Galeran wanted to ask whether Jehanne had truly taken Lowick as her lover, but of course she had.

He wanted to ask whether she had truly taken him to her bed within days of the news of her husband's possible death, and the certain death of her son. But she had done that too, or she could not have born a babe a nine-month later.

Why?

Why?

Why?

It was, he discovered, not something he could talk about yet, not even with Matthew. So he asked another question. "Matthew, tell me honestly, what do you think caused my son's death?"

"The honest truth, my lord, is that I don't know. I'm no believer in spells and wizardry, but something like that is the only explanation."

"Such things do not exist."

"Miracles do, my lord."

"Perhaps."

"Then why not works of the devil?"

Galeran sighed. "An excellent question."

"One thing I do know, Lord."

"What?"

"It would have been better if Lady Jehanne had taken to her bed with grief alone instead of with Sir Raymond."

Galeran didn't want to know more, but the man continued doggedly. "The very day the babe was buried, she slept the night with Lord Raymond, and all knew it."

Galeran turned away, blocking talk he could not yet bear. "Where is Gallot buried?"

"In the churchyard, near the wall, lord. There's a stone."

Galeran waved the man away and stayed on the battlements for a while, his mind wandering aimlessly in random patterns over his shattered life. It did no good, however, and so he went and prayed by the stone that marked the brief life of his child.

Someone had planted a rosebush there, but it was young and feeble yet. However it, unlike his son, would grow.

Galeran spent an hour in the darkening garden seeking the spirit that was his flesh and blood but finding nothing. He forced himself to leave the small grave and to return to the solar. He'd prayed and thought through most of the last night, and when he'd slept he had been cramped in the open air. It would be foolishness to do it again when he needed strength and wits to cope with all his problems.

All the same, he was reluctant to face the chamber he'd shared with Jehanne. He wasn't sure he could sleep there with the memories of past pleasures for company, but he couldn't face the talk he'd cause by sleeping anywhere else.

Jehanne and her closest ladies would be sleeping in the smaller room with the babe. He could summon her. . . .

No. On top of all the other reasons, exhaustion had swamped lust.

He stripped off his clothes and settled into the bed.

He almost leaped out again. The feel of the mattress and sheets, the smell of fresh air and herbs, all carried him straight back to this bed before he left.

With a groan he rolled over and buried his head in his arms. He'd convinced himself that it was God's will he take the cross, that it was God's will that he leave England, home, and wife. But if this situation was God's will, then the deity had a very nasty sense of humor.

Galeran woke rested, but heavy with too much sleep. The angle of light on his closed eyelids and the noises rising from the bailey all told him it was late in the morning and he should be up. He was in no hurry to open his eyes and stir, though. To rise was to face myriad problems.

He didn't want to go back to sleep either, for his dreams— though scarce remembered—had not been pleasant. He'd been back in Jerusalem at one point, with Jehanne by his side. There'd been a child crying, but always too far away to be reached, too far away to be saved from German knights and a river of blood.

Even the thought of those dreams was unbearable, so he opened his eyes . . .

. . . to see Jehanne sitting cross-legged on his bed, watching him.

She wore just a delicate silk kirtle and her hair hung long and loose around her, some wisps stirred gently by the summer breeze.

His heart began to pound as his body tightened and swelled. "Have you bewitched your guards?"

"I convinced them I was as secure in here as in the next room. A guard is outside the door."

"They might have given thought to my neck."

Color rose in her face, and not prettily. It was rare that Jehanne looked awkward, but now she did. "Since you let me shave you, they must know you don't fear that."

"I was awake then."

"I have never wished you harm, Galeran."

"Then you are remarkably clumsy, aren't you?"

As if slapped, she looked down and he found he hated this, hated seeing her so ill at ease. He'd rather she fought him.

"What do you want?" he sighed.

She did not look up, and two fingers and the thumb of her right hand moved in small anxious movements against the cream silk. "Raoul de Jouray . . . He told me of your vow."

Galeran silently cursed his helpful friend.

When he said nothing, she looked up, chin raised, almost her old self. "Perhaps you'd rather I sent a maid."

Pride and dignity said send her away.

Prudence echoed it.

Everything else in the universe made him flip back the sheet in silent welcome.

She caught her breath and a light shone briefly in her eyes. A cool, logical part of his mind warned that a clever woman in Jehanne's situation would make swift moves to reestablish herself with her husband, including getting with child if it were possible.

Jehanne was very clever.

He seemed to be split into three separate parts, though, and the cool, logical part was only one.

The second part was the man who loved Jehanne of Heywood too deeply for prudence.

The third part was an animal, consumed by scarce-contained lust for this woman.

She slid down to join him in the bed, stripping off her kirtle at the last moment. She would have covered herself, but he held the sheet away.

So she surrendered to his eyes.

He ran a hand gently over a belly that was a little more rounded.

"It's from carrying the babe."

"I don't mind." But he minded that reminder.

Then he let his hand wander up to her fuller breasts and darker, longer nipples. When he gently rolled a nipple, a drop of milk appeared. Milk for the child whose brains he should dash out against the nearest wall.

And a small, primitive, raging part of him wanted to.

Kill the bastard, the cuckoo in the nest.

Get rid of him at least.

Get rid of Jehanne's only living child.

He pushed these thoughts away and concentrated on the immediate. Her skin was as pale and translucent as that drop of milk, and against it his hand was darker than it had ever been, showing its exposure to hot sun. The only darkness on Jehanne was the bruise on her face where he had hit her. He touched it softly. She looked at him without reproach, and indeed she had no right to reproach him.

But he wished she would.

He stroked her breasts again, feeling the difference in them. She must have fed the babe recently, for they were not full of milk, but they were different.

To his relief, his lust was somewhat under control, perhaps because it knew it would soon be assuaged. He was hard, and every nerve was humming, but he could wait.

A little.

For some reason, it seemed important, now the moment had come, that he not just rut like an unruly stallion.

He moved his leg over her slender ones while exploring with hand and lip the wonderful softness of her skin, the curves and edges of her bones, the silk of her hair. . . .

He buried his face in her hair, fighting tears at the familiar feel and smell it, the stuff of dreams during exile, the stuff of torture now, as he shivered and his mind fell apart.

She had been passive, but suddenly her arms went around him, drawing him close, stroking down his back, over his buttocks, urging him over her, drawing him into her, so that—shuddering with agonized relief—he was home without intent or consciousness.

He wept as he found his release, and wept afterward in her arms, feeling her own tears trickle down onto his skin.

They lay together in silence, speaking through their skin, renewing their senses in the taste and smell of each other.

Then Galeran laid his head against hers. "Why?" he whispered.

She shook her head. "Not now, not here." She slid down and took him in her mouth, licking, tasting, tormenting. . . .

After a moment he found the strength to drag her back up to face him. "Are you trying to whore away your guilt?"

Her eyes sparked anger in her old manner. "Are you afraid I'll bite it off?"

He could keep demanding answers, but he saw in her face that he wouldn't get them here, not even with torture, so he settled for what he could get. He let her drive him wild with her lips and tongue and clever fingers, then entered her again in a fierce, violent passion that set the bed shaking and started her breasts pouring milk.

Their bodies slithered against each other, lubricated by the milk, and he started to laugh. She gave up trying to stop the flow and laughed, too, as she rose to meet him.

He licked the sweet milk off her, and she off him, as yet more spurted out to drench them and fuel their wild laughter, fuel their wild passion.

At the time of his last mighty thrust, there was a crack, a jolt, then one end of the bed collapsed, tumbling them, still interlocked, to the floor. Jehanne squealed, Galeran cursed, and the guard dashed in.

He stared. Then retreated, grinning.

After a frozen moment, Galeran and Jehanne dissolved into laughter again, rolling with it like children, wet and sticky among the ruins of the great bed.

When they finally sat up, however, Galeran's mind was clearing. "It would have been a clever move to half saw through that joint."

Jehanne's lingering smile disappeared. "By the Rood, Galeran, are you going to suspect every move I make?"

"Why not?"

She erupted to her feet. "Because of who I am! And anyway, I half expected you to whip me and send me to a convent, so why would I plan this pretty scene?"

"You were always capable of planning for many opportunities. And I might still. Whip you and send you to a convent, that is."

"I might prefer it to living with suspicion." She turned to the bed and wrenched back the mattress to inspect the wood. Then she swung to face him. "Look. Worm!"

He leaned closer. It clearly was worm, but a sour madness had taken control of him. "Not very good housekeeping," he pointed out. "I suppose it was merely good luck that the bed didn't collapse under you and Lowick."

And that was what really ate at him—the thought that the last time she'd joined in passion here it had been with another man. That she'd explored milky sex with another man . . .

She froze, half turned from him. "We never used this bed."

His relief was out of proportion to the words. "Why not?"

She walked away and pulled on her shift. "Probably because it was wormy."

Galeran sighed and rose to his feet. Another door slammed

in his face. He watched her slip on her clothing, enjoying the way it settled over her damp curves as much as he'd enjoyed her nakedness. "You're going to have to talk to me soon, Jehanne."

She spun to face him, and the stark agony on her face silenced him. "I'm sorry," she whispered, and left. But where another woman would have run, she walked from the room with dignity.

But what are you sorry for? Galeran wondered as he surveyed the shambles. The bed was quite an accurate reflection of his life—messy, rot-riddled, yet full of the essence of his love, his life, his wife.

Jehanne.

He inspected the bed and found worm in other parts. A new one would be needed. He couldn't regret it. Even if Jehanne and Lowick had never used this bed, it was part of something past, not present.

He froze, hands tight on the wood.

Jehanne and Lowick.

It had been a distant thing before. But now, now he could see them, hear them, *smell* them. Everything Jehanne had done with him today she had done with Lowick. She'd held him, guided him, nuzzled him, kissed him, sucked him, bit him. . . .

Galeran realized he was trying to snap the side of the bed with his bare hands. Since it was four-inch oak, it was more likely to snap him first. He made his hands relax and release, then examined the grooves and bruises he had made there.

What terrified him most was that one day he might turn this rage on Jehanne. She had to be made to talk to him, to let him understand and forgive, or one day he might snap her with his bare hands.

Pushing to his feet, he called for water and John to shave him. He couldn't take any more of his wife's ministrations for the moment. He dug out more clothes and was soon ready to face the day.

He wasn't ready for an encounter with Jehanne's cousin Aline, but that was what waited outside the door. Eighteen forceful years old, Aline of Burstock was short and plump, but had Jehanne's coloring. She shared Jehanne's temperament in many ways, but whereas Jehanne was a sword, Aline was a club.

"I'm sure hitting her made you feel better," she stated.

"You're usually more astute." He actually liked Aline, and was suddenly grateful to have her here with her common sense and her habit of speaking her mind. Although that didn't mean he wanted to discuss his affairs with her.

"I suppose you might as well get into practice, since you'll probably have to beat her to clear the air." Her worried frown showed that her words were bait dangled to see whether the fish would bite.

"You should get to know Raoul de Jouray. You two seem to think alike."

Bright color rose in her cheeks. "Alike! That one's a heathen. He'd scarce washed off the dirt of his travels before he found Ella."

"Or Ella found him." Galeran couldn't help but grin. "But then, Raoul could probably find the most amenable woman in any castle inside five breaths."

"Then he should get *her* to bathe him," said Aline, glowering.

"He expected you to?" Galeran tried not to laugh. He wondered if Raoul had guessed that Aline had strict notions about modesty and had deliberately teased her. "I'm sure he didn't insist on it when you objected."

"No. Jehanne assisted him."

All urge to laugh vanished. It was only proper that Jehanne bathe a well-born guest, and such matters had never bothered him before. Now, however, he wanted to squeeze his friend's throat between his hands.

"I'll bathe him next time he asks," Aline said, her blue eyes sharp as a hawk's.

He hated being so transparent. "There's no need . . ."

"*I'm* not going to be cause of more trouble with my silly scruples."

"I know such things are important to you, Aline. One of the other women . . ."

"That wouldn't be right. It would be an insult to a friend of the castle's lord." But then she frowned at him. "If you don't trust him, though, he's no friend."

"And if I don't trust her, she's no wife."

"Friends can be disowned. Wives cannot. Or not as easily."

Galeran leaned an arm against the stone wall and surrendered. "So, cousin, what do *you* think I should do?"

She looked up at him steadily. "She never stopped loving you, Galeran." Then the frown settled again. "But if you ever find that Brother Dennis, who brought news of your death, you could maybe cut out his lying tongue!"

"I didn't think you were so bloodthirsty."

"There are times when violence is called for, as with Christ in the Temple." With that she walked off in her typical brisk manner.

"Aline."

She stopped and turned.

"Is the child a girl or boy?"

"A girl. She's called Donata." Suddenly her lips quivered. "Don't hate her, Galeran."

Then she swung on her heel and went on her way.

Was it hate to wish a creature did not exist?

Galeran continued around the screen into the main part of the hall. He found his father in a chair, feet on a stool, nursing a cup of ale. Galeran took the other chair, gesturing for a servant to bring him food and drink.

"Rather late to be breaking your fast," said his father.

"I'd been three days without proper sleep."

"Ah." Lord William rubbed his bristly chin, and his dark

eyes picked over Galeran like a starving gleaner. "You're thinner."

"Did anyone expect taking Jerusalem to be easy?"

"You've been months coming home with nothing to do but eat."

"Shipboard rations."

"I hear you lingered in Constantinople and Sicily."

"Foreign food," Galeran countered, rather enjoying bandying words with his father once again.

"Bruges is a fine city, and they eat honestly there."

"I wanted to be home." Galeran took ale, bread, and cheese and gave the serving wench a smile. It was the pretty, plump one. She smiled back, but a touch of pity in the grin turned it sour.

He turned back to his father. "So, tell me how England goes these days."

His father opened his mouth to object to the change of subject, but then clearly thought better of it. "Badly. Rufus wants money, money, and more money, all to waste on his unnatural friends. And now he's sent Ranulph Flambard up here to squeeze us dry."

"Raoul said he was Bishop of Durham. Does he still run England for the king?"

"Aye, the weasel." Lord William spat into the rushes. "I tell you, it doesn't sit easily to have him at my backside. He and I have had a run in or two already. It was Flambard's clever idea, or so they say, that the king leave bishoprics vacant and pocket the rents and tithes. Wish he'd kept to it. Now he's milking Northumbria dry with double and triple taxes on laymen and churchmen alike."

"At least you can't accuse him of favoritism." Galeran bit into the warm, crunchy bread, filled with a sudden gratitude for simple pleasures. Surrounded as he was by the comforts of home—good bread, strong ale, and cluster of fine dogs—Rufus and Flambard could wait.

His father leaned forward to poke him. "It's a bad situation and getting worse, lad. No man's safe from the king's favorites. We've done well up here, being far from their activities, but now . . ."

Galeran dragged his mind back to the practical. "Will anyone oppose Rufus and Flambard?"

"There's talk."

Galeran sighed. The last thing he needed was involvement with a rebellion. "Talk won't stir anything."

"Probably as well," said Lord William, slouching back in his chair. "If anything happens to Rufus, the country'll be thrown to the wolves again, with his two brothers snarling over the Crown. God's breath, why couldn't he get some sons?"

Galeran raised a brow. Everyone knew why Rufus had no sons, had not even married.

"It's a simple enough matter," grumbled his father into his pot, "to sire a few male brats . . ."

Which wiped away amusement.

Lord William looked up and groaned. "I'm sorry, lad. But at least . . ." Then he thought better of what he had been about to say. "What are you going to do?"

They were no longer talking politics.

Galeran lounged back in the chair and Grua put her nose on his knee. He stroked her warm head. "What do you think I should do?"

"Hell's flames! Do you want to keep her?"

"Yes, if she wants to be kept."

"If she wants . . . ?" his father spluttered. "If you keep her, she should thank you on her knees daily!"

Galeran looked at him. "Can you imagine a decade or two of such bitter gratitude?"

His father fell silent. It was not so long since Galeran's mother had died, and all the world knew she and Lord William had been devoted. Mabelle of Brome had been steady as a rock and warm as a hearthstone, the loving heart of a rambunctious family. Galeran wished she were still alive.

Mabelle might have been able to see a way through this tangle.

Lord William eyed his son. "Perhaps it would be better, then, for you to put Jehanne aside. We'll find you a steadier wife. If Jehanne goes to a convent, we might be able to hold on to Heywood. . . ."

"If I break the marriage, I assume Jehanne will marry Lowick."

"Marry Lowick!" his father exploded, then hastily lowered his voice. "If you have her put to death, she'll not marry anyone."

"I couldn't do that. And neither could you."

"I could put her in a convent so tight, she'd never so much as set eyes on a man again."

"True, but Lowick could still petition to marry her on the basis of their true attachment, which resulted in a child. He might even be able to fabricate a case of prior betrothal that would satisfy a Church court. I couldn't swear old Fulk never thought about it before his sons died. And in that case, Lowick would get Heywood, at least as guardian for his daughter."

"The sun's fried your brains if you think I want that scoundrel sitting on my borders!" Red anger tinged Lord William's face. "Even in this last year he's been disputing rents, interfering with my tenants. . . ."

"Has he? Then perhaps you'd better help me restore my marriage."

Lord William stared at him, caught mouth agape. "You cunning fox!" Then a glint entered his eyes. "Right, then. But she can't get off unscathed. You'd better start by disciplining her. A daily whipping for a month should tame her."

"By all means. Why don't you order it?"

His father growled at that. "Don't think I don't know why you hit her, boy." He worked his jaw anxiously. "Well, what in the name of St. John are you going to do, then?"

"Try to understand."

His father shook his head. "There's nothing to understand. She always panted after Lowick. Half the girls in the shire did, including two of your sisters. With you gone and her needs untended, she grew weak, as women will. You know I thought it unnatural for all you men to be going away for years. It's surprising the whole of Europe isn't littered with bastards! If I'd realized earlier—"

"No matter how sex starved," Galeran interrupted, "do you really think Jehanne would slide into Lowick's bed the day of her child's burial?"

William looked at him steadily. "She did, though, didn't she?"

It was like a shower of ice. For she had, hadn't she?

"So," repeated his father, "what are you going to do?"

Galeran hadn't the slightest idea. "For the moment I'm going to let her out of custody so she can resume her work. Unless you object. It was for attacking you she was confined."

William shook his head. "A gnat to an ox. And she had a point. I should have told you."

"Yes, you should."

"Mary's womb, but she's a difficult woman sometimes! She came to me when there was news of your death, you know. Cool as water from deep in the well, but for all of that, I'd swear she was distressed at the possibility."

"I'm sure she was. Did you see her after the child's death?"

William shook his head. "Not soon after. It was a full week before we had word, and when I came here, it was as if nothing—no," he said abruptly, "it was not as if nothing had happened. She was like a walking statue. But she was taking care of business as if nothing had happened, and apparently had been doing so since the day after the death. Looks funny, that."

"And talk had already started."

"Aye, though at that time none spoke to me of her liaison with Lowick."

Galeran fought the urge to get up and walk away. He was going to have to get used to talking about these things. "When did you find out about that?"

"That's a good question." His father worked his jaw again. "It's been a busy year, lad, what with one thing and another. The Scots have been bothersome. The weather's been chancy. And then there's Flambard. . . . When we had word of your death, I sent messages abroad, to the Pope and to Constantinople, hoping to hear better news. Lacking good news to share, I didn't seek out Jehanne."

He reached for his ale and took a deep draft. "Turns out Will's wife heard rumors, but didn't want to stir up trouble, the silly besom. But it was too late by then, anyway. First I heard for sure was when Lowick petitioned the king that you be declared dead so he could marry your widow, who was expecting his child. I came here only to be refused admission or explanation! I was much of a mind to take the place then, but it makes no sense to put a castle through a siege if it can be avoided. Especially one that's in the family. So I went south to oppose the petition."

"What happened?"

"It was tangled up in courts and chanceries. After a while I left them to it, for I could see nothing would happen soon. What's more, I'd spoken to one sailor, who swore he'd seen you alive in Constantinople. So I sent off more messages to seek the truth."

"Did Lowick get any support from Rufus?"

Lord William's smile was grim. "There was nothing in the case worth the cost of offending me, though Flambard tried to sway the king. The bishop's had some long-nosed cleric hereabouts asking questions, but since I had that sailor tell his tale, no one wanted to be hasty. I fear the bishop's man will be back now, though, at the least looking to fine somebody for something."

"Money is the least of my problems."

"Hah! With Rufus and Flambard picking over England like crows in a cornfield, money'll soon be a problem nobody has!" William pushed up out of the chair. "Which reminds me. I'd best get back to Brome and take care of my own affairs. Unless you need me here."

Galeran rose. "No, of course not."

"You'll have a care . . ."

Galeran met his father's worried look with a bland one. "I don't feel particularly violent, and if that changes, Raoul's bigger than I am. He seems to have appointed himself my watchdog, and he's as tender toward women as you are."

Lord William just harrumphed and went on his way. The army had already broken camp, and it didn't take long for the orderly file of men and wagons to disappear over the hill. Galeran looked out from the walls as if for the first time. Heywood certainly seemed more like home without an army encircling it.

The enemy, of course, was within.

He sent an order to remove the guards he'd placed on Jehanne and to tell her she was free to take up her duties but was not to leave the castle. Though he hated to do it, he also spoke to Walter of Matlock, making it clear that Jehanne was to be prevented, with any necessary force, from leaving.

Next, he summoned the carpenter and commanded a new bed, ordering a new mattress as well. He hoped it symbolized a fresh start.

Then he ordered out his best palfreys, gathered his hounds, two promising hawks, and four men-at-arms, and set out to show Raoul his estate and a bit of hunting. The trip could take days if he stopped to talk to his larger tenants and the village headmen. Of course, if he traveled to visit the other smaller estates that belonged to Heywood, the trip could last weeks, but that would be taking cowardice too far.

Seven

When Aline heard that Galeran had left, she hurried in search of her cousin, silently berating people who ran away from situations that needed to be faced. She was sure that Raoul de Jouray had something to do with it. He was just the sort of slippery, smiling fellow who would rather go hunting than tackle a thorny problem.

And thorny it certainly was. She'd never forget the clash of joy and raw terror she'd experienced when Galeran had appeared two days before. She was only just beginning to believe that it wouldn't be instant disaster. She wasn't at all sure disaster could be avoided entirely.

Eventually she found Jehanne on the walls, staring after the riders. Aline stopped at a distance, reluctant to intrude on a moment she scarce understood at all.

She knew her cousin well and loved her deeply. Some might think that stony face showed indifference, but Aline knew it was a mask to cover Jehanne's deepest pain. It was unfortunate, though. The mask was too easily misinterpreted.

As it had been when Gallot died.

Aline still felt guilt over that. She'd adored the child, and had been so distraught herself that she'd given little thought to the mother's pain. Instead, she'd fled to the chapel to seek solace in prayer. Perhaps if she'd stayed to comfort Jehanne, her cousin would not have ended up in Lowick's arms, would not have ended up trapped by Donata.

If that night had been different, then Galeran's safe return could have been a time of wondrous delight. Instead, she remembered with a shudder the time between Galeran's appearance at the gates and the morning after, when he'd entered the castle.

When a guard had burst into the hall with the news of Lord Galeran's approach, Aline had thought Jehanne might finally faint, though even she wasn't sure how much of the pallor had been fear, how much shock.

Lowick was simply furious. It didn't take him long, however, to realize that staying was certain disaster. Certain death.

Right there in the hall, Jehanne calmly urged him to leave. Aline wanted to shake her cousin, to tell her to say something warm about her husband's return. Instead, she was sounding like a woman urging her beloved into safety.

At least Jehanne was publicly refusing to go with him, stating before all that she would not flee her legal husband. It hardly sounded loving, though.

"Jehanne. My lady!" Lowick protested, and he at least sounded genuinely moved. "How can I leave you here to face him? You must come with me, or I fear for your safety, and for the safety of our child."

"Donata is too young for a wild journey, Raymond."

"Then leave her. Aline can hide her."

"She's at the breast."

"A wet nurse . . ."

"I will not give my child a stranger's milk, especially not to save my skin."

"There will be no milk if he strangles you!"

He tried to seize her then, but Jehanne whipped out her knife, and her men in the hall drew their swords. Lowick's men drew too, but they were heavily outnumbered, and so they and their lord headed for the postern gate in the dead of night.

With men of her own to protect her, Jehanne accompanied them down to the small door in the walls. Aline went too, wanting to make sure the chief cause of their problems left.

At the door, Lowick tried one more time to persuade Jehanne to flee with him. Failing at that, he fell to his knee to kiss her hand. "God protect you, then. And I will go to the bishop and beg his aid. He will speak to the king for us. I will find a way to protect you, a way for us to be together."

Jehanne, unfortunately, said nothing.

Aline muttered, "Good riddance," and prayed Lowick would quickly find some other propertied lady to prey on.

That wasn't fair, though, she thought as they all hurried back into the keep. Raymond was genuinely devoted to Jehanne. Perhaps that explained why Jehanne seemed so weak with him.

And there was reason for Lowick to fear for the safety of Jehanne and Donata. Men were not kind to adulterous wives and bastard children, and that knowledge haunted Heywood through a long, sleepless night. Aline, helping to prepare to open the castle to its returning lord, prayed earnestly to Mary Magdalene, patron of sinful women.

Dawn was welcomed as an end of waiting, though no one felt confident of what the day would bring. Jehanne, still outwardly calm, spoke one last time to her officers, making sure they understood their orders, and then tidied herself and went to wait in the hall.

When Aline realized she meant to greet her husband bastard in arms, however, she finally protested. "Donata is the only innocent in this, Jehanne. You can't put her at risk! Give her to me."

"No." It came out breathily, and Aline realized then that her cousin was almost faint with fear. Which meant she was not thinking clearly.

"Be sensible, Jehanne. You can't expect a man to be careful at a moment like this."

She tried to take the child, but Jehanne held on. "I won't hide her. . . ."

"It's not a matter of hiding. Give her to me!"

But then Galeran was there, looming in the doorway, an ominously dark shape against the dawn sky. With a hiss of anxiety, Aline retreated a few steps, telling herself that Galeran had always been a rational, good-hearted creature.

For a man.

Aline had five brothers and few illusions about the male of the species.

Anyway, was this man the Galeran she knew? He looked a mess—ragged, gaunt, bearded, and filthy, with new scars on his face.

She almost wondered if it *was* him, until the dogs raced forward to welcome him home. He gave them their due, then looked up. As he walked toward Jehanne and the baby, Aline sucked in a fearful breath.

This man was not the Galeran she knew. . . .

It had not gone too badly, though, all in all, Aline reflected.

And yesterday he and Jehanne had spent time together at the bath. Then this morning Jehanne had been in the solar with him for quite a while, though she'd emerged stone-faced again.

Hardly surprising. Aline couldn't ignore the new darkness in Galeran's eyes and the sense, emanating from him like heat from a fire, of choked-off rage. She couldn't forget that blow.

Perhaps Jehanne was relieved to see him riding away for a few days.

She went forward to interrupt whatever thoughts held her cousin captive, and saw something else. "Tears?" Immediately, she regretted mentioning them. Jehanne hated to be seen crying. "Donata's hungry."

Jehanne wiped her eyes, then turned. "I'm sorry. I lost

track of time." Calm again, she led the way down the steps to the bailey.

Aline hurried after, wishing Jehanne *would* cry in public, and often. It would soften the men up in no time. "What's going to happen now?" she demanded.

"I don't know."

"Didn't you ask Galeran?"

"No."

"Why not?"

Jehanne stopped and looked back at her. "Because he probably doesn't know."

Aline rolled her eyes. "You could have *asked* him. You were together this morning."

"We hardly spoke."

"But you were in there for ages! Oh!"

"Quite."

Aline could feel relief like a warm poultice to her heart. "Is everything all right, then?"

But Jehanne sighed. "No, Aline. Sex doesn't mend problems like this."

"What does, then?"

"I don't know." And Jehanne turned again to make her way across the bailey.

"You can't just put it out of your mind. You have to be prepared. What will Raymond do now?"

Jehanne stopped dead. "Raymond?"

"You remember Raymond," Aline said caustically. "The tall, blond one? He won't give up. He's probably doing as he said and trying to get the king's interest in his case."

"I suppose he is," said Jehanne, but her frown was thoughtful. "What gain to the king, though, in supporting Lowick against Galeran's family? And a returning crusader at that. They are the closest thing we have to living saints."

"So he'll have to give up?"

Jehanne turned pale. "So he might think of correcting

fortune's move." She lifted her skirts and ran up the stairs to the hall, Aline pounding after.

"What?" she gasped as Jehanne shouted for her scribe. But then she heard the hasty note her cousin was dictating—a warning to Galeran to beware of sneak murderers in the woods.

"He'd try to *kill* him?" Aline asked as the scribe hurried off to give the letter to a fast rider.

"Why not? Why not?" demanded Jehanne, pacing the hall in a swish of skirts. "With Galeran dead, Raymond would once again be in an ideal situation to claim me." She suddenly stopped, hands gripped together. "Oh, if only I could ride with that note myself!"

"To protect him? Jehanne, he can look after himself, especially now that you've warned him. And he has that Raoul de Jouray alongside as well. All that brawn must be of some use."

Jehanne calmed and even laughed. "True. And I am resolved to have done with my fierce ways. Look what they have brought us to. I am going to put my trust in God."

Aline hugged her. "Then there is hope. And Donata is waiting, as you can hear."

Aline accompanied her cousin to the crying babe, sending up her own most earnest prayers for Galeran's safety.

Galeran was surprised by the note. He could read no particular affection in the terse words, but surely they must mean that Jehanne preferred him to Raymond.

Unless she simply feared to be judged an accessory to murder.

With a grimace at his thoughts, he pulled up his coif and rode on, keeping a watchful eye on the surrounding countryside.

They slept that night at a monastery, one that prospered

under the protection and endowments of Heywood. In fact, many of its riches came from Jehanne's petitions for a child.

The Lord gives to his people, but He also demands sacrifices in season . . .

Was that a part of the answer? Had his disgust and lack of faith at the taking of Jerusalem angered the generous God, and caused Him to take back his gift? Galeran was not accustomed to thinking of God as petulant, but he wasn't used to thinking of him as cruelly unjust, either.

As he and Raoul sat in the guest parlor finishing a fine meal, Galeran said, "You're being remarkably tactful. No questions? No advice?"

"Do you want advice?"

"Yes."

"But will you take it?"

Galeran grinned and mopped up a delicious gravy. "Probably not."

"Then it may be harmless to give it. Put her aside. She's a sorceress."

Galeran stared at him. "A *sorceress?*"

"Scoff if you want. No one who's under a spell knows it. It's clear the people in the castle think she uses magic."

"The people in the castle think she's strange because she doesn't always act like other women. She does not use magic."

"Then how did she get into your bed today?"

Galeran burst out laughing. "You can ask that? I was like a stallion with a mare in season. She had only to touch me."

Raoul leaned forward, jabbing a finger to emphasize his point. "That's because she persuaded you to that vow of fidelity. I always said it was unnatural."

"I persuaded myself to it, Raoul. It seemed right, considering what we were asking of God. And," Galeran admitted, "I've never wanted or taken another woman."

Raoul's mouth slackened with shock. "There. You see! Bewitched."

"Raoul, *you* might see that as a sign of bewitchment, but it's only a sign of devotion. If ever a woman conquers your wandering affections, you'll probably feel the same way. I met and loved Jehanne before I had much interest in wandering. And she is a special woman." He saw Raoul gather breath to speak. "But *not* a sorceress. She's the most down-to-earth woman I know. Which reminds me. Don't embarrass Aline."

Raoul's brows rose. "Your wife's bantam cousin? What have I done to her?"

"Asked her to bathe you."

"Why not?" Then Raoul flashed Galeran a wary glance. "I didn't *ask* your wife to attend to me, however. I suggested she send one of the other women."

"That would hardly show proper respect to a guest."

"The situation would never have arisen if the little cousin had attended to it. Why didn't she?"

Galeran poured the last of the wine into their goblets. "Aline's always been very modest around men, despite being the only girl in a family of boys. A few years back she went to live at St. Radegund's convent, thinking to take vows there. She left only because Jehanne needed companionship whilst I was away."

"Then if men make her nervous, it's time she returned to the cloister."

Galeran smiled wryly. "She's doubtless staying on guard. She's a fierce creature for one so small. But once she's sure I won't hurt Jehanne or the babe, she'll doubtless take the veil."

Raoul sipped the last of his wine. "It seems rather a waste."

"Why? She's an ideal nun—clever, practical, and with no interest in men."

"I can't quite envision it. But I suppose since nuns are

supposed to be brides of Christ, He should get some of the pretty, lively ones."

Galeran almost choked on his wine. "One day, a thunderbolt will come down from the sky to turn you into a cinder." But then he considered his friend. "So," he added thoughtfully, "you find her pretty and lively, do you?"

"Oh, no!" Raoul raised his hands. "Keep your mind on your own affairs. Pretty and lively doesn't mean I want to become entangled with her."

"But—"

"But what *are* you going to do about your wife? Do you think you can just say, 'There, there, we'll forget all about it'?"

"That's turning the conversation with a heavy hand. . . ." Galeran took a moment to wipe his knife clean, first on the remains of the bread, then on the linen cloth. "No, I don't suppose I can brush it aside when she has her brat at the breast."

He regretted the word *brat* as soon as it was out. None of this was the child's fault—Donata's fault. He must think of her as Donata. *Donata* should not suffer for her mother's sin.

"Ah, well." Raoul looked at him far too shrewdly. "Perhaps you'll see your way in time."

By silent agreement they went off to their beds.

Once there, however, Galeran couldn't help but think of Jehanne. Their loving that morning had eased him, yet could not touch a deeper hunger—the hunger to be with her in harmony as in the past, playing with each other as musicians play with instruments, drawing tunes both new and old simply for the joy of it.

After a sleepless hour, he left the bed and went into the chapel to kneel before the altar and pray.

First he rubbed away the stain of doubt that had crept into his mind. God did not snatch back gifts just because humans were frail. Galeran knew he had done his best in the Holy Land, that he had played his part in all the battles. As for his revulsion at the extent of the slaughter in the streets of Jerusalem, his sudden conviction that a true God would not call for this . . . Well, it had either been a valid insight or a weakness of faith, and God would redress the first or forgive the second.

He would not kill a child in revenge.

Galeran continued to pray, and peace settled on his soul.

Jerusalem and Jehanne had both shaken his faith in religion, but they had not touched his belief in divine goodness. In fact, the Holy Land had brought him a deeper, richer vision of God.

There, for the first time, he had truly believed that Jesus of Nazareth had existed—not the glorious lord of the manuscript pictures, but a man, like other men. As a child He had played with friends in the dust of Bethlehem as Galeran had played at Brome. As a youth He had set out to take up His place in the world. As a man He had died in Jerusalem as Galeran had nearly died.

The Christ had built and mended things, laughed and cried, loved and been betrayed by his closest friend. He had suffered temptation and doubt both in the desert and in the Garden of Gethsemane. Though He had never fathered a child, Christ had grieved for Lazarus in the grave. He, if anyone, could understand Galeran's pain, and light a path through the dark.

The next day they went on their way, still wary. The expedition proved peaceful, however. Day after day the sun blazed from a clear blue sky, but God granted His children the boon of puffy white clouds and breezes to relieve the heat. Even Raoul began to think more kindly of the English climate.

Everywhere, insects, animals, and people labored against harsher times, and the workers in the fields both blessed and cursed the life-giving sun. On the moors the sheep were glad to be free of their heavy fleece. In the valleys the peasants rejoiced as the first hay was formed into stacks. Cattle grazed stoically on thick grass whilst back in cottages and manors their rich milk became butter and cheese. Little armies of geese, chickens, and ducklings swarmed from spot to spot under the command of children, fattening for the autumn slaughter.

The countryside was bursting with food, and Galeran's hawks regularly brought him tasty birds. Each evening the men and hounds chased rabbits and hare for the pot, and for the joy of the sport.

This was his land, this was his life, and Galeran found its health and welfare healing.

He didn't forget Jehanne's warning, however. In every hamlet he asked about strangers, but consistently he was told that none had been seen. Gradually, he relaxed his vigilance. At this busy time it would be hard for armed men to move though the country unobserved, and it offended him to ride on his own land as if among enemies.

In each village and hamlet he made it known that he was home, and available to his people. He was greeted with heartwarming joy and offered new cheese, ripe fruits, and fresh-caught fish.

Yes, it was sweet to be home even if he felt surrounded by a silent question. *And what does this mean for the Lady Jehanne?*

No one mentioned Gallot. Perhaps it was too difficult a subject, or perhaps it seemed a sorrow too long past. Children died. It was no great event. Except to the parent.

The parent who had never known the child.

He heard no direct complaints about Raymond of Lowick, and it was clear that in general Lowick had managed matters well enough. It was also clear, however, that he had ruled with a heavy hand and had not been above taking more than Heywood was entitled to.

That was not so uncommon in Rufus's England, but it wasn't Galeran's way.

As the days drifted by, and the journey took them farther from Heywood, Galeran found that the simple people had heard little of events at the castle. Though they knew there had been trouble, they knew nothing of Jehanne's infidelity. If they'd heard of her second child at all, he was congratulated about it. Presumably they couldn't count months, or had no idea how far away he had been.

Doubtless they thought the Holy Land was somewhere not far beyond Wales.

Sitting on the ground beneath a tree, earnestly discussing just where one village's fields should end and another's begin, Galeran could almost envy these people their simple lives. But then a case would be brought before him for judgment, and he'd realize that in their way a village's problems were just as complex as his own.

Biddy of Merton was a thief, the people of Threpton said, who had no right there anyway now that her man was dead. It seemed to be so, but looking at the defiant young woman, with her sneering mouth and cocked hip, Galeran saw someone alone and frightened. How was she to survive all alone without stealing?

On the other hand, she didn't strike him as a naturally honest sort, either.

Biddy clearly couldn't remain where she had become so unpopular, so he sent her to Heywood to be employed there. He promised that if she behaved she could have a place, or he'd find her a new husband. If she stole again, she'd be whipped and driven out to fend as best she could.

As Gil and others wanted to have Jehanne whipped.

As the churchmen would doubtless want to have her whipped if they became involved.

But the Church would be more merciful than the civil courts, who would probably want her burned to death.

People at all levels had a relentless desire to see justice done.

The next case brought forward for judgment was a complaint against Tom Fetler, who had allowed his animals to escape and get into the corn before harvest.

That was simple enough. Galeran levied a fine.

Then the village headman laid complaint against the miller, that he took more than his share. Nothing new in that, and it couldn't be proved, but Galeran made sure the man understood that if he were caught at it, he'd rue the day. From an incautious remark the miller made, Galeran suspected that Lowick had been willing to take a cut of the extra profits in return for protection.

So, Raymond of Lowick had been filling his purse at the expense of Galeran's people, had he? It was not uncommon, but Galeran was pleased to hear it. He knew Lowick had many good qualities, but he wanted reasons to despise him thoroughly.

Before leaving the village, he inspected the millrace to be sure it was properly maintained, and checked some hedges and a footbridge the village was responsible for, then he rode on, wishing he were not such a coward and was home in bed with his wife.

It was at the end of the third day that the woman was brought before him, babe in arms. He thought his heart would stop.

She was nothing like Jehanne, being stocky and dark, but something in her fearful defiance made him think of his wife waiting for him in the hall, and he was not surprised when told she was an adulteress.

Here, however, the case was different, for the woman would not say whose child it was. She had tried to claim that it was her husband's, but he—a quite elderly man— swore he'd never had his wife.

The local priest had been brought into the matter and had preached long and hard at the woman, begging her to name the father. Now Father Swithin repeated his exhortations, explaining to the woman that if her husband could not fulfill his duties, the marriage could be annulled and she could marry the true father of her child.

She remained stubbornly silent, and everyone looked to Galeran for judgment.

Once he would have been impatient with such a silly business, but now he wondered if there were as many complicating factors in this case as there were in his own.

In this village he was sitting on a bench near the inn, under the shade of a spreading beech tree. Raoul and his men were off to one side, enjoying a hearty meal of ale, bread, and cheese.

Taking a draft of his own ale, Galeran called the women to sit on the bench with him. She came, hesitantly, still carrying her bundled baby.

"What's your name?" he asked, offering her some raspberries from the dish that had been set alongside his bread.

"Agnes, Lord." She took a few berries warily, but then shoved them in her mouth.

"Do you know who the father is, Agnes?"

She swallowed the berries in silence, and he thought she wouldn't answer, but under the pressure of his gaze eventually she nodded.

"Is he married?"

She looked down, scowling. "Lord, I'd rather not say."

"Why should he avoid his responsibilities? At the least he owes a fine and should support his child."

"Edric always said he wanted a child of me. Why shouldn't *he* support it?"

"Edric's your husband?"

"Aye, Lord." She flashed a scowl at the sinewy white-haired man, who scowled back.

Galeran beckoned the man forward. "Edric, do you have any children?"

"Nay, Lord. My first wife never caught."

"Not surprising," muttered Agnes.

"Be silent, woman," said Galeran sharply, and Agnes settled warily to eating the raspberries. Her babe suddenly stirred and turned to her, and she lowered the loose neckline of her tunic to put him to the breast. The tiny, dark-thatched infant latched on and suckled greedily.

Galeran looked up at the husband, whom he caught eyeing the child rather wistfully. "He looks to be a healthy lad. He could be a support in your old age. . . ."

The scowl returned. "I'll not raise another man's brat, Lord, with all the village laughing at me."

"If you'd not made a fuss," Galeran pointed out, "no one would have known."

That was a choice he would have welcomed.

"She told me in public, Lord Galeran! That she were with child. It were a shock."

Galeran turned to the woman. "Agnes, why did you do that?" When she remained silent, he said, "Speak, or I will have you whipped."

She flashed him a resentful look, but muttered, "I never thought he'd admit his failing, Lord."

"Ah. So you thought shame would keep him silent so you could keep both husband and lover."

Betraying color rose in her round cheeks.

A merry coil indeed, but Galeran felt some sympathy for a young woman tied to an old and impotent husband. "Edric, why marry a young, lusty wife if you've no interest in swiving her?"

"Oh, I've interest, Lord," said the old man, raising a laugh from the bystanders. "I thought a young 'un 'd spark me up, like."

Galeran turned to Agnes. "And why did you marry Edric? Were you forced?"

When she hesitated, a burly man stepped forward. "She was not, Lord Galeran. I'm her father, for my sins, and it was her will entirely to marry Edric."

Galeran waved him back. "Well, Agnes?"

She was still scowling, but he thought her lips trembled. Despite her sturdy build, she was surely younger than Aline. "He's a well-to-do man, Lord. I didn't know about his problem. He should have said something."

"True enough. And, as the priest has told you, if you want to complain of your husband's inability, it could be grounds for breaking the marriage so you could marry the father of your child."

She stared straight at him. "Nay, Lord. I'd not want that!"

"Why not?"

Her eyes slid around, perhaps hesitating for a moment on a florid, black-haired young man who seemed to be finding this inquiry amusing. "I don't like him," she muttered at last.

"Then why lie with him?"

"He's lusty and I itched for a man."

Galeran was distracted by the notion that such a simple itch might explain Jehanne's behavior. But no. She had at least as much willpower as he. Perhaps more.

"So," he asked the woman. "What's going to happen next time you itch?"

She sniffed. "I don't know, Lord. I plan to be a better wife, but I do miss the swiving."

It would be nice, thought Galeran, if England had a version of the Arab harem but with one woman having a number of husbands. Agnes could have a husband to support her and help her raise her children, and a lover to ease her itch and conceive them with her. As it stood, there was no neat solution.

"Perhaps I can give your husband a few suggestions that might help matters a little," he said. Both husband and wife looked at him with cautious hope but then scowled at each other with resentment.

"Well, Edric?" Galeran said to the sour-faced old man. "You deserve a penalty for making a foolish marriage. Will you take her back, babe and all?"

"If I take her back, I'll have a rod to her first. A man has his pride!"

Galeran saw Agnes stick out her tongue at her husband, and was tempted to kick her under the table to try to make her behave. He felt less like a lord in judgment than like a nurse trying to govern two unruly children.

"That's between you and her," he said.

"Nay, Lord, it ain't," protested Edric, "for she's stronger than me, and faster too. I can't catch her!"

Galeran was hard pressed not to join in the laughter of the crowd. "Well, Agnes? Will you stand still long enough to be beaten?"

He thought she'd refuse, but her round face twisted in thought. "He's to beat me only the once?"

"He'll get my help to do it only the once."

She looked up at her husband. "Will you always be on at me about it? Will you be nasty to the child?"

"Nay," said Edric grudgingly. "I'll forget. And I'll not take it out on the child. It's true enough that a healthy son'll be a good thing to have. You shouldn't have spoke it out in front of the village, Agnes. You should have given me time to think about it."

She sighed. "Aye, I reckon that's true. For that I deserve the beating." She stood, dumped the grubby baby in Galeran's arms, and went to kneel in the dirt. "Go on, then, Edric. Lay it on. You'll not get another chance."

"Right, then!" said Edric, a light in his eyes. "Someone get me a stick!"

As the old man rolled up his sleeves, a grinning woman came forward to relieve Galeran of his burden, but he shook his head. He'd never held his own child, or the new one—Donata. It seemed right to hold this black-thatched mite.

He didn't like this business at all, though, for it cut too close to his own case. Everyone was grinning as if at a festival, happy that justice would be done; relieved, perhaps, to have a problem wiped away.

Within moments a whippy green branch was put into Edric's hands. Accompanied by laughter and cheers, he laid about his erring wife's back with great ferocity. Galeran noted that the black-haired lover cheered along with the rest and marked him in his memory. If the lout ever crossed the law, he'd get an extra dose of punishment.

Not that Agnes was suffering much. She was shouting mightily, but Galeran reckoned that with at least three layers of clothing on her back, the flexible stick, and the old man's weak arm, she wasn't coming to much harm. It would sting, but nothing more than that.

It was all for show, to salve Edric's pride and put matters right again in the eyes of the village. A wrong must be redressed.

He looked down at the cause of the trouble, and the boy looked up with huge dark eyes, his mouth working slightly in hope of food.

"Mother will be back soon," Galeran said, hearing Agnes's wails reach a crescendo, begging for mercy.

Sure enough, the noise stopped except for the merry cheering and laughter. Agnes was immediately surrounded by women and helped to her feet as if grievously hurt.

Edric, rosy from exertion and with a spring in his step, came over to Galeran. "You had some suggestions, Lord?" he asked hopefully.

Galeran gave him some advice about pleasing his wife despite his impotency, including a few ideas he'd picked up in the Holy Land and not been able to test yet. When Agnes came over to take her child back, he suggested a few things she could do that might help her husband's problem. Since it all seemed to be news to both of them, it might even do some good.

Or perhaps the next time Agnes took her itch elsewhere and conceived, Edric would pretend it had. It could be so, for the old man had taken the babe from his mother and was holding the lad proudly, as if it were in truth his own son.

And perhaps, after the little scene, the child was legitimate as far as their neighbors cared. Certainly the villagers had gathered around the small family and were driving them toward the inn to celebrate the healing of the wounds. Galeran declined an invitation to join the celebration. After a brief word with the headman, he mounted and led his party onward.

Raoul's eyes were sharp with interest, but he was wise enough to keep silent.

Eight

Though he was plagued by disquieting thoughts, Galeran found the journey gave him a chance to settle into his new reality. The loss of his son was a wound, but one that had begun to heal. The situation with Jehanne, however, still festered and would do so until it was handled. It ate away at him, and he knew it was a raw wound in the community.

No man liked the thought of adultery. Even less would he tolerate the idea of another man's child in his wife's arms, stealing a share of his property.

So every man expected adultery to be sternly dealt with. Galeran didn't fear the opinion of other men, for if they made an issue of it, he'd kill them, but he feared official action against Jehanne. He couldn't kill Church or Crown.

He knew the way to avoid official interference was to take firm action himself. Yet he couldn't do it. He couldn't send Jehanne to live a penitent's life behind walls. He couldn't send the child away. He couldn't even give her a simple beating to clear the air. That one blow had shown him that.

Wending his way back to Heywood, he went over and over the problem in his mind. As Lowick had found, Church and Crown were unlikely to concern themselves in such a domestic matter unless they saw advantage in it. Unfortunately, there were a number of ways the Church and the king might see advantage in meddling in Galeran's affairs.

Or, rather, in his family's affairs.

Spurred on by this thought, Galeran stopped at Brome on the way home.

Brome and Heywood were the two castles in this area with stone curtain walls. The difference between them was that Heywood commanded a natural rise, whereas Brome sat on a high motte near a river, using the river to form a moat around the walls. The site had been chosen because it overlooked an important ford.

It gave the Lord of Brome power in the north, but also made him and his family the subject of political interest.

Galeran's father came out of the mews to greet him, hawk on wrist. "You're looking more yourself, lad! What do you think of this beauty, then?" He stroked the hooded bird lovingly.

Galeran slid off his horse with his own hawk on his wrist. "A fine peregrine. Have you flown her yet?"

"Any day. Any day." Lord William led the way to the hall. "So, any problems with the estate?"

"No. It's in good heart. Doubtless you've been keeping an eye on things."

"Here and there, lad, here and there." Lord William placed his bird on a hawk stand and fed it a tidbit before calling for ale. "Wasn't sure I could trust a woman with such matters, and I didn't like having Lowick running things. Never did trust that one. Too slippery-handsome. Was sniffing after both your sisters at one point, you know."

"Yes, I remember." Galeran settled his own hawk on another stand. "But he'd probably be no worse than the next man if he once gained the land he yearns for."

"Then he can go seek it elsewhere."

It was Raoul, taking the ale offered by a servant, who said, "We're wondering if Lowick *will* go elsewhere."

Galeran flashed him an irritated glance. He hadn't wanted these matters raised, or not yet, at least.

"What choice does he have?"

"He has a child here," said Raoul.

"What can he make of that?"

"Very little. As long as Galeran's alive."

"Raoul," said Galeran. "Enough of this."

Lord William took a deep drink of ale. "What basis would Lowick have for a duel?"

"A duel?" Galeran laughed dryly. "I'd have to be mad enough to challenge him. Raoul is worrying about more sneaky ways."

"No man would. . . . I'd gut him," his father snarled, "and strangle him with his own entrails!"

"You'd have to prove it first. When a man's already in the grave, sometimes it's simpler not to rake the coals."

"I'd rake them, never fear!"

"I'm glad to hear it, but I'd still be dead. All I want at the moment is a few men of Brome to add to the garrison at Heywood."

Lord William thumped down in his great chair, still frowning. "Why?"

"Most of the Heywood garrison has been there for years," said Galeran, wandering over to soothe his restless hawk. "Many of the men are Heywood born and bred. Their allegiance should be to me, but it could be to Jehanne and even to Lowick, whom they knew as a lad. He has his charm. If anything happens to me, I want to be sure that he doesn't claim the castle. I want a few men there whose task it would be to bring Jehanne and the babe to you."

"So I can strangle her?"

Galeran just raised a brow and his father shook his head. "I know, I know. It's a weakness in me, this softness I have toward women. I was a stronger man before I married your mother. Now I can just see the look in Mabelle's eyes if ever I even think of it. . . ." He glared at the two younger men. "Be wary with women. They'll tie you in knots."

"Not Raoul," said Galeran. "He just ties them in pretty love knots and leaves them cooing."

Lord William's glance was scathing. "You'll have no luck

with that game here, sir. Our northern women are too sensible for your Frankish games."

Raoul put down his tankard. "If you'll excuse me, I think I'll test your theory." With that, he sauntered over to one of the maids.

"What?" said Lord William, gaping after him. "What in the name of heaven . . . ?"

Galeran laughed as he took a seat opposite his father. "He's just tactfully leaving us to discuss family business, Father. I don't think even Raoul can seduce a sensible northern woman in the time we have here."

Lord William harrumphed, but was willing to return to his main point. "Why did you hit Jehanne? Did you think I would, and harder?"

Galeran stared into his ale. "I suspect I hit her because I wanted to. My excuse was to turn you soft toward her. I didn't think you'd beat her, no, but . . . She needed someone, and I wasn't sure then that it would be me."

"And now? She has you?"

"Yes," said Galeran simply. "To death and beyond."

Lord William relaxed back. "She's explained it all, then. Rape. Was it—"

"She's explained nothing, but I very much doubt it was rape."

"Explained nothing!" exclaimed Lord William, surging to his feet. "Hell's cinders, Galeran, *make* her explain!"

"How?"

"But . . ."

Galeran rose more slowly. "I'd better ride on if we're to reach Heywood before dark. Just promise me, Father, that you will care for her if need be." Galeran kept his voice calm as he brought the hawk back onto his wrist. "A pretty beauty, isn't she? And sharp-eyed. It would be a shame to feed her to the dogs."

William spluttered for a moment longer, then said, "Of

course I'll care for her. And I'll make sure Lowick never profits from his deeds."

"And promise me that she will keep her child."

"Who else would want it?" snorted William. "A bastard girl."

Galeran looked up from the hawk. "Lowick would want a crippled monster if he thought it could give him a toehold in Heywood."

Lord William worried his lip with his knuckle. "In that case, I've some news you'd best listen to carefully."

A short time later, as Galeran mounted his horse, he wondered whether there had been a true purpose in visiting Brome, or whether he had just been putting off his return to his troubled home. Certainly now he was reluctant to continue the journey. He pulled himself together and gave the command to ride out. Two of his men had been left at Brome, and four of his father's most trusted men were now riding behind him.

"Why the glum face?" asked Raoul. "Did your father have bad news?"

"Not particularly. But it's sure now that Lowick is in Durham with Bishop Flambard and being received warmly. I can't imagine even Flambard trying a crude assault on a castle connected to Brome, but it's always dangerous to become tangled with the Church."

"If he won't attack Heywood, what can the bishop do?"

"Claim to have jurisdiction over the matter of Lowick and Jehanne. It is a matter of sin, and even connected to the crusade—thus a Church matter."

Raoul whistled. "Dangerous."

"Indeed. The time for drifting is over. I'm going to have to take action."

"I don't know. This bishop won't lightly take on your family. Perhaps time will heal."

"Will it? Look at that woman in the village."

"Peasants," said Raoul dismissively.

"We're not so different. When there's a wound, it must be treated. If left unattended, it will likely get worse rather than better. And a festering wound will certainly draw the attention of the local guardian of moral right."

They rode toward Heywood at a steady pace, stopping at three more hamlets. Sometimes they halted to speak to laborers in the fields or those traveling along the road. Galeran thought whimsically that he was like a dog marking his territory, making sure that everyone knew he was back, alive, well, and in charge. He was hoping by his relaxed manner also to convince his people that all was right in the world and that they need fear no unrest.

His people, however, were shrewd enough in their own way, and he could read doubt in their manner. At the last village, Hey Hamlet, which sat at a crossroads scarcely out of view of Heywood, he sensed a distinctly uneasy atmosphere. Galeran chatted of the weather and the harvest, waiting for the people to voice their concern.

Eventually the headman said, "Were you thinking to find the Lady Jehanne in the castle, Lord?"

Galeran's heart missed a beat. For a frantic moment he couldn't think what to say, but knew he couldn't avoid the truth. "Yes. Why? Has she left?"

"Aye, Lord," said the man in the blank manner the simple people always used to mask uneasiness. "Rode by not long since with a small party, including some women and a babe. Heading toward Burstock, I'd say."

One track through Hey Hamlet led toward Brome and another toward Burstock, a half day's ride away. Burstock Castle belonged to Jehanne's uncle, Aline's father.

"I see," he said, as nonchalantly as he could. "I had best follow her, then. It is late for her to be on the road."

It took almost more willpower than he possessed, but he did not race to his horse. He even took time to accept a

handful of bilberries from one shy woman and thank her.
Then he led his troop at a trot along the wooded Burstock
road, passing his hawk to one of his men as they rode.

Once out of sight of the village, he kicked the horse into
a flat-out gallop. Jehanne was running off to her lover.

He'd kill her.

No.

But this time he *would* beat her, and keep her in close
confinement.

He'd kill Lowick, though. He'd spit him before her eyes.
But even that might not quench the rage in him.

He charged around a bend in the road to see the party
far ahead, out of the trees and onto the open moor. They,
too, were riding flat out, doubtless having heard the beat
of pursuing horses.

Galeran drew his sword.

Raoul raced up beside him. "Think, my friend!"

But Galeran just kicked his steaming horse into greater
speed.

The crossbow bolt clipped his helmet, twisting his head
back, jerking his rein hand so his horse reared, almost un-
seating him. The next thunked into his shield, passing a
finger-length through the iron-reinforced wood.

His men immediately swung into a circle around him,
shields high, but the assault stopped as abruptly as it had
begun. An eerie stillness settled. No other projectile flew.
No armed men charged out of the suddenly silent woods.

Galeran looked once at his distant, rapidly disappearing
quarry, then broke the shield wall to drive through the scrub
into the woodland.

Crashing noises marked his assailant, ahead and running
for his life. Galeran chased after, being careful only not to
ride his horse into a bog or crevice. His hounds gave voice
and flew with him. He bellowed for his party to fan out,
to stop the man from sneaking off to one side.

The next bolt might have found its mark had not his

horse tossed up its head. The quarrel pierced it in the eye, killing it instantly.

Galeran kicked clear, but landed sprawling in fallen leaves, almost slashing himself on his drawn sword. He scrambled to his feet, discarded his shield, and ran straight at the bowman, who was fending off snarling dogs with his two bows.

A swing of Galeran's sword took off the man's hands. Before the bowman had time to scream, Galeran ran him through. Then he dragged the corpse up by the hair and hacked off the head.

Blood poured from it onto blood-soaked ground . . .

. . . as it had in Jerusalem, where the streets had flowed blood and the same metallic stench had risen to sicken him. Where his sword had killed because it was kill or be killed. Where he'd killed women and children because they, too, had fought. Where he'd charged a group of German knights.

Raoul had dragged him back. . . .

Raoul was dragging him back from the bloody mess, seizing his sword hand and twisting viciously.

Galeran dropped the sword, wondering why Raoul was doing such a thing. He blinked to clear misty vision. His friend looked angry, as he had in Jerusalem. . . .

Were they in Jerusalem again?

He'd thought he was back in England, which was nice, but for some reason there was pleasure in the thought that he might be still overseas. . . .

Raoul had knocked him out in Jerusalem, knocked him out of his mind. Was he still out of his mind . . . ?

"Galeran, give it up. You don't want it."

Raoul seemed to be trying to pull something from his left hand. But he'd dropped his shield. . . .

Galeran focused and saw he was holding a grimacing head by the hair, blood still trickling from the severed throat.

With a shudder he dropped it.

Raoul kicked it toward the corpse around which the hounds hovered uncertainly, drawn by blood, repelled by the human scent.

Taking in the mess that had been a man brief moments before, Galeran turned to retch. It was as if he spewed out madness, for when he straightened, he was sane. He knew he was in England, he knew about Jehanne, and he knew what he had just done.

Beginning to shiver, he wondered what would have happened if he'd caught Jehanne in that mad rage. Would he have attacked her with the same mindless violence? Snatched the babe from her arms to spit it on his sword?

Now it seemed unthinkable, but now it seemed unthinkable that he had slaughtered someone he could have taken prisoner. It was even more unthinkable that he had decapitated a corpse and clung to the head as a trophy.

Raoul passed Galeran a wineskin. "I assume that wasn't Raymond of Lowick."

"God, no." Galeran rinsed out his mouth, then drank deeply. "You'll know Raymond when you see him. He's tall as you, with golden hair and a noble demeanor. The sort women go silly over." He leaned against a tree, still shivering as if it were January.

"Then it would have been convenient to question the wretch."

"What point? It was clearly Lowick's plan."

And Jehanne's? Galeran's quivering mind was asking.

Had she led him into this trap? He could feel frantic sweat trickling cold down his back.

"A witness, at least, if it comes to law."

Galeran looked around at his men, who were beating back the dogs and pretending nothing much had happened. "We have witnesses if we need them. The man was abroad with two crossbows. What other purpose than to kill?"

Raoul looked down for a moment. "Perhaps he was just guarding your lady's back?"

"With two crossbows? He couldn't hold back a troop. At the very least, an ordinary bow would be better because he could fire more arrows. The crossbow is a murder weapon, as all know, and the only effective one against a mailed man." Galeran pushed away from the tree, passing the wineskin to a man. "Bogo, Godfrey, dig a grave and put that in it."

Then he walked back toward the road.

Raoul walked with him. "What are you going to do now?" he asked in a carefully neutral tone.

Galeran flashed him a look. "Don't worry. The blood lust has left me. I'm just curious to see whether anyone comes back to count corpses."

"Then you can have your sword back."

Galeran took it and cleaned it on some leaves before sheathing it.

"So you think it was a trap?" Raoul asked.

"The bait was attractive, and he was waiting."

"I don't think your lady—"

"Don't speak of it."

Galeran couldn't bear to hear his thoughts on another's lips, even to deny them. If it wasn't spoken, it would have less power.

As they halted at the edge of the trees to study the deserted road, birds began to sing again. After a while a rabbit cautiously hopped across the road. One of the dogs whined hopefully, but Galeran stayed it with a hand signal.

"Well?" asked Raoul sometime later. "The sun is starting to set. Are we to stay here all night?"

Galeran sighed, accepting that staying there was pointless. He was just reluctant to progress to the obvious step. "Of course not. We ride on to Burstock and visit my wife's uncle."

Galeran took Bogo's horse, sending the man back to Heywood, but under orders not to speak of this event. Then he led his troop along the road in the fading light. Recent rains had turned the dirt soft enough to hold hoofprints, so it was clear Jehanne's party had not stopped or turned off.

Could it just be an innocent trip to visit relatives? Galeran would like to believe it, but Jehanne's party had been traveling in haste, and had speeded when pursued. Moreover, he had left clear instructions that his wife was to stay in the castle.

And, of course, there was the bowman.

He didn't want to think about that bowman.

Night settled and the moon was clouded, so they slowed to a walk as they crossed the moors. Galeran heard the nearby convent bell sounding lauds as they came in sight of Burstock.

Burstock Castle was a simpler structure than Brome or Heywood, developed twenty years earlier around an old manor house that sat near a river. A motte had been thrown up behind the house, but it was still crowned only by a simple wooden watchtower. The family lived in the comfortable wood manor house within the palisade.

At this time of night, of course, the gates were firmly closed.

"Will they let us in?" Raoul asked when they drew up some distance away.

His friend's patience was beginning to wear on Galeran's nerves. "Probably, but I think we'll camp here for the night."

"Why?"

"I want to see what happens in the morning."

"We've no food and precious little wine."

"Pretend it's Lent. No fires."

The men weren't happy with the situation, but there were no complaints, which wasn't surprising after Galeran's berserker rage. They must wonder when next that kind of violence would erupt, and who would be on the receiving end.

Galeran wondered too.

He took care of his horse, cooling it, then leading it back a short distance to a stream to drink. He unsaddled it and hobbled it so it could graze on the low moorland growth. He drank some water himself, and washed the blood off his hands and face. There was gore all over his mail and braies, but there wasn't much he could do about that.

He spotted some brambles and pointed out the fruit to his men so they could gather some if they wished. Then he allocated watch hours to each man, with special instructions to wake him if anyone entered or left Burstock.

Having run out of things to do, he rolled up in his cloak. He could sleep this way if he had to, but doubted he would sleep tonight. He could have kept watch all night, but feared his mind would wander. And anyway, he didn't want to have to talk to Raoul.

One question tormented him: Was Lowick in Burstock, awaiting his leman? Were they even now in a bed, pumping together hot and sweatily, and lamenting that Jehanne had needed to whore with her husband to deflect his suspicions?

His whole body burned again with that desire to kill. He desperately forced himself into calm, seeking more palatable explanations.

He could not think of a one.

Jehanne could have no good reason to leave the safety of her home, where she had been commanded to stay.

Perhaps she knew about the bowman, knew he had been tracking Galeran for days, waiting for an opportunity to kill him and still escape to claim the reward. If Jehanne had been waiting for news of her husband's death, then news of his safe return could have thrown her into a panic, causing her to flee to the nearest refuge.

Though the explanation had a certain plausibility, it didn't sit right in his mind. It didn't fit with what he knew of his wife, and it left Jehanne's warning letter unexplained. Of course that could have been a skillful attempt to deflect suspicion.

Hell's flames, nothing made sense anymore!

Galeran wasn't sure he would recognize sense these days if it snarled in his face.

A few days ago he would have sworn that Jehanne was the same honorable woman he had always known, that her sin had somehow been an aberration. Now he couldn't help but wonder if he'd been duped by hopes and lust.

He went over and over her behavior, from the moment he'd found her waiting for him in the hall to when she'd left him alone with a broken bed. He sought truth, he sought understanding. He found only confusion.

Eventually he did sleep, to be woken by the dawn chorus poorly rested and chilled by the dew. Spots of rust were already mixed with the dried blood on his second-best mail. Cuthbert would have yet more reason to complain.

He stood and stretched, then went to study Burstock, determined to have done with foolishness.

As soon as he decided what foolishness was.

Lars, the guard on watch, shook his head to indicate nothing had happened yet. But cocks were crowing, and somewhere inside the walls a dog barked. As the sun turned the sky pink and gold, people straggled up the road to the castle from the nearby village, and the great gates swung open to let others out. Two came out on horseback.

Galeran tensed and studied them, but didn't think they were men of his.

They certainly weren't Jehanne and Lowick riding south.

The sun rose higher, and in fields down by the river work began. Raoul had come to stand beside Galeran, and his stomach growled. Doubtless all their stomachs were complaining. There was no point in staying here until they all starved to death.

"Very well," Galeran said, "let's go down and see what the story is."

They saddled the horses and headed back aways to rejoin the road out of sight of the castle. Then they rode up to the gates, banner unfurled.

Believing that Jehanne had taken refuge there, Galeran expected to be stopped, but the guards at the gate just raised their spears in acknowledgment and waved them through. Too late, Galeran wondered if this was another trap, but in a world turned crazy, he'd still be ready to swear that Jehanne's uncle Hubert was incapable of base deceit.

He looked around cautiously, however, trying to sense betrayal. All he saw was the ordinary bustle of a peacetime castle.

The bailey here contained the old manor house as well as the usual shelters for animals and workshops for the craftsmen. In fact, it was more like a small village than a castle compound. People chatted as they passed, children played among strutting poultry, women pummeled wash in big tubs.

Stable grooms ran forward to take the horses even as Hubert of Burstock came forward to welcome them. Aline's father was a short, compact man of great strength and shrewdness known far and wide for his bluff honesty.

With dangerous suddenness, Galeran relaxed. How could he ever have thought Hubert would be party to a meeting of illicit lovers? If the women had convinced him Jehanne was in danger of her life, he would take them in. But Hubert did not look wary so much as worried.

"A bad business, Galeran," he said with a frown.

That was certainly true. But to what business did Hubert refer?

"Is Jehanne all right?" Galeran asked, thinking it was the most noncommittal question that made sense.

"Yes, yes. Upset, of course, but unharmed. Come along in. Have you broken your fast?"

"No."

"Then you must eat! Come along." And Hubert shepherded them all toward the wide doors of the thatched manor house with no hint that he thought ill of Galeran. It was all very strange.

When Galeran walked into the long, beamed hall, supported along the sides by huge wooden posts, he immediately searched out his wife, but she was not to be seen.

Had Hubert lied to him?

But Hubert of Burstock never lied. Then it occurred to him that Hubert had not actually said that Jehanne was here.

Since he wasn't ready to search the place by force, and was almost faint with hunger, Galeran allowed himself to be steered into a seat at the long, fixed table, and plied with bread, meat, and ale.

Hubert sat by him. "What action are you planning?" he asked quietly, toying with a pot of ale of his own. "It's a delicate situation."

Galeran concentrated on a sausage. "True enough. What would you advise?"

"It might be no bad thing to be rid of the babe."

"Do you say so?" Galeran flashed the man a puzzled look. Was he recommending murder?

"The brat would doubtless be well enough cared for, and once you fill Jehanne again, she'll soon forget it."

"I'm not so sure of that."

A grimace told him Hubert agreed. "If it stings her, she deserves it! After her sin, what right has she to put her own concerns before those of the rest of us?"

Us? Galeran queried silently. This conversation wasn't making sense, but he was reluctant to confess as much just yet. But how could Hubert be jeopardized unless he thought he might have to go to war with Galeran over Jehanne?

"And," said Hubert, "once Jehanne bears another child, preferably a son, any claim this one might have to Heywood would be greatly weakened."

"That's true. But I have plenty of evidence that getting sons and having them survive is not always easy."

Hubert waved a hand. "That's in the past! Sometimes a woman needs loosening up for it to work right. And perhaps Jehanne's learned her lesson and will act more the gentle woman. That'll help the babes stick."

Galeran couldn't resist saying, "Gentle, like galloping over here as if the hounds of hell were after her?"

Hubert gave a sharp crack of laughter. "True enough. But it was the only thing to do, if you ask me, despite the affront to the Church."

"It's hardly a sin for a woman to ride at a gallop." Galeran wondered whether his earlier blood madness was with him still. This conversation was making no sense.

"Some might disagree with you there, Galeran. But," Hubert added testily, "you know what I mean. Flambard's not going to like Jehanne having carried Donata away. And he'll doubtless not be pleased that I've given them both shelter here. I don't like being at odds with the Church."

It was like a key turning in a lock. Galeran put down the remains of the sausage. "The Bishop of Durham wants Donata?"

"Aye. You know that, surely? Though how the idiots expected to care for her without women or wet nurse—"

"Galeran?" Jehanne burst out of one of the private rooms along the back of the hall. "Oh, praise heaven! What have you done about it?"

Galeran rose to take her hands, grateful not to meet her with dark suspicions on his mind. "Nothing," he said. "I came straight here."

"Why?"

It was an excellent question. With his wife and her child safely elsewhere, he should have stayed behind to deal with the importunate churchmen. If, that is, he'd had any notion of what was going on.

"We had best talk privately."

Hubert waved his permission, and Jehanne led Galeran back into the room. It was small, but had a large window onto the castle herb garden, letting in morning sunshine and sweet aromas.

Aline was there, holding Donata. She immediately rose to leave, but Galeran stopped her. "Give the babe to me."

She stared at him from under her severe brows, making no move to obey.

Jehanne said, "Do it, Aline."

Aline passed over the child, along with a warning scowl, and left the room.

Galeran looked down at big dark blue eyes, long but pale lashes, and a sucking blister on the upper lip. "Aline fears me."

"No. But we all wonder when your rage will strike, and where."

Nine

Galeran looked up. "Including you?"

Jehanne sat on a bench by the window as if her legs had given way. "I almost wish it would. That your rage would strike. I can't believe it won't. . . . The waiting is hardest."

He didn't tell her his rage had already broken out. "Then let that be your penance."

The child made a mewling sound, and her tiny mouth worked anxiously while she stared up at him. No matter what her origins, he couldn't hate such an innocent.

She had her mother's delicate skin, and he could believe, if he chose, that the golden fuzz on her head was her mother's heritage too. Perhaps it was a blessing that Jehanne and Lowick were of a similar type. Galeran would never have to search for the father's features in the child.

Then the baby screwed up her face and let out a sharper cry. Galeran jiggled her a little, but she squalled louder. Frustrated, he scowled at Jehanne. This might not be his child, but did the babe have to reject him so openly?

"She's still hungry," Jehanne said. "I was feeding her when I heard you had arrived."

"Then why didn't you say so?"

She didn't reply, but *because I was afraid* floated in the room, making his heart ache. When she learned of his berserker rage, she'd fear him even more.

With reason. As he passed the babe to her, he remembered his foolish youthful wish that Jehanne would fear him.

He could have wept.

She raised her tunic and he saw that her gown was slashed down the front to free her breasts. She put Donata close, and the babe grasped the nipple with her gums to suck lustily.

Just as the peasant child had.

Just as Gallot once had . . .

Galeran pushed back that thought. "Can you talk as you feed her?"

"Of course."

He put a foot on a chest and leaned on his raised knee. "When did the bishop's men arrive?"

"Yesterday, quite early." A tense pallor in her face was a memory of fear. "I suspected something, so I insisted that the men-at-arms stay outside the walls and permitted only the three monks to enter. Brother Forthred seemed taken aback to find that you weren't there." She flicked him a wary glance. "I think he assumed you would support his case."

"And let him take the child?"

She nodded, stroking her babe's hair in a protective gesture Galeran thought entirely unconscious.

"Jehanne, I took the cross and traveled to a war half a world away to give you a child. Do you really fear I will let one be torn from your arms?"

She looked up then, eyes wide, and glossed by unshed tears. "Truly? It would be—"

"Truly." After a moment he straightened. "You could look more delighted."

"I am, I am. But I see blood in it, Galeran."

He took to pacing the room, for he did too. "Because of the bishop's men? Tell me what happened."

She made an effort to compose herself. "Raymond has made confession to the bishop, who has decreed he should do penance for his sin. But the penance is that he raise the child he misconceived. They came to take her to him!"

Galeran stilled and nodded. "Cunning."

"I couldn't let them take her! I protested on any number of grounds, but Brother Forthred went on and on about sins and perdition. Then he promised damnation for all who abetted me. I was terrified that the people of Heywood might give him Donata just to stop his ranting!"

"So how did you escape?"

"I pretended to give in and went to get her. But I sent a message to Walter of Matlock. I . . . I wasn't even sure he would support me against the Church, especially when you'd left orders I was not to leave the castle. But he did, thanks to Blessed Mary. He openly sent out a small group of men, saying they were to search for you and inform you of these matters. Then he accompanied me, Aline, and the babe out of the postern gate and down the road. Aline and I took two of their horses and we all rode here. Forthred will come after us, though. I've been racking my brain to think where we could go next." She stared at him. "Galeran, no one can oppose the Church! What are we to do?"

"This far north, it's amazing what a person can do."

"Not for long. And Flambard has the power of the Crown in his fist as well! Oh, I am weak in these matters! Too weak to do as I should."

A thousand sharp suspicions cut at him. "What do you mean?"

He thought she wouldn't answer, but then her eyes slid past him to rest on the wall. "When I found I was with child," she whispered, "I resolved to do away with it. I saw then what tangles it could weave around us. I . . . even prepared the herbs." Her gaze skittered over him and down to her child. A tear fell to splash in the babe's hair. "I could not take them."

"It would have been a sin," he said gruffly. "Adding one sin to another cannot create good."

"But think what could have been. . . ."

"You could have concealed your adultery, you mean?"

"No!" she protested, looking up. "I mean we could have avoided this bitter taste to your return. Not by concealing my stupidity, but by not having such public ignominy, and not having a child to confuse matters. I would have told you. I have never lied to you, Galeran, even by omission."

He was taken aback by that. "Perhaps I would rather you lied to me about such a thing."

She frowned, clearly disapproving of such a weak thought, and he was tempted to laugh at the strange twists and turns of their relationship these days. Just then, however, the child fell asleep and slipped off the nipple. Jehanne rearranged her clothes and rose to pat the babe on the back. With a little bubbly burp, Donata smiled as if she had sweet dreams.

Ah, to be so innocent again.

He held out his arms. "I would like to hold her again."

She looked at him with a slight frown that reminded him of Aline. "Jehanne, if you even imply that I will hurt her, I will be grievously hurt."

She hastily put the child in his hands. "I implied nothing! It's just that she's wet."

Galeran realized that was true. Wet, and smelly as a dye yard. With a rueful smile he passed the babe back. "You can see that I'm a very inexperienced parent. We'll have to stop reading the worst into each other's every act."

Flashing him a very startled look, she said, "That won't be hard for me."

She laid the baby on a cloth on the floor to change it. He watched in fascination as she removed the wet clothes from the tiny body, marveling at the fragile yet perfect limbs. Donata didn't wake, and was soon dry again and wrapped in a secure bundle. Then Jehanne laid her in the cradle.

"I wonder often," she said softly, "why this happened to us. To you in particular . . ."

"If God had given us a child in the early years of our marriage, our lives would have been different. Perhaps it is God's will."

"Not at all," said Jehanne sharply. "It is all the result of my willfulness and pride, and it is I alone who should suffer for it."

"But not by giving up the child?" he asked dryly, taking a seat by the cradle. The tiny mite fascinated him.

Jehanne's hands flexed in a sudden, desperate movement. "If Brother Forthred had brought a wet nurse, even . . . Babes do not thrive on pap, Galeran!"

"So, if Brother Forthred had brought a wet nurse, you would have handed Donata over without protest?"

She turned away, and after a moment put her hands to her face. "No. No, I *wouldn't*. I try, Galeran, but I cannot be meek and mild!"

Galeran laughed. "Nor do I want you to be. But don't start lying to yourself, Jehanne. Since we are not willing to give Donata to the wolves, we had best put our minds to handling all our problems, hadn't we?"

The babe stirred, perhaps because of her mother's raised voice. Galeran put out a foot and rocked the cradle, and in a moment Donata settled back to sleep.

Jehanne had turned and was staring at him as if he were a puzzle. "How can you just accept her? How can you just accept everything?"

He met her eyes. "How can I not? Do you want to be whipped? Locked away? Burned at the stake? Do you want me to throttle this child . . . ?" He bit off the increasingly violent words. "Don't, Jehanne. Don't push me. Let's handle the simple problems first. Was Lowick with the monks?"

"No," she said, distinctly pale. "Didn't you speak to Forthred at all?"

"No."

"Had he left?"

"I don't know. I never returned to Heywood. I heard you had come this way and followed."

She looked him over as if seeing him for the first time. "Why are you so bloody?"

There was no place in this for lies. "Someone tried to kill me."

She sat on a bench with a thump. *"What?"*

"Yesterday. On the road between Heywood and Burstock, when you appeared to be fleeing me."

"What?"

Galeran's heart eased. Jehanne was clever, but she was not capable of faking such deep confusion.

"Do you mean *you* were the horsemen pursuing us?" she asked. "I thought it was the bishop's men!"

"Pity you didn't have anyone with Raoul's sharp sight."

"It wouldn't have mattered. We weren't about to stop and study matters. We just rode here as fast as the horses could bear. But," she asked painfully, "what is this about someone trying to kill you?"

The action of rocking the babe was strangely soothing. "There was a man on the road with two crossbows and the plain intent to kill me."

She paled. Distinctly, she paled. "Sweet Savior! Where is he now?"

"Under the earth."

"Praise be!" Then she frowned again. "It might have been better, though, to preserve him for questioning."

"I wasn't thinking very clearly. But if we knew who was behind it, it might carry us into deep water."

"Raymond," she whispered.

"I can't imagine who else wants me dead."

"Sweet Mary, help us. I can hardly believe it! He is not a bad man." Something of Galeran's feelings must have shown on his face, for she added, "He isn't, Galeran. You must know that."

"He tried to have me killed, Jehanne."

She closed her eyes. "Desperate," she sighed. "He isn't a saint, either." Then she studied him again. "Was there only one man? You seem to be wearing a great deal of blood."

"There's a great deal of blood in a man." A lightning-flash vision of blood pouring through the streets of Jerusalem made him shudder, and then he saw blood on the babe's white blanket.

After a heart-stopping moment, he realized it had merely rubbed off his gory mail when he'd held her. He rose, suddenly aware of his own stench. "My rage broke free, Jehanne. I didn't just kill the man, I butchered him. Walk carefully around me. Please."

Outside in the hall, Raoul saw Aline leave the room, then turn to study the closed door. He could not see her face, but her whole body expressed concern. Her short, compact, well-rounded body was extremely expressive.

He suspected it would be expressive in bed. . . .

How strange to think that way about the little nun.

He strolled over to her. "Lady Aline. You are troubled?"

She swung sharply. "There are matters enough to trouble anyone who has a mind above base pleasures." Her eyes flicked down to his crotch, and then she turned pink.

Raoul began to think the Lady Aline was mistaken in her vocation to a life of chastity. "Are there? Perhaps you could sit on this bench and explain these matters to me."

She stepped back. "Do you take me for a fool, sir? You know perfectly well what is going on."

She would have walked past him, but he caught her wrist. The way she froze, the way her color deepened, told him she was rarely touched by men. It intrigued him. She tried to snatch her hand away, but he had her shackled just tightly enough to prevent it.

"Sirrah!"

"I do not know what is going on, Lady Aline, and I think I should."

She looked him in the eye searchingly, clear-headed despite her fluster. "How can you not?"

"Because for three days we've ridden around the estate and received no messages. And before we could return to Heywood we were told that Lady Jehanne had come here, so we followed. Your father seems to have told Galeran some interesting things, but since they spoke quietly, I am left in ignorance. Pity me."

Judging his moment, he released her. She pulled her hand close to her body and rubbed her wrist even though he knew he had not hurt her.

"Very well." She walked briskly over to a bench, her firm, purposeful step having the unaccountable effect of making Raoul want to kiss her into limp dazedness.

He shook his head and sat beside her, but not too close. He had not lived to the ripe age of twenty-eight by seducing virgins in their father's houses.

"So," he said, "what caused the Lady Jehanne to flee here?"

Aline's pretty face turned sober and her gaze direct. "Raymond of Lowick, may God rot him in interesting places, has decided on a new line of attack. He's made devout confession to the bishop and accepted penance. Seeing what turmoil his ungoverned lust has caused—I quote almost verbatim from the unctuous Brother Forthred, you understand—Raymond is resolved to ease the situation by taking upon himself the burden of raising the unfortunate product of his liaison."

Raoul leaned back against the wall behind and whistled. "Clever. His own plan, do you think?"

"I don't know. He's not totally stupid, but I'm not sure he would think of such a circuitous route to his goal. Perhaps the bishop . . . Though how it would serve Bishop Flambard, I can't tell."

"Ah, yes, Galeran mentioned this Bishop Flambard. The Church dearly loves to have men in its pocket, and I gather Galeran's father is a thorn in the flaming bishop's side. What sort of man is he?"

Though Aline's hair was almost as blond as her cousin's, her brows were darker and inclined to make a severe line. When she frowned, as now, they were formidable. "No one even knows where he came from, but he served the Conqueror and now holds the highest position under William Rufus. His chief talent is squeezing money for the king and himself. His name is virtually a curse with layman and churchman, for he spares neither."

Raoul wanted to smooth those creasing brows with his thumbs, but he kept his mind on the issue in hand. "So he survives because he is protected by the king?"

"Yes, though it's rumored that last year some men managed to seize him, intending to kill him. He escaped, unfortunately, and now he goes nowhere without heavy guard." She scowled at Raoul as if everything were his fault. "It is most unfortunate that those men made a mess of it."

"Very." He cut to the point. "If this Brother Forthred had succeeded in taking the child, would the Lady Jehanne have gone too?"

"How could she do otherwise, when no wet nurse was provided?"

Raoul nodded. *"Very* clever."

Her eyes widened. "You mean the intent was to seize Jehanne, not Donata?"

"I very much doubt an elderly prelate and a young lord have much interest in a six-week babe."

Her face relaxed at last, but into deep concern. "Sweet Savior, but this frightens me." Before he could even think about offering comfort, she frowned again—this time while staring at him. "You are very bloody, sir. In fact, not to put too fine a point on it, you stink of it. Is there fighting over this already?"

He looked down and realized he was well stained with gore. That's what tussling over severed heads did for a man. "There's no fighting yet, but you're right about my deplorable state. Perhaps if I take off my armor, it could be cleaned. I have no wish to offend your nose, Lady Aline."

"Much good that will do. Most of the gore is on your braies."

Strength and good intentions can take a lusty man only so far. "Then I suppose they must be cleaned too. Doubtless the blood has gone through to my skin, since my clothes are stuck to me in places. I fear, to be really worthy of your company, dear lady, I need a bath."

Seeing the trap too late, she stared at him like a startled bird. "Oh, no!" But then she turned bloodred herself. "Of course. Come. We have a room set aside for bathing here."

Intrigued, amused, and not too seriously aroused, Raoul followed her to another corner of the hall and through a door, to find a small room equipped with braziers and a wooden tub. Since it was summertime, the braziers were unlit, but a stone hearth in one corner radiated heat. Two large kettles hung over it, full of hot water ready for anyone wanting to bathe.

"An excellent arrangement," he said.

Aline had her head bowed over a chest from which she was taking the necessary cloths. Her lovely, ample rump drew his eye, therefore, especially as it was covered by rich red cloth. No nunlike clothes for Aline. He wondered why not.

It might be safer for everyone if she were marked as Christ's.

"There are advantages to these old halls," she said. "It's easy to have small private rooms when building with wood." When she stood and turned, he saw she had regained most of her composure. "Of course, even with the palisade, it's not well suited to defense."

"And thus was taken by your Norman forbearers, I assume."

"Not at all." She pushed springy curls back from her round, heated cheeks. "My grandmother was left a widow by the battle at Hastings, and given in marriage to my grandfather. They were happy, to all accounts, and Burstock has never been fought over."

"A place of blessings." After a moment he said, "Perhaps, Lady Aline, you could summon people to help with my armor."

She flushed again, this time with embarrassment at her own neglect. It was as well, he thought, that flushing suited Aline. It was so easy to bring color to her cheeks.

Now, however, she pulled on efficiency like a cloak, opened the door, and called orders in a lusty voice.

In moments, two men arrived to strip off his mail and carry it away to be cleaned, then two others poured water from the huge kettles into the tub and took the empty vessels off to be filled.

Women hurried in with jugs of cool water, bags of herbs, and even a vial of oil.

Raoul eyed the oil with interest, but he let his better side take command.

"You are to be a nun, Lady Aline?"

"That is my intention."

"Then perhaps it is against your rule to assist a man at his bath."

She stared at him for a moment, temptation clear in her eyes, but then she shook her head. "No. There is nothing sinful in such a courtesy."

"But you have a sister-in-law here who is responsible for this household, do you not?"

She nodded. "Catherine. She's away at St. Radegund's convent on business."

Raoul decided he had done what he could to be virtuous. He certainly wasn't going to suggest Jehanne assist him at a time like this, and to demand lower aid would be to insult

Aline, who was now rolling up her outer sleeves in a businesslike fashion.

Perhaps whatever qualms had troubled her were eased.

Perhaps, he thought with some affront, she had previously believed him so ill bred as to be indecent in this situation. He bent to unlace his braies, intent on showing her that he knew polite behavior.

In hindsight, he wished he hadn't accepted the willing Ella's invitation that first night at Heywood. He had not imagined, however, that there was a lady in Heywood whose opinion would concern him—especially a modest, excessively virtuous, lushly rounded almost-nun.

He suppressed a smile, wondering why Aline intrigued him so. Perhaps just because she was such a contradiction.

She was so brisk and practical that she reminded him of his mother, who could manage a large household to perfection and dabble in a hundred other matters at the same time. But Aline was also young and easily flustered around men. She had in truth offended against the laws of hospitality in refusing to assist him to bathe at Heywood.

He'd be flattered to think that he alone had this effect on her, but he'd heard it was not so. She was skittish with all men, especially young ones. It was strange in a girl with five brothers. People seemed to accept that it was her vocation to the holy life that made her prudish, but Raoul wasn't sure.

In truth, he found it hard to imagine Aline of Burstock as a nun. A dictatorial abbess, yes, ruling a community of both men and women, and large properties as well. But it was necessary to go through the process of learning to be a nun in order to end up an abbess.

He peeled off his linen leggings, using force where blood had stuck them to his skin.

She looked up from where she was testing the temperature of the water. "Are you injured, sir? I apologize. I should have asked."

He looked over to see that her genuine concern had banished embarrassment for the moment. "It's someone else's blood."

"Galeran's?" she asked with alarm.

"No. Someone we encountered on the way." He pulled off his shirt so he was dressed only in linen drawers, and glanced at her.

She had modestly turned her head and now moved away from the tub. Of course it wouldn't be polite for a lady in this situation to ogle a man's parts, but her avoidance of the sight of his body was extreme. She must have seen many male bodies in her time.

She was clearly ideally suited to be a nun, and he should accept that fact. It was as well that servants continued to come in and out, refilling the big kettles, building up the fire in the hearth, and filling the jugs of rinse water. He wouldn't even be tempted to be foolish.

He stripped off and sat down in the tub, finding it a little small for his length, but otherwise ideal. The water was exactly the right temperature, seasoned by the herb bag, and with a film of oil that would linger on his body.

Though she might avoid the task, the Lady Aline was clearly skilled.

She turned cautiously, first eyes, then head, then—once she was sure he was decently covered—her whole body, suddenly brisk again. She picked up the pot of soap and a cloth and moved to wash his back. He took another cloth, had her soap it, and washed his own legs, chest, and arms. In fact, as was usual between strangers, he washed the parts he could reach.

It was sweet to feel her rubbing his back, but he'd rather she were where he could see her.

"So you still intend to be a nun, Lady Aline."

"Of course."

"What rules must you obey during this time away from the convent?"

"None. I never took a novice's vows."

Interesting. "Why not?"

"I was about to when Galeran went away and I went to Heywood to be with Jehanne."

"Do you miss the cloister?"

"Of course." But her voice did not carry conviction.

His lips twitched. "I'm sure it must be hard to be meek and obedient." When she was silent, he added, "Especially if the orders are foolish. We encounter that, sometimes, in battle."

Her hand paused. "And yet you obey?"

"Generally. That is how armies work. And religious communities, I suppose. I wonder why you wish to be a nun."

"Why not?" Her hand picked up its task again. "It is a productive life."

"Some would say it is a sterile one."

"Only those who think of nothing but rutting." She stood and tossed the cloth on the floor. "Are you ready for rinsing yet?"

"In a moment." He made a business of cleaning his feet, pleased that she had moved where he could see her. Really, with her cheeks flushed, tendrils of her hair damp with steam, and her garments clinging to her generous curves, she was completely luscious. He felt his body respond, and decided he'd better stay in the water a bit longer to control himself.

A serving woman, bringing extra drying cloths, studied him with a sliding look and winked. Another Ella. She was tempting, but he ignored the invitation and leaned back against the rim of the tub. "What productive work do you hope to do in the nunnery, Lady Aline?"

"Prayer, of course," she said warily, "and care for the unfortunate." Then she added, "Also work with numbers. Accounts."

A light in her eye told him he'd found her true vocation. "A useful interest for a wife too, surely?"

Her lips curved in a cynical smile "What man would let

his wife know all his business? Most certainly not a man of our class. I know only of merchant's wives who share fully in the trade."

"Perhaps you should marry a merchant, then." He was talking just to keep her where he could enjoy the sight of her, and also, perhaps, to teach her to be at ease with him.

"I would marry a merchant, and willingly, but Father would never permit that."

"So you wouldn't mind marriage?"

That set her blushing again. "Are you not ready for rinsing yet, Sir Raoul? The water must be getting cold."

"Another moment, if you please. It is pleasant to relax here. So, will you be returning to your convent soon, now that Galeran is back?"

Her eyes slid away. "As soon as matters are settled."

"But can you do anything to help settle them? I think not."

She looked back at him, eyes clear and unflustered. "Why are you here, then, Raoul de Jouray?"

"Just to be with a friend."

"And that is why I stay too."

"Ah." He stood, deliberately catching her unawares. "I am now ready to be rinsed."

Her eyes skittered wildly and her color danced around her face, but she brought him the clean water—eyes averted—so he could pour it over himself. Then she held out the warm drying cloth and he stepped out of the tub into it.

They were alone for the moment, and he couldn't resist. Once he had the cloth wrapped decently about himself, he ran a finger gently over her rosy, averted cheek. "Thank you."

She turned to look at him, her large eyes huge. "I have only done my duty. . . ."

"But you do it well. And I know it was against your inclination. I hope I did not upset you."

"No, of course not . . ."

"I'm glad." He wondered how long he could hold her spellbound. "I must seem large to you. Your father is not a large man."

Her gaze sank down to take in his broad chest—which meant that she had to look forward rather than up. Then she broke free, turning swiftly to begin picking up cloths. "A man is a man. Size doesn't mean much."

"Alas. And I am so proud of my generous attributes. . . ."

She swiveled to stare at him. So, the little Aline was not naive.

"It is generally an advantage," he went on smoothly as he dried his legs, "for a fighting man to be big and strong."

He glanced up to see that she was staring at his body as a rabbit stares at the dog that will kill it. It made him suddenly ashamed of his teasing.

"If you would do me a kindness, Lady Aline, I have clothes on the pack horse that are a little cleaner than those I took off. . . ."

"Oh, of course." And she bounded out of the room just like a rabbit unexpectedly released from the hound's jaws.

Raoul dropped his modesty cloth and, hearing noises in the bailey, wandered over to the window as he pondered the encounter. He was a mischievous wretch to tease a lady so, especially one who wished to be a bride of Christ. But, in fact, he had some doubts about that. . . .

It sounded as if someone was arriving, but he couldn't see the bailey from here.

He wondered what the effect would be if he told Aline that his family had many mercantile interests. . . .

She dashed back in. "Forthred's here!"

Then she stared at his naked body.

He was some distance from any scrap of clothing, and he'd be damned if he was going to cover himself with his hand like a nervous boy.

She just stood there, mouth agape, studying him inch by

inch as if he were a fascinating manuscript. He felt himself begin to respond.

He walked over, turned her around, and propelled her toward the door. "Then I need some clothes. Does Galeran know?"

"Father's gone to tell him—them. What are we going to do?"

"If you don't get me some clothes, I'm going to walk out into the hall naked, which should at least cause a distraction."

He pushed her through the door, and with a wild giggle she ran off to find his pack.

Galeran listened to the full story of Jehanne's encounter with Brother Forthred, then he and Jehanne set to considering various ways of handling the crisis. No action was particularly appealing to people who didn't want to mortally offend the Church.

He had not taken the time to remove his armor or clean himself, and when Hubert came to say the monk had arrived, it was too late. So he walked out into the hall knowing he looked unkempt and stank of blood.

All in all, it might be a good thing.

Hubert certainly eyed him with concern. "It would bother me mightily to offend the representative of Christ here, Galeran."

Galeran didn't think Bishop Flambard deserved that elevation, but he knew Hubert was devout. "With God's blessing, that won't be necessary." He went to the big hall doors and saw three tonsured clerics on mules trot into the bailey, followed by five sturdy men-at-arms.

He wished Hubert had been as cautious as Jehanne and made the soldiers stay outside the castle, but Hubert had too much respect for men of God.

Despite the simple robes, Galeran had no doubt that one

monk at least was a man of some importance. There was intelligence written on his smooth face, and he bore himself like someone who knows his worth.

Brother Forthred, no doubt.

Hubert went forward. "Greeting, Brother. Welcome to Burstock."

"Blessings upon this place, Lord Hubert," said the monk smoothly as he dismounted. "We have come from Heywood, since the Lady Jehanne was called away, apparently to visit her family here. We have business with her. Business of the bishop."

Galeran stepped forward. "Then you have business with me, Brother. I am Galeran of Heywood."

It was only an extra blink, but Galeran knew he had surprised the monk, which was useful.

"Greetings, my lord. I am Brother Forthred, dean to the bishop. My companions are Brother Aiden and Brother Nils. On behalf of Bishop Flambard, may I congratulate you on your blessed journey to the Holy Land, and on your safe return."

"My thanks to his lordship. I have some items from Jerusalem at Heywood. If circumstances permit, you must take one back with you for the bishop."

The monk absorbed the hint of bribery. "He will be most grateful, I assure you, my lord. If circumstances permit."

But despite the proviso, Galeran guessed that even haughty Brother Forthred wasn't above awe of crusaders. In fact, he was looking more uncomfortable by the moment.

"You said you had business with my wife? If Lord Hubert permits, perhaps we could go into the hall and discuss it in comfort."

"By all means, Galeran," Hubert declared, and shepherded them into the hall, where Galeran found Aline busy laying out wine and sweet cakes, assisted—improbably—by Raoul.

Jehanne was out of sight, as he had directed.

As he passed close to Raoul—a sweet-smelling Raoul in relatively clean clothes—Galeran murmured, "How is it that you *always* get a bath before me?"

"Charm. Sheer charm! What do you make of this business? Should I put my armor on again?"

"We can't take up arms against a bishop. Let's see how much *my* charm can accomplish."

Galeran moved on to where Brother Forthred was seated on a bench, sipping the wine. His two assistants stood uneasily close by, one holding a wax tablet ready to write an account of the proceedings.

"So," said Galeran, taking a seat nearby, "what business calls you to these parts, Brother? As you know, I have only just returned to England, but if in my absence some tithes have been neglected, or if my people have offended the Church in any way, you can be sure it will be set right."

A tinge of color entered the monk's lean cheeks, and he actually looked lost for words. But he soon gathered himself. "My lord, there has indeed been offense. Word has come to the bishop of a grievous irregularity in your household, one which might cause discord among some of our greatest men. He has sent me to investigate it."

"I see. And what investigations have you made?"

The monk cast a harried glance around the busy hall. "Perhaps we should continue this in private, my lord . . ."

"Not at all," said Galeran, smiling amiably. "It is always instructive for simple people to see matters put aright."

Brother Aiden, looking as if he was concerned for his neck, carved rapid marks into the wax.

Forthred put down his wine and sat straighter. "Has the bishop been misinformed, my lord? To be blunt, he was told your wife has played the harlot and borne a bastard."

"That *is* blunt," said Galeran coolly. "It is true that my wife has borne a child who is not mine. I would not take kindly, however, to anyone—in or out of Holy Orders—who called her a harlot."

Forthred blanched and Aiden dropped his stylus.

"Indeed, my lord . . ." stammered Forthred. "Perhaps in that we were . . . but still"—he gathered his dignity—"the Lady Jehanne has clearly sinned!"

"Have not we all? She has been forgiven."

He was aware of a distinct stir among those close enough to hear.

"By God?" demanded Forthred.

"That, you must ask of God. She has been forgiven by me."

"That is, indeed, noble of you, my lord."

Galeran met suspicious eyes. "I have recently walked in the footsteps of our Savior, Brother Forthred. Did he not say that only those without sin on their soul should cast stones at others? And I believe in that case the sinner was a woman taken in adultery."

"Very true, my lord. But in these troubled times we have to be more practical. . . ."

Galeran let his gaze wander to the smoky rafters. "Why do I feel that Christ Himself was pressured by those words?"

"My lord, this is no time for levity! Bishop Flambard is concerned that you might make this abuse of your marriage and your home excuse for acts of violence."

Galeran focused on him again. "You may assure his lordship that I won't—as long as it is not repeated."

"Moreover," said Forthred, clearly having arrived at his prepared text, "he feels that the presence of the evidence of sin might well stretch even the most tolerant man's forbearance. . . ."

"But, by God's grace, will not break it."

Forthred rose to his feet. "My lord, I have been instructed to take charge of the bastard child, and bring it with me to York, where it may be cared for until this matter is settled."

"What matter requires to be settled, Brother Forthred?"

"The ownership of the babe."

At that, Galeran rose too, pleased to still be in armor,

and bloodstained armor at that. "Who claims the child other than her mother?"

Forthred stepped back. "The father, of course."

"Who is?"

"You . . . you do not know?" Forthred was suddenly like a man who strides boldly along the road, only to sink into a quagmire.

"Why don't you tell me?"

The monk looked around uneasily, seeking wisdom of those around. He received none, though there were plenty of smirks.

He turned back to Galeran, narrow-eyed. "Sir Raymond of Lowick confesses to being the father of the babe, my lord. He admits his sin, but declares that both he and the Lady Jehanne believed you dead when the child was conceived. He rejoices in your safe return, and is truly repentant for the sin committed. As penance—recognizing the irritant his daughter must be in your household—he will take upon himself the burden of raising the child."

Galeran let a thoughtful silence run before saying, "I would think his penance should be somewhat more severe than that."

"My lord bishop has also fined him twenty shillings and imposed many prayers upon him."

Galeran nodded. "My wife already prays earnestly for God's mercy, but she certainly should pay the same fine. My Lord Hubert, could we borrow coin from you?"

"Why, yes," said Hubert, an alarmed look in his eyes. He sent a servant off with a message.

Galeran turned back to Forthred. "As to the babe, we insist on bearing the penance of raising it."

The monk paled, seeing the trap before him. "That is to place a burden on you, my lord, who carries no blame at all."

"Ah, but is that true? Did I not leave my wife unguided for many a long month? Even holy Pope Urban, who called for the crusade, had doubts as to whether married men should take part. As always, our Holy Father is wise in matters both spiritual and temporal."

"But any sin on your soul has been wiped out by the crusade, Lord Galeran."

"Then I'm sure Our Savior will grant me the strength to bear one small irritant in my household."

Forthred's cheeks were mottled red. "My lord, the bishop insists that the child be given into his care until this matter is settled!"

Galeran rested his hand on the hilt of his sword. "Brother Forthred, the child cannot leave her mother, for she is at the breast."

"A wet nurse could be found. . . ."

"I do not believe in feeding a highborn child the milk of inferior women."

"Well, then . . ."

"Nor will I entertain the notion of my wife going off to Durham with the babe. I am just back from crusade and require my comforts."

Forthred's thin lips curled back in what was very close to a snarl, but his arguments seemed to be exhausted.

Galeran took the opportunity to summon Jehanne out of hiding. In moments she was at his side, head slightly bowed, a perfect picture of womanly demeanor. "You sent for me, my lord?"

"Yes, wife. It appears Raymond of Lowick has confessed his sin to the Bishop of Durham and been forgiven upon payment of twenty shillings and the promise to bear the penance of rearing little Donata. It seems only fair that you pay the same penalty."

When he'd mentioned Raymond raising the child, her color had come and gone with panic. But then she took in the rest of his speech, and her eyes widened. He saw her have to fight a wild impulse to laugh.

He had to control his own lips' tendency to twitch.

Hubert's steward arrived with a purse. He presented it to his master, but was waved over to Galeran. Galeran took the purse, but then dropped it in Jehanne's hands.

With a deep breath she turned to the monk and knelt. "The bishop is wise and merciful, Brother Forthred. I willingly give this money for his holy works and beg his prayers and yours to aid in my petition for forgiveness from our almighty and merciful Father in heaven."

Once the dazed monk had taken the purse, Galeran raised Jehanne with all courtesy. "I, too, thank the bishop for acting as peacemaker between myself and Raymond of Lowick, who so heinously took advantage of my absence. In return, I promise that I will not raise my hand against Lowick unless he offends again. May we consider this matter closed, Brother?"

"I doubt it," snapped the monk, who then strode out of the hall followed by his two companions. Brother Aiden paused a moment to pack away his tablets and flash them a rather awe-filled smile. Galeran and Jehanne strolled after to watch the monks remount their mules and ride through the gate, trailed after by their armed guard.

"Galeran," Jehanne whispered, "how did you *do* that?" And she looked at him with perhaps the most undiluted admiration he'd received from her in his life.

He smiled, feeling as if he'd slain a mighty dragon. "Oh, just charm. I'm tempted to try my charm to get a bath and some unbloodied clothes, but I really think we should be safe back in Heywood before the next thunderbolt strikes."

Ten

Galeran was pleased to have a large body of armed men to accompany them back to Heywood, for he remembered the bowman. If the first bolt had struck a finger-length lower, he could be beyond these earthly cares.

In a spiritual sense he should welcome death, but he shuddered to think what might happen to Jehanne if she were left unprotected. He wore coif, helmet, and shield, therefore, and took care to ride well away from Jehanne and the child in case of more projectiles.

So, who was responsible for the bowman? If he'd been following Galeran's party for days, he could have found any number of chances to kill. More likely, he had come with Forthred, part of the same plan.

Flambard's plan.

Without Jehanne's swift action, Forthred might well have succeeded in taking charge of the child at Heywood. Without Galeran's presence, he would almost certainly have succeeded at Burstock. In that case, Jehanne would have felt impelled to accompany Donata.

At one stroke, Flambard would have the two pawns he wanted. If at the same time Galeran had been killed in the ambush, the whole affair would have been over before anyone could object. With the authority of the Church behind him, Lowick would have been married to Jehanne and installed in Heywood within days, and there would be little his father, or even the king, could do about it short of war.

In fact, the king would be more likely to support Flambard. So if Galeran's father objected to Lowick's possession of Heywood, Rufus would have a reason to come north and break the powerful family of William of Brome.

Raoul rode up beside him. "Why the frown? You don't really think there'll be another attempt on your life, do you?"

"It's unlikely, but I don't discount it. For all I know, a healthy price has been put on my death, and it's easy enough to kill a man. That crossbowman was simply unlucky. But I'm not exactly quaking in the saddle."

"Then why the frown? You routed that cleric cleverly."

"It won't stop there." Galeran glanced at his friend. "I gather you've never heard of Bishop Flambard."

"Aline explained something of the case. An unpleasant creature, but under protection of the king."

"He's more than that. He's the king's right-hand man. For years, he's been virtually running the country, and now that the king's raised him to the bishopric of Durham, he and my father are contestants for power here in the north."

"I'm still not sure why the bishop would think it worth supporting Lowick, though. Such a powerful person can't need such a weak ally."

Galeran shook his head. "Look at the situation here. The bishopric of Durham controls a sweep of the north from Carlisle to Durham itself. On the other hand, my father holds many estates, including Brome, the major barony in the area and with a castle that commands a crucial ford. Close by are the baronies of Heywood and Burstock, both closely allied to Brome, since I am married to Hubert of Burstock's niece, and another niece is my brother Will's wife. Did I mention that my mother's brother holds the coastal lands, including two important ports?"

Raoul whistled. "So your family has this part of the country in its fist and a real ability to interfere with the bishop."

"Exactly. And my father is not the type of man to take abuses in silence."

"But if the bishop can control Heywood, he will have significantly weakened the power of Lord William of Brome."

"And if my father objects, the king has an excuse to break him."

Raoul scanned the countryside with his sharp eyes. "The bishop and his pawn will be back, then, one way or another."

If there were other murderers lurking in the woods, however, they were too cautious to attack such a large and alert troop. The party arrived safely at Heywood in the early afternoon.

Making a show of it, Galeran went to take the babe from Jehanne so she could dismount, and carried Donata into the keep.

"Galeran," said Jehanne as they entered the hall. "I would give her up for you. I would. Don't pledge yourself to her cause."

He returned the babe to her. "I have already done so. She is an innocent, Jehanne. I wouldn't give a serf's babe over to wolves, and I will not give Donata to Flambard and Lowick. At the very least, she was born in my castle and is under my protection. Go tend her. And then," he said with a smile, "I would like a bath."

Jehanne left Galeran with anguished love in her heart. At times it seemed to her he was good to the point of madness, and she wanted to berate him as she had when they'd been young. But she knew his strong sense of justice didn't blind him to reality, and that his wits were sharp.

As he'd proved today.

But he was idealistic, and that was dangerous.

As she called for her women, she remembered all too well those times when her father was alive and Raymond had visited Heywood and flirted with her. She'd always been terrified that Galeran would take offense and make it a fighting matter.

What if it came to fighting now? Galeran was a good soldier, but no match for one like Lowick, who was bigger and known throughout the north for his fighting skills.

She'd spoken the truth earlier. Though it would tear her heart into tiny pieces, she would give Donata to the wolves rather than see Galeran die to protect her bastard child.

Her women brought warm water and clean cloths and she let them change and bathe Donata as she washed and drank some ale to refresh herself from the journey. She knew she hovered too close to Donata. She was in the habit of doing nearly everything for her, but now she made herself stand back. The time might come when she would need to be able to act on cold logic.

Distance might help.

Then Donata cried, her milk gushed forward in response, and she reached for her babe with joy and despair in her heart.

Galeran had John take his armor for cleaning, then went to praise Walter of Matlock for his assistance to Jehanne.

"I knew well enough, Lord, that you'd not want either of them snatched away to Durham."

"Would you do the same, though, if the bishop excommunicates me?"

"Would he be so foolish as that, Lord? To try to unbless a crusader?"

"Ah, yes. I keep forgetting that I'm supposed to glow with glory."

Having the Holy Land brought to mind, Galeran went to find his packs, and carefully unwrapped several items. The wrapping itself might appeal to Jehanne, for inside the leather outer layer he had used a fine cloth from the east called *qu'tun,* which held dyes well.

The precious items, however, were inside.

Reverently, he took out rolled palm leaves from the road to Jerusalem, a silver cross holding water from the Jordan, a withered branch from the Garden of Olives, a pouch of dust from Calvary, and a chip of stone from a place supposed to be the Holy Sepulcher.

He contemplated another package, a spherical one, with hesitation, but in the end he unwrapped to revealed a small skull. "The skull of John the Baptist as a child, Lord!" the eager seller had whispered. "For you only . . ."

It had made him want to laugh as few things had then, so he'd bought it to share the joke with Jehanne. He hadn't needed to bring the skull, of course, to tell the tale—especially since others had bought the same relic without realizing the absurdity—but he'd intended to see how long it took her to realize what an impossible item it was.

Miracles could perhaps preserve vials of the Virgin's milk, or wine from Cana, but it would take more than a miracle to preserve the childsize skull of a man who died in his thirties.

Now, however, there was nothing at all humorous about a baby's skull. He ran a hand over the smooth white bone, tracing the edge of the eye sockets, thinking that doubtless a mother had grieved over this child's death as Jehanne grieved over Gallot.

As he himself grieved, or could . . .

He wrapped the skull again. It was the ideal gift for Ranulph Flambard, for he wanted rid of it. With luck the bishop would not see the absurdity, for many clever people did not. It would satisfy Galeran to see the man build a rich reliquary for it. If Flambard did see it for a fraud, he could read into it what he wanted.

After all, Galeran had only promised the bishop something from the Holy Land, and it was that.

He had the scribe write a courteous letter. In it, he thanked the bishop for his assistance in smoothing the problems between himself and Raymond of Lowick, and begged him to accept the gift and remember all in Heywood in his prayers.

Jehanne joined him just as he was dispatching the messenger. He told her what he had done, but didn't tell her what the relic was. When, he wondered sadly, would the freedom to share such a joke return to their lives?

"I suppose it's wise to thank him," she said, inspecting the other items reverently. "Though it seems a waste."

More and more he wished he could tell her, and was even tempted for a moment, but—taking strength from Christ on the mountain—he resisted.

She felt the leathery palm fronds. "What sort of tree is a palm? These are more like the leaves of a bullrush."

So he described palm trees to her as the bath was prepared, and olive trees as well. He told her of heat and desert and how ordinary Bethlehem was.

"Were you disappointed?" she asked as she supervised the addition of cold water to hot.

"Only for a moment. Then I liked the thought that our Christ lived as an ordinary man. Not the glowing prince of the manuscripts, but a man with dust on his skin and calluses on his hands."

He spread his own hands thoughtfully and Jehanne took them, turning them to trace the tough pads of skin created by a lifetime of training for war. "How else would a man's hands be?"

"It sustains me," he said, "that thought. That Christ really was a man for a time, and perhaps understands men."

"I feel the same way about Christ's mother." She helped him off with his shirt, shaking her head over the blood. "Though I don't like this new idea that she was a virgin."

"It does seem strange. . . ." Galeran sank into the water with a pleased sigh. "Two baths inside a week. Luxury!"

As she began to help him to wash, Jehanne said, "Tell me more about those baths in Constantinople."

So he did so, and went on to talk of other matters such as the food, and the costumes of the various lands he had seen. He avoided all mention of fighting, though.

When he was drying himself and the servants were emptying the tub, Jehanne said, "I wish we had a bathroom like the one at Burstock."

"It would have to be out in the bailey near the kitchens, I think. What's wrong with the arrangement here?"

"Nothing, I suppose." She smiled. "I'm really thinking that I'd like a sunken marble bath big enough to swim in."

He smiled back. "I'd give you the moon and the stars if I could, Jehanne, but a sunken marble bath is beyond me."

She blushed and laughed, and it was the first time he'd heard her laugh like that since his return.

She glanced once at the bed. His body reacted, but he stayed where he was. Though it would be sinfully easy to slide back into their old ways, he mustn't until he had made sense of it all.

"Jehanne. I need to know exactly what happened between you and Raymond."

She paled. For a moment he thought she wouldn't speak, but then, clearing away damp cloths, she said, "I never betrayed you in my heart, Galeran. I never desired him. Can we not leave it at that?"

"No. Did he rape you?"

She stared at him. "No!"

"If you didn't desire him, and he didn't force you, what did happen?" When she remained silent, he said, "Jehanne, how I handle this matter in the future, what I can expect Lowick to do, all depends on what happened here the night of Gallot's death."

It was as if she'd turned into a painted statue, standing there clutching a damp drying cloth. But then she dropped it and sank to kneel by him in a swirl of colored cloth. "I'm afraid you'll hate me."

He wanted to gather her in his arms and reassure her, but her fear sparked fear in himself. Jehanne was not stupid. He'd forgiven her for infidelity, so why did she fear that the details would be beyond forgiveness? "I am slow to hate. You should know that. And I love you."

She rested her head against his leg. "As I do not deserve to be loved . . ."

"Jehanne. Tell me. Explain to me."

"I don't know if I can. Perhaps it is simplest to say that I was mad."

"Not too surprising, that." He stopped his hand from reaching to stroke her hair. "You had just lost your babe."

"And it was possible that I had lost you as well. When I heard that news, I began to think that God had taken you as exchange for a child." She looked up. "I *never* meant that, Galeran!"

"Nor would God be part of such an evil bargain."

She grimaced. "I knew you wouldn't understand." She rested her head against his thigh again, so he couldn't see her face. "I'm not good like you, Galeran, and I make God in my own image. I bargained with God that I would send you on crusade in exchange for a child. I knew you didn't want to go, but I pushed you to it anyway. When I heard you were dead, I didn't really believe it, but I wondered . . . I wondered whether God had taken more than I'd offered. Or if I'd offered more than I thought. I prayed for your safety. Every day I prayed. But then Gallot died . . ."

He did touch her hair then, for it seemed she weighed heavier against his leg.

"It was so sudden, so inexplicable . . . I decided God had answered my prayers that way, switching items like a cheating huckster at the fair . . ."

"Jehanne!"

"I hated God." She looked up fiercely. "I did. I *hated*

Him. I wanted comfort, yes, and a brief oblivion. But mostly I wanted to do the most evil thing I could imagine. So I seduced Raymond."

Galeran didn't know whether to rage or cry. "That was the most evil thing you could imagine?"

"Other than murdering my child, and perhaps I'd already done that."

Chill shot through him. "What do you mean?"

Her eyes widened. "I didn't! But it seemed some act of mine, some thought of mine . . . those prayers . . ." She leaped to her feet to pace the room. "Babes don't die for no reason. Perhaps my prayers for you were answered. Perhaps I could have either Gallot or you, and I'd chosen you. . . ."

"That's nonsense. How can you be sure Raymond didn't kill him?"

She stopped to face him. "As I said before, I'm not a heavy sleeper. When have you ever left our bed and I not wake?"

"True. And you could not have been given a drug?"

"I would have known. And anyway, he would not have done such a thing. He was fond of Gallot. He would play with him. . . ."

Now Galeran leaped to his feet. "For the mercy of God, Jehanne! Is it not enough that he took my place in your bed without him dandling the son I never saw?"

It was as if he'd hit her again. "I can only tell the truth."

"Then let's not speak of it."

"Galeran . . ."

"Go away."

"Galeran!"

"Go!"

She ran, which showed wisdom, for he could feel the rage building like a fire capable of consuming everything in its path.

Galeran sank back onto the bench, trembling with it. Jehanne was right. They needed truth to clean these wounds, but not yet. Not yet. Truth such as today's revelations was more than he could bear.

He'd had little direct contact with young children, but he could still imagine Raymond of Lowick—handsome, charming Raymond—bouncing an infant on his knee. He could hear the infant laughing, thinking of this golden god as his father.

He pushed to his feet and dragged on the clothes Jehanne had laid out for him. It was time, anyway, for him to preside over a meal in his hall, to convince even the doubting that peace and harmony reigned in Heywood.

His hands paused in the tying of his braies. Peace and harmony, indeed.

She'd seduced Lowick because she hated God? It was madness, but it was just the sort of thing Jehanne would have done in her willful youth. He'd thought she'd grown out of such wild ways.

Finishing the knot, he saw the ivory rose on its table. The cracked petal was straight again, but he didn't dare touch it. She'd not meant to break it all those years ago, he was sure. Her frustration had just exploded.

More recently, in a more cataclysmic way, her grief had exploded into rage. Shattering rage against God. He could believe it, and he sent up a prayer for her forgiveness, and another that she never confess such a sin in public.

As he put on the floor-length tunic of blue silk-embroidered wool that Jehanne had selected for him and added a gilded belt, he began to feel some comfort from their talk, bitter though it had been. He did understand now. His problem, he thought, choosing a silver and gold chain to wear around his neck, was how to convince the world that there was no need of punishment.

A good start would be an impressive appearance as lord and lady. He summoned Jehanne back and told her to dress more richly.

She exchanged her workaday linen tunic for one of silk,

and her braid girdle for one worked with gold thread and pearls. She dressed in silence and without looking at him at all.

"Don't fear me," he said. "I'm in control again."

She paused in the tying of the girdle to look at him, and it wasn't fear he saw in her eyes, but a frowning concern. "I must fear you, for then I will be cautious. If you were to hurt me, Galeran, you would never forgive yourself."

She knew him too well.

As he knew her.

"I hit you." There was still a faint yellowing on her face from that blow.

"And it bothers you still, doesn't it?"

"Deeply."

"So I must be careful for you. But if it serves a purpose to beat me, I hope you will."

"It is the last thing I want to do, Jehanne." But he told her then, while she rolled on fresh stockings, about Agnes and Edric. She smiled at some parts of the story, but she understood.

"You know," she said, standing to adjust the folds of her gown, "in a strange way I might even welcome a whipping." She came over to fuss with the hang of his garment. "Do you think that sort of thing heals the soul like a penance after confession?"

"No," he said, seizing her busy hands. "Have you confessed your sin?"

She became very still. "No."

"Why not?"

"How can God forgive . . . ?"

"God can forgive anything. And perhaps if the priest gave you a suitable penance, you'd stop wanting me to."

He'd meant it as a joke, but she sighed. "Am I anything to you but a burden?"

"Dear God!" He pulled her roughly into his arms. "You are *everything* to me, Jehanne. Everything. But it will take time to grow out of this." He held her close, closer, knowing he must almost be suffocating her. "Let us give ourselves the time," he whispered into her hair.

She pulled back enough to look up at him. "As long as the fates will give us."

She meant, as long as the world—the community, the bishop, the king—would give them. As if speaking for the world, the horn sounded to announce the meal, and he had to let her go, had to take her hand and lead her out to preside at the castle meal.

Everyone was there except the guards on watch and a few servants needed elsewhere. At the raised head table sat Raoul; Aline; Matthew, the steward; and Brother Cyril, the scribe. Galeran and Jehanne took their places in the central chairs. It was all as it had been for most of their married life.

The rest of the household sat at tables running down the sides of the hall, Galeran's knights closest, with Jehanne's ladies mixed among them. Beyond, the upper servants of the castle were placed—the falconer, the head stable groom, the mistress of the looms, and the smith.

Lower still were the other servants and the men-at arms.

The kitchen varlets entered with jugs, bowls, and platters, presenting the food first to the head table.

Galeran courteously chose good pieces and placed them on Jehanne's trencher. She smiled her thanks and did the same for him. He couldn't help thinking, though, that this would have gone somewhat better if she'd not stirred his jealousy of Lowick. Lowick and Jehanne ate at him like a canker. He wouldn't experience any true peace or happiness until he came to terms with it.

Thus far, he had discovered that Jehanne had seduced Lowick because she hated God. To many people that might seem insanity, but he understood her enough to see that she might have thought that way. Jehanne had a very human picture of God. For her, He was a person to be admired in good times, blamed in bad, and to be cautious of always.

Rather like a king, actually, Galeran thought, glancing sideways at her and drinking from the goblet they shared.

Because he was turned that way, he noticed that Raoul and Aline were being much more successful at presenting the appearance of a happy couple.

Raoul and Aline?

Galeran loved his friend almost like a brother, but he had few illusions about his behavior with women. Surely Raoul would never be so foolish as to attempt to seduce a virgin lady. Especially one like Aline, as good as pledged to the Church.

If he did, it might end with Galeran having to discuss it with him at sword's length. That he certainly did not need.

Aline was pink. Was Raoul embarrassing her?

Aline didn't know if she was in heaven or hell.

Truly, Raoul de Jouray was just the type of man she disliked, and the fact that he was handsome and charming only made it worse! He probably expected all women—lowborn or high—to crumple at the mere sight of one of his slight, teasing smiles.

But ever since the bath that morning, it had been as if she'd an itch on her skin, an itch made worse whenever he came near her, or whenever he caught her eye across the room. Her normally clear thoughts were constantly tangled, probably because she couldn't think of anything except when he would appear, and what he would say or do when he did.

For some reason, having seen his naked body once, his clothes, even his mail, had become transparent and she could see it all the time.

The ride from Burstock had been exquisite torture, since he had ridden by her side the whole way. She'd tried to ignore him, but he had asked questions about the countryside, forcing her to answer. When she was reluctant to speak, he had told her of his own homeland in France and his travels to Spain, and to the Holy Land.

Footloose, she'd tried to tell herself. A wandering free lance really, without property or prospects. Though why that should bother her, she didn't know, since she was going to be a nun, and had no interest in Raoul de Jouray.

Or no interest she couldn't rid herself of with a bit of willpower.

Now, at the meal, Raoul wasn't flirting with her. He sent her no special looks, gave her no teasing touches. He was not praising her skin, her eyes, her lips, her hair. . . . They were just talking and eating.

So why did she feel hot and twitchy?

He was speaking of Flanders. "I think you'd like it, Lady Aline. They are a very practical people, the Flemish."

"You think I'm practical?"

His eyes crinkled. "Yes. Don't you?"

"Not at the moment," she blurted out, and felt another layer of heat rise in her cheeks. Oh, why had she said anything so stupid?

He leaned back and smiled at her. "But it's very practical at your age to be interested in a man."

At this direct attack, Aline stiffened her spine and glared at him. "I have no such interest!"

"Then you are notably different from the rest of the human race, Lady Aline. Young women are interested in young men, and young men in young women."

"What about old men?" she asked tartly. "Such as yourself."

Something flashed in his eyes, and then he laughed. "We are interested in women of many ages. But we ancient specimens have a great deal to recommend us, you know. We are patient, and we have more self-control than striplings."

"Really?" she queried, letting her gaze move pointedly to buxom Ella.

He blushed! She'd swear he blushed. It was as sweet as victory in battle.

"When we have need to be, Lady Aline."

"Ah." With great care she chose a gooseberry tart. "You mean you are patient about seduction, sir, but impatient when the game is won."

"Never." He smiled at her, lazy-eyed. "I promise you, Lady Aline, I am *never* impatient with a woman."

Pest! There went her color again, flying in her cheeks like a banner. "Some women will not be seduced, Sir Raoul, no matter how patient the hunter."

"So a good hunter learns to choose his quarry with care. More wine, my lady?"

She watched him pour wine from an earthen jug into her silver goblet, a thrill going through her at his words. Was it a thrill of terror or excitement? "You think *I* could be seduced?"

"Do you think you couldn't?" He poured wine into his own goblet, not looking at her at all.

"Yes!"

"Perhaps you are right." Then he looked at her, and something in his hazel eyes was like the trumpets of battle. "Do you wish to find out?"

"No!"

Calmly, he turned to the plate of gooseberry tarts and chose another to offer her. "Then we will not play the game."

She took the tart, studying him. "What game?"

"Seduction." Before she could protest, he added, "Of course, we couldn't actually take it to its conclusion, fair lady, for that would ruin your chance of becoming a bride of Christ. And it would quite likely land me in more trouble than I want."

And that was true. Her father and brothers would chop him into tiny pieces if he dishonored her. And by that time he would be glad to die.

Aline studied him as she nibbled on the tart, her heart beating fast. She was well aware that Raoul was acting like a hunter and setting lures and traps. But it was such exciting sport and ultimately completely safe.

"So it would be just a game . . ."

"Exactly. Like the mock battles men fight when training for war. In fact, like those battles, it could be useful practice for you. I suspect you need training in defense."

"What do you mean?"

"Why do you not like assisting men at their bath, Aline?"

It was the first time he'd used her name without "Lady" in front of it and she knew the game had started. "I am modest. . . ."

"The sight of a man's body cannot be a shock to you."

"No. . . ."

"Well, then?"

She couldn't manage the tart, so put it down. "I rarely need to perform that duty, so it flusters me."

"I don't think it's the duty that flusters you, Aline."

She glared at him. "Very well. I find men arousing— young, healthy men. I have tried to fight it, but I never seem able to, so I prefer to avoid the occasion of sin."

His smile said he had won in some way. "It is not always wise to avoid our occasions of weakness. As you discovered this morning, it can leave us vulnerable. It's like a man-at-arms who avoids climbing walls because he fears heights. One day he will need to climb a wall in battle, and doubtless die for his folly. Fighting men need to be strong in all ways. They need to train away every weakness, to have their skills constantly well honed."

"I'm sure you are very strong, and your skills well honed."

"Oh, yes. See." Without warning, he took her hand and placed it on his bare forearm, pressing her fingers against iron-hard muscles.

She snatched her hand back. "So,"—she wished her

voice were not so breathy—"let me understand you. You are offering to train me in the skills I will need to avoid carnal temptation?"

Carnal temptation. She wanted, quite desperately, to feel his arm beneath her hand again.

"Not precisely." He adjusted the heavy gold bracelet he wore on his wrist. She was sure it was solely to draw her attention back to his muscles. "I suspect you need a lady to teach you those skills. I am offering to stage some mock assaults to test your defenses so you will know which skills you need to improve."

Mock assaults like that bracelet, that arm . . .

"In fact, Lady Aline, I am beyond offering and am now promising. You had better start reenforcing your walls and stocking up on arrows."

She forced her eyes back up to his teasing face. "Whether I agree or not?"

"Whether you agree or not."

She focused her most severe frown on the wretch. "I should complain to Galeran of your behavior."

"That would put him in a very awkward position, and it is not necessary. Remember, Aline, you have my word that I will not invade your citadel, even if it lies wide open to me."

Aline gaped at that blatant image, but then snapped, "Very well. But I warn you, sir, my defenses are very strong indeed. And sometimes assailants suffer more than the citadel they attack."

She then turned to watch four of Jehanne's ladies perform a dance, an intricate weaving dance whose sole purpose was to show off their grace and charm to the watching men. Why couldn't Raoul play his games with one of them?

She'd be after them with a knife if he did.

Oh, dear. Her defenses were straw and sticks and she feared he knew it.

As a beleaguered citadel, her first line of defense should

be to call upon her liege lord to handle this unruly assailant. But Raoul was correct. That would put Galeran in a difficult position.

One of the ladies smiled at Raoul, and he winked back at her. Aline didn't know which of the two she most wanted to throw a pitcher of icy water over.

She also had to accept that having Galeran control Raoul wouldn't be much fun.

Suddenly, she wanted some fun.

Soon, probably before Christmas, she would return to St. Radegund's. Since she'd turned eighteen, she would be expected to take her novice's vows. This could be her last opportunity to explore the strange, frightening world of men and women. As virtually a promised bride of Christ, she shouldn't *want* to explore the strange, frightening world of men and women. . . .

But, on the other hand, the temptations of the flesh would never go away. He was right. She should build her defenses.

The ladies sat down and Galeran's knights started to dance, as unashamedly performing for the women as the women had danced for the men. This was a fiercer dance, allowing them to show off their nimbleness and strength as they acted out a very explicit hunt.

One of the younger knights—dark-haired and with a wicked eye—smiled straight at Aline and did a fancy sequence of steps. Normally she would have ignored it, but this time she smiled back.

A hand gripped hers beneath the table. "Aline," said Raoul. "You are not yet ready to take on one like that."

"Am I not?" She slid a look at her partner. "But I am able to handle you, you think?"

"Not in this millennium, my sweet. It is just that I shall be using blunted weapons, and that bold adventurer is whetting a fine edge to his sword."

* * *

Galeran nudged Jehanne. "I fear Raoul is flirting with Aline."

Jehanne slid a look sideways. "A somewhat pointless exercise."

"Perhaps it is just that—exercise. You think she's invulnerable, then?"

"Aline has always been wary about men."

"Aline was fourteen when she decided to become a nun. She spent only a year in the convent before coming here to be with you. Perhaps she has just been slow to develop an interest."

Jehanne glanced sideways again and her lips twitched. "If her interests lie that way, surely it is as well that she find that out now."

"She is not pledged to the Church?"

"No. It was completely her own idea. Uncle Hubert is pleased, of course. Being devout, he likes the idea of having a daughter to pray for his soul. But if she changes her mind, no one will force her to it."

"I fear Raoul is just amusing himself, though. I can put a stop to it if you wish."

Jehanne thought about it. "No. As I said, it will be as well for Aline to discover her true nature. She may still choose to take vows, but at least she will do so knowing her weaknesses. I assume we can trust your friend not to ruin her."

"I believe so. But I'll make sure of it. He might hurt her feelings, however."

"Break her heart? That is excellent training for life."

Galeran concentrated on draining his wine. What did that mean? Though he stamped on its every appearance, deep inside he still wondered whether Jehanne loved Lowick and would rather her husband were dead.

Eleven

As the trestles were broken down, the household relaxed, chatting and flirting. Jehanne watched Galeran strolling among his people, taking time to talk to each and catch up with their news. She had missed Galeran during his absence. Selfishly, she had not thought of how much he must have missed Heywood, or of the many events that had taken place while he was gone.

She'd been sorry he'd missed Gallot's birth and brief life, but she knew he would also have wanted to be here for the hilarious courtship of Hugh and Margaret. He was laughing now as he was told the tale, but he'd have laughed more if he'd lived through those weeks.

And he'd want to hear the story of how Sven lost his hand, and how Ann rescued a child from the river. . . .

With an ache in her throat she turned, and saw the way Aline's eyes kept flickering to Raoul. Oh, dear. She strolled over to her cousin. "Raoul de Jouray is certainly a handsome man," she said casually. "Unfortunately, he knows it."

"It would be hard not to. Just as you know you are beautiful."

"Since you are very like me in looks, you must know your own charms too."

"But no one will ever describe *me* as slender as a willow wand." For the first time, Aline sounded rather glum about it.

"Poetic nonsense. Would any sensible man want his lady to behave like one of those sweet, gentle willow maidens?"

"Probably," said Aline with a grin. "She'd be less trouble. She'd wait patiently at home while her man went adventuring. Or she'd obligingly put herself into danger so her hero could show his prowess. And when her swain declared that he was unworthy of her, she'd not tell him how true it was." She sighed. "Being the only girl in a household of men warps a woman, I fear."

Jehanne laughed with relief and hugged her cousin. "I suppose you could do worse than to test your vocation against Raoul de Jouray, for he's tempting as the apple in Paradise. Just take care not to go too far. And never think he'll marry you. Landless men like that cannot marry."

"He'd make a sorry husband, anyway, with his roving eye." And Aline glared at the handsome wretch who was teasing a giggling lady.

It seemed Aline still had her sensible head set right on her shoulders. All the same, when Jehanne declared the midday rest over and sent everyone about their work, she went out of her way to catch Raoul before he left the hall. "If you hurt my cousin, sirrah, I'll gut you."

He looked down at her with a raised brow. "Galeran has already given me that message, my lady, though rather more doucely."

Jehanne felt color rise in her cheeks. "I can be sharp-tongued."

"Lady Jehanne, virtue comes not from confessing our faults but from trying to correct them." He walked away, leaving her gaping.

Galeran came to her side. "Did Raoul say something to offend you?"

"No." She looked at him. "How can you love me? I'm not lovable."

His hand went to his knife at his belt. "What did he say?"

"Nothing to offend, but . . ."

"But?"

"But I *do* take pride in my vices. I don't try to change them. I like to speak my mind. I'm afraid to be weak, afraid to depend on you. . . ."

"Why should you want to be weak? And I could die tomorrow."

"I've already proved unable to handle that event well."

He sighed. "Jehanne. We have to stop picking at all this like the scab on a healing wound."

"When it heals, there will be no scab. If it heals." She studied him, trying to see beneath the calm exterior. "Everyone is still waiting for you to do something."

"Perhaps one day they will stop. The well needs dredging, I'm told. I'd better set some men to it."

Jehanne sighed and went off to supervise the scouring of the corn bins. She sympathized with Galeran's desire to let time heal, but she doubted that time alone would wipe her sin away.

The days were still long, so the evening meal came late, but not so late that people were too tired for entertainment. When the trestles had been broken down, music began, and then stories were told in the russet light of the setting sun.

Because Galeran and Raoul had been to mystic lands, their stories were much in demand. In addition to tales of the Holy Land, Raoul could also tell of Spain, both the Christian north and the Moorish south. He told of a meeting with the famous *Cid Compeador,* Rodrigo Diaz de Vivar, mightiest warrior of Spain, who had spent his last years opposing the Moors in his own crusade.

"Perhaps I could sing you a song of Spain," Raoul said at last, looking around at his rapt audience.

A great shout answered him. He called for a gittern and plucked a tune from the strings, a delicate, floating melody.

"Some say this is the song *El Cid* sang to the Lady Jimena when he wooed her. In it, he tells her she is as beautiful as the almond blossom, as pure as water from the snows of the sierra, and as sweet to the lips as a plump, juicy grape.

He began to sing in a rich, expressive voice, and though he did not look at Aline, and she understood none of the Spanish words, she felt as if he sang to her alone. As if she were as beautiful as the almond blossom, as sweet as a juicy grape, and as pure as the water from the snows of a sierra.

When he finished and refused to entertain further, he came to sit on the floor by her knee. Why that should seem so much more intimate than him sitting by her side, she did not know.

"Did you really sing the words you said?" she asked.

He glanced up at her. "Of course, though that is just the refrain. In the verses the warrior relates his pursuit of his beautiful lady. How he adored her from afar. How he undertook dangerous exploits in order to be worthy of her. How he slew any who endangered her. And all because she was as beautiful as a blossom, as pure as mountain water, and as sweet to the lips as a plump, juicy grape."

"Why do I suspect that grapes are actually sour as unripe gooseberries?"

He twisted to look at her fully, resting his arm across her thighs. "Are you so suspicious? The grapes in Guyenne are sweet as honey. Perhaps grapes can be found in London and other southern ports. One day, I promise, I will feed you a plump, juicy grape."

Dry-mouthed, Aline turned her attention back to the center of the hall, where a knight was telling a tale of monsters and magic. Raoul's arm stayed where it was, invasive, powerful, but strangely comforting.

She even found herself wanting to put her hand on his

broad shoulder. She could imagine how hard it would feel
beneath the cloth. How reassuring . . .

She was quite relieved to be able to retreat to the lady's
chamber, where she slept safely guarded by Jehanne's five
ladies.

After spending an appropriate length of time with their
household, Galeran led Jehanne to their chamber. It was
like so many other evenings, and yet unlike. Too many problems sat between them for ease. The nurse immediately
brought Donata, and Jehanne sat to feed her. As soon as
the babe had finished her meal, however, she called for the
woman to take her away again.

Galeran decided not to comment. He removed his belt
and robe, so he was only in braies and shirt. "Would you
like to play chess?"

She looked directly at him. "I would like to make love."

Heat swept through him. "So would I." He held out his
hand and she rose to place hers in it. He pulled her into
his arms for a kiss, tasting her—he realized—for the first
time in so long.

After, holding her tight in his arms, he said, "Sweet Savior, we didn't kiss. Last time, we didn't kiss!"

She clung as tight to him as he to her. "I know. I noticed.
Why is kissing both the first and the last thing?"

He raised her face and rubbed his thumb over the fading
bruise there. "Perhaps the kiss is universal. Even those pledged
to chastity kiss, if only in peace."

But now, like a fever, he needed more than kisses. He
undid her girdle and tossed it aside. Then he slid his hands
beneath her tunic to find the openings provided for the babe
to feed.

She gasped, relaxing back against his arm as he pleasured
her breasts, first with hand, then with mouth, until she was
clutching at him. Then he toppled them onto their new bed.

Loosening his braies, he pulled up her skirts and thrust into her moist heat, unable this time to hold back, or be gentle, or thoughtful. This time he could only let the wild flames consume them both, and revel in every scorching moment.

When his strength returned, he drew the curtains around the bed, enclosing them in a private world where evil could never intrude. In that darkness he stripped the clothes from her limp, sweaty body, moving her limbs as if she were a child, kissing and nipping at each bit of skin exposed.

By the time she was naked, her energy had returned and she stripped him in the same way, teasing every part of him until he was ready again. Before she could mount him, however, he tried one of the eastern tricks, and pulled her to kneel over his mouth so he could torment her with his tongue.

"Galeran!" she gasped at the first touch, and then braced her hands against the head of the bed and went silent as the tension gathered in her body. He would not let her be silent, though, and held her prisoner until she cried out.

Only then did he let her down to fill herself with his flesh, so she could ride them both into blessed oblivion.

"Oh, but this is heaven," she murmured weakly at last, tucked close into his arms. "Or hell, considering the wickedness you just practiced on me! Delicious wickedness, though. If only we could stay in this hot, spicy cocoon forever."

That was impossible, and they both knew it, but they didn't expect the next day's news.

William of Brome rode into Heywood when they had only just broken their fast. "The king's dead," he announced as he stamped into the hall, cloak billowing, setting the dogs to barking.

Galeran abruptly abandoned a discussion on the well and waved the wide-eyed men off to get on with the work.

"Rufus is dead? How?"

"An arrow while hunting. Can you believe it?" He lowered his voice. "Can you believe it an accident?" He jerked his head toward the solar.

Without a further word, Galeran led the way there.

Jehanne and Aline were in the solar with the baby and her nurse. They all immediately rose to leave, but Galeran said, "Jehanne. You should stay."

When the three of them were alone, Galeran said, "Now, Father. Tell us what's happened."

Lord William thumped down onto a bench, hands braced on strong legs. "I've only had the official word plus a bit of gossip. Two days ago Rufus went hunting down near Winchester. Among the party was his brother Prince Henry, Wat Tyrel—who's connected to the Clares—and the Beaumont brothers. Wat Tyrel managed to put an arrow through the king."

Jehanne gasped. Galeran could have gasped himself, but only said, "How very convenient."

"Hah!" said his father. "You see it without squinting! No sooner was Rufus cooling than Henry raced off to Winchester with the Beaumonts to seize the treasury. I'm summoned to London to help choose the next king, but it hardly seems worth the trip."

"He'll have been crowned by now, unless there's been a mighty move to object to him. Unlikely, with Rufus so unpopular and the other brother, Robert, not well thought of either."

"But Robert's the eldest," said Jehanne. "Will he contest this?"

Lord William nodded. "That's what I want to know. You must have met him on the crusade, Galeran."

"I served in his force most of the time. I came back with him too, separating only when he decided to dally in Sicily."

"A dallying he may live to regret."

"Do you really think so? I suspect that if Robert had come home sooner, Rufus would have died sooner."

A silence settled on the room, then Jehanne said, "Henry had his brother killed?"

Lord William nodded. "It's hard to believe otherwise. Henry Beauclerk has always wanted England. Since he's the only son of the Conqueror born here, he's always thought it his birthright, but he was only nineteen when his father died and in no position to contest it. Now he's thirty-two and a clever, skillful man. He's doubtless just been waiting his chance."

"Chance? It looks like murder."

"Accidents can happen in hunting, Jehanne," Galeran said. "It all bears considering, though." He sat on the edge of the bed. "I arrived in Bruges with a small group of crusaders, and some of those men were heading for the south of England rather than the north. In the last week or so, Henry has received word that his brother is returning healthy from the crusade, and covered with all the glory of one who saved Jerusalem from the infidel. What's more, Robert acquitted himself quite well over there—better than he had at home. To Henry, it must have seemed that even if he managed to dispose of Rufus, Robert might be chosen king of England. Intolerable. So perhaps he had to be crude."

"The question is," interrupted Lord William, "what do we do now?"

Galeran turned to him. "What choice do we have?"

"We can support Robert's claim."

Galeran flicked a glance at Jehanne, and saw she shared his alarm at this. "Why should we?"

"For right! Hell's flames, Galeran, are you so lost to right and wrong that you'd support a fratricidal villain on the throne?"

"I'd support the best king."

"And you think that's Henry?"

"Yes. We don't want England a province of Normandy again."

Lord William slumped down. "True enough. But it sits uneasily with me, I tell you true."

"Rufus sat uneasily with me, with his unruly followers, and his greedy thievery through men like Flambard."

Lord William frowned at him from beneath his bushy, grizzled brows. "Are you sure you're not just thinking this is a fine way to stop Ranulph Flambard from interfering in your own affairs?"

"I admit that has its appeal. Without Rufus's protection, I think Flambard's torch will be extinguished. But as far as the king goes, what choice do we have?"

Lord William rubbed uneasily at his lip with his knuckle. "Like I said, I've had gossip as well as the official messenger. Some men are already moving to support Robert."

"God save us all, then. Are we to have war over it?"

"We can't flinch from the right for fear of fighting."

"I've had my fill of fighting."

"No man can escape it," stated his father. "We have to do what is right. But it can wait. It can wait." He shrugged off his cloak and studied them. "Now, speaking of Flambard, what's this I hear about him trying to seize the child. And a bowman?"

Galeran grimaced, though he'd never really had a chance to keep the news from his father. "It all came to nothing. How did you hear?"

"Hubert sent me a message. Just as well, since my own son tries to keep me in ignorance."

"I didn't want to bother you."

"Bother me?" Lord William surged to his feet. *"Bother* me! What do I have in life but bother? And why would Flambard want the brat?"

"It's more a case of Lowick wanting Donata."

"Why?"

"Because Jehanne would have to accompany her babe."

Lord William directed a fearsome stare at his daughter-in-law. "He still lusts after you, does he?"

She flushed, but answered calmly. "He lusts after Heywood."

"God's toes," Lord William muttered, seeing the plot. "And Henry Beauclerk will be no friend of Flambard's, so this event spells Flambard's ruin, and that of Lowick too. . . ."

"Precisely," said Galeran. "So, once we declare our support of Henry, I can go to him and ask him to sort out the situation regarding Donata, and be reasonably sure of his support."

Lord William sat back down. "He'll have to heed the law, and a man has a right to his children."

"A man who has been wronged in his own house has rights too. But you'll be the turning point, Father. If you are Henry's staunch supporter here in the north, he'll not want to alienate you. You would be alienated, I assume?"

Lord William scowled at him. "It'd be easier to just drown the brat." But then he flashed a guilty look at Jehanne.

"Perhaps," said Galeran, "you should meet your new granddaughter. Jehanne?"

She left, even as his father spluttered, "She's not my granddaughter!"

"You might as well get used to treating her as such." When Jehanne returned with the baby, Galeran took her and placed her in his father's arms. Surely it was the hand of God that had ensured Donata was at her best—dry, awake, and not hungry.

He sent a silent message, and Jehanne slipped out again.

The babe stared up at ruddy-faced William of Brome and stretched her mouth to squawk, almost as if she wanted to talk.

"Hey, hey. There's a little bird, eh?" said Lord William,

giving her a stubby, callused finger to grasp. "She looks quite like her brother at the same age, I must say."

That reminder of the son he had never known was like a blow, but Galeran managed to be impassive when his father cast him an embarrassed glance.

"A good strong grip on her too," said Lord William hastily. "Pity she'll not be handling a sword."

"Being Jehanne's daughter, I'd swear no oaths to that."

"True enough!" said his father with a bark of laughter. Then he shot Galeran a searching glance. "All right between you two, is it?"

"It is as it is. I will not renounce Jehanne, or let anyone hurt her. I will not let her child be taken from us."

Lord William looked down at the baby and waggled his eyebrows at the fascinated child. "Load of trouble, you are, for such a tiny mite. Right, then," he said, looking up. "What's Lowick likely to do now?"

"Short of trying to seize Jehanne and Donata by force, I don't know. And if he cannot kill me, his chances of getting Heywood are small even with them in his power."

"If Lowick were to get his hands on Jehanne and the babe, you'd fight him, wouldn't you?"

"I'd have to."

"And if he killed you, his path would be smoothed."

"Apart from the enmity of my family."

"What if he throws his lot in with Duke Robert? Then if Robert invades and carries the day, the enmity of your family will be scant protection."

"Father, I know both Henry and Robert. If Robert prevails, it will be the wildest freak of fate."

Lord William looked him in the eye. "Like the Conqueror succeeding against all odds, and like a hunting arrow killing Rufus? Fate plays a strange game with the kings of England, Galeran. Don't ever expect these matters to follow logic."

He stood and gave the babe back. "I'm for London, then, to take my oath. Perhaps you should come with me to put your case directly to Henry before anything else happens to upset the apple cart. We'll be a strong party."

Donata wriggled, and so Galeran tried putting her against his shoulder as Jehanne had done. She settled, head resting trustingly close to his. "When do you plan to leave?"

"Within days."

"Women and a baby will slow you down."

"I don't mind traveling slow. I just don't want it to *look* as if I've dallied."

"I see." Galeran gently rubbed Donata's tiny back, and it seemed as if the babe relaxed even more. It was tempting to stay safe in his castle and hope the world would ignore this tiny, defenseless child. Like most temptations, it was foolish.

"We'll travel with you," he said.

As soon as Lord William left, Jehanne appeared at Galeran's side. "I didn't stay to hover over Donata. Did you note that?"

Galeran continued to stroke the sweet burden on his shoulder. "Was I supposed to?" he teased.

"I was trusting you!"

"So I would hope." But Galeran smiled at her intensity. It doubtless hadn't been easy for Jehanne to stay away completely.

At the sound of her mother's voice, the baby turned slightly and gave a mewing cry. "Hungry again?" asked Galeran, lowering her to look into her eyes. "You're a greedy miss."

"They get hungry at this age," Jehanne said, and Galeran heard anxiety in her voice. Would she ever completely trust him with the child?

"Will you be able to travel?"

"Of course. Feeding her is easy, and her appetite should settle again soon. Why?"

"My father is going to pledge to Henry. He travels south within days. I said we'd go with them."

"Why?" She'd tensed, but kept the question mild.

"To put our matter before the king. We need it settled."

He could see she feared this as much as he did. But not to act was just as dangerous.

Donata squawked again, and Jehanne took her, jiggling her. "But why so quickly? Surely Henry's hold on the throne is no sure thing."

"Jehanne, we can't delay. With matters disordered by the king's death, Flambard might decide to use force to impose his judgment. I don't want to have to take arms against the Church. At the very best, it will cost us a fortune in fines."

"But won't the king put the matter before a Church court?"

"If he does, it will be under the Bishop of London."

"But what if *he* decides against us?"

"We can't hide in a hole, saying 'What if . . . ?' " He put an arm around her, around them both. "Trust me?"

She stared up at him. "Of course I trust you. I didn't come out to hover over Donata, did I?"

But it had been conscious trust, frayed by effort. He wanted more than that. He wanted what they'd once had. . . .

Perhaps responding to his silence, she added, "I'm trying. I'm determined to change, to not be so difficult."

He kissed her cheek. "Don't change too much, Jehanne. I love my sharp-tongued, combative wife. I've no mind to find myself married to a honey-voiced, docile creature who would faint at the sight of a wild boar."

She blushed, which pleased him, and tried to hide it by looking down at the babe. "Your father's mad," she confided.

Then she stared at Galeran, appalled.

He made himself smile. "In all but blood I'm her father. But not mad."

* * *

Aline walked into the solar, but when she saw Galeran and Jehanne talking in such an intimate way, she whipped back into the hall and slipped down to the bailey. Without reason, her heart beat wildly just from witnessing such a tender moment.

Why had she ever thought she wasn't interested in earthy matters? After Mass this morning she'd spoken to Father Robert, embarrassing herself dreadfully as she tried to explain her tangled feelings. She'd half hoped to be told that any contact with Raoul was wicked, that she should go straight back to the convent.

The priest's advice had been quite different. "Lady Aline, you've made no vows. You should take time to learn where God wishes you to serve Him. Experiencing the temptations of the flesh does not make it impossible to be a nun. Those in Holy Orders can be tempted, but learn to resist. In that they find new strength."

So Aline was left wondering whether her alarming feelings for Raoul de Jouray were a message from God telling her she was to marry, or a temptation of the devil sent to strengthen her.

At the same time, she fretted over whether Raoul had any feelings for her at all. Was she just a challenge, mere amusement for an active man stuck up here in the north?

She walked over to the far corner of the bailey, to the training ground, knowing she would probably find Raoul there. What a man he was for military exercise. The previous day she'd watched from an arrow slit as he'd taken on two men-at-arms wielding axes. Though he'd been in mail and armed with sword and shield, her heart had nearly stopped a time or two.

Today, in view of their personal challenge, she refused to watch from concealment, but walked boldly up to the training yard.

Then she saw that they were practicing the quarter staff. Half naked.

It was a warm day and the exercise had clearly heated the men, for most of them had stripped off their shirts. It was only Raoul's torso, however, that made Aline's heart race. She'd seen him naked when he'd bathed, but she'd been more intent then in *not* looking at him than in appreciating his attractions.

Today, in the light of their challenge, she felt obliged to assess his weaponry.

Oh, my.

She had five strong brothers, but came from a short family. Raoul's height balanced his strong build, making him the most impressive man present, but it was his movement that captured her. He was graceful and agile as an animal as, one after another, he winded, tripped, or knocked down the men without being touched himself.

"Come on!" he suddenly bellowed. "Why are you lining up like nuns for the Eucharist! Try to take me!"

The ten men looked at one another, then attacked together from all sides, grinning madly at the thought of downing this demon. Still, it took them a while, and a good number of cracked shins and bruises, before they had him beneath them in the dust.

Aline had her hand over her mouth, sure he must be dead.

But the group dissolved and he leaped up, spraying muddy sweat from his hair and dirt from everywhere. Then he saw Aline and grinned, teeth white in his dirty face.

"Care for a bout, my lady?"

Aline turned and fled back to the hall.

Jehanne looked up from where she sat embroidering, cradle by her side. "What's happened?"

"Nothing!" Aline tried to straighten her veil and slow her breathing.

"Something must have." A sudden smile twitched Jehanne's lips. "Let me guess. Raoul de Jouray."

Aline silently cursed her tendency to turn red. "It just frightened me. Ten men attacked him. . . ."

"Good heavens. Why?"

"Because he told them to, the silly man." Aline sat down and made herself calm enough to pick up her distaff and spin wool as she made the encounter into a funny story.

At the end Jehanne said, "He's the kind of man who loves nothing more than fighting and hunting."

Aline concentrated on the evenness of her thread. "Is that a warning?"

"Perhaps. But I shouldn't have said *nothing* else interests him. I'm sure love-play absorbs him, too."

Aline met her cousin's eyes. "There's no question of anything like that between us."

"Good." But Jehanne did not sound convinced. "However, if he was as dirty as you say, he'll doubtless want a bath."

Aline knew she was blushing again, but she said, "I suppose so," and went to make sure there was hot water ready, a wicked tingle of excitement building within her. Her words to Jehanne about love-play had been a lie. There was already love-play between them. She hoped. And she hoped there would be more.

After a time, when Raoul did not appear, she went in search of him. She found him sitting among the men, shirt on, chatting and laughing as they all attended to weapons. Raoul looked reasonably clean, and was sliding a whetstone down his sword blade with all the care of a lover.

Catching sight of her, he sheathed his sword and came over. For once he looked a little somber. "Lady Aline. I'm sorry if our rough play offended you."

"Of course it didn't."

"Then it was my invitation. I apologize even more."

"So you should. It was lewd." Aline knew she was frowning when she didn't really want to.

"Not at all." A warning twinkle sparked in his eye. "You just misunderstood. I would be happy to train you in quarter-staff work if it interests you."

"Oh, you are impossible!" She looked him over, trying not to notice how his simple braies and shirt showed off his marvelous body. "How is it that you are so clean?"

He looked down at his still-grubby clothes with a grin. "The clean bits are courtesy of a few buckets of well water. Am I clean enough to kiss?"

Aline stepped back. "Of course not!"

"I feared as much. If you're not going to kiss me, sweeting, I had better go back and tend my more appreciative sword." And he did just that, leaving Aline feeling abandoned and intensely dissatisfied.

She soon lacked time to fret about such things, however, for Jehanne needed her help to prepare for the journey.

"Aline," said Jehanne the next day as they went through chests selecting suitable clothes. "There's actually no need for you to come with us. You could return to Burstock, or even to St. Radegund's."

Alarmed, Aline looked up from a pile of shifts. "But I've never been south, and I've always wanted to." It was as good an excuse as any.

"It will be a long, arduous journey, with possible danger at the end. After all, Duke Robert could invade."

"I don't mind the journey, and surely with Lord William and Galeran to protect us, we'll be in little danger. And Raoul de Jouray as well," she added, praying that her interest didn't show. "I suppose he will be with the party."

"I believe so. Galeran said something about him wanting to find grapes. He must be missing his home in the south of France."

Aline hid her red face in the depth of a chest, alarmed at how determined she was not to be left behind.

In a small, cozy parlor in the Bishop's Palace in Durham, Ranulph Flambard unwrapped a package, peeling off layers of leather and cloth until he revealed a small white skull.

A stocky man of middle years, with a heavily jowled face and sallow skin, he was intelligent and shrewd, and both qualities showed in his features. He was also ruthlessly avaricious, which was well known by his actions.

The letter that accompanied the gift had told him what to expect, but he was still considering the implications. Coming hard on the news of King William Rufus's death, the strange gift was especially disturbing.

Rufus's death was a serious blow, but Flambard was not one to worry over what could not be changed. His only concern now was how to maintain his wealth, power, and influence.

He'd prefer to continue undisturbed under Henry Beauclerk, but the new king had never been well disposed toward him. To be sure, Henry—like Rufus—was going to need money, and Ranulph Flambard was very good at squeezing out money, but he still couldn't depend on that to maintain his place.

Which left Henry's brother, Robert of Normandy, who was a less clever man, and thus a more likely tool. If Robert was to win England, however, it would be through war, which meant he'd favor men with military power over those with administrative skills. Flambard could not have true power in the north unless he destroyed William of Brome.

He contemplated the skull, then sent for Raymond of Lowick.

The man who arrived not long afterward almost had to duck beneath the stone lintel, and his muscular breadth took up too much of the room. Flambard found Lowick an annoying mix of ambition and scruples, but with his blond hair, massive chest, and proud bearing, he was generally considered appealing, especially by women. And it was a woman who was at the heart of this matter.

"My lord bishop, you have news for me?"

He stood, hand on sword hilt, as if ready at this unlikely moment for battle. Bishop Flambard sighed, wondering why tools always came in such inadequate form. He recounted Brother Forthred's adventures at Heywood and Brome.

Raymond frowned. "How could such a simple matter be so miscarried?"

"Lord Galeran is rather more clever than you gave me reason to think, Sir Raymond."

"What has cleverness to do with it? You said I had a right to my daughter."

"But mother and child cannot be separated—a fact we counted on—and Lord Galeran claims a right to his wife's attentions."

Raymond's well-shaped mouth tightened. "It can be little better than a rape, my lord bishop. Jehanne has always loved me. She never wanted her marriage. Her father had to whip her to the altar to say her vows to that runt."

Flambard had heard that story from other sources, so it could be true. It was not, however, supported by recent facts. "Yet she did not leave the castle with you when she had the chance."

"She felt her marriage vows too strongly." Lowick stood even straighter. "I honor her for that."

"It is indeed honorable," said Flambard, adding dryly, "if a trifle belated. According to my information, she was not intimate with you throughout her pregnancy or afterward."

Lowick flushed. "I honor her for that too. She is not a sinful woman, my lord bishop. We were weak, but only once."

"Yet I'm sure you tried to persuade her to sin again."

"I have confessed it to you."

Flambard studied his tool uneasily. Surely Lowick was right, and Jehanne of Heywood preferred him to her husband. But in his experience, women were not given to such noble scruples, especially when they think their husband is dead. If the Lady Jehanne was merely afraid to flee her husband, that could be solved by the man's death. If she sincerely repented of her sin, however, she could take herself—and her property—to a convent, which would not suit at all.

Jehanne of Heywood could be the means to break the power of William of Brome and secure Flambard's undisputed power in the north. She could also prove to be a disaster, and what he'd learned of her worried him. He much preferred stupid, docile women.

"Brother Forthred brought back a story of Lord Galeran being attacked near his home."

"Brigands?" asked Lowick without great interest.

"Doubtful. The attacker was a lone crossbowman."

That jerked the man out of his thoughts. "A crossbow! That's the devil's tool. What would such a wretch hope to achieve?"

"Lord Galeran's death, I assume."

"Was Galeran injured?" Flambard could not detect a trace of hope in the man's face.

"Scarcely at all."

"I give thanks for that. No man should die in such a dishonorable way. By the Holy Cross, if I could get my hands on such a low rogue as that . . ."

"It has already been dealt with, Sir Raymond. Lord Galeran dispatched him, with considerable vigor, or so I hear."

Lowick nodded his approval. "He is capable in his own way."

Flambard eyed the noble fool. "It would not have been completely inconvenient for Galeran of Heywood to have died there, you know."

Lowick frowned again, but this time with puzzlement. "What has that to do with it?"

Flambard abandoned that line of debate. "You gave me to understand that Lord Galeran is not a notable warrior."

"How could he be, so small as he is? But it takes little brawn and skill to execute a villain."

"It seems Lord Galeran fought well in the Holy Land."

The man frowned in genuine perplexity. "Have I ever suggested otherwise?"

"You have never shown a high opinion of his fighting skills."

The frown tangled the golden brows even further. "I merely mean that he has no great taste for it and is lacking in stature. I am sure he would do his part in a battle."

"But you still think you could defeat him in a court battle?"

The frown cleared. "Without a doubt, my lord. I would regret the necessity, but for the sake of Jehanne and our child, I would do it."

Flambard was no longer sure he could depend on this success, though Lowick was known as a formidable opponent. He had a prickle of uncertainty about this whole affair. The lord of Heywood's reactions upon his return had not been normal except for that one blow. Anyway, court battles were always chancy things, best avoided if there were safer ways.

He tossed in the next piece of information without warning. "The king is dead."

It clearly took a few moments for the new idea to penetrate. "Rufus? How?"

"Unlike the lord of Heywood, he did not escape the convenient arrow."

"*The king* was with Galeran?"

"No," said Flambard, holding on to his patience. "He was with his brother Henry in the New Forest. Henry, I assume, has seized the throne by now. Unfortunately he is no friend of mine. We must hope that Duke Robert arrives back in Normandy soon."

"You think the duke would be more likely to support my case?"

"For the promise of your support, yes." Flambard spelled out the situation. "If William of Brome throws in his lot with Henry, Duke Robert will be looking for a staunch supporter here in the north. That could be me, and you, once Galeran of Heywood is dead and his widow is your wife."

Watching Lowick stand taller at the thought, Flambard ran his hand over the smooth white skull on the table.

"What's that?" asked Lowick with distaste. "A child's skull?"

"The skull of John the Baptist as a child."

Lowick promptly sank to one knee. "My Lord! May I touch it?"

Flambard sighed again. "Of course."

Raymond reverently touched the white bone, then kissed it, his face softened almost to childish wonder. "Where did you obtain such a miracle, my lord?"

"A miracle indeed. It is a gift from Galeran of Heywood, to thank me for bringing peace between him and you."

At that, Lowick surged to his feet. "A bribe, you mean! I see it now. You are supporting his cause against mine."

Flambard picked up the skull and contemplated it. "Such a course does have its appeal, I must admit. But no. I see no future in it, for his family would not join with me for any consideration." He replaced the skull on its cloth and addressed his tool in simple terms. "We must turn Rufus's death to our advantage, but no matter what we do, the key is still the death of the lord of Heywood."

"I will be happy to kill him in honorable combat."

"You are unlikely to have the chance unless he challenges you."

Lowick laughed. "He has not the courage!"

"Be careful how you speak, Sir Raymond. Never forget that Lord Galeran is a crusader. He is held in high respect."

Lowick paced the room, his cloak and scabbard buffeting small objects. "Just for being there? I wish I had gone. I'd have shown them true heroism!"

"I'm sure many share your wish." When the scabbard almost toppled a candlestick, Flambard snapped, "Stand still, please!"

Lowick obeyed and Flambard continued. "Listen carefully. I hear that William of Brome and Galeran of Heywood are planning to journey south to declare themselves for Henry. They hope for his support in their case, of course. The Lady Jehanne and her child are to accompany them. You, too, must ride south with all speed and try to establish yourself in favor before they arrive. I will send Brother Forthred to assist and advise you, since he seems to feel he has a score to settle with Heywood."

"But I thought I was to take oath to Robert of Normandy."

Flambard waved a hand. "There will be many in London pledging allegiance to Henry but keeping an eye out for Robert. After all, Robert has dallied in Sicily and it might be some weeks before he returns. I, too, will set out for London tomorrow, but will not be able to make as much speed as you."

Lowick nodded. "So what must I do, my lord?"

"Appear to support Henry, and gain as much favor in that quarter as you can. As soon as the lord of Heywood appears, try to bring the matter to a challenge and kill him. Since God will have spoken through your sword, Henry will have little choice other than to give you the Lady Jehanne and her castle. Then, if Robert makes war over the Crown, you will be excellently placed to support him and rise high under his rule."

Raymond's ambitious eyes glowed at the thought. "Killing Galeran will be easy, if only I can push him into making a case of it."

"Do your best. If nothing has been achieved when I arrive in London, I have some other ideas. All that is required is that you eventually do your part and kill him. God go with you, Sir Raymond."

Raymond fell to his knee and reverently kissed Flambard's ring and then the relic before sweeping out on his holy mission.

The bishop picked up the skull. "What a useful test of men you are, to be sure. But I wish that in this struggle I had Galeran of Heywood on my side rather than Raymond of Lowick."

Twelve

Two days later, Galeran's party left Heywood.

Though he felt rather foolish about it, he had agreed to extreme security for the short trip to Brome. The area all around had been scoured, and everyone had been put on the alert for strangers. Today six of Lord William's men-at-arms had come over to Heywood to bolster the eight Galeran was taking on the journey.

Since the group also included Jehanne, Aline, and a maid with Donata, all riding their own horses, and ten pack horses to carry the baggage, it was an impressive entourage.

Raoul was driven to tease. He rode back to where Galeran was placed securely in the middle of the line. "We could always carry you in an iron-bound litter, safe from all harm."

Galeran scowled at him. "I could always make you stay behind to hold Heywood."

"You have no power over me," his friend declared cheerfully. "I wouldn't miss this jaunt for the world."

"Jaunt? I'm hoping this will be nothing more than a dull journey followed by tedious paperwork."

"Alas, you do not have the soul for high adventure!"

"True. All I want is a quiet life on my own lands with my family around me, prospering." He looked at Raoul thoughtfully. "Do I detect restlessness? Once this excitement is over, will you be off adventuring again?"

"Perhaps." But Raoul turned to stare ahead as if a vista of swaying horses' rumps enthralled him.

"What else?" asked Galeran curiously. "Much though I love the north country, I hardly see it holding you."

"You're right there," said Raoul with an artificial shudder, for the weather had turned dull again, and there was a hint of rain in the air. "Before winter sets in, I'll be off to sunnier parts. But I've lost taste for holy wars and pointless battles. Perhaps your example is making me think of settling down."

"My example!" Galeran laughed out loud. "I'd think my experiences would suggest a long journey far away from women."

Raoul glanced sideways. "And yet you do not have the look of a completely unhappy man."

"True enough," said Galeran, laughter lingering as a smile. "If we can just settle the matter of Donata, and deal with Lowick so I can ride through my own land without fear of ambush, I'll be as happy as any man has a right to be."

"Why do you grudge me the same, then?"

Galeran concentrated, alerted by a seriousness in his friend's tone. "I don't. But I do wonder if you have the temperament for domesticity. For fidelity." After a moment's thought, he decided to charge the issue head-on. "Surely you are not thinking of settling down with Aline? Quite apart from her intent to become a nun, she is a northern girl, born and bred. What of your beloved sun, then?"

"I'll have to try seducing her with southern fruits. . . ." Raoul glanced sideways, a rueful smile tugging at his lips. "I really do fear the Lady Aline is running so fast from my wicked ways that she just might catch me."

Galeran raised his brows. "I think this will be an interesting jaunt after all."

They stayed the night at Brome, and then set out in an even more impressive cavalcade, heading to Richmond, where they would join the remains of the ancient road that headed straight as an arrow south.

That night they asked the hospitality of a priory, but it had only separate dormitories for men and women, so Jehanne and Galeran had to part. "It's perhaps fitting," he said, "that we be chaste on this journey."

Her eyes searched his features with a shadow of concern. "I might begin to think you are growing fond of chastity."

"Never think that." He stroked her cheek with his knuckles. "It is because it's hard that it will be a suitable offering to God."

"You think we need His aid, then?"

"Don't we always?"

"And yet, you haven't been much given to sexual abstinence in our marriage, Galeran."

"And you have always had a saucy tongue. Now, if you were to *insist* that I perform my marital duties, we could probably find a suitable corner. . . ."

"Oh, no!" she said, capturing his teasing hand. "You won't make me into your Eve. By all means let us suffer. In your case it can be a votive offering. In mine it will be penance."

Galeran shook his head as he watched her cross to the well-separated women's quarters. Jehanne would never lose her sharp edge.

Thanks be to God.

He took a moment to slip into the chapel to offer his abstinence to God, and to pray for His assistance in this tangled matter.

Raoul made sure that he assisted Aline down from her saddle, and escorted her to the entrance of the women's dormitory.

She looked at the sturdy door with a rather smug smile.

"I fear this journey will not provide much opportunity for your assault of my citadel, Sir Raoul."

"Do you think not? But it is a soldier's skill to find the weakness in any defense."

Her eyes flickered to his and her smile wavered. "I doubt you will find one here."

"No? In most religious houses the chapel is common ground."

Her lovely blue eyes widened. "No one would conduct dalliance in a *chapel!*"

"Do you think not?" Now it was his turn to smile smugly.

"If you were to do such an irreverent thing, it would only strengthen my defenses, I assure you."

"Then why do you seek to dissuade me?"

She raised her pretty, round chin. " 'Tis merely that I fear for your soul, Sir Raoul." Then she moved to open the door.

He seized her hand, stopping her. "Don't fear for any part of me, Lady Aline," he said, raising her hand for a kiss. "Unless it be my heart that swells with what might be the beginning of love for you."

She snatched her hand away. "If any part of you is swelling, sirrah, I'm sure it's not your heart!" With a sharp look at his genitals, and a rapid blush, she flipped the latch and marched into the dormitory.

Raoul laughed. She had him there, but the swelling had not begun until she had—so to speak—raised the subject with her sharp tongue and bold look.

The thought of tongues and eyes did little to ease him, so he went off to check the horses and use up his energy in purposeful work.

Aline stormed into the dormitory in a daze, berating herself for stooping to low badinage and unchaste looks.

Raoul de Jouray seemed to have that effect on her.

Wicked, wicked man.

And of course she wasn't going to meet him in the chapel.

On the other hand, it would be pleasant to say her nightly prayers in the sanctified chapel, and she should not let a low rogue keep her from God.

For all his bold words, the man couldn't really try to seduce her before God's altar.

Could he?

All the time she was assisting Jehanne and Winifred, the maid, with the baby, she struggled with this mix of fear, rebellion, and rampant curiosity. It was as if she were a puppy with a skein of yarn, tangling herself further the more she twisted.

There were three other women in the dormitory—a merchant's wife and daughter, and a mason's wife. The merchant's family was returning from Nottingham, where they had heard definite news of Henry Beauclerk's coronation.

"I fear events when the Conqueror's oldest son returns home," said thin Dame Freda, shaking her head. "I was a child when the Normans came into England, but I remember it. Terrible times, and the north country still not recovered. I wouldn't go south just yet, ladies."

"Duke Robert is still far away," Jehanne told her.

"He'll move fast when the news reaches him," said the dame. "I'm staying in the north."

When Dame Freda and her pale daughter settled in their beds, Aline said quietly to Jehanne, "Do you think Duke Robert will invade?"

"No. The Conqueror spent a mountain of gold to seize England, buying soldiers with coin and with promise of land here in England. That land is now held by strong men of Norman descent who are not likely to give it up. Unless the barons turn on Henry, Robert has no chance."

"You're saying he wouldn't succeed, not that he wouldn't invade."

Jehanne sighed. "True. And I don't think he's a wise man. But he's still dallying in Sicily, which is south of Italy and many weeks away. Whatever he does, it shouldn't affect our journey."

"No. Your enemy is Ranulph Flambard, with Raymond of Lowick as his tool. I wonder what effect this new king will have on them."

Jehanne grimaced. "We can do nothing but hope and pray. Are you ready for bed?"

As if impelled by an outside force, Aline rose and straightened her skirts, "Speaking of prayers, I think I'll visit the chapel."

"Very well. But don't pray the night away. We leave early in the morning."

Heart beating fast, Aline went to the small door that led into the chapel. There was a squint next to it for ladies who wished to observe Mass without venturing farther. She paused with her hand on the chilly metal latch and peeped through. Beyond a distant metal grille, the altar candles showed two cowled monks praying.

The squint, however, did not show the body of the chapel. With a deep breath, she pressed down the latch and slipped through the door. She almost laughed. She was in a small separate chapel, divided from the main body by that metal grille which contained no gate at all. Clearly the monks had made sure that there was no danger of females sneaking out in the night to invade their chaste quarters.

That meant, however, there was no danger of Raoul de Jouray staging an attack from the main chapel upon her tower of virtue.

Suddenly ashamed of her wanton thoughts and her impious reason for coming here, Aline knelt before the minor altar and prayed earnestly for the strength to be good. She gazed intently at a wooden plaque set above the altar and draped in silk. In the dim light she could see a carving of the Blessed Mary with her child on her hip.

Assisted by that image, Aline addressed her prayers to Christ and His mother, said now to have remained a virgin despite her motherhood. As she prayed, however, her mind wandered around the subject of virginity and virtue.

She knew in her heart that goodness did not equal virginity, whatever the priests might say. Her mother had been a very good woman despite bearing eight children, and Lord Hubert was as good as one could expect a man to be despite siring them.

Galeran was good too.

Raoul de Jouray, however, was anything but. . . .

Angrily, she thrust the thought of that man out of her mind.

Perhaps it was lewd enjoyment of sex that sapped a person's goodness. But she knew that her parents had taken pleasure in their bed, and she was sure Jehanne and Galeran had, even since his return.

Now the Church said that virginity was the ideal state all men and women should aim for, even within marriage. The abbess of St. Radegund's supported that view strongly, but Aline didn't think many ordinary people did. For a start, it was a daft way to organize a community that needed children.

She was disturbed from her thoughts by singing, and realized the monks were arriving for compline, the service before nightly rest. She looked across to watch the column of cowled figures arrive in the chapel, and so saw Raoul de Jouray kneeling not far away.

At least he was securely on the other side of the grille.

She stared at him, expecting him to look at her, to do something that would constitute an attack, but he seemed completely absorbed in prayer. She continued to watch him warily until the beauty of the familiar, floating music caught her and she prayed with it for peace and security during the coming dark.

And for freedom from lewd thoughts.

When the service ended and the monks began to leave, she looked again at Raoul.

But he had gone.

In the morning he came to help her check her horse. "I hope you slept well, Lady Aline."

"Very well, thank you. And you?"

"Restlessly, to think of you so close by." She was standing close by her horse, and in checking the girth, he managed to let his hand slide down to touch her hip.

Aline stepped back. "At Heywood we were somewhat closer, I think."

"You felt closer last night, perhaps because we are in an alien world."

She moved around to put the whole bulk of the horse between them. Being short, she could not see anything of him other than his boots. "This is not an alien world to me, Sir Raoul. I am used to religious houses."

"But it is a place that is strange to us all, quite different from your home or your cloister."

Aline decided she'd made a tactical error. Hearing just his voice seemed more intimate than standing close by his large body.

"As the days go by," he continued, "everything will become stranger still. Thus, the familiar—the people you are with—will seem more intimate, more necessary."

Aline ran her hand restlessly down the horse's rough-silky neck. "You are depending on this strangeness to make me seek you out?"

"I am depending on it to bring about changes. I have traveled often, Lady Aline, and this always happens. The traveling group, no matter how disparate they seem to begin with, become close. A company. Almost a family."

She ducked under the horse's neck to face him. "It is quite possible to detest a member of the family."

He met her smile. "How true. I must introduce you to my grandfather one day. But by the time we reach London we will all be closer than ever before, whether bound by love or hate."

He led the horse over to the block so she could mount. Once seated there, and with a rare advantage of height, she asked, "What were you doing in the chapel last night?"

He looked up, not so very far below her after all. "Praying, Lady Aline."

"You said you would be there to pursue your attack on me."

"Attack." He frowned. "Picture me rather as a petitioner at your gates." Quite casually, he laid his hand on her thigh. "Beseeching you to open and let me in."

"Last night," she said, all too aware of her spread thighs, "last night you asked me nothing. . . ."

"Perhaps last night I was seeking aid of your overlord." His hand did not move, but it was as if it moved. She could imagine heat pouring from it, penetrating her thick woolen tunic and sturdy linen kirtle, trickling between her legs. . . .

She put her hand down to move his, but he captured and turned it, pressing a kiss into her palm. "Your overlord—and mine—gave me reason to hope."

Aline snatched her hand away. "Do not bring God into this! This is just a game, and a foolish one at that."

His hazel eyes seemed brighter gold than usual. "Many men think war is just a game, Aline. It still leads to both death and glory."

With that he walked away, leaving her wondering whether she was steady enough to keep her seat on the horse.

At Baldersby he gave her flowers.

At Wetherscot he presented wild strawberries.

At Knottingly, where they stayed for two days to give extra rest to the horses, he stole a kiss.

* * *

Raoul had persuaded her to walk from their lodging to a nearby leaf-hung stream, where they watched fish rising, surrounded by the abundance of birds, insects, and flowers, enjoying all the beauty of an English summer evening. There he spoke to her of his native land, where flowers, he assured her, were even more abundant, birds more beautiful, and fish plumper. And where there were fields full of juicy grapes.

She was so entranced by his stories that he was able to trap her in the cleft of an old sycamore tree.

Arms braced on two of the three great trunks, and entirely blocking her escape, he asked, "Don't you think you would like to travel, Aline, and see these places for yourself?"

If she didn't acknowledge that she was trapped, perhaps he wouldn't take advantage. She leaned back against the third trunk as if comfortable. "Nuns sometimes travel. . . ."

"But not often."

"I wouldn't care for a wandering life."

"There is a difference between travel and wandering."

"Is there?"

"Of course. Travel implies a place to travel from and return to. Wandering is a rootless life."

"And do you have roots?"

"Yes. Do you?"

Aline thought about it. Burstock wasn't really her home anymore now that her sister-in-law ruled there. She knew, too, that shy Catherine had been delighted to see Aline leave for the convent. They didn't dislike each other, but Aline couldn't help organizing things, and thus supplanting Catherine's authority.

As soon as Aline and Jehanne had turned up at the gates of Burstock the other day, Catherine had remembered an urgent errand to St. Radegund's, and left to avoid any conflict. Catherine hated conflict, but in her own quiet way was determined to rule her house.

So. Where was her home?

St. Radegund's, she supposed, but she had never felt that to be her home either. Or not yet.

"Where are your roots?" she asked Raoul.

"In my home. In the Guyenne and my father's house there."

"Yet you travel."

"I'm curious."

"And you have older brothers."

"Just one. I own property near Jouray and will settle there one day."

That was interesting. She'd thought him landless. "But you will not settle just yet?"

"I need a reason, perhaps."

Bark rough against her back, she met his eyes. "Is that supposed to tempt me?"

He plucked a spray of leaves and tickled her chin with them. "I would like to show you my home. I think you might find it good soil in which to put down roots."

She batted the leaves away. "But if I didn't, I'd have to anyway, wouldn't I? That is the fate of women, to be sent to live with strangers."

He dropped the leaves. "Am I a stranger?" Slowly, his hand slid around to the back of her neck, beneath her plaits.

She shivered. "I don't know you. . . ." But then she leaned back into the size and strength of that warm hand, which tilted her head up to his.

"I think you do." His lips were as warm as his hand, and perhaps as strong, for they seemed able to make hers part so their breath mingled. His other hand rested against her waist so that he seemed to encircle her.

Like a besieging army encircling a castle, breaking down its walls . . .

She twisted her head away. "This isn't right!"

To her surprise, and perhaps disappointment, he moved back, sliding his hand free. "True. I'm supposed to be helping you develop defenses, aren't I, not just charging in and taking the fortress."

"Taking!" Aline snapped. "If you think conquest will be so easy, sirrah, you are vastly mistaken!" Flaming with embarrassment, she pushed at his solid chest, and he moved back to let her pass. Even walking her fastest, however, she could not outpace him.

"Let us review this incident and see where your strategies could be improved," he said in exactly the tone of a teacher.

"I don't even want to speak to you!"

He ignored her. "To begin with, you should not have agreed to walk with me apart from the others. Your defenses are far too weak as yet for single combat."

Aline hissed with annoyance, but knew better than to stop and argue. Anyway, he was completely correct.

"Having walked with me, you should never have allowed me to trap you in that tree. Elementary strategy, my lady."

"I thought I could trust you!" she retorted, not slackening her pace.

"Yet another error. Never trust a declared opponent."

"I thought we were friends." Then she cursed the hint of tears she heard in her own voice.

He seized her arm and swung her to face him. "We are friends."

"How can we be, when I cannot trust myself alone with you?" Tears did escape, and she brushed them furiously away.

He frowned thoughtfully. "When I train with Galeran, would either of us be friends if we did not test each other, push each other to the limit? How else would we improve?"

"You could kill each other doing that."

"That is always a possibility."

She looked up at him, all too aware of his hands on her shoulders. "And with us?"

He gently brushed away a lingering tear. "Yes, Aline, we play a very dangerous game."

The next morning, Aline saw the truth of Raoul and Galeran, for the men decided to use the rest day for training. The small manor house that housed them had a training ground of sorts, but since they'd had a morning shower of rain, soon the place was a rutted sea of mud churned up by furiously gleeful men. Even Lord William was taking part.

Jehanne came over to watch, the baby in her arms. "It's as well there's a river here. I fear there's not enough water in the well to clean them all."

They shared a look and chuckled.

Then the men spread into a circle and one of Galeran's knights took on one of Lord William's. The latter was an older man who was clearly less agile, but who proved to be both skilled and cunning. The swords were blunted, but even so, soon both men had bleeding wounds and doubtless numerous bruises.

Aline and Jehanne ceased being amused.

Lord William called an end to it before the contestants were flat on their faces with exhaustion, thumping them on the back. "Good men! You've not let your skills grow stale. Off and clean up." Then he turned to Galeran. "What about you? Must be months since you raised a sword with serious intent."

"Not quite," said Galeran with a strange expression, and Aline remembered him turning up at Burstock covered in gore.

"Still," said Lord William, "I'd like to see that you are up to combat."

Aline heard Jehanne suck in a breath and understood the reason for all this. Lord William had called for this one-on-one exercise for this reason alone—to assure himself his son was able to defeat an opponent in a court battle if necessary.

An opponent like Raymond of Lowick.

Surely it was impossible that Galeran defeat Raymond.

Galeran was already in mail. Now he pulled up his coif, pushed on his helmet, and drew his sword. "Raoul and I have kept each other in fighting trim, Father. But it's true we've not exercised in too long."

Raoul was already in the muddy circle, sword and shield ready. "I think you've been avoiding me, midget."

"I didn't want to shame a guest, you great hulk."

"Men!" said Jehanne under her breath, but when Aline glanced sideways, she saw that her cousin was pale.

"They won't hurt each other," she comforted, but she wasn't surprised that Jehanne was worried. Galeran could never prevail against such a huge opponent. Even if he escaped injury, he was going to be embarrassed.

Soon, however, her concern changed and she winced at each clang of metal, each grunt of effort from the men.

Galeran was strong for his size, and he was both more nimble and quicker to react than Raoul, who was himself both agile and quick. Some of the larger man's blows seemed sure to be lethal until they were blocked or avoided. Galeran, too, swung ferociously at his friend, stopped from doing serious injury only by a miraculous deflection.

There. That smashing overhead blow could have crushed Galeran's skull except for a sidestep and a raised shield. Galeran's counterstroke sent a chip of Raoul's shield spinning into the air.

Aline silently echoed Jehanne's comment. Men!

She included Lord William in that, for under her father's rule such dangerous play had never occurred at Burstock. On the other hand, none of her brothers had ever been in imminent danger of a court battle. With a shiver she remembered a case not long ago when accusations of treason had been settled with the sword. The loser had not died in the battle, but since the battle had proved his guilt, he'd lost his eyes and his balls afterward.

The watchers were silent now, all surely holding their breath as she was, praying that there be no disaster.

Then Donata cried.

Galeran's attention slipped sideways for a second. Raoul's sword took him on the helmet.

"God take your soul to hell!" Raoul bellowed, sliding in the mud as he twisted to weaken his own stroke.

Galeran was knocked sideways to the ground. Raoul slid to his knees screaming at his fallen friend. *"How could you do that? Christ's crown . . . !"*

But Galeran was already struggling up, feeling his head and wincing. "How could I not? Thank you for not beheading me."

"I was as close as . . ."

Both men turned to stare at Jehanne, and it was then that Aline realized she'd gone. She turned to see her cousin running toward the manor house, a screaming baby in her arms. She picked up her skirts and chased after.

She caught up in the hall just as Jehanne thrust the screaming child into Winifred's arms and the wide-eyed woman hurried away with her.

"I almost *killed* him!" Jehanne cried. "Is there no end to the damage I can do?"

Thirteen

Aline gripped her cousin's arms. "Raoul wouldn't have killed him. And it wasn't you. The child cried."

"I squeezed her. I was so terrified, I was squeezing her. She probably could sense my fear. . . ."

Aline moved away to splash wine into a goblet and press it into Jehanne's shaking hands. "Drink! You're taking this too seriously. If men play at war games, it isn't our fault if they get hurt."

"Is it not? All this is my fault, Aline. *All* of it. I realized, standing there, that one day it will be a real fight, and I will be the cause of someone's death!"

"It doesn't have to be that way. . . ."

"Doesn't it?"

In the distance, Donata was still shrieking, in the piercing manner of a frantic baby. "Oh, God," Jehanne said. "I'd better feed her."

She thrust the wine goblet back into Aline's hands and hurried away.

Aline drained the wine herself, then went out again, thinking that it was remarkable that the human race survived. No sensible woman would get involved with men and marriage when the orderly, rational world of the convent was available. There a woman had time to study, to create beauty, to think without distraction. . . .

The muddy area in front of the manor house was once more the domain of chickens, pigs, and peasants, though in the distance, beyond the palisade, she could hear the men. Had they taken their silly battles to the fields?

She climbed a ladder to the walk along the top of the wooden palisade and saw them.

They were washing off sweat and mud in the river.

Naked.

Naked men were not a mystery to Aline, but since becoming a woman she had regarded the interest they sparked in her as a weakness to be suppressed. Raoul de Jouray was successfully teaching her that weakness could be ruinous, so perhaps she should study these naked men as representative of the enemy she must learn to defeat.

To her relief, she found that the assortment of bodies stirred no feelings in her at all. Thin to fat, bowlegged and knock-kneed, barrel- or sunken-chested, furred or nearly hairless, they were just bodies and no threat.

Most splashed at the water's edge, getting rid of the mud. A few, however, were swimming.

With alarm, she realized she couldn't see Raoul or Galeran. Had the injury been serious after all?

Then she saw two heads in the water, racing down the river.

Competing again, and this time Raoul was clearly winning.

Men!

Raoul reached a spot where a fallen tree hung out over the river and reached up to catch the stub of a branch to stop himself. Then he hauled himself out one-handed.

"Showoff," Aline—sister of five brothers—muttered, but she was impressed in spite of that. Raw muscle power seemed to make her heart beat faster, and when Raoul pushed to his feet and stood on the log in all his arrogant, golden-skinned nakedness, she knew her cheeks had flushed with color.

And not with embarrassment.

He'd told her of the hot sun of his native land that often

made clothes an inconvenience rather than a necessity. Now she noticed that he was dusky gold all over. The other men—true Englanders—were paler, or dark only in patches. She could spot the crusaders by the darkness of their arms, their lower legs, and sometimes of their chests.

Raoul, too, was darker in some places, but he was gold everywhere except around his man's parts with their thatch of brown curls.

Aline blushed to think that she was staring and even assessing. But she didn't stop. He was, as they put it, well hung.

Then Galeran reached the tree. Raoul knelt to give him a hand and he, too, rose from the water in a show of mutual strength.

Galeran, of course, was of slighter build, but naked, his strength was clear. He was sun-browned in places, too, but his upper legs and loin area were much paler.

As was only decent.

Aline did feel it was wrong to study her cousin's husband, and so she turned her attention back to Raoul. His nakedness stirred alarming sensations inside her, which she understood perfectly well. It was the physical need for a man. She'd felt it before and trained herself to suppress it. It had never been so strong, however, before she'd encountered Raoul.

But, as Father Robert said, such feelings were normal. She was not wicked to feel them. She would be wicked only if she let them conquer her.

Or if not wicked, weak.

Surely looking at the cause of her weakness would help her fight. In time, all things become ordinary. . . .

They were wrestling now.

Really, she thought with irritation, didn't the two of them realize Jehanne was upset and needed assurance that Galeran was unharmed? That Jehanne did *not* need Galeran brought back to the manor even more damaged by their wild games?

Hands slipping on wet skin, feet firm on rough bark, the two men twisted, pushed, and levered, cheered on by the others. At one point Galeran slipped down onto the log, and Aline thought with satisfaction that he must have scraped his behind.

In straightening up, Galeran managed to lever Raoul off the trunk. Raoul, however, grabbed a wrist as he fell and took his friend with him to crash into the water.

Moments later they climbed out onto the bank, arms around shoulders, laughing.

Men.

When they separated, Raoul stretched and shook water from his hair, a healthy animal looking around in obvious satisfaction at the world.

Then he looked toward the palisade.

Too late, Aline remembered his gift of sharp sight. She was trapped. He could doubtless see all the color in her cheeks, perhaps even the lust in her eyes. She would not turn tail and run, though. This was part of their battle.

He smiled and just stood there, naked, hands on hips.

Though it hurt her cheeks, Aline smiled back. When he didn't flinch, she let her gaze wander over his shameless body.

Which is why she saw his shaft begin to swell and rise.

She looked hastily up at his face.

He raised his brows.

Aline *couldn't* turn away and give him the victory.

Why in heaven's name didn't he give in and cover himself? A quick glance showed her Galeran already in his braies.

Determinedly she looked back at Raoul's shaft, hoping to shrivel it with her bold study.

It showed no sign of shriveling at all. Quite the contrary. She swallowed nervously but would not surrender. . . .

Then he was gone.

She blinked, and realized Galeran had knocked his friend down into the muddy bank, where Raoul lay laughing.

Galeran looked up at Aline and just pointed a sharp command to go.

Aline fled.

Sweet Mary, Mother of us all! What she had just done must be some sort of sin. It wasn't a sin to look at a naked man, but that *had* to have been a sin.

As much for him as for her, she thought rebelliously, and *he* wouldn't be suffering pangs of conscience.

Aline wondered nervously what Galeran might do or say, and prudently took refuge with Jehanne, who was jiggling the still-fretful baby. It wasn't the safest haven, however, for Galeran soon appeared, damp but clean.

He had a darkening bruise on his forehead where his helmet had bitten in under Raoul's blow, but no other sign of hurt. He shook his head at Aline, but didn't seem particularly angry. "Jehanne, would you walk with me?"

Jehanne looked anxiously at Donata, who wailed again. "Oh, I don't seem able to help her, and she won't feed. Perhaps she'll be better without me." She gave the baby to Aline and left.

Jehanne picked her way around the edge of the muddy manor yard, trying to sense her husband's mood. She had nearly killed him, and he must know it.

He led her out onto the grassy meadow near the river. Peace had returned now that the men were back at their tasks, but the water was still muddy from their games.

"I'm not hurt," he said.

"I can see you are."

He touched his brow. "This is nothing. I've bruises to match it in various spots."

She was determined to make him face the truth. "You could have been hurt. And it would have been my fault."

He smiled reassurance. "Of course not. A baby cried."

"That baby wouldn't exist if not for my folly!"

His humor faded. "So you accept blame for everything? If so, you can accept my thanks."

"Thanks?"

He sat on the grass and tugged her into his lap. She struggled. "Am I to be cuddled out of my concerns like a child?"

With a sigh he tightened his hold. "I am merely trying to save your gown from the damp grass, frugal husband that I am."

She stopped struggling and surrendered, even daring to tease. "So you really have no wish to have me in your arms?"

"None at all," he teased back. "It makes it hard not to ravish you."

She relaxed against his chest. "Oh, Galeran, I couldn't bear to think that I'd caused you more pain."

He stroked her hair. "Don't grow foolish on me, love. You've stitched wounds, dug out bits of wood and metal, and poulticed my twisted limbs. I'm a fighting man when I have to be."

She tilted her head to look up at him. "But I could always feel sure those fights were silly men's affairs. This one is mine."

"We wouldn't be on this tedious journey if men didn't have their silly fingers in it somewhere. Which brings me to thanks." He appeared serious.

"What do you mean?"

"I want to thank you for causing that distraction. The purpose of a training fight is to find weaknesses so they can be worked on and eliminated. Next time I'll know better than to look away when Donata—or any baby—cries."

"I would hope so!"

"So you see"—he kissed her soundly—"it was excellent that it happened as it did."

"It still terrified me."

He met her eyes seriously. "If it does, you must hide it. Don't weaken me, Jehanne."

"I never used to weaken you."

"No, you didn't."

"Have I changed, then?" She ran over it in her mind, trying to contrast herself now with herself two years or more ago. "Perhaps it's motherhood that's turned me soft."

He slid a hand down her side. "You seem firm enough to me." Then he touched her breasts. "Especially here." Then his hand stilled. "Sweet Savior. Are you all right?"

She moved his hand off her rock-hard, tender breast. "Donata was too fretful to feed properly. I should go back and try her again."

He rose and set her on her feet. "Does it hurt to be like that?"

She touched the bulge in the front of his braies. "Does it hurt to be like that?"

He laughed. "Somewhat, yes."

"I suspect it may feel the same, though the relief won't."

With rueful laughter they hurried back across the sheep-scattered field to the manor house, and Jehanne knew Galeran must be thinking of making love as much as she was. But the small manor house offered no privacy, and they weren't of a mind to couple in a crowded room.

Penance and votive offering, she reminded herself. And anyway, at the moment her milk would flood the house.

By the open hall doors, just before they parted, Galeran said, "Jehanne, watch Aline."

"Aline? Why?"

"She's playing some game with Raoul, which means she's playing with a sharp-edged knife."

"Control your friend, then!"

"I trust him, within limits. You might want to explain to

Aline that throwing out challenges to men can be fool-
hardy."

Jehanne stared at him. "What on earth do you mean?"

"Just ask her about the river."

Pondering that, Jehanne went to Donata, but found her
at last asleep. The poor infant still looked flushed from her
crying, and it would be cruel to waken her.

Being in some pain, Jehanne squeezed out enough milk
to relieve the pressure. She couldn't help wondering if
Galeran might be relieving himself in a similar way.

As she expressed the milk, she pondered Aline's situation.
Could she be seriously involved with Raoul? If so, Jehanne
had been too distracted with her own affairs to notice.

"Where is Lady Aline?" she asked a servant.

"I don't know, my lady."

Aline was almost as devoted to Donata as Jehanne was.
What had she found that was more important? It all seemed
disturbingly unnatural, and she wondered if in some way
they had steered their lives into entirely the wrong paths.

When she was as comfortable as possible, Jehanne went
looking for her cousin and found her in the stillroom inno-
cently helping Lady Marjorie, the elderly lady of the manor
in preparing simples. She couldn't help noticing, however,
that her cousin frowned as she pounded leaves.

"Why the black look?" Jehanne asked, taking up a bunch
of borage and beginning to pinch off the petals. "Are you
still worried about the fighting?"

"No," said Aline, twisting the pestle viciously in the mor-
tar.

"Then perhaps you have a headache."

"I never have headaches."

"Anything can change as circumstances change. Perhaps,
then, it is your feelings for Raoul de Jouray that bother
you?"

Gray-haired Lady Marjorie glanced across with a twinkling smile.

Aline stopped her pounding and glared at Jehanne. "Not at all."

"It is not very Christian to have *no* feelings for another human being."

Aline settled back to her task. "You know what I mean."

"Yes, I do. And I think I know more than that. I am in some way responsible for you, as is Galeran. It would shame us both to have you act foolishly."

Aline turned her head to look at Jehanne, clearly thinking that Jehanne had little right to guide in matters of acting foolishly.

Though she knew she was coloring, Jehanne ignored the silent reproach. "What were you doing down at the river?"

"I wasn't down at the river." Aline pounded at leaves that were almost slime. Lady Marjorie gently removed them and replaced them with fresh ones.

"You were close enough to see, I have no doubt," said Jehanne. "Aren't you a little old to be peeping at the men from the bushes?"

Aline turned, hands on hips. "Who said that? If it was that—"

"No!" Jehanne threw up a hand. "I'm just guessing. Have pity, Aline, and tell me. What *did* you do?"

For a moment it seemed her cousin would refuse, but then she said, "I just looked out from the palisade, that's all. I was worried about Galeran. I wanted to be sure he was all right."

"But after it was clear he was uninjured, you stayed to watch." Jehanne, too, stopped the pretense of working. "Aline, one man's body is much like another."

"Is Galeran's like any other man's to you?"

Jehanne caught her breath. "Have you fallen in love with Raoul, then?"

"Love? Of course not!" But Aline turned to pick up a willow branch and pick away its bark. She halted with one long strip in her fingers, twirling it. "I would be lying to say that I don't find him arousing, though." She tossed the bark on a pile and stripped off more. "I am determined to conquer such feelings, so I am practicing on him."

"Practicing . . . !" Jehanne stared at her cousin. "What kind of practice, pray?"

Aline looked up, bold but red-faced. "He is trying to seduce me, and I am learning how to resist."

"Seduce!" Jehanne tossed down her bunch of sprigs. "You're mad! What if he wins? You'll be ruined."

"Perhaps if I lose I would deserve to be ruined. Just as Galeran would deserve to be dead if Raoul could defeat him."

Jehanne snatched the willow twig out of her cousin's hand. "One slip and Raoul injured him. And could easily have killed him. Aline, this is far too dangerous a game to play when your life is at stake."

Aline faced Jehanne seriously. "It's no game, Jehanne. If I'm to be a nun, I must know I'm strong enough to resist the most potent temptation of the devil."

"Most potent . . ." echoed Jehanne in sinking dismay. Galeran was right. This was a perilous situation. And yet Aline had a point. What if she *weren't* suited to a life of chastity?

But Raoul de Jouray? It was like a person who had never ridden deciding to use a war stallion for their first attempt. Jehanne wondered exactly what had been attempted?

"So," she asked, "what happened down by the river as part of this battle of yours?"

Aline's eyes suddenly twinkled with wicked mischief. "I merely showed Raoul that he could flaunt his proudest possessions in my face all day long and not impress me at all!"

After an appalled moment, Jehanne had to laugh, and she saw Lady Marjorie covering her lips with her hand.

But in the midst of all their other troubles, she didn't want to have to deal with this.

* * *

The first action Jehanne took was to speak to Raoul. As Raoul had pointed out once before, it was Galeran's job, but the men might both think it a great joke.

As the sun began to set, and the household gathered for the evening meal, she threaded her way through servants loading the tables with food. She came up beside Raoul, where he chatted with one of the manor's men-at-arms.

"Sir Raoul."

He turned to her with a smile, and the other man bowed away. Jehanne thought she detected a watchful look in Raoul's deceptively smiling eyes, however. Because she had been so absorbed by her own problems, she hadn't really noticed what a dangerously attractive man he was.

Though she was completely enamored of a man of lighter build, she could recognize that a tall, well-muscled man who handled his body with skill and grace had a certain elemental appeal. Clean bones under golden skin, white teeth, and lively eyes were all made worse by a distinct flare in his southern garments. And in addition to all this, he had that aura that Galeran had—an undefinable power that caught any woman's interest, and held it if she were free.

He was no training partner for someone like Aline.

"Sir Raoul, I am somewhat concerned about your behavior with my cousin."

He drew her gently out of the way of a man bearing a large bowl. "Has Lady Aline cause to complain of me?"

Jehanne realized she was being sparred with too. "She has made no complaint. But you must know that she plans to pledge herself to God."

"That is a worthy calling. For those who *are* called."

"You think she is not?"

"I think it wise for her to find out."

Jehanne found him altogether too arrogant. "The fact that you can heat her blood does not mean she lacks a vocation to the religious life!"

"Surely that depends on the amount of heat generated." He looked frankly into her eyes. "Lady Jehanne, would you want Aline stuck within the convent walls if it does not suit her nature?"

"No one has ever forced her to that. It is her own choice. . . ."

"Sometimes people change their minds. Sometimes they are fortunate, and have not yet committed themselves. Don't you think we should let Aline explore her feelings before she decides?"

Jehanne fixed him with a steely gaze. "Just make sure, sirrah, that her feelings are all you explore, or your exploring days may well be over, crusader or not!"

Raoul watched Jehanne swish away to join Lady Marjorie, then worked his way around the crowded hall to come up behind Aline, where she sat pensively rocking Donata's cradle with one foot.

"You don't play fair, my lady."

She jumped, then swiveled, a charming and revealing blush flooding her cheeks. "What?"

"Setting your cousin to threaten to cut off the bits of me that most alarm you."

Her color deepened. "I did no such thing!"

"So you do admit their power?"

She turned away, nose in the air. "I believe I showed you earlier that your manly attributes have no power over me."

He bent down to whisper in her ear. "We were interrupted. Care for a rematch?" She was a genius with perfumes, the pretty witch. Rose, vervaine, and others too subtle to detect wafted from her skin to tantalize his senses, a sweet eternal promise of womanliness to balance the harsh world of men.

"Don't be silly," she hissed, rather denting his romantic

musings on sweetness. "If you had any decency at all, you wouldn't have flaunted yourself like that!"

He straightened. "I was swimming, Lady Aline. An innocent activity. A virtuous one after dirty work. If you had any decency at all, you wouldn't have stared."

She avoided his point by reaching down to fuss with the baby's blanket.

"Perhaps we should repeat the match on more equal terms," he said. "Naked to naked. See who blinks first."

The sound of stifled laughter made him smile. Ah, but he loved a lass who could laugh at such matters. Gently, he touched the nape of her neck where her short veil showed golden curls springing free of her thick plaits. The image of what she would look like, her lush curves naked except for the mass of her hair, tended to keep him awake at night. Or his wakefulness could just be because he'd not had a woman since Ella.

She had quieted beneath his touch.

"But," he said, still teasing at that sensitive spot, "as your trainer, I think you should avoid my naked body until you are more advanced at basic maneuvers."

She twitched from his hand and looked up, eyes wide and steady, though she could not control her color. "Raoul de Jouray, you could dance in front of me stark naked without giving my willpower any trouble at all! I doubt the same could be said in reverse."

Raoul burst out laughing. "Oh, Aline. You are the most foolish, flaunting, green cadet I have ever encountered."

Even while discussing teething problems with Dame Marjorie, Jehanne watched the encounter between Aline and Raoul with a frown. It was like seeing a summer storm gather, knowing nothing could stop the lightning. One could only pray it would do no harm.

She could send Aline back to Burstock, but to give her

sufficient escort meant weakening their own party, and she would let nothing endanger Galeran.

She could tell Galeran to get rid of his dangerous friend, but apart from the discourtesy of it, she liked the fact that her husband had such a warrior at his back.

And anyway, there was some validity to Raoul's arguments. Everyone had accepted that Aline wanted the religious life, that she had little interest in men and marriage. If that was not true, better she learn it now than when she had taken her vows.

She was distracted from her worries by a serving woman who gave her a small roll of parchment. "From whom?" she asked.

"I dunno, Lady. The gateman said it came for you."

Jehanne unrolled it, glad that she could read, even though her skill at writing words was severely lacking.

At the sight of Raymond's name, her breath caught.

The note said simply: *I wish no harm to you and yours, but will not lose you and my child. Bring Donata to the church in the village before blood is shed.*

Almost she went—though alone—thinking she could protect the men she had entangled. But then she remembered that Raymond might have tried to kill her husband and was plotting to steal her child. He did not deserve her protection.

She went instead to Galeran. "I need to speak with you."

He excused himself from his father. "What is it?"

She passed him the note.

He must have read it three times before he looked at her. "How did you get this?"

"A servant."

He studied her. "Were you tempted to go?"

How much she wished such questions were impossible. "Yes," she said honestly. Then, seeing his expression, she quickly added, "But only to protect you."

"Protect me?"

She turned away distractedly. "Protect *both* of you. If anyone suffers for all this, it should be me."

He gripped her arm down to the bone. "You would protect Lowick?"

She looked back at him, seeing how her honest words were like daggers in his flesh. She'd shield this man from every hurt, but she kept having to wound him with honesty. Despite the pain of his grip, she spoke steadily. "Yes, but I would never choose to protect him over you."

He let her go. "I will never understand you, Jehanne. How can you . . . ?" But then he shook his head. "I'm going to check out this church. You are not to leave the manor."

She caught his sleeve. "Don't go alone!"

"Do you think me a complete fool?" It was not an idle question.

She quickly let him go. "I can't stop worrying over you, Galeran. Don't take it amiss."

He sighed. "Forgive me. My male pride pricks at me sometimes." He touched her cheek gently with his knuckles. "At least, even if you thought about it, you didn't dash off to try to handle this single-handedly. For that, I thank you."

"I'm studying hard to be a proper woman."

"Heaven help us all." But it was said with a smile.

When he left the hall with four of his men, she did not follow, but went, as a proper woman should, to sit by her child's cradle and spin.

There she prayed that her husband wouldn't kill or be killed by the father of her child.

Fourteen

The village of Knottingly straggled along the river close by the manor compound. Small, stone, but with a thatched roof, the simple church sat slightly back from the water between the two, surrounded by its graveyard. The priest's cottage must be part of the village, Galeran saw, for there was no other building on the site.

Search as he might, the area appeared deserted, the only visible creatures being the sheep that cropped all over the area. The light was fading, though, and could conceal a great deal. Perhaps he should have brought Raoul of the excellent eyesight.

Raoul had tried to insist on coming along. In fact, he'd wanted to lead the expedition while Galeran stayed in the manor house. Galeran, however, was heartily sick of skulking in safety, and so he hadn't even told his father what was going on. He'd left Raoul behind and brought just four men-at-arms, itching for a fight with Raymond of Lowick. If Lowick was able to kill him, so be it.

Perhaps the best man would win.

Perhaps it would be God's will.

Perhaps Jehanne would prefer it. . . .

He didn't really believe that, but the suspicion gnawed at him day and night. When he'd turned up at the gates, Jehanne had had no real choice other than to stay and face him, for to flee with Lowick would make them both outcasts and fugitives. Her staying didn't prove devotion. And

Lowick was like Raoul, one of the tall, Godlike men whom women, even sensible women, went silly over. As a young man at Heywood, Galeran had always felt insignificant beside Raymond of Lowick.

However, he'd put all that behind him. Or so he'd thought. After all, it didn't take long to realize that Lowick was not clever, and that his vanity handicapped him as he tried to make his way in the world. He was aware of no one's concerns but his own.

Galeran's sparring with Raoul had helped, too, convincing him that brawn didn't always win.

But perhaps deep down he'd never quite overcome his wish to be as big and broad as his brothers and Lowick. Perhaps that was why he could think for a moment that Jehanne might prefer—all things being equal—to be with Raymond of Lowick.

After all, look at Aline, who had seemed impervious to men all her life. A few encounters with Raoul, and she was a blushing ninny. Galeran wondered how *she'd* reacted to Lowick. She'd never mentioned him.

Impatiently, he focused on the problem at hand and made plans.

He was greatly tempted just to saunter up to the church and smash his fist into Lowick's even, white teeth. It would be impossible to approach the church in concealment, however, and he had too much to lose by such bravado.

So the first thing to do was to find out how likely it was that anyone be there. Galeran and two men stayed back in the trees while the other two skirted the church to go into the village. There, they were to ask about strangers nearby and find out who had brought the message up to the manor.

The sun continued to sink behind distant hills, turning the world to russet shot through with dangerous shadows. There was no sign of movement from the church, but Galeran made himself wait until the men appeared on the road near the village and signaled all was clear at that end.

If strangers had passed by the manor, the watchman would have noticed. If no strangers had passed through the village, it looked very much as if the note had been a hoax, or some other kind of circuitous plot.

All the same, Galeran and his men approached the church with drawn swords and ready shields, all with a clear memory of crossbows.

Still no movement or sound.

They dashed the last few yards to press back against the rough stone walls, safe from projectiles.

Then Galeran edged up to the oaken door, flung it open, and charged into the church.

It was empty except for the wooden altar and two priedieux for the lord and lady of the manor.

The stone walls, crudely painted with biblical pictures, contained one door close to the altar. Galeran opened it cautiously but found, as expected, the sacristy, empty except for a few locked chests for the priest's vestments and vessels.

He sheathed his sword and looked around again, wondering just what the point of all this was. With great care he peeped out of one of the small windows, wondering if the attack would come as they left. There was too much open space here, though, for any kind of sneaking approach.

Looking out over the river to the rising ground beyond, he saw only fields striped with crops and crowned by a coppice of trees. Someone could watch from there, and with good eyesight they'd see most of what went on.

Had this just been a joke?

No. If anything, it had been a test.

Perhaps Lowick was up there watching to see if Jehanne would obey his summons. If so, Galeran thought with satisfaction, he wouldn't like what he had seen.

One of his men called a warning from the other side, and he ran over. It was only his other two men jogging back from the village.

"No nobles have been this way, Lord, other than your party," one reported. "The message was brought by a lad from Bartletor, the village on the other side of the river. We could go by the ford and fetch him."

"No," said Galeran, leading the way out into the evening, still looking around for some sign of his enemy. He still thirsted to cross swords with Lowick. "The boy probably just received it from some other. We could follow that trail for days."

He shielded his eyes from the flaming ball of the sun and peered once more at the tree-topped hill. In this light not even Raoul could have spotted anything. "Let's return and eat."

As they walked back up to the manor, the sun dipped and dusk suddenly arrived. Crows settled noisily into their roosts and bats swooped out to feed.

It was a time of day to make a man uneasy, and Galeran was. He had a hard time believing that Lowick would plan this sort of event as test or joke. His idea of amusement was to tie pigs' tails together, then watch them squeal.

No, this had the mark of Ranulph Flambard. But what had the bishop hoped to gain from it?

Flambard received his man in the prior's parlor at the priory of Hitchinborough, Prior Joseph having declared himself delighted to give up his quarters to his eminent guest. Even if the ingratiating smile hadn't reached his eyes.

"So?" he asked, choosing a piece of roast duck with great care.

Lucas, a burly, competent man of middle years, stayed kneeling. "No woman came near the church, my lord bishop."

"Ah." Flambard popped the meat in his mouth and savored it. He was not a glutton, but what he ate he expected to be of highest quality. He dabbed his lips with the cloth. "Did anyone?"

"Aye, my lord. Three men approached the church and burst in. Two ordinary soldiers and a highborn man."

"Of what build?"

"Of average build, my lord."

Flambard used his silver spoon to sup some greens in sauce. "Burst in, you say. If there had been anyone there, do you think they would have done him harm?"

"Aye, my lord bishop."

"As I thought."

So Jehanne of Heywood had taken the note straight to her husband. That cast further doubt on Raymond of Lowick's tale of the woman's love for him.

Why were people so stupid? Look at Rufus. He'd *warned* him about Henry, that Henry would stop at nothing to gain England, but Rufus—arrogant Rufus—had not listened. Flambard hoped he was roasting in hell.

He turned his mind, however, to the future. "Thank you, Lucas. Make sure a careful watch is kept on the Heywood party and report their movements back to me."

The man rose and bowed himself backward toward the door. "Aye, my lord."

"And, Lucas . . ." The words halted the man as he turned to exit, swinging him back. "I'm afraid I might have given you a wrong impression." Flambard picked up a honey cake. "I would be distressed to hear that any harm had come to Lord Galeran on his journey."

Lucas stared at him. "You would, my lord?"

"It is so hard to explain away a crossbow. That, Lucas, was a mistake."

The man blanched. "I see, my lord. But . . ."

"But?"

"I thought you wanted the man dead, my lord."

Flambard took a bite of the sweet almond-filled pastry

and savored it. "It is not for man to seek justice when the hand of God is available."

"I see, my lord," said Lucas, who clearly did not.

"I received a report from the manor of Knottingly, about a trial of arms between Lord Galeran and his large friend. The friend won."

"Perhaps to be expected, my lord."

"Quite. Raymond of Lowick hopes to fight a court battle with Lord Galeran on the matter of the Lady Jehanne. It would be unfortunate, I think, if anything were to prevent that request for divine judgment."

Lucas was not a stupid man, and a twitch of a grin marked his understanding. "Ah. It would indeed, my lord. No one could argue with the hand of God, could they?"

"Exactly." Flambard waved a hand and the man bowed out.

Much more elegant. Much less dangerous now that it was sure that Lowick would win. The only lack in the plan was that the Lady Jehanne might not suffer enough for thwarting him. Flambard resolved to try to do something about that. It was his right, as a representative of the Church, to ordain punishment.

He had been laggardly in his progress to London, but tomorrow he would make better speed. He didn't want to miss the moment of triumph.

The next day the Brome party moved on south. After the ominous affair of the message, everyone wanted to make all possible speed to London. The weather was ideal for traveling—warm but not hot, and with a light breeze—but they were all on edge.

Jehanne was untypically nervous, and the baby still fretted, seeming to break only to catch breath before wailing again. The women passed Donata between them as they rode, but though each change seemed to soothe her for a little while, the peace didn't last.

They'd scarce gone a mile before Galeran decided that a baby's cry was the most wearing noise in creation.

When he rode back to ask if Donata was all right, Jehanne snapped at him. "She's hungry, but she won't eat. Perhaps she has the gripe. I'm bursting with milk and she won't take enough. I've been up most of the night because she won't sleep, and so have all the other ladies. Dame Marjorie must be delighted to see us leave!"

He could almost laugh to see Jehanne in such a state. "Perhaps a strange hand will soothe her. Give her to Raoul to carry for a while."

"Raoul? What does he know of babes?"

"He seems to have a rare ability to charm females." He called to his friend, who cantered up.

Raoul took the baby into his large hands without hesitation, cradling her neatly against his mail chest. Donata hiccuped and went silent, staring up at him wide-eyed.

"It won't last," Jehanne predicted, almost peevishly.

But it did.

With a sigh of relief Galeran turned his horse to ride the line, checking on the order of everything.

A half hour later he returned to the center where the women and pack horses were grouped, and found Donata fast asleep in the crook of his friend's right arm.

"How do you do it?" he asked.

"It's a magic gift," said Raoul with a grin. "But I think I should pass her on. If I hold her much longer in my arm like this, I might be stiff if I need to fight." He kneed his horse over toward the women. Galeran noted with a sigh that he stopped by Aline, not Jehanne.

"Do you think you could extract this infant from my arm without waking her, Lady Aline?"

Aline looked at him warily. She had tried not to react to his taunt that she was a green cadet, but it was true and she knew it. She suspected that if he turned his full strength and armory upon her, she would be as helpless as if they fought with swords.

That didn't mean, however, that she was going to hide behind her walls and offer no challenge at all.

"Is a tiny babe too heavy for you?" she asked, halting her horse next to his enormous beast.

"A great burden indeed." His eyes crinkled with laughter. "She certainly has mighty lungs. I'm rather anxious not to wake her."

He twisted down and she reached up, and they managed the transfer without waking Donata, though the baby stirred and her lips began to work. "If she is of a mind to eat, Jehanne will be glad of it." Aline then looked up at Raoul. "Just think. A life in a convent spares a woman from the tyranny of these little monsters."

"So it does. And I'm sure you have no desire to hold a babe of your own in your arms."

Typically, he'd scored a neat hit. As a last child, she had not been close to a baby before entering St. Radegund's. Since going as companion to Jehanne, she'd seen the births of Gallot and Donata and held them both through good times and bad. Held one of them dead. She didn't have any rosy illusions about the perfection of babies, but she wanted one. Indeed she did.

"What of you?" she asked as they moved forward to keep up with the party. "Do you want a babe of your own?"

"The idea of filling you with a babe of mine is certainly tempting."

Only he would dare say such a thing! "My family would make you marry me."

"I'd rather marry you before the event, Aline."

With that, he cantered away.

As if triggered by his absence, Donata's face screwed up

ready to wail. "Oh, don't be such a silly little female," Aline snapped. "He loves to tease, that one. He loves to conquer. But he has no lasting interest. As soon as the castle is his, he'll be off to the next one. Next time he takes you in his arms, Donata, you are to scream as you've never screamed before."

Donata opened her mouth, then shut it again, amusingly, as if she gaped at the mere notion.

Aline maneuvered over to Jehanne. "She might be ready to feed if you want to try."

Jehanne took the baby and tucked her under her cloak, giving her access to a breast. In moments it was clear that Donata was feeding steadily for the first time in days. Jehanne gave almost a shiver of relief, and after a little while switched the hungry child to the other side. "Thanks be," she said.

Aline scowled at Raoul de Jouray's back. "Brilliance is not an attractive trait."

Jehanne shook her head. "Aline, I can only warn you in plain language. You are well on the way to being conquered. I have no way of knowing if that is what you want or not, but you should know what is happening. To me, you do not appear to be a castellan holding a fortress. You seem more like a foolish lady who lets a troop of armed men in her castle merely because they smile and profess good intentions."

Aline sighed. "If only I knew if he truly wants to conquer me."

"What else?"

"Perhaps when I open the gate, he'll simply ride away laughing."

Jehanne's look was understanding. "If you suspect that, you should be doubly on your guard."

"But wouldn't that be virtuous of him, not to take advantage of the foolish lady?"

"It would be virtuous of him to leave the foolish lady alone."

Aline huffed out a breath. "It's amazingly difficult to decide what is right and what is wrong!"

"No, it isn't," said Jehanne, switching the baby yet again. "The right thing would be to put the matter to your father and abide by his decision."

"But my father isn't here."

"Then behave yourself until you are back in his domain."

A month or more of tender assaults. "Surely you and Galeran are his deputies here."

"Oh, no," said Jehanne with a wry smile. "We have enough burdens. You might try Lord William if you need mature advice."

Aline knew Jehanne thought she wouldn't take her up on that suggestion. Just to be contrary, she said, "Why not?" and turned to ride back to Galeran's father.

Solid as a rock in his richly decorated saddle, fine-woven cloak spread over his horse's hindquarters, Lord William looked exactly what he was—a mighty baron and a shrewd man. Aline thought perhaps this wasn't the best idea, but she wouldn't back down.

"Good day to you, Lady Aline," he said. "How are you liking our journey thus far?"

She placed her horse neatly beside his. "It has its pleasures and its pains, my lord."

"Most journeys do." But he had a twinkle in his eye that suggested he understood some of her particular pleasures and pains.

Was it so obvious to everyone?

She plowed on. "Lord William, Jehanne suggested that I speak with you on a personal matter."

"Indeed. Well, I am the leader here."

"And my father is far away." Aline stared fixedly between her horse's ears. "I am wondering if you would recommend

Raoul de Jouray as a husband." Then she looked to see his reaction.

Shrewd brown eyes studied her. "For whom, Lady Aline?"

"For any lady."

"Too loose a question by far. Surely in God's wide world there is a maid for every man, and a man for every maid."

Aline wrinkled her nose at him. "For me, then."

"Ah, well. It would depend upon his property—if he has any other than his horse and sword—and the amount you can bring to a union."

"Property? Dowry? Is that all that matters?"

"Not at all. But until that's settled, there's no point in going on to other concerns."

"Very well." Aline steadied her nerves and cantered forward to come up with Raoul.

"Yes, little one?" he said from the lofty height of his horse.

"It's not my fault that my horse is a full two hands shorter than yours!"

"It's not your fault that you are a full two hands shorter than me. It's just a fact. Did you ride up here simply to argue size with me?"

"No. You mentioned marriage. I think it's time to straighten out some details."

He eyed her sideways. "My mention of marriage was rather hypothetical."

"So is my question about details."

"Very well."

"Do you have any property other than your horse and sword?"

"Yes. Do you have any property to bring to a marriage?"

"Yes. What property do you have?"

"Land near my father's home in Guyenne. And you?"

"The rents from an estate in Yorkshire. How much is your land worth?"

"Perhaps fifty marks a year. And yours?"

"About half that."

"Adequate, then." The teasing humor in his eye almost made her want to smile at him, but she resisted and rode back to Lord William.

The older man raised his brows. "You're going to tire out your horse, Lady Aline, making him do a double journey."

Aline ignored that. "He has an estate in France worth twice my dower property."

"It would have to be looked into, for it's too easy for a foreigner to lie about such things, but if true, he is a suitable husband for you."

"But there has to be more to it than money."

"Of course. There's temperament. A house full of disagreements and misunderstanding becomes tedious after a decade or two."

Aline looked forward at Raoul's broad back. "I don't think that would be a problem."

"Even if he has a wandering eye?"

Aline frowned at Lord William. "It's not so much the eye that bothers me."

His eyes still twinkled, but he said seriously, "There are some women who don't care a great deal if their husband eases himself elsewhere, as long as no insult is offered them in their own house. There are others who are deeply hurt, and perhaps driven to strike back in some way. Temperament, you see."

And Aline did see. She'd always thought of herself as a calm, easy-natured person, but she wasn't at all sure she could be calm if her husband—if Raoul eased himself elsewhere. "Thank you, Lord William. I'll think on it."

She rode back to Jehanne's side, only too aware that there had been no mention of a third possibility—that Raoul de Jouray be a faithful husband.

* * *

Galeran was aware of the strange maneuverings between Raoul and Aline in the next days, but he put them out of his mind. He trusted his friend to marry Aline if necessary, and there were more important matters to be dealt with.

As they neared London, the heavy traffic toward the city spoke of excitement and acceptance of the new king. The closer they got, however, the more uneasy Lord William became.

Speaking quietly as they rode into Waltham, Galeran's father said, "Once we take our oath to Henry, it is settled."

"Henry will make a better king than Robert."

"Not if he's cursed. I let my dislike of Bishop Flambard and my concern for you push me into supporting Henry, but I'm not sure it's right, lad."

Galeran looked at his father. "You can't go to Westminster and not swear to Henry."

"I know, I know. In fact, I feel a terrible pain coming on. . . ."

And by the time they stopped at the abbey for the night, he was groaning and swaying in the saddle.

Once he was settled and being treated by the monks, Jehanne came over to Galeran. "Is he really sick?"

"With any luck he will be after taking those medicines." Galeran flipped open a satchel with considerable irritation. He looked up at Jehanne and saw she already guessed the truth.

Having checked that no one was close by, he said, "He's never been easy about Rufus's death. It was Flambard's interference in our affairs that pushed him into supporting Henry, then he stuck with it to aid us. Now, however, his conscience balks. His opinion—and he could be right—is that no enterprise built on murder can succeed."

"No enterprise supported by Bishop Flambard can be worthy!"

"I feel the same way, but it's not logical. Good and bad men often end up on the same side."

"What will it mean to us if your father stays here?"

"As long as he doesn't openly support Robert's claim, it could be all right. Henry will have to try to woo him. I hope."

"We will go ahead, then, without Lord William?"

"Of course. We need this settled, and these early days are probably best. I suspect Henry is promising anything to anyone to gain support."

She let out an exasperated breath. "Your father is right. There should be more to this than expediency. If it weren't for me, you would both have a freer choice."

He touched her cheek. "Jehanne, I have forgiven you. It would be pleasant if you could forgive yourself."

She closed her eyes, clearly close to exhaustion, but of the spirit more than the body. "It's not so easy. Just think how it could have been. . . ."

He ached with the need to heal all her hurts, but he could do nothing more than he was doing. "Not so very different, love, especially as far as the question of who should be king goes. I know Robert, and I don't want him as king of England no matter who fired that cursed arrow." He put an arm around her, to support and guide. "Come on. We'd best go and find Aline and Raoul before they get up to mischief."

The abbey was crowded with travelers heading to London, however, so there was little danger of Raoul and Aline finding privacy even if they wanted to. In fact, they were on a low cloister wall making music on cheap reed pipes.

"Raoul bought them from a packman," said Aline when she'd finished a little trill. "There's quite a fair out there, he says, sprung up to amuse the crowds. Why don't we explore?"

Galeran and Jehanne shared a glance, agreeing that it would be preferable to sitting in one of the crowded guest rooms worrying.

Evening shadows were lengthening, and the local people

hurried home for their suppers, but the acrobats and jongleurs still hung around the square outside the abbey hoping to attract pennies, and some merchants and packmen had not yet put away their wares.

Galeran bought pasties from a pieman, and they ate as they wandered among the impromptu stalls delighting in pots and platters, beads and carvings, shoes and hoods.

One merchant had fine bolts of silk for sale, but the traveling party were in no mood to burden themselves with such as that, so he tempted them instead with ribbons. Galeran bought Jehanne an ell of blue, and Raoul chose white for Aline.

Aline knew she should be wary of the flamboyant southerner who could never be for her, but she wanted a gift from him to cherish through the long lonely years.

"For purity," he said with a teasing grin as he skillfully tied the long strip into an elaborate knot.

"Somewhat tangled purity," she remarked as she took it.

"Pretty, puzzling, challenging. Like you."

Aline glanced at him warily. "Is today the day for flattery exercises, Sieur Raoul?"

"You guessed! I delight in a quick-witted opponent."

Heart speeding, Aline fired back. "Then I must confess that you, too, are handsome and challenging. But not particularly puzzling. Your intent is clear."

"Is it? It's not even clear to me, sweet Aline."

"Then I have reason to worry indeed."

"Yes, you do."

She twirled the pretty white ribbons. "I seem to receive so many of these unhelpful warnings. So," she said, looking up at him, "here I am, safe within the walls of my purity and resolution, and unlikely to open the gates just because of pretty words. What would an evil attacker—a hypothetical evil attacker—do to harm me? In what skills do I need to be trained next?"

"I am beginning to think I should build myself a sturdy

keep and huddle! However," he said, steering her onto another stall, "one option for your enemy is to lay siege. But that could take a long time."

As they strolled past a tinsmith, she asked, "Is my castle not worth time, sir?"

"Undoubtedly, but time is not always available. What if your suzerain were to approach with supporting troops?" He cast a meaningful glance at Galeran and Jehanne, who had paused to watch a fire-eater.

"In that case, I suppose my enemy would need to decamp. Unless he could find a speedier means of assault."

"You have an excellent understanding of warfare, Lady Aline! But to charge straight at such a well-defended fortress would be suicidal, don't you think?"

She looked up at him. "Then I'm safe? I didn't think war was so easy." Or so disappointing. Aline was aware that she did not want her besieger to fold his tents and ride off to find an easier target. Not at all.

He leaned against the tinsmith's cart. "No castle is safe from a truly determined assailant. With time your attacker could mine the walls, burrowing underneath, supporting the passages with timber, then setting fires to bring them down."

Aline was powerfully tempted to lay her hand on his very broad chest. Did a besieged castle ever just throw open the gates and invite conquest? "But our hypothetical attacker does not have time . . ."

He took her hand, rubbing his thumb gently against her skin. "In which case he could attempt assault from a distance. He'd use projectiles, attempting to batter down the walls."

"That sounds rather dangerous to me. Wouldn't I be on the walls hurling things back?"

"And we all know how formidable you are on walls. . . ."

"Oh," she said, lips twitching, "were you *hurling* yourself at me?"

When he'd stopped laughing, he raised her hand and kissed it. "The other approach, of course, is betrayal."

He switched his grip on her hand, seized her around the waist, and swung her behind the cart so that in a couple of whirling seconds she was out of sight of the others, trapped by his body in a shadowy corner, his hand shutting off her cry.

Aline stared up at him, both terrified and thrilled. Jehanne had warned her. Were the warnings to come true?

He eased his hand away from her mouth, but immediately sealed it with his own, a hot, overpowering kiss that had nothing to do with courteous wooing and everything to do with conquest.

His whole hard body pressed against her, drowning her in power and danger and a spicy smell of horse and leather. With a sudden shift he pulled her skirts up and thrust his thigh between hers. Despite her stifled shriek, he raised his foot onto the wagon wheel so her feet left the ground.

She had to clutch at his shoulders for balance, as she was stretched wide, pressed open against him.

Then a jolt of something shot right through her.

Panicked by her own feelings, she pushed desperately at his chest, but all her strength didn't move him one inch. He just rocked his leg beneath her, and stretched her mouth, overwhelming her with tongue and thigh and arms until her resistance weakened and she could scarcely think, never mind fight.

Then she kissed him back and found that surrender was much more rewarding than resistance. . . .

At last, at long last, he released her lips with very flattering reluctance, and kissed the tip of her nose. "Are you conquered yet, little castle?" It was hardly a question, but a smug announcement.

Aline pricked him in the back with the knife she'd slid out of his sheath. "Are *you?*"

Shock wiped away the smile, but then it slowly returned,

though his eyes were a great deal more alert. "Feint, then attack. Excellent tactics. There are dangers to taking prisoners you can't handle, though."

Aline prayed for a steady voice despite her absurd position, still straddling his thigh. "I can handle you, Raoul de Jouray. I'll let you go for ransom, just as long"—she pushed the knife in a fraction farther, so he hissed—"you admit that you were as overwhelmed by that assault as I."

"More, my fair opponent. Or you'd not have my knife."

She hadn't expected such full capitulation.

Warily, she moved the knife, watching for retaliation. But he simply eased her to the ground, then stepped back and held out his hand. She placed the knife in it and straightened her clothes, distressingly aware of a heated ache where his thigh had been, an ache that made her want to seize his belt and haul him back to her. She looked down, concentrating on the precise arrangement of her gown.

"You are a remarkable woman, Aline of Burstock."

She looked up. "Because I am not driven totally witless by your kisses?"

"Because you can keep your wits under pleasure." He slid the knife slowly, very slowly, into his jeweled sheath. "Do you deny the pleasure, Aline?"

She wanted to, but her dry mouth and aching crotch said otherwise. They had stripped another polite layer from themselves, and lying was no longer possible. "No, I don't deny it. But I am angry that you expected to be unaffected."

"I never expected that. I merely underestimated your armory. So," he said with his usual warming smile. "I am your prisoner. What ransom do you want?"

"What do you suggest?"

"Tush, Aline. That is foolish."

"Not at all," she said with a grin, "I merely meant to take your figure and treble it."

He trapped her against the cart again, but gently. "A hundred kisses."

She stared up at him, already sliding under his aura. "Our lips would wear out."

"We could spread the three hundred over many years."

She looked down at his chest, at a fine piece of gold embroidery around a gleaming yellow stone. His fancy, high-colored dress reminded her that he was a foreigner. "But before winter you will be back in the land of grapes and almond blossoms."

"You could come with me."

They were the words she had wanted to hear, but now the reality frightened her. "No, I couldn't."

"Why not?"

"I couldn't leave my home, my friends, my family."

"I see." He sounded annoyingly calm. "Ah, well, it is probably as well that we put aside our games for now and concentrate on our friends' affairs. Jehanne and Galeran need us clear-headed and willing to act. . . ."

See how little he cared! She pushed out of his arms. "Exactly. So, no more of your assaults, sirrah. You can see I'm a well-defended fortress."

"Adequately. Unless a strong force moves against you."

She began to walk around the cart, back to the light, fighting tears. He could at least have tried to talk her out of her decision.

"Aline . . ."

His touch on her arm froze her still in shadows. She did not speak, however, waiting, heart beating high and fast. Perhaps now he would beg.

"Don't become a nun."

Teeth gritted, Aline continued into the light, where flam-beaux and the fire shooting from the mountebank's mouth seemed more like the illumination of hell than saving light. She shivered under the danger and the weighted memory of Raoul's sensual attack. She'd spent her life paddling in ponds and was now being towed out into the wild sea, which both thrilled and terrified her. Even worse, he did not seem to want to stay with her there.

If he didn't want her, what right had he to decide she should not take vows, and to try to destroy her will to do so?

Right or not, he was succeeding.

Galeran saw Raoul spirit Aline behind the cart and noted when they emerged, noted, too, the aggrieved set to Aline's firm chin. He'd rather expected her to be kissed into a daze. What particularly interested him, however, was the expression on Raoul's face. He looked dazed enough for two.

Jehanne had noticed as well. "He really shouldn't . . ."

"Nor should she."

"He's a great deal more experienced!"

"True, but Aline has her eyes wide open."

"Just so long as that's all she has open."

Galeran raised his brows at her. "I really can't see Aline giving up her virginity in a brief encounter behind a cart, Jehanne."

She laughed and shook her head. "I know, I know. And with all our worries, I don't know why I'm fretting about her."

He rested his hand on her nape and rubbed there. "Perhaps because it's easier than fretting about more serious things. We should be in London tomorrow."

He felt her shiver. "I think I'd be happy to just wander. I'm afraid, Galeran."

"With reason." He didn't stop massaging her tense neck. "Do you want to take ship? Doubtless Raoul would give us refuge in Guyenne."

She turned to look up at him, her beauty turned wild by the fire-eater's flames. "You would do that? Leave England for me?"

Her move had brought his hand to the side of her face,

and he ran his thumb down her beautiful jaw. "I would do anything for you."

"Oh, Galeran! It's tempting. I'm terrified of having to watch you die."

"Do you fear for me? I'm terrified that some punishment will be imposed on you. It is, as you say, very tempting to run away."

Her expression firmed. "But a sin. We can't."

"No, I don't think we can. I hope we don't live to regret it, though." He kissed her lightly on the lips. "But I do regret our vow."

"So do I." With a mischievous glance, she pressed a little closer and touched his chest. "Shall I play Eve, then? There's apparently a dark corner behind that cart."

His mouth went dry. Dignity argued against it, but he pulled her swiftly over to the cart and behind it, to find that dark and private corner.

"Not Eve," he whispered, loosening his clothes. "Just Jehanne." Then he was in her hot wetness, her legs tight around him, her hands clutching his shoulders as her body clutched his.

"Oh, God," he groaned, knowing his thrusts were probably rocking the cart at her back. "We're mad."

"Don't stop. Just don't stop!"

How she thought he might, he had no idea. The world could crash to an end around him and he wouldn't stop before the blinding relief of shooting his seed into her.

As his heart rate settled and he lowered her slowly back to the ground, he realized she'd not found her release. She made no complaint, but when he slid his hand between her thighs, she spread them and leaned against him. In moments her breathing fractured and her fingers dug deep into his flesh. Then her teeth sank in him, too, as she muffled her cries.

He felt himself begin to harden again. In a peaceful bed he'd be in her again before she recovered, and it was a spicy notion, but enough was enough. He drank the last of her passion from her lips, then led her out a long way around, hoping no one would know just who had been making that cart shake.

By the time they blended in with the crowds, Jehanne still looked dazed. Galeran thought almost kindly of the problems that had brought them to a tinsmith's cart in Waltham, for they'd never before made love like that, in fierce, surreptitious urgency.

But there were too many hazards for him to be grateful. It was those hazards, even including death, that had driven them into that brief madness. He'd settle for security and love in a bed any day.

When they joined Raoul and Aline, his friend gave him a knowing grin, and Galeran could feel himself blush.

At least Aline hadn't noticed. She seemed enthralled by a sword swallower. "Ugh! Why would anyone want to do a thing like that?"

"Perhaps he has little choice," Galeran said, tossing the man a coin. "Perhaps it is just his destiny."

"Oh. Like a vocation," said Aline, not looking at Raoul at all.

And when Galeran looked a question at Raoul, his friend just seemed very thoughtful, and even unhappy.

The situation could be interesting if Galeran had interest to spare.

Fifteen

The next morning Galeran visited his father, who was trying very hard to look frail.

"This is better, anyway," said Lord William. "Keep him unsure of us."

"Not hard when you don't know what you plan to do."

"Don't scowl at me, lad! In the end all that matters in this world is our honor and our soul. I have to think on this."

"I understand, Father."

"Watch out for Flambard. He'll do what he can to break us." Lord William gripped his hand. "I'll be praying for you."

Galeran went to mount his horse, reminding himself that he believed in prayer, and believed in a just but merciful God. He'd rather have had his father by his side, though. No monarch would reject William of Brome's support if offered. A monarch unsure of it, however, just might decide the best course would be to break the family's power entirely.

He could imagine Bishop Flambard urging that.

The road into London teemed with mountebanks, merchants, gentry, and lords, doubtless woven through by all kind of thief. They could have used the horses to force a path, but with women and a babe in their midst that wasn't so easy, so they went with the slow-moving flow, reminding Galeran again of his thoughts about destiny. He was grateful, at least, to have lodging. Raoul had distant kin—wine merchants—living in the city, and had sent a messenger ahead to ask hospitality. They'd just received word that Hugo and Mary would be delighted to house their party, though they warned space would be tight.

Still no opportunity for a peaceful, private night with his wife, he feared. Galeran found that he wanted his peaceful life at Heywood perhaps more than ever before. It was so close—so nearly in his grasp—yet could be snatched away at the king's whim.

It hardly seemed possible, but within the city walls the crowds were worse. In places, the crush of people clogged up entirely and Galeran had to order his men to use horse and whip to break up the blockage. It took them hours to reach Corser Street. Their hosts apologized for the limited space in their narrow house, but Galeran knew they were fortunate.

While Jehanne and Galeran arranged their party in the two available rooms, with the grooms and men-at-arms left to sleep out in the sheds behind the house, Raoul undertook the task of finding any news.

He returned in an hour with a basket of pies and a net of cherries. "The king's holding open court," he said, dusting off his clothes. "Of course, the point of it is to accept homage from as many people as possible."

"What's the mood out there?" Galeran asked, pouring his friend some of Hugo's wine.

"Favorable to Henry, I'd say. Your old King William wasn't any more popular here than in the north and the general tone seems to be 'good riddance.' Especially with King Henry making that special declaration on his coronation day, reestablishing the old laws."

Jehanne was off with the baby, but Aline was present, struggling to untie the net to liberate the plump cherries. She stopped her work and frowned at them. "I hope he's not *too* keen on law and order."

"Why not?" asked Raoul, strolling over to slash the net with his knife. Galeran noticed that even that simple operation seemed to generate a great deal of tension and colored cheeks. How Aline could think she still wanted a religious life, he didn't know. But perhaps if Raoul would not commit to her . . .

He put such matters out of his mind.

Aline picked up a cherry and moved away from Raoul. "What if the king wants to enforce laws against adultery?"

Raoul speared a cherry on the sharp tip of his knife. "Is that likely?" he asked Galeran, then put the cherry into his mouth. He never took his eyes off Aline.

Cheeks cherry-red, she popped her cherry into her mouth.

"I hope not," said Galeran, wanting to bang their heads together. "No one has ever accused Henry Beauclerk of being tenderhearted in judgment."

"Hah!" Aline spat a cherry pit into her hand and looked at Galeran. "An understatement. He threw a man off the battlements of Rouen with his own hands for opposing him!"

"A clear lesson about opposing the will of princes."

Aline's severe eyebrows settled lower. "You can't really find this funny."

"No, of course I don't. We have to trust to Henry's good sense and his desire to have my father on his side. Raoul, did you find out anything else of interest?"

Raoul sheathed his knife. "Not really. I asked about Raymond of Lowick, but no one knew anything of him. Not surprising, really. I heard news of the Bishop of Durham, though. He arrived here yesterday."

"Flambard's here already?" said Galeran with a chill of unease. "I hoped he'd move more slowly. I'm sure he stands our enemy. Apart from his ambitions in the north, he'll never forgive us for thwarting his plans."

"He may be toothless. It was clear in two words that he's a hated man."

"Oh, yes, he is that. But hatred hasn't stopped him yet. He seems almost magically able to slither out of trouble."

"You choose interesting enemies," said Raoul with a grimace. "And no one I spoke to was sure his day was over. His appeal seems to be a rare skill at obtaining money. What king can ignore that?"

"Henry won't dare support someone so unpopular," said Galeran, but again he was merely concealing his fears. Ranulph Flambard was a very clever man, and as Raoul said, kings had a fondness for men who could provide them with money.

Raoul shrugged. "I assume you'll attend the court tomorrow and seek an audience. We'll get better information then."

Jehanne came in on those words, carrying a contented baby. Her pale face became even more drawn. "Tomorrow? So soon?"

Galeran went to put an arm around her. "We didn't come haring down here to sit twiddling our thumbs, love."

"Oh, I know," she said, bouncing the baby nervously. "But I can't help but worry. I wish I could come with you. . . ."

"I don't really think that would help."

She grimaced at him. "I know, I know. I just feel so *helpless*. Can I at least talk strategy with you?"

It would clearly soothe her, so Galeran agreed. Raoul spread out his pies and cherries, and the four of them sat to eat and discuss plans for the morrow, though there weren't really any choices. Galeran would dress his finest, take gifts—including items from the Holy Land—and hope. If the king gave him a private audience, he'd lay the situation before him.

Unless he gained the impression that someone had been before him and laid traps. But he didn't say that, for he had no strategy for that situation other than his wits.

As he and Raoul went to share the chamber set aside for them, Galeran asked, "Do you want to come tomorrow?"

"It might be better if I stay behind to guard the women."

"I think the farther you stay away from the women, the better."

Raoul contemplated his bed as if it were a mystery. "I asked her to marry me."

"And she said no?" Galeran didn't know which surprised him most.

"She doesn't want to leave her home."

"That's foolishness. I'm sure you can persuade her."

"I wish I were as certain. So," he added more briskly, "you want me to accompany you?"

"Why not? Lowick will hardly try to snatch the baby from this busy household, and Flambard has no jurisdiction here. I'd value your opinion of Henry Beauclerk."

That night, Raymond of Lowick rapped at the door of the Bishop of Durham's sumptuous house near Westminster. An armed guard opened it, doubtless necessary for such an unpopular person. Since coming to London, Raymond had realized just how unpopular Flambard was. He wished he didn't have to deal with such a man, but who else could support him against William of Brome?

It was for Jehanne, he reminded himself. Beautiful Jehanne, who had been forced into her marriage even though she was as good as betrothed to himself. After all, old Fulk had mentioned it a time or two.

And now she was in danger. Galeran was surely only biding his time. He'd shown his true feelings when he'd struck Jehanne down. Raymond cursed the fact that he'd left her behind to face such violence.

And what of the child? Raymond was genuinely fond of the babe, or as fond as any man could be of such a tiny creature. She was his first child as far as he knew, and he felt honor bound to protect her. Galeran was a good man, but no man could forget the origins of such an infant. At his most merciful, he'd give her to some peasant to raise.

Raymond wished it need not come to death, but feared there was no other way. He knew of no other way to protect Jehanne and Donata.

And to have Heywood. That was a less noble goal, he knew, but it burned in him all the same.

Just as King Henry had thought England his from birth, Raymond had thought Heywood his from the moment Fulk's last son had died. He was Fulk's favorite. He was acknowledged to be one of the finest young warriors in the north. Who else deserved to marry Jehanne?

When Fulk's interest had turned to Brome, Raymond had fanned his friend Eustace's faint interest in the holy war against the Moors. It had been easy enough, and had left the coast clear.

Or so he'd thought.

To see Heywood and Jehanne presented to that scrawny runt Galeran had almost made him choke on his bile. It wasn't right. It couldn't be right. God had showed that by denying Galeran a son until the crusade, and then by taking that son to give Raymond his chance.

As Raymond was ushered into the presence of the bishop, he was firm once more in his belief. It was God's will that he have Heywood, Jehanne, and Donata. Even at the cost of Galeran of Heywood's life.

"My lord bishop, welcome back to London. . . ."

It took Galeran and Raoul half the next morning to progress out of the walled city and along the long curve of the Thames to Westminster Hall, where the king kept his household and held court. The churned-up road was thick with lordly trains, hopeful merchants, and the merely curi-

ous. The congestion was worsened by unauthorized stalls
lining every road, and by a small army of beggars.

The river might be an alternate route, except that it, too,
was crowded with all manner of vessel, and thus much more
hazardous.

Troops of soldiers regularly forced through the crowds
to knock down the stalls and chase off the beggars, but as
soon as the guards moved on, the hawkers and mendicants
popped back, crying out to the passing lords so the noise
seemed a physical presence.

It was like swimming through mud, thought Galeran daz-
edly, tossing some coins to a cripple who looked genuine—
surely those scarred stubs where her legs had been couldn't
be fake.

Eventually, however, they emerged into the open space
around the great Westminster Hall and its sister building,
King Edward's noble abbey. Here, too, people gathered in
huge numbers, but the space could accommodate them and
their noise.

Where did so many hawkers come from? Galeran wondered as a man thrust horse bells at him, extolling their
quality. Create a crowd, and the people who catered to
crowds popped up as if sprouting from dragon's teeth.

There was a kind of organization here, though. A number
of well-disciplined men-at-arms patrolled the area, and tem-
porary stables had been set up to one side for the lordly
visitors' mounts. The merely curious and the more unruly
sellers were regularly driven back out of this enclave into
the jammed streets.

With space to breathe, Galeran began to find all this interesting. He'd been to London only once—to join the crusade. This time, however, the atmosphere seemed different.
The mood was lighter, and under the chaos lay a sense of
limits or even order. It could reflect already the nature of
the new king, and he had to consider whether it promised
good or ill. A lighter mood was surely good, but as they'd

discussed the day before, a very strong inclination toward law and order might not be the best thing for his cause.

He led his party over to the stables, and they gave their horses into the care of the grooms there.

Then a cleric came forward, bearing wax tablets. "Your names, kind sirs?"

Galeran's nerves twitched, but he replied calmly. "Galeran of Heywood in Northumbria, and Raoul de Jouray from the Guyenne."

The man noted their names without expression. "His majesty King Henry is most gratified that so many wish to pay homage to him and congratulate him on his accession. The sheer numbers, however, make it impossible for him to give private audience to everyone at this time. If you will enter the hall, my lords, the king passes through from time to time."

He moved on to greet the next party.

"Very interesting," said Raoul as they walked toward the huge wooden building, which was finely carved and painted and hung with banners. "Your Henry seems to like organization."

"And be good at it, which is more to the point. If his hall were full of people all chivvying for a chance at a moment alone with the king, feelings would be much sourer. This way, those not given audiences won't feel too disgruntled."

Raoul grinned. "You think as I do. The names are sent to the king and he chooses whom to see. Well, let's go in and see if you are chosen."

"Probably not. My father would be, but I do not have his power."

"You're his son."

"If anyone knows that. I might have made a point of it, but I doubt there's any chance today to have a private audience. We may have to wait weeks, and that might not be a bad thing."

"Or perhaps you just want to put off the moment. If need be, I could give you refuge in Guyenne."

It was the first time lighthearted Raoul had mentioned such a thing, and Galeran's throat seized up. What did Raoul sense here that led him to make the offer?

Having returned safe to England, he had no wish to leave her shores again, but if it were that or Jehanne at the stake, of course he would flee into exile. Given the chance.

They joined the stream of handsomely dressed lords passing through the open great doors of the hall, and found the main chamber full but not oppressively so. It was a huge space and could handle the crowd and even the noise of many voices.

"What's the betting," Raoul murmured, "that when the crush reaches its limits, the king comes out to appease everyone and send them on their way?"

"I'm sure you're right, but at least the waiting is to be civilized."

Musicians played in one corner, tables were laid with food, and servants passed around with cups of wine. Galeran and Raoul took one each, tasted, and raised their brows at each other. It was good.

Galeran worked his way toward a space near a window and said quietly, "I'm vastly grateful that I'm not trying to fool Henry Beauclerk."

"Perhaps he just has efficient servants."

"You can tell a man by his servants."

Galeran leaned against the wall and tried to relax. He knew he could be here for hours. He'd grown accustomed to this kind of time-wasting while on crusade. It irked him, but there were occasions when just being present was essential to favor and welfare. He had no doubt that a record was being kept of who was here, and how speedily they had come.

And who had not come.

His father's absence would already have been noted, and he did not know what consequences there might be to that.

He was sure, too, that some of these men were king's men, here solely to listen to conversations. Probably that was obvious to everyone, for all he could hear was safe talk of crops and horses.

Then he heard one mention of Duke Robert—a speculation as to what he would do.

"If he's got sense," said a sinewy man with a hooked nose, "he'll keep his fingers out of England. It's not 1066 now."

"But what if some here want him?" murmured a plumper man, eyes sliding around as if he could spot a spy. "Not me!" he added hastily. "But I've no mind to see us up against each other."

"I doubt anyone wants that. That's excellent reason to make it plain that Henry Beauclerk is rightful king."

Perhaps to avoid this dangerous talk, the sinewy man turned and introduced himself to Galeran and Raoul—a Robert of Keyworth, near Nottingham—then settled to talking safely of the weather and the price of wool.

Then Galeran thought to ask, "I wonder if you know a Raymond of Lowick, who married a woman near Nottingham."

"Why, yes. His wife was a distant cousin. Sadly, she died."

"So I heard." Trying not to sound particularly interested, Galeran asked, "Do you know the cause?"

"The spotted fever. She was never strong."

A small suspicion could be laid to rest, at least. Lowick had not murdered his wife as part of a long-laid plan. "Poor lady."

"Indeed. And Sir Raymond was much distressed, as I remember. You know him well? A fine soldier."

"Very fine. He is a distant connection only."

"Ah. It will not be long now, I think, before the king comes out," Robert remarked. "The crowd is pressing."

Before Galeran could comment, a touch on his arm caught his attention. He looked sideways to see a young man, perhaps a page. "My lord of Heywood?"

"Yes?"

"If you would come with me, my lord, someone wishes to speak with you."

"My companion, Raoul de Jouray?" Galeran asked, heart already speeding.

"That is as you wish, my lords."

They parted from Robert of Keyworth and followed the youth through the crowds, risking no more than a look between them. It could be that some friend, or a friend of his father's, had spotted them and sent a servant to fetch them. But Galeran half hoped, half feared that he was being taken to the king.

Now that the moment had come, he wasn't sure he was ready to put his case, Jehanne's case, to the master of all this efficiency.

To the man who had thrown a miscreant off the walls of Rouen.

To the man who might have arranged his brother's murder.

The youth led them across the hall, but not to some distant acquaintance. He carried on through a side door and out into the fresh air. From there, he took them around the building to a well-guarded entrance that opened into a small chamber.

Westminster Hall, like Burstock, was a wooden building and thus able to have any number of small rooms around the central great chamber. This room contained two armed guards, a monk at a desk which held a large book, and a number of young men coming and going. Even as they entered, one youth left on a errand. Shortly after, another came in with a set of wax tablets. The monk took them and scanned them quickly. Then he murmured a message, and the clerk hurried off.

The monk then looked at them. Know a man by his servants. This one was healthy enough to be a soldier, with shrewd eyes in a lined but quite genial face. Though he wouldn't allow himself the indulgence, Galeran felt he could trust him.

As long as he wasn't up to mischief.

"My lords," the monk said, "the king is pleased you have come so speedily to pay homage to him. Please go on through."

The next room also contained two guards, who eyed them with swift competence. Then one opened a farther door and let Galeran and Raoul into the king's presence.

This large, richly decorated solar chamber was nearly as crowded as the hall, and wherever the king was, he wasn't in his great chair on the dais. That sat empty. Galeran scanned the room and found Henry simply by the fact that no one had their back turned to that one spot. Then it was easy because Henry was wearing his crown.

It was not really remarkable for a monarch to wear the crown at an important occasion, and yet Galeran felt it to be significant. Day after day under that metal contraption couldn't be pleasant. It was a clear statement of possession.

He'd seen Henry Beauclerk a few years before, and he hadn't changed much. He was perhaps a little stockier, but looked healthy and athletic at thirty-two, with good high color. His dark, glossy hair curled onto his shoulders in the latest style.

He smiled at everyone, and Galeran thought that smile was genuine. It wasn't so much a smile of pleasure at meeting anyone, but one of sheer delight at having finally achieved his ambition and become king of England, and at having half the world desperate to kneel before him and acknowledge the fact.

What would this man make of Galeran's affair, though?

Galeran fingered the pouch containing the palm leaves and the chip of rock from the Holy Sepulcher, and continued to assess the room.

It was easy to spot Henry's close companions from those come to pay their respects. They were more relaxed, less overdressed, and instead of staring at the monarch, they moved about the room, chatting to this person or that.

It occurred to Galeran that they were probably a household in the true tradition, companions bound to their leader by oaths, and loyalty almost impossible to break. Such a household worked to a common cause, living or dying as their leader lived or died.

It was the traditional English way, but had weakened under the Normans.

Robert of Normandy had favorites rather than a household. During the crusade, Galeran had learned that those favorites were more inclined to stab at one another in a search for advantage than to work together to advance their lord. He'd heard that Rufus's friends had been of the same mettle.

More than before, Galeran didn't give much for Robert's chances of grabbing England out of his brother's hands.

His thoughts were disturbed by a tall, dark-haired man of about his own age. "Lord Galeran of Heywood?"

Galeran admitted it and introduced Raoul.

"I am FitzRoger," the man said simply.

Galeran recognized the name and absorbed the complex powers neatly covered in dark garments. This was one of the foremost tourney fighters of the age, and a close companion to Henry Beauclerk. He was his champion as well. Champions were often chosen for simple physical prowess. This man had brains.

Know a man by his servants.

FitzRoger's clothing was quietly magnificent, but it was his bearing that spoke of inner and outer power. "Your father, Lord William, does not accompany you?"

Straight to the point. "He came south, sir, but was taken ill at Waltham Abbey. He will come on as soon as he is able."

Clever green eyes studied them for a moment, and Galeran didn't doubt that FitzRoger recognized a convenient indisposition. What would he and his lord make of it, though?

"The king will be sorry to hear of it, but pleased that you are here, my lord. Unfortunately, with so much to do, it won't be possible for him to travel to the far north for some time, so he is eager to hear of affairs there. Please, come with me."

He easily made a way for them through the room and seemed to alert Henry to their presence by will alone, for he neither spoke nor touched, and yet Henry turned.

The king still smiled, but his fine, dark eyes were keen as a hawk's, stripping them both to the bone in seconds. How exhausting it must be, Galeran thought, to have to judge men day after day, when those judgments meant the success or failure of a life's dream, and perhaps even life itself.

Of course Henry had his household, men like FitzRoger, to judge people ahead of time. Probably there was some subtle sign to convey that a man was suspect, or not worth the trouble. He wondered if some sign had been given about himself.

He did kill his brother.

The certainty came into Galeran's mind so sharply that he feared for a moment that he'd spoken the words, or at least let them show on his face. It was a conviction, though, now that he'd met the king. Henry Beauclerk would let no scruple stand between himself and what he wanted.

And what did that imply for his own cause?

He and Raoul knelt, but were immediately raised. Galeran was kissed on the cheek. "My dear friend!" declared Henry. "I call you that, for your family have stood friend to my family since we all came to England."

"We consider it our privilege, sire."

"Good man! And you are recently returned from the Holy Land. You must tell me of it. How I wish it had been possible for me to join God's Enterprise."

There had, in fact, been nothing to stop Henry other than lack of funds and his primary obsession, his desire for England. But Galeran did not say that, just took the opportunity to present his gifts.

As Henry opened the pouch with his own hands, an extra touch of color in his cheeks suggested that he was not immune to the mystique of the crusade. He touched the items reverently, showing them around to all. "We will have shrines built to these, Lord Galeran," he said, "and we most sincerely thank you."

As Henry gave the items into a monk's care, Galeran thought that at least something was going right. Perhaps it was a promise for the future.

"Now," Henry said, drawing Galeran aside slightly, "tell me of affairs in the north. What of the Scots?"

He then put Galeran through a smiling but efficient catechism of northern affairs, showing a good understanding of matters there.

"I was born in Yorkshire, you know," he said at last, and Galeran judged that he said it often. It was one of his chief claims to the throne, that he was a trueborn English prince. It wasn't just a political move, however. There was real feeling behind it.

Galeran still had no indication of how Henry would react to the matter of Jehanne and Donata, and the king was already turning away to greet other people.

"Sire," said Galeran.

Henry turned back, eyes narrowed. "Yes?"

"I have a matter to put before your judgment, at some convenient time."

There was no surprise on the royal face. "So I understand. Tomorrow at terce, we will hear you. I understand the Bishop of Durham has an interest, and some other man. . . ." He looked around.

"Raymond of Lowick," supplied FitzRoger.

"Ah, yes. Tomorrow, Lord Galeran."

With that, he turned to a party from Devon, smile back in place. Galeran let out a breath as he and Raoul eased backward toward the door under FitzRoger's courteous care.

Galeran decided he needed more information. "Bishop Flambard has already spoken to the king?"

"Yesterday, briefly."

Galeran wanted to ask if Henry favored Flambard at all, or hated him as much as everyone else did. That would be going too far, however.

"And Lowick?"

"The man has paid his respects in the great chamber."

Not admitted to the sanctum, in other words.

At the door, FitzRoger added, "You seem to have a very forgiving nature, Lord Galeran."

So, the king and his household knew the story already. There was a genuine expression of curiosity on FitzRoger's features. Galeran supposed he'd have to get used to that.

"Is it not our Christian duty to forgive the penitent?"

"Especially the adulterous, I suppose, with Christ's example so clearly laid before us. It is an aspect of Christianity many men find hard, however."

Perhaps rashly, Galeran decided to send a message to the king. "It is not hard to forgive one who erred in a time of great stress," he said, "especially if one loves the sinner. It is, however, hard to forgive those who hurt the ones we love."

FitzRoger raised a brow but merely nodded. "God go with you, Lord Galeran."

They were passed back through the anterooms and into

the fresh air. Galeran took a deep breath and rolled his tense shoulders. "Well? What do you think?"

"I'd like a bout with FitzRoger."

"Don't you ever think of anything but fighting?"

"It's my job. But what I would like is to judge the man by his servants. If FitzRoger lives up to his reputation and the impression I just had of him, it says a great deal that he serves the king."

They headed toward the stables. "He may not have much of a choice. He's a bastard."

"He has choice," said Raoul with certainty. "As for your king, I judge that he'll do whatever he must to keep the crown of England on his head. After that, I assume he'll do whatever necessary to make the country safe and prosperous."

"What you're saying is that we have to hope that my affair doesn't threaten any of the above."

"Of course. But it doesn't, does it?"

"Not as far as I can tell. Unless Henry decides he needs Flambard more than he needs my father."

Raoul slapped him on the shoulder. "That would be foolish. Cheer up. All in all, I have a good feeling about things!"

In the house of the Bishop of London, Ranulph Flambard lay in a huge tub, considering his situation. He had attended the king the previous day, and experienced little difficulty in obtaining an audience with Henry. He was a bishop, after all.

However, the audience had been short and the king had shown no warmth whatsoever.

Flambard had expected nothing else, but it was still a shame. He admired Henry. It would be pleasant to retain his place under him.

As it was, without the king's absolute protection, London

was uncomfortable. The unruly mob had voiced their feelings, which was that King Henry should do away with Ranulph Flambard, and it would be good riddance to bad rubbish.

He did hope they were wrong.

He believed they were wrong, though he did not deceive himself that Henry looked upon him kindly. The king wouldn't dare move against a man of the Church without cause, however, and in time Henry would realize he needed Ranulph Flambard's skills.

Henry, however, was in the early days of his reign. He had not had time yet to assess his brother's successes and failures, or to detect who had been responsible for them. Nor had the king had time to realize just how much he needed the money Ranulph Flambard could obtain for him.

On the other hand, some of Ranulph's means of obtaining that money had been . . . unusual. And Henry had promised to uphold the laws.

The bishop reached for the goblet of wine standing close by his right hand. Everything hung in the balance.

A servant slipped into the room and bowed.

"Yes?"

"Raymond of Lowick requests an audience, my lord bishop."

A possible weight in the balance.

"Send him in. And bring more wine and another goblet."

Sir Raymond stalked into the small chamber with a great excess of energy and dignity. He was not in armor, thank heaven, but his sword still threatened various objects as he moved. The servant presented the goblet of wine and was thanked curtly.

It was amazing, thought Flambard, how men of such minuscule importance thought themselves so grand.

"My lord bishop," said Lowick, "Galeran of Heywood and his household are in London."

"Are they indeed? That is hardly surprising."

Lowick stopped his restlessness and fixed a surprisingly knowing look on Ranulph. "Lord William of Brome is not with them. He was taken ill at Waltham."

Ranulph put aside his wine. "Indeed? That *is* interesting. Do we know what kind of illness?"

"No, my lord."

Flambard considered for a moment, then said, "You must ride to Waltham and discover just how ill Lord William is."

"But Jehanne and my child are here, only lightly protected at the house of Hugo the Vintner in Corser Street. Is this not a good time to seize them?"

Ranulph decided he must have been mistaken about that flash of intelligence. "Not at all. I have no jurisdiction here. Knowing where they are is good enough for now. I have already mentioned your case to the king and hope that he will order that my judgment be obeyed. He is not keen to offend the Church at this time. . . ."

With a knock, the servant intruded once again.

"What?"

"Begging your pardon, my lord, but a messenger comes from the king."

"Then send him in, man! Send him in!"

The messenger was a neatly made young clerk of the type Henry seemed to favor. "My lord bishop, I bring greetings from the king, who sends to inform you that tomorrow at terce a case will come before him that could hold interest for you."

"What case?" asked Ranulph, not letting a scrap of interest show, though Lowick, damn him, was flaring and sidling like a stallion scenting a mare.

"A matter raised by Lord Galeran of Heywood to do with his wife and his wife's child. You did mention this matter to his majesty, my lord."

If this young rapscallion was his servant, he'd whip him for impudence. Ranulph sipped his wine. "Ah, yes. I remember. A minor matter, but Lord Galeran was less than cooperative."

"The king invites you to attend the hearing and put forward any aspects of the case as you see fit."

"The king is most kind and just. Sir Raymond here has an interest, too, being the father of the child. Unless I hear to the contrary, I will bring him with me."

"I will report as much." The clerk bowed himself out.

"By Saint Michael, it has come!" declared Lowick, hand on sword hilt.

"And may well go in moments if the king is so minded," Ranulph snapped. "He's a man with a quiver full of bastards, so he may not look upon fornication and adultery seriously."

"You think we could lose, my lord?"

"Just in case, I have prepared another weapon."

"A weapon, my lord?"

"You are Jehanne of Heywood's lawful husband."

"No, I'm not."

Flambard pointed to a document on a side table. Lowick picked it up, but said, "I don't read." He made it a declaration of worthiness.

"Then put it down again," said Flambard with a sigh. "It is your betrothal document, duly signed by a number of witnesses."

"But I was never formally betrothed to Jehanne."

A profound desire to hit Lowick over the head with something astonished Flambard. The current tension must be rotting his brain. "It was Lord Fulk's intent, you say, and I have made that intent real. The document, Sir Raymond, changes everything. It means *you* can challenge Lord Galeran."

Lowick contemplated that. "But if I issue a wrongful challenge, God will not be on my side."

Flambard closed his eyes briefly. "You must look to the

truth, not just what happened. Truly, you were promised Jehanne as your bride, weren't you?"

"Yes, but . . ."

"Does not that promise invalidate her later betrothal to Galeran?"

"Does it?"

"Yes," Flambard lied.

"Oh. So if their marriage is invalid . . . she is mine!"

"Quite. Now, we will not produce this document unless we need to, but it means we cannot lose. One way or another you will fight him and kill him, yes? For your lady and your child."

Lowick stood tall. "For my lady and my child!"

The volume of his declaration almost made Flambard's head ache, but he smiled. "However, it would be useful to know exactly what William of Brome is up to, and it's no great distance to Waltham. Get you there, sir, and discover what you can. If Lord William is malingering, that's another pennyweight on our side."

Once the knight had left, the bishop drained his goblet of wine, then sent Lucas to check on the house of Hugo the Vintner in Corser Street.

When the man returned, he had very interesting news.

Sixteen

Galeran and Raoul collected their horses and worked their way back to Hugo's house, which took longer because they were moving against the flow of traffic. They stopped partway along at a tavern to eat and wash down the city dust.

It was a relief to arrive back at Corser Street, until Mary ran out, wringing her hands, her veil and circlet all askew. "Lord Galeran! They have all been carried off!"

"My wife? The babe? By whom? Lowick? Flambard?" He grabbed his horse's reins back from the man who was leading the animal away.

"It was the king's men!" Mary gasped. "They came with full authorization. There was nothing we could do!"

"The *king!*" Galeran's mind spun madly. Henry had heard Flambard's story the day before. Did this mean he was on the bishop's side? Was it time to flee?

"Where have they taken her?" he asked, gripping his sword hilt.

"St. Hilda's convent. It's off Aldersgate Street, not far from here." Mary gave quick instructions and Galeran's fears eased a little. A convent was a suitable place, as long as they didn't want to lock Jehanne up there forever.

He turned to leave the house, and Raoul stopped him. "Shall I come?"

"No. You'd better stay here."

"Take some men, at least. Don't forget the original plan."

Galeran turned back. "What?"

"The last time someone tried to seize Jehanne and the baby, your murder was part of it."

"But this time it's the king's men."

"But the game could be complex. Flambard might still know about this convent—the king may even have told him. He could still plan an ambush."

"In the middle of the city? I doubt it." Galeran's mind was on another track. "As soon as Henry knew I was at Westminster, he sent men to take Jehanne into custody. I don't like it. He's probably already decided what his judgment will be, God rot him."

Raoul gripped his arm. "Cool your tongue before you go in public, Galeran, and look to your own safety. Jehanne is not in any direct harm, but she needs you alive and well to defend her."

"She's in custody." Galeran twisted free. "What happens if Henry and the Church decide she should be punished?"

"You could never have stopped them."

"I'd have found a way. I might still." With that Galeran swept out into the street, judging that a man on foot would make better speed than a horse. Any escort could follow or not as they pleased.

St. Hilda's was a solid establishment covering many acres and surrounded by high wooden walls. An excellent prison, Galeran thought, but not impregnable. He was already considering ways to liberate his wife.

Behind the walls, Galeran could see the tops of some thatched roofs and a stone bell tower, presumably part of the convent's chapel. Nothing about the place was militant or defensive.

Of course, a religious house was protected by God and man, and anyone who invaded it would suffer dearly.

He tugged on the bell rope that hung by the heavy oak door, and a small peep door slid back.

"I am Galeran of Heywood, come to see my wife."

The little door slid closed and the large one immediately opened. Galeran's fears began to subside. The thin portress said, "You must speak to our mother superior, my lord," and led the way across a pleasant cloister garden full of herbs and flowers.

Galeran's heart eased even more. St. Hilda's was not a dungeon or a place of terror. Doubtless the king had felt it safer to have the cause of contention kept out of sight. Perhaps it had even been an attempt to protect Jehanne and the baby from the Church.

Though she could be said to be in the hands of the Church . . .

The mother superior's office was stark—plain whitewashed walls, plain benches and tables, and for ornament, just one ivory crucifix. It spoke of virtue of the more severe kind. The mother superior was equally plain, with sallow skin and a mighty nose, but like the room, her plainness gave her a kind of majesty.

"Lord Galeran," she said, gesturing toward a bench.

He didn't sit. "I wish to speak to my wife."

She folded her hands neatly on her desk. "For what purpose?"

"To ensure that she is well, and content to be here."

"And if she isn't?"

"Then to remove her."

The woman's bushy brows rose, pushing up her pristine veil. "Against the king's orders, my lord? I am ordered to hold the Lady Jehanne here until all matters concerning her and her child are settled."

"Are you ordered to prevent me speaking to her?"

The woman considered him a moment. "No," she said at last. "Wait here a moment, my lord, and I will see if she wishes to receive you."

If she wishes . . .

Galeran stared at the closed door, wondering for the first time whether Jehanne was pleased to be here, away from all the stress of their tangled situation. He put his hands to his head. Old suspicions of her feelings for Lowick still hid in his brain, waiting to ambush him at the slightest provocation.

He couldn't think straight about any of this anymore, but he had to. Tomorrow he had to convince the king that it was right to let matters be, to leave Jehanne untouched and to leave Donata in their care.

The mother superior returned. "She will see you. By our rule, Lord Galeran, you may not touch each other."

"I understand." He followed her along one side of the roofed cloister-walk to a door, which she opened to let him into a tiny room. A small high window let in little light, and it took him a moment to see a narrow bed, a bench, and a prie-dieu before a wooden cross.

This was no guest room. This was a nun's cell. Jehanne stood there alone. Where were Aline and the baby?

"Are you all right?" he asked, silently cursing the fact that the mother superior had entered the room with him. If not for that, he would have held her, rule or not.

"Yes, of course. It was a bit of a shock. . . ."

"I'm sure it was. The king is to hear our matter tomorrow morning, so this shouldn't be for long."

"This is an excellent place to pray about it."

"I suppose it is." Something was wrong. This wooden calm was very unlike Jehanne. "Where are Donata and Aline?"

"In another room. They bring the baby for feeding. There's no problem, Galeran. Privacy gives me a chance to meditate and pray."

He didn't believe her, and yet he could see no problem other than the fact that she was a prisoner, and that would only be for another day.

Unless the king ordered her kept here for life.

Galeran would burn the place down before he'd permit that.

He put on a smile. "Don't worry. We can probably be on our way home tomorrow."

And she smiled back, a smile that traveled into her eyes. "Have pity! Having come so far, perhaps we can stay a day or two and enjoy the celebrations."

"If you wish, then we will." Galeran blew her a kiss and turned to leave, but she spoke again.

"When is the case to be heard?"

"At terce."

"Will I be able to attend?"

"What do you have to say that I cannot?"

"There might be something. . . ."

Galeran knew his Jehanne. She was keeping something from him. But he also knew she couldn't easily be made to tell it, especially with the nun as witness. He rather feared that Jehanne's new resolution to be a good, quiet woman and let the men handle things was proving hard to hold by. That could be disastrous. Galeran hoped to convince Henry that Jehanne had sinned out of weakness, overwhelmed by her loss.

"Jehanne," he said with heavy meaning, "leave this in my hands. I won't let harm come to you or the child. I promise it."

She frowned, almost as if in pain. "Of course I trust you, but . . . Oh, I know you will do what is right."

"Just pray, Jehanne," he said, "and wait patiently until tomorrow."

When he left, the mother superior turned a heavy key in the lock.

"That hardly seems necessary, Mother."

"I am following my orders, Lord Galeran. You cannot deny that your wife has sinned. Such little pains as she is now suffering will help save her soul, perhaps help save you all."

He wanted to protest that, but there hardly seemed much point. If he gave in to his impulses and released Jehanne by force, he'd end up either exiled or in custody himself, which wouldn't help anyone. "I would like to see the Lady Aline and the baby, to be sure that they, too, are well."

With an audible sigh, the mother superior led him across the garden to the other side of the cloister.

"Wouldn't it be more suitable for them to be housed nearby?" Galeran asked.

"These were our only two empty rooms, my lord. Many people have asked for hospitality during the king's visit."

But do you lock all your guests in? Galeran wondered as the nun again unlocked a door. It wasn't worth fighting over. Jehanne was safe, if rather tense. As long as Aline, Winifred, and Donata were also well, he'd let it be until tomorrow.

The mother superior ushered him into another small room very like Jehanne's, but this time crowded with two narrow beds and a cradle. Aline leaped to her feet with fretful energy. "Galeran! Thank heavens."

She would have flung herself into his arms, but the mother superior stepped firmly between them. "Conduct yourself properly, young woman!"

Aline pulled a face, but settled down. "A troop of men brought us here. They had the king's seal and—"

"Yes, I know," said Galeran. "Don't worry. It will all be settled tomorrow. How's Donata?"

Aline looked toward the cradle in which the baby slept. "Well. But I don't know why they've split us up. We're to call when she needs feeding, then one of the sisters will take her over to Jehanne."

Galeran looked at the mother superior. "Well?"

"I was told to keep the Lady Jehanne alone so that she could contemplate her sins in peace, my lord. Children are not peaceful. She has stated that she appreciates every aspect of the arrangement. The child will be taken to her whenever necessary."

It was all stupid, but no more so that a hundred other incidents in which government had become embroiled. What worried Galeran was that such matters could get out of hand. He didn't want to worry the women, however, so he smiled at Aline and Winifred. "Probably Jehanne will be the better of some tranquility. She's had little enough of it the last year."

With that he left, and allowed himself to be herded out of the convent with only one backward look at Jehanne's locked door.

Aline sat back down on the hard bed, thinking. She wished she'd been able to talk to Galeran in private, for she didn't like this situation at all. She needed to talk to Jehanne as well and make plans. What if some silly judgment were made to give Donata to Lowick? They had to be ready to act!

In the short journey from Corser Street to the convent, Jehanne had ordered Aline to keep Donata safe at all costs. But how could such a young baby be safe away from her mother?

No, if the worst happened, they had to be ready to escape together. It shouldn't be impossible. The convent wasn't guarded. All that held them was locked doors.

She went to inspect the door, and discovered locked doors could be quite formidable. This one was thick, iron-strapped oak, and the lock was heavy iron too. It seemed strange that a convent would have such secure rooms, but perhaps they were often called upon to hold prisoners.

Winifred just sat looking quietly miserable, but Aline paced. Perhaps it would be better to wait patiently for the morrow. Any attempt to escape could be seen as rebellion against the king's orders.

She didn't know enough about such things.

She desperately needed to confer with Jehanne.

Donata began to stir, and Winifred picked her up, obviously pleased of something to do. The baby looked around, chewing on her knuckles.

"She'll want feeding in a moment or two," said Winifred. "I'll change her."

Then Aline had an idea. She picked up her embroidery materials and the babe's blanket. With quick stitches she worked along the edge the message, *What do you want to do?* adding some ornamental stitches to disguise the words. Surely Jehanne would notice that the work was new and decipher the message.

When Donata was ready, Aline wrapped her in the blanket, making sure the stitchery was visible but not too clear, then went to the door and called out. In moments a smiling nun took the baby, cooing to her, and carried her away.

Aline was reassured by the nun's friendly manner, but it made this imprisoned separation even more peculiar. What was behind it, and did it have any implication for the crucial hearing before the king?

It would be a while before Donata returned, for Jehanne would surely keep her as long as possible, so Aline sat and took up her more normal embroidery. She kept making misstitches, though, for her mind wasn't on it. In addition, the light from the small, high window wasn't really adequate for fine work. She wished she had her distaff. She could spin thread in the dark.

One problem suddenly occurred to her. She didn't think Jehanne had any needlework materials with which to reply.

Winifred lay on her bed and went to sleep. Aline envied such placidity.

* * *

Jehanne saw the embroidery immediately, but she settled to feeding Donata, in part because the middle-aged sister was hovering, gazing besottedly at the baby. Another nun who perhaps was not suited to her life? Jehanne decided Raoul was right, no matter what his motives were. If Aline wanted a husband and children, she should find that out before committing herself to the veil.

Donata, bless her, did not seem to be finding her situation bothersome. She nuzzled impatiently at Jehanne's breast, then latched on to it and settled—with an amusing sigh of relief—to filling her belly. Sister Martha left, and Jehanne could loosen the blanket to smooth out the new embroidery.

She laughed out loud. Clever Aline!

Her amusement faded, however. It was an excellent question. What *did* she want to do?

Jehanne had made, and intended to keep, resolutions to stop being so militant. Days earlier, she had promised to leave matters in Galeran's very capable hands.

But in this crisis she was not sure he was capable. He'd told her about Agnes, the woman taken in adultery, and the solution that had come from her punishment. Even so, he couldn't, or wouldn't, see that their situation was the same.

Jehanne knew she had to suffer some punishment for her sin, and as she had said, in a way she would welcome it. It was not just that the community must see matters put right; she herself must feel that the balance had been made even again. Until she did, she wasn't sure she could let herself be happy again.

A court battle would do nothing to put matters right in her heart. Especially a court battle between the two men who had given her a child, a battle in which one of them must die. She simply could not live with that.

Thanks to Bishop Flambard, however, Jehanne now had a means to ease her soul, and possibly to prevent any fighting. But she couldn't do it by patiently staying here until it was all over.

When Donata was satisfied, Jehanne unwrapped the babe and laid her on the bed. As she played games with her daughter, moving her arms in time to nonsense songs, she considered the bishop's unexpected involvement with her imprisonment.

The king had ordered their detention here, but Bishop Flambard had ordered this solitary confinement and close guard. Apparently he had only to tell Mother Eadalyth of Jehanne's wicked sin to get the woman on his side.

It was Flambard, too, who had ordered Jehanne's specific punishment—ten strokes of the rod every three hours. She did not thank him for that, but it could well save them all, in more ways than one.

Mother Eadalyth had no kind thoughts about Galeran, either. "A man who would permit such sins to go unpunished is a sinner himself," she had declared while rolling up her sleeve for the first serving not long before Galeran's arrival. "He is like Adam succumbing yet again to Eve. You are to be pitied, my child, for being so poorly ruled."

Jehanne wondered if the mother superior had modified her views at all on meeting Galeran. He wasn't the convincing picture of a weakly doting husband. But as long as he refused to punish her, that was what everyone would think.

And of course he *was* doting, she thought, smiling sadly at her bastard daughter. Though not weak about it. He doted on her just as she doted on him. They would both fight and die in the other's cause.

That was the problem.

But since she'd caused the disaster, it was for her to sort it out and to suffer any pains, even if Galeran were furious afterward.

She grimaced, acknowledging that she was failing in her resolutions of being a proper woman, able to wait patiently for the men to sort it out. It wasn't her nature, though, and so she could do only as she saw right and pray God to guide her.

What was right at the moment was to accept her punishment, galling though it was, and then use it as a weapon against the bishop. But that meant she must attend the hearing the following day to show her back, to show the king how Flambard had overridden his orders.

The mother superior would never permit it.

Galeran wouldn't cooperate, either. In fact, if she let him know about the beatings, he'd put a stop to them. But Raoul might be more practical if she could get a message to him. The only way of doing that was through Aline. She couldn't imagine how, but it was the only chance.

She had no embroidery tools with her, unfortunately, so, leaving Donata to kick and chortle by herself, she searched the room for anything that would make a mark. She found nothing, but the floor was simple beaten earth, and so she made mud with a little drinking water and laboriously printed a message on the blanket.

Jehanne could read, but did very little writing, and with the inadequate materials the message looked more like a mess than words. She could only hope Aline would decipher it. Hearing footsteps, she hastily wrapped Donata again, and handed her over to Sister Martha.

Then she went to her prie-dieu to pray, and to wait for Mother Superior Eadalyth's strong right arm. In simple honesty, she offered her pains up to God and His mother, seeking forgiveness for her sin, but, more important, protection for Galeran and Raymond. She cared not at all for Raymond of Lowick, except as someone she had known most of her life, but she knew that she had entangled him in this mess.

In order to strike against God.

She shuddered at the thought.

Oh, yes, she deserved every stroke Bishop Flambard had ordained for her. She could almost bless him, if not for a certain crossbow attack, which she was sure was Flambard's work. Raymond would never stoop so low.

Sometime later she heard the lock turn and the door open. A faint rustling told her the mother superior was rolling up her wide outer sleeve.

"May the Lord forgive his wretched sinner," intoned Mother Eadalyth, and the rod cut.

"Amen," Jehanne responded as steadily as she could.

Dear Mary, help her, but the strokes hurt more on her already-sore back. She gripped the wood of the prie-dieu and strangled all noise other than a gasp at each stroke. She counted them silently.

Another four.

She could endure another four.

Another three.

Two.

Last one.

It almost broke her and made her weep, the relief that it was over.

For this time.

In another three hours, however, or another six, she would cry out. All people had limits. Her pride shuddered at the thought of wailing under the blows, but pride was a silly thing.

As the lock turned behind the departing mother superior, Jehanne lowered her head and prayed, offering her pain for the safety of all, and victory in the end.

Aline had watched the sun's reflection move a quarter way around the room before Donata returned, sleeping peacefully. Aline took her, glad now that Winifred was snoring. She put Donata in the box that served as a cradle and gently unwrapped her blanket, substituting a fresh one.

At first it just looked as if someone with dirty hands had handled the blanket, but then she saw that the dirt was writing. She shook her head. She had learned to make letters in the convent, but Jehanne had always used scribes, and it showed.

Still, allowing for awkward shapes and strange spelling, the message seemed to be *I must go to hearing. Raoul.*

Aline let out a breath and rubbed the blanket together so that it looked merely dirty. So, Jehanne wanted to go to the hearing. Since she'd specified Raoul, she clearly didn't think Galeran would help her.

Aline sat on the edge of her narrow bed and thought.

She was sure that judicial hearings before the king were not usually attended by women. Perhaps this was one of Jehanne's less inspired ideas, coming out of her need to always be involved in whatever was happening.

On the other hand, Jehanne had begun to come to terms with that fault. Aline really didn't think she would be trying to attend the hearing out of willful impulse. She had something of importance to contribute, something that couldn't be achieved by a simple message.

However, they were all prisoners, and though the convent was not a formidable prison, it was strong enough.

Aline sighed. In view of Jehanne's message, she supposed she had to try to engineer an escape.

Then a new range of problems came to mind.

Jehanne could not separate from Donata for any length of time, and escaping with a baby would be very tricky indeed. Moreover, if Jehanne wanted to attend the hearing, it would be best if she escaped not long before it. Trying to hide all night from a full hue and cry, screaming babe in arms, was enough to make anyone quail.

Aline saw why her cousin had mentioned Raoul. He was just the sort of man who might be able to arrange all this, and there was the additional benefit that he was foreign. If the king flew into a rage at their behavior, Raoul could flee back to his native land.

Alone.

Aline pushed that thought away and settled to making real plans. By the time the nuns emerged from the nones prayer, she had a strategy of sorts. It would have to wait for vespers, though, and so she sat to unpicking her message from one blanket, and stitching another in a clean one, explaining briefly what she intended.

Late in the afternoon Sister Martha came for Donata, and Aline sat, fidgeting, to wait.

The trouble with her plan was that it depended upon so many uncertainties. The other trouble was that it terrified her.

When the nun returned with the babe, Aline clutched her belly. "I don't feel very well," she moaned. "I think I might be ill. I don't know what it is, but I'm worried about the baby. She might catch something. . . ."

"Oh, my. Oh, no!" exclaimed the nun, looking around for help. But the bell was ringing for vespers and through the open door, Aline could see the community filing toward the chapel. At least the timing was working right.

"Perhaps the infirmary . . ." Aline gasped, covering her mouth as if about to vomit.

"Yes!" exclaimed the sister. "We can't endanger the baby." She grasped Aline and dragged her out of the small room before locking the door.

Aline leaned against a wall and sent up a prayer of thanks. She sent up another prayer that the infirmarian be at vespers.

Having done her best for the safety of the baby, Sister Martha became her usual friendly self, and put an arm around Aline. "You poor thing. Come along to the infirmary. There's a privy there, and as soon as vespers are over, Sister Fredeswide will find you something to help."

Thank you, oh, Blessed Mother, Aline said silently. There was a chance she would be left alone.

The small, whitewashed room held six beds, all empty. Another cause for thanks. Perhaps God and His mother smiled on this enterprise. Aline collapsed onto one bed with a moan. Sister Martha, unfortunately, sat on another.

"Do you have a pain in your belly, Lady Aline?"

"Yes. A bad one."

"I'll get you a bowl."

But that only took the nun to a cupboard at the end of the room.

Aline took the bowl and mumbled her thanks, thinking hard. "Perhaps I can sleep," she said after awhile. "Please don't feel you need to miss vespers."

"I am excused for now to see to our guests."

Guard us, in other words. Aline thought frantically. "Don't you think you should go to where you can hear Winifred if she calls? What if Donata turns sick too?"

Sister Martha leaped to her feet. "Oh, dear! Indeed! The poor precious mite. Perhaps I should get Sister Fredeswide . . ."

Before Aline could think of an objection to that, the nun muttered, "But she has such a tongue on her, and hates to be bothered unnecessarily. . . ."

Aline waited, praying.

"I'll sit in the cloister," said Sister Martha with a nod. "I'll be able to hear you or the baby's nurse if you call." She hesitated for a moment. "Are you sure you'll be all right?"

"Yes. I'm sorry to be a trouble."

The nun patted her hand. "Don't you worry, dear. You'll soon be healthy again."

Once she was sure Sister Martha was out of sight, Aline slipped out of bed to reconnoiter. This room had three doors. One led out into the cloister. From behind the other she heard chanting. It must lead into the chapel, which was common enough. It meant that the door could stand open during services to allow the sick to worship.

The third door, when she gingerly opened it, proved to open into the infirmarian's still room. It was rich with the smells of herbs and potions, and its other door—*thank you again, Blessed Mother*—stood open into the herb garden.

The herb garden, however, was no escape. It had only one other exit—an archway back into the cloister, where Sister Martha presumably sat.

With a *humph* of frustration, Aline studied the wooden wall that sheltered two sides of the garden. It was the outside wall of the convent, but was at least twice her height. Though it had some cross-bracing on her side, she really didn't think she could climb it. She'd never been the sort of girl attracted to climbing and or other rough activities.

On the other hand, she had to get out of here.

She turned to consider the infirmary building itself. The peak of the thatched roof was a little higher than the wooden wall. Perhaps from up there she could let herself down.

Her heart started to thump with nervousness at the mere thought, but if she were going to try, it had to be now. As soon as vespers were over, the infirmarian would come to physick her, probably followed by a suspicious mother superior.

She remembered Raoul calling her a green cadet. He hadn't been talking of this kind of challenge, but the memory challenged her. She could do it. She could do anything if she put her mind to it.

Aline ran back into the infirmary and brought out a sturdy stool. Standing on that, she found she could almost reach the first ropes of the low-hanging thatch. With a jump and a pull, she was spread-eagled on the thatch, praying to whatever saint guarded foolish climbers.

As her heart steadied, she realized the roof was quite shallow, and with the thatch ties at regular intervals, it was easy enough to creep up to the crown—as long as she didn't look down.

When she reached the top, however, she had to peep over to see what Sister Martha was doing. She was sitting in the cloister garden, praying.

It was a long way down.

"God bless you and keep you, Sister, and may you not get into too much trouble over this."

Aline began to edge sideways along the peak of the roof toward the wooden wall, muttering with irritation as the layers of her clothing kept snagging on straw.

At the wall, Aline found she was still blessed, for on the other side was a quiet, narrow street. People passed along occasionally, but it was often deserted.

The drop, however, was still twice her height.

Jumping was completely out of the question.

She wished Raoul were here to train her. She was sure he knew any number of ways of getting down a wall. In fact, he'd think the task trivial, and laugh at her fears.

"Hah!" muttered Aline. "I'll show you, Raoul de Jouray."

Heart pounding with fear, she unknotted her woven girdle and tied one end securely to one of the thatch ropes. The girdle was more than her height in length. If it held, it should make the drop quite small.

If it held.

Praying that the bell for the end of vespers wouldn't start yet, Aline waited for a time when no one was in sight. Then, whispering a continuous litany to her favorite saints, she wriggled her legs and hips over the wall, holding on to the cloth for dear life.

"Mary, Mother of God, aid me."

"Saint Anne, pray for me. And give me stronger arms and hands!"

Muscles screaming, feet braced against the wall, she worked hand over hand down the stretching, straining strip of woven cloth.

"Saint George, mighty warrior, come to my support!"

Her hands ached and weakened, and she was sure she would lose her grip.

"Saint Thomas, let me not doubt that this cloth will hold me. . . ."

The girdle snapped.

Aline let out a squeak of terror, but in fact she was so close to the end that she just dropped with a thump on her behind.

After a shaken moment, she leaped up, dusted herself off, and grabbed the torn strip of material off the ground.

She was just in time. As she hurried down the lane on shaky legs, a man carrying a heavy sack on his back trundled in. He passed her without a glance, and her heart began to steady.

Stopping for a moment to catch some deep breaths, she heard the convent bell signal the end of prayer. She hastily wrapped the remains of her girdle around her waist and threaded her way into a busier street to put distance between herself and pursuit.

She couldn't help smiling. She'd *done* it! Wait until Raoul heard about this! After a little while, however, in the anonymity of a crowded, clamorous market, Aline had to admit she was lost.

Never imagining a city as huge and crowded as London, she'd thought that if she wandered a little, she would soon come across Hugo's house. She had walked up and down a score of streets, however, and seen nothing she recognized at all. She wasn't sure what kind of search would be made for her, but she had been confined at St. Hilda's by order of the king. Perhaps the whole city was even now being put on the alert.

She could imagine criers appearing in the street, bellowing, "Seek out a maid of eighteen years, one with blue eyes and fair hair under a plain white veil. Her plump body is covered in a cream-colored kirtle and a red and brown overtunic, finely worked. She is a fugitive of the king's. Detain her with all necessary force!"

She looked around, but no one was staring at her yet. In fact, it being close to the end of the day, everyone seemed intent on their own business, and in a hurry to be home.

Customers were making last-minute purchases, and vendors were beginning to pack away their wares. She doubted they'd notice her if she were stark naked.

That gave her an idea. Stepping into a quiet corner, she pulled off her richly woven tunic and bundled it up in her plain veil. Then she tied her girdle around her simple kirtle. With uncovered head and simple gown she wouldn't look so out of place. Nor would she so obviously fit any description.

What next, though? It was ridiculous, but she couldn't remember the name of the street on which Hugo had his home and business. In smaller northern towns, even in York, to ask for the house of Hugo and Mary, the vintners, would surely gain her directions, but in London? She doubted it.

Moreover, there were so many sly-seeming people here, so many rogues and ruffians, she hesitated to announce to the world that she was a lost stranger.

She let the press of the crowd move her past the stalls, remembering Waltham and the tinsmith's cart. If only Raoul would appear out of nowhere to help her.

Appear out of nowhere to kiss her?

That kiss, those feelings, and her rejection of his offer of marriage all troubled her mightily, but now was not the time to dwell on them. Instead, she sent a short, fierce petition for help up to Christ's mother.

Like an answer, the words popped into her brain. Corser Street.

Her knees almost gave way in relief. Sending a fervent prayer of thanks, Aline worked her way over to a pleasant-seeming women loading jars of honey and baskets of honey cakes into a little wagon.

"If you would be so kind, mistress, could you tell me the way to Corser Street?"

"Lost, love?" asked the woman. "Not surprising, the crazy way everything is these days. I'll be glad when it all settles back down again, even though it'll be bad for business. Corser Street?" She turned and called to the black-pudding seller next to her. "Davvy! Corser Street. Where is it?"

The man never stopped packing away his remaining sausages. "Over near Fetters Lane. Down near the river."

The honey woman turned back. "Well, love, you're aways from home, and that's the truth. But you follow this road to Cooper's Lane. Turn left there and it'll take you to the river. Corser Street's in that direction. You'll find it." She picked up a small honey cake and pressed it into Aline's hand. "Here, love. It'll keep up your strength."

Aline could willingly have hugged the woman for caring, but she just thanked her and hurried on. Or, rather, she would have hurried if the crowd had permitted it. As it was, she had to go with the flow of people, squeezed and buffeted by those trying to hurry anyway.

There were doubtless quieter streets nearby, but she was afraid of losing her way, and anyway, she was well hidden in such a crowd. To be even less conspicuous, she made herself stroll along and nibbled on the honey cake, trying to understand exactly what was going on.

She wondered why Jehanne felt she must be at the hearing, but knew that if her cousin was convinced she had something of import to tell the king, she was probably right. Jehanne was formidably clever.

Jehanne was probably also right in thinking that Galeran would stop her from appearing before the king if he could. This gave Aline some problems. Galeran was also formidably clever. If he thought it best that Jehanne not appear, he might be right.

So, should she go to Galeran and explain the situation, and leave it in his hands? Or should she go to Raoul and hope he'd help get Jehanne out of the convent tomorrow morning?

And how was that to be done?

Aline saw the words *Cooper's Lane* on a wall ahead, illustrated by a stack of barrels. She brushed the cake crumbs off her hands and worked through the crowd so she was ready to turn off when the street appeared.

The change was so abrupt that it felt as if Cooper's Lane were deserted, whereas in fact it was reasonably busy. It was clear, however, that few used it as a thoroughfare, perhaps because of the stacks of barrels standing outside each house. The people here were either the coopers and their apprentices and families, or purposeful businessmen inspecting products and placing orders.

Casks.

Wine.

The coopers surely knew all the vintners.

When one middle-aged man came out to roll a barrel back into his workshop, Aline spoke to him. "Excuse me, sir, but do you know the vintner Hugo who lives on Corser Street?"

The man straightened and looked her up and down. But then he winked and smiled. "And if I do, pretty maid?"

Aline's instinct was to shrink away, but she knew he was just teasing, so she made herself smile back. "I'm a new maid there, sir, and I've lost my way. Can you tell me how to get back?"

"From the country, I reckon," he said, eyes bright with curiosity. "From the north, I'd say."

She could have screamed with impatience, but he was clearly proud of his deduction. "How did you guess that?" she asked admiringly. "Yes, sir, I come from near Durham."

"A long way from home, and not surprising you're a mite lost. Right then." He touched her arm, but only to turn her to look down the street. "Go on down here until you come to that house that hangs out over the street. The one with the red trimming. See it?"

"Yes."

"There's a ginnel running between the houses there. Follow it through and you'll be in Ironmonger's Lane. There's another cut-through almost opposite. Take that and you'll be in St. Mark's Road. Turn left there a bit and you'll find Corser Street. You got that?"

"Yes," said Aline. "But why can't I go straight down here and turn right?"

"You're a canny one, aren't you?" he said admiringly. "This goes down to the docks, sweetling. I'd not send a pretty girl like you down there. You go the way I've told you."

"Thank you," she said sincerely. "Thank you very much."

He patted her arm. "Off you go, then."

Aline waved and skirted barrels down to the narrow passageway between the houses. As the cooper had said, it led to the ironmongers with their forges and clanging hammers, then into a wider street with varied merchants and inns.

"Left," she muttered to herself as she turned, already scanning the side streets for the one she sought. If only anything were familiar. But how could it be since she'd not ventured out of the house other than to be brought to St. Hilda's?

After a while she stopped and looked backward, wondering if she might have been wrong. Should she have turned right . . . ?

"Aline?"

Seventeen

The touch on the shoulder made Aline squeak and jump, but even as she whirled, she recognized the voice. She almost threw herself into Raoul's arms in the middle of the street.

"Are you all right?" he asked, steadying her with a hand on the arm, scanning her for damage.

"Yes, but Jehanne—"

He covered her lips with his finger, then wrapped an arm around her and led her off in what she believed to be the wrong direction. She felt wonderfully safe, though, and relished it as only a person who has experienced danger can do.

"Isn't Hugo's house the other way?"

"The king's men are there already, seeking you. I presume, having climbed the wall, you don't want to return?"

"Not at the moment. But I've got to tell you—"

Again he shushed her. "Not yet." He scanned the area, then turned her sharply to enter an inn.

"Ho, Paul!" he called out cheerfully to the enormous innkeeper, keeping Aline hugged indecently close to his side. "Any rooms to spare?"

The man's small eyes took in the two of them, then his belly bounced with his wheezing laughter. "You know I keep a few for emergencies, my friend. Down the corridor. Second on the right."

Raoul spun him a silver coin. "And a jug of wine."

The innkeeper turned a spigot on a huge cask and filled an earthenware jug with wine before handing it over with a wink.

Aline, still forced against Raoul by an unbreakable hold, tried to remember that she was on important business and Raoul was probably only trying to keep her safe. But the thought that he knew this man, and knew that he kept rooms free for men and their whores, made her want to scratch his eyes out.

In moments they were in a small room—a partitioned alcove really—containing a bed, a bench, and a table. And a settled-in stink.

Raoul let Aline go, and she stalked over to the bed and flipped back the covers to expose dirty sheets. "I hope you don't intend me to use this bed."

"Of course not. The wine's probably safe, though." He poured some into the two wooden beakers and passed one to her. "Drink. Then you can tell me what's going on. Quietly, though. These walls hardly deserve the name."

Aline clutched the beaker, fighting to calm her rage and keep her mind on important matters.

And failing.

"You find Ella as soon as you arrive at Heywood," she hissed, "and this place as soon as you arrive in London!"

"I wouldn't use that bed, either, Aline."

He looked not the tiniest bit guilty. Aline just turned away.

"Jehanne," he reminded her.

So she had to turn back and talk to him anyway. She did it, but with a scowl. "Jehanne is a prisoner at the convent," she said in the softest possible voice. "We all are, I suppose, but she is kept apart, and I don't like that."

He drew her over to his side so he could speak into her ear. "Galeran said as much. He doesn't like it either, but he spoke with her, and there didn't seem to be anything seriously wrong. He expects the matter to be over with by

tomorrow. He believes the king will favor his side over
Flambard. The bishop daren't even appear in the streets of
London for fear of his life. There's no reason for the king
to support him."

Aline resisted the temptation to cuddle up against his
broad chest. "Jehanne wants to attend the hearing."

"Let her want."

Aline frowned up at him, making her neck hurt. "She's
not a fool! She couldn't say why she has to be there, but
it's important. It's not some whim."

He lifted her to sit on the rickety table, more on a level
with him and face-to-face. "She's in the king's custody,
Aline. It will hardly turn him to her favor for her to escape
and confront him. Nor will your escapade. I thought the
idea was to convince the world that Jehanne's a weak
woman, distressed into foolishness by the death of her
child."

To be close, he was standing between her legs. Since he
seemed to think nothing of it, Aline tried to do the same.
"I know," she murmured, then swallowed to clear her throat.
"It bothers me too. But she is determined on it. So, should
we tell Galeran?" Unable to ignore their positions, she wriggled away slightly, causing the whole table to sway.

He put his hands on her hips. "Stay still. Telling Galeran
seems the reasonable thing to do."

"She doesn't want that, though."

Why couldn't she ignore his hands on her hips? It wasn't
an indecent contact. . . .

The way their bodies pressed together was, though, despite the layers of clothing between them. He didn't seem
to be disturbed at all, however. His mind was entirely on
Jehanne and Galeran's problems.

As it should be.

As hers should be . . .

"If I had to stake my sword on it," he said thoughtfully,
and his thumbs moved against her hipbones, making her

want to wriggle again, "I'd say the Lady Jehanne loves her husband as much as he loves her. Am I right?"

To tell him to stop that little movement would reveal how much it was affecting her. "Of course you are."

He frowned into her eyes. "So why doesn't she want him to know of her intentions?"

"Because he'd try to stop her, I suppose."

It was another battle, she realized. Whether he was aware of that movement or not, she would not admit that it had any effect on her.

He nodded. "So her purpose must be to stop him from facing Lowick in a court battle. Just as he's trying to prevent her becoming the focus of the case, and perhaps being punished for her sins. Ah, love," he remarked with a wry smile. "It leads even clever people into strange paths."

Aline was extremely glad that she hadn't let him know how his touch, his smile, his presence, could tangle her brain into love knots. "How fortunate that we are free of it and can think clearly," she said. Unfortunately, loudly.

He put his fingers over her lips, hushing her. But he was laughing. At her? At least he'd moved one of his hands.

She stopped herself from biting him, and when he removed his hand, merely said, "So, what shall we do?"

He became suitably somber. "First, find you a better place than this to stay. Not easy, London being as it is." He kissed her quickly, lightly, burningly.

As if it didn't matter.

"Wait here for a moment."

He slipped out the door and Aline leaped down off the table, almost upsetting it. It was horrible of her to be more concerned about Raoul and whores and her lust for him than about Jehanne and the king. But she seemed to have no control. She could force her logical mind to worry about Jehanne, about Lowick's claim to Donata, but deep inside was a place where Raoul was the only important person in the world.

And he couldn't keep his horse in its stall for more than a couple of days at a time!

She sat miserably on the bench.

Young men were allowed to spend their seed on whores or easy servants. Since it wasn't practical for many of them to marry, what else were they to do? She'd known her brothers were doing that sort of thing and it hadn't bothered her at all. She wanted Raoul, however, to live as pure as a hermit. Or to spend his seed with her.

A hot, curling ache between her thighs made her leap to her feet just as he returned.

"What is it?" he asked, looking around for trouble, knife springing into his hand.

"Nothing! You'd just been gone a while."

He slid the knife back in its sheath. "Just long enough to go to the public room and get an address from Paul." He suddenly pulled her into his arms, rubbing gently at her back. "Don't be afraid. I won't let anyone hurt you."

You could hurt me, she thought. You could hurt me by going back to your sun-bright home alone. You could hurt me by taking me. You could hurt me by stealing my virtue. You could hurt me by leaving me pure. . . .

He pushed her gently back, studying her with his all-too-perceptive eyes. "Better?"

She nodded, wondering why life wasn't as simple as it was supposed to be. If she had to fall in love, why hadn't it been with a sensible northern man?

He had a blue cloth in his hand and held it out. "Put this on."

She wrapped it around her head, hiding her hair entirely.

"Good girl. Come on, then."

He guided her out into the warrenlike inn and took a different path, so they emerged into a backyard complete with pig. They picked their way through a number of similar yards until they emerged through another tavern onto a wide street.

"Cheapside," he said, and steered her across it and into a side street. Halfway down, he stopped to knock on a door.

It opened and a gaunt woman looked them over.

"We want a room for the night," said Raoul.

"Sixpence."

Raoul handed over the coin, and the woman led them down a corridor and up some rickety stairs. The place was as dingy and cramped as the other one, but at least it smelled clean. When the woman reached their room, it even had a door of sorts, held on to the wall by leather hinges.

She walked off without a word, and Aline looked around. Table, bench, and bed. Just like the other place. But clean. She checked the sheets and found, as she expected, that they looked and smelled fresh.

"Definitely a better class of place," she said, but couldn't help sneering.

"So it would seem. I'll have to remember it."

Aline gritted her teeth but resisted the urge to comment.

"Now," said Raoul, "I'm going to visit the convent to see if I can get in to talk to Jehanne. I need to find out—"

"You can't leave me here!" Aline was ashamed of the weak words as soon as they escaped, but she was adrift in a strange world and terrified.

He took her hands. "Hush, love. You'll be safe here. Men come to this house with a companion, not in search of one. And according to Paul, Mistress Helswith runs this place like a tight ship. If she has trouble, she has a clutch of strong sons next door at the farrier's."

His words were reasonable, but Aline would still like to cling to him and never let him go. She made herself smile up at him and say lightly, "Oh. All right."

He touched her cheek. "That's my brave girl. . . ." Hand curled around her neck, he kissed her lips. Then—almost with a sigh—he gathered her into his arms to kiss her more thoroughly.

Aline's conscience and her sense of caution commanded that she resist.

She lacked the will.

She suspected that if he tumbled her onto the bed, she'd probably lack the will to resist there too.

As she savored the taste of his mouth and pressed closer to the hot strength of his body, she began to think of tumbling *him* to the bed!

He drew back from the kiss, slowly, like a person pulling out of honey, and she felt the same sticky attachment protesting their separation. "Don't go." The words escaped from her heart, from her demanding desire. "Oh, don't listen to me!" she added quickly. "I know I'm safe."

"Do you, indeed?" he murmured, arms still around her. "I'll have to come back here for the night, you know."

She knew why he made it a warning.

There really wasn't any choice, however, except returning to the convent. "I wouldn't want to spend the night here alone."

"That's what I mean."

"But you'd better go."

"Yes."

They were talking like idiots, or drunkards deep in their pots.

Aline braced her hands on his chest and gave a mighty shove so his hold broke, and he fell back a step. Suddenly he grinned. "Remember that push later. Here." He gave her his knife, a long, gleamingly sharp blade with a hilt of chased silver set with amber. "Can you use it if there's trouble?"

"Yes."

"I thought so. But don't knife one of the king's guards if they find you. That's just for rapists." He turned at the door. "Including me."

"You couldn't rape me . . ."

"I wish I had such absolute faith."

". . . because I can't imagine resisting."

He closed his eyes briefly. "Then God help us both."

"Amen," whispered Aline to the closed door.

Raoul made his way through the London streets, trying to keep his mind on the serious matters at hand, aware only of aching desire and a luscious maid who perhaps wouldn't fight him hard enough in the night.

He wanted Aline, but he wanted her as his wedded wife. He didn't want to dishonor her. But he wanted her in a way he'd never wanted another woman in his life.

He groaned aloud, gaining him a funny look from a merchant hurrying by. Galeran and Jehanne, he said silently to himself.

Almost having to move his lips to make his mind concentrate, he went over recent events. The king had agreed to hear Galeran's case. Galeran intended to ask that Jehanne be forgiven by society as well as himself, and that they keep Donata. There was no reason to think the king would deny these petitions, but then, why had he seized Jehanne and Donata?

Organizing an escape, however, was very dangerous. Galeran had returned from the convent concerned and angry, but he still seemed to think the confinement there of little importance. He was confident that the king would approve his case and Jehanne would go free.

So why did Jehanne want to be rescued so she could intrude upon the king? Aline was right, Jehanne was no fool. Nor, despite her past mistakes, was she foolishly willful. Raoul very much feared she was intent upon offering herself up for punishment to prevent Galeran from having to face Lowick at sword's length.

If Raoul aided and abetted her in that, he'd probably end up facing his friend in combat himself!

When he arrived at the convent, he rang the bell hanging

beside the portal. When the peep door opened, he asked, "I come seeking news of the Lady Aline. Has she been found?"

"No, sir."

"May I come in and speak to the mother superior on the matter?"

Somewhat reluctantly, the convent door was opened fully so he could step through. In moments he was in the mother superior's plain room.

"You have news of the silly child?" the mother superior asked, annoyance warring with concern.

"I came with the same question. She is not used to such a city. I fear for her."

"As do I," snapped the woman. "I have no idea what can have possessed her to do such a thing. And she almost a nun herself!"

"Could I speak to the Lady Jehanne? I wonder if Aline has relatives or friends nearby with whom she might have taken refuge."

The mother superior frowned at him for a moment, but then nodded and led him out of her room, around the cloister, to another. Raoul took in as much of the place as he could.

She unlocked a door and led him in. Jehanne was kneeling in prayer, but when spoken to, she jerked around as if startled.

"Does she know?" Raoul asked. He tried to make it soft, but Jehanne heard anyway.

"Know what?" she asked, rising sharply and giving a gasp, almost of pain.

"That Aline has disappeared," Raoul said, watching her carefully.

She was steadying herself with a hand on the prie-dieu, and looked paler than usual. "Disappeared? How? What is going on?" Her very blankness told him she was hiding something. Then she added, "Donata?" But Raoul knew she had no real fear for her child.

"The child is safe with her nurse," said the mother superior. "For some reason, your cousin tricked her way out of St. Hilda's and has not been seen since. London is a city of many dangers."

Jehanne's eyes moved to Raoul, seeking truth. He deliberately didn't give it to her. "I wondered if she might have friends or family in the city."

"No. None that I know of." Her hand on the prie-dieu tightened so her knuckles shone white. "Oh, God help her. . . ."

He couldn't torment her like this. He gave a tiny nod.

She almost gave them away then, but covered her sigh of relief by turning it into a sob, covering her face. "Oh, by the sweet Virgin, what other disaster can there be? And it is all my fault, all my fault!" She pulled down her hands and stared at him. "Find her, Raoul. Help us!"

That last plea, he knew, was not about Aline.

He was still troubled by the whole matter, especially about keeping secrets from Galeran, but he nodded. "I'll do my best. The king has men out searching for her too. Do you have any idea why she might have run away?"

She shook her head.

"You know that the king is to hear your case tomorrow?"

"Yes. I wish I could be there."

That was direct. "I doubt you will be called to attend. And I doubt Galeran would want it."

"Galeran seems to want to pretend I had no part in this."

"Even he cannot hide it. There is no reason for you to attend. You have nothing to offer or prove."

"Perhaps not." But her eyes sent a different message.

Raoul saw the mother superior growing impatient at their talk. "If you have a message for Galeran, I could take it to him."

"You can tell him I want to be at his side during the hearing, but I doubt it will sway him."

Raoul nodded. "And meanwhile you are all right? I feared some mistreatment had made Aline run from here."

"I am content."

With that, he had to leave. It was getting dark—the bells of compline sounded as he left—and he must return to Aline. He stopped at Corser Street to find Galeran pacing, haggard.

"Aline is safe," Raoul said.

"God be thanked!" Galeran grasped his arm. "Unharmed? Where is she?"

"In a safe place. I didn't feel able to bring her back here."

Galeran ran his hands through his hair. "No. I wouldn't be surprised to find the house is watched. I wish I understood what is behind all this."

"I think I should return to her. She is rather frightened."

"Then why flee the convent in the first place?" Galeran was relaxing enough to be irritated, but—thank heavens—too distracted to pursue his own question. Instead, he looked sharply at Raoul. "Are you intending to spend the night with her?"

"In a manner of speaking."

Galeran pulled out his silver cross containing water from the River Jordan. "Swear on this. Swear that you will not dishonor her."

Raoul looked at the relic. "You might trust me, my friend."

"I do. I trust you not to break your sworn oath, no matter what the temptation."

Raoul placed his hand on the cross and made the oath, feeling a comfort from it, from the reinforcing of his good intentions. This made him wonder yet again about the wisdom of keeping secrets from Galeran.

Ah, well. He had a night to consider it, since he wouldn't be doing more interesting things.

"I also stopped by the convent," he said, "and spoke to Jehanne. She seems well, though rather strained by it all. That's hardly surprising. You look stretched tight as a bowstring yourself. Everyone is safe for now. Get some sleep."

Galeran laughed and rolled his shoulders. "Yes, nursemaid."

"You may have to fight tomorrow. You need your wits sharp and your body rested."

And, by God, thought Raoul, he could sympathize a little with Jehanne. Standing by to watch Galeran face death would be harder than facing the ordeal himself.

In the convent, the mother superior returned to the cell, armed with her rod. "What is your foolish cousin up to, Lady Jehanne?"

"I don't know."

"I think you do. You are a wickedly willful woman, and you need to pay for her peril as well as for your sins."

Jehanne turned to kneel, accepting the mother superior's judgment. She had not considered how Aline was to recruit Raoul's help, and thus had put her into danger. She'd do it again, though, to keep Galeran safe.

"May the Lord forgive his wretched sinner."

"Amen."

Jehanne sincerely prayed for forgiveness as the strokes began, applied this time with considerably more vigor. By the fifth stroke, her control broke, and she cried out.

Raoul returned to Helswith's house by a circuitous route, making as sure as possible that he wasn't followed. As he went he considered the options. He'd assessed the convent, and it would be child's play to remove Jehanne from it. Violating a church establishment, however, was not a risk to be taken lightly.

Even if he extracted Jehanne without penalty, he would then have to escort her to Westminster and into the king's presence, thus proclaiming the sinful crime to all. He found it hard to imagine that this would make the king more likely to favor their case.

Underlying, or perhaps overlaying, all these concerns was the thought that he was about to spend the night with Aline, who strained his control to breaking point.

She'd accomplished her mission and contacted him, so she could be returned to the convent. There were two arguments against that. One was that she might be punished. The other was that one of his plans for liberating Jehanne involved returning Aline tomorrow morning.

And, of course, there was the fact that he wanted this night, tormenting though it promised to be.

Just a night to talk.

A night to hold her.

A night to teach her a little more about her wonderful body . . .

He cursed softly. He was already hard.

He gave thanks for his sworn oath to Galeran which made weakness impossible.

In Cheapside, he bought a wineskin, a roasted rabbit, and a loaf of bread. He was hungry, and he didn't think someone with Aline's rich curves would be a sparse eater.

Dame Helswith let him into the house, which now hummed like a beehive with illicit activities. Laughter, gasps, groans, bumps . . .

Hurrying up to Aline, he berated himself for not finding a better place. But what other place? He was sure the king's men would have checked the inns, and even if he knew other private households well enough to ask for lodging, they would not want to house a fugitive.

No, this was best, but it offended him mightily that his future wife even enter such a place.

He rapped gently on the door, saying, "It's me. Raoul," before entering. He had no desire to be knifed.

Even with the warning, Aline was standing ready, knife grasped competently and held close to her body, ready for a killing thrust.

He grinned with delight. "Ah, Aline, you are a splendid woman."

"Am I? I thought I was a frightened one." And her eyes were still wide with fear.

"It's what people do when they're frightened that really matters." He put his purchases on the table. A rather more substantial one than the rickety assembly of planks in Paul's crude room. He could sit her on this one. . . . "Do you want to keep the knife?"

She looked at it, then shuddered and tossed it on the table. "No, thank you. If anyone attacks, you can handle it."

As long as it's not me.

He used it to cut the bread, then tore the rabbit into chunks. "Eat. Drink."

She picked up a thin leg. "What happened at the convent?"

"I was able to reassure Jehanne that you were safe. She also managed to tell me directly that she wants to be at the hearing." He squirted some wine into his mouth and swallowed. "You're right. She seems serious about it. Not at all petulant."

He passed her the wineskin, but she just clutched it. "Jehanne is never petulant. You probably haven't seen her at her best. She's so strong. So brave . . ."

"I'm not sure women are supposed to be strong and brave." He was partly teasing, but he knew that a woman like Jehanne was not the wife for him.

"You prefer them weak and timid?" Aline asked, turning rigid with affront.

"Perhaps just a little less likely to rush into trouble."

She raised the skin and tilted it to shoot a stream of wine into her mouth. "I see," she remarked, wiping her mouth. "But of course we women aren't supposed to mind when men—driven by their strength and bravery, not to mention their pride and boneheadedness—rush into trouble, then come limping home to be soothed and mended."

"I'd like to limp home to be soothed and mended by you, Aline."

She stared at him, face softening into confusion. She had the uncapped wineskin clutched in her arms and must have squeezed it. A stream of wine shot out to hit the wall.

He laughed and rescued it. "Let's not argue or talk of things that can wait. Eat, and then we'll try to get some sleep amid all the noise."

She colored slightly as she pulled a bit of meat off the rabbit. "I've never heard people be quite so noisy about—"

"Perhaps they feel less inhibited here than in the castle hall."

She popped the meat into her mouth and chewed. "But I've heard groans and screams. . . ."

As if to confirm her point, a choked wail echoed through the house, building then fading into irregular yelps. Raoul felt his own face heat. "It's probably an indication of pleasure not pain, Aline."

"Pleasure?"

"Oh, Christ's crown, we can't stay here." Raoul had never been a great user of houses of convenience such as this, so he'd not realized just how intrusive the other inhabitants would be. It wasn't merely that it embarrassed Aline, and even embarrassed him a bit. It was too arousing.

He gathered the food and drink. "Come on."

"Where?" Aline moved quickly and put herself between him and the door. "Where? I know as well as you that word will have been sent to inns and hostelries. If you're going to take me anywhere, it will have to be back to the convent."

"Perhaps that would be as well."

"I don't want to go back. I know the mother superior's type. She is doubtless ready with her rod."

"She wouldn't dare. . . ."

"She would probably claim that I'm as good as a nun and thus under her jurisdiction. We stay here."

"I doubt we'll get much rest."

"I can sleep almost anywhere, under almost any circumstances."

It would be foolish to leave, and so he gave in. "Very well. We stay." He spread the food out again and sat on the bed to eat. As he'd thought, she had a hearty appetite, and did her fair share of the damage. After a while it did become possible to ignore the surrounding noises except the occasional shriek or wail.

"Are you sure . . . ?" she asked after one sharp cry.

"Yes." He wasn't entirely, but he didn't feel up to explaining to Aline the peculiar ways in which some people found sexual pleasure.

She shook her head and chewed on the last of the bread. When it was all gone, he pulled back the thin covers on the bed. "Come on. In you go."

She did look wary at that, but slipped under the covers, wriggling over against the wall, the bracken in the mattress rustling with every move.

"It's all right. You can have the whole bed."

"You can't sleep properly on the floor."

"I'll manage."

"Raoul de Jouray, stop being foolish. You need a good night's rest too. Get into bed. I promise to scream and fight if you try to rape me."

He couldn't help laughing. "Truly?" he teased.

"Truly. I have no intention of losing my maidenhead in a place like this."

She was completely serious, and being Aline, she would fight like a she-wolf. He eased into the bed, keeping as close to the edge as he could. "Perhaps I do like women who are strong and brave after all."

"Of course you do. The other sort are useless." With that, she rolled over to face the wall, giving all the appearance of someone about to go to sleep.

Raoul turned slightly to stare at her back. He didn't know what he'd expected, but it wasn't this. She should be flustered, embarrassed, restless under the same needs that tormented him. He had intended to at least hold her in his arms as they talked, as they suffered sleeplessness brought on by the noisy house.

A change in her breathing, and then a slight snore on each in breath told him she really had gone straight to sleep.

He grinned up at the ceiling. Aline of Burstock was a remarkable women in every way.

To his surprise, her regular breathing lulled him to sleep far sooner than he'd expected. And if he woke in the morning resting comfortably against her, her warmth and subtle perfume soothing his senses, at least nothing had happened in the night to violate his oath.

Eighteen

The house was silent now, but faint sounds from the street and the light cutting through a gap in the wooden wall told him it was early morning. Time to attack a crucial day.

He put out a hand and shook Aline gently, nobly resisting the temptation to stoke along the curve of her side, hip, and thigh. He expected to have to be more vigorous, but with a grunt, her breathing changed and she sat up, blinking.

"Is it morning? Already?" She pushed strands of hair off her face and shook herself like a puppy climbing out of the water.

Then she looked at him and suddenly, devastatingly, colored from collar to hairline.

"Good morning," he said.

Her eyes darted around as if expecting to find something new and different in the plain cubicle. Then they settled on him again. "I went right to sleep."

He managed not to laugh. "You said you would."

"What did you do?"

"Eventually, I went to sleep too."

Her eyes did their nervous dance again. "So you didn't . . . ?"

He sat up and captured her face in his hands, turning her so she had to look at him. "Aline, when I make love to you, you will know all about it. And remember it. I promise you that."

She stared at him, pupils so huge as to almost make her blue eyes dark. "Truly?"

He was again tempted to laugh, or perhaps even to get angry, but he did neither. "Truly."

She pulled out of his hold, took a deep breath, and blew it out. "That's all right, then. I'm sorry. I suddenly thought, you see, that it might be impossible for a man to be so close to a woman in a bed for so long without his baser instincts taking over. Of course," she added with a sliding look, "I suppose it depends how much he wants to . . . Could you let me out, please?"

With an exhale almost as noisy as hers, Raoul grabbed her shoulders, forced her down, and rolled on top of her.

"What—"

"Stop chattering. If you force your skittering mind down to the lower part of your body, you should be able to feel just how much I want to make love to you. If I'm going to be so painfully noble, I at least want the credit for it."

Her eyes were still beguilingly dark, and now her full lips parted softly, temptingly. "Oh."

This must surely, thought Raoul, be the most challenging, the most difficult thing he had ever done in his life. Despite his thundering heart and a proof of devotion that was beginning to protest urgently, he kept his voice calm. "I desire you, Aline. Very much. As soon as other matters are settled, we are going to talk about the future and see if there is a way we can be together. The tortures of the damned, however, would not push me into dishonoring you, especially without your consent, and without you waking up. Which, when I think about it, would be just about impossible."

"Oh," she said again. "I'm sorry. But I couldn't know for sure. . . ."

"I suppose not."

She licked her lips, which would have been wickedly cruel if she'd had any idea of how it affected him. "What constitutes dishonoring?"

"Aline!"

"I was just thinking that perhaps you could kiss me. . . ."

"Just how strong do you think I am?"

"Infinitely." And she meant it, poor, deluded maid.

He pushed off her and rolled off the bed. "At the moment I feel as strong as Donata. Come on. Get up and let's get out of here. We have actions to take."

She scrambled off the bed, tidying her clothes and looking ridiculously deprived. He was very tempted to spank her, for he didn't believe she was nearly as innocent about all this as she pretended to be.

"What are we going to do, then?" she asked as she wound the blue cloth around her head again.

"I'm not going to get Jehanne out of the convent."

Her hands stopped. "What? Why not?"

The end of the cloth began to fall loose, so he caught it and tucked it in, glad of any excuse to touch her, despite the dangers.

"Since I didn't go instantly to sleep, I had time to think. It can't do any good to thwart the king in that way. On the other hand, I do believe that Jehanne has something of import to add to the hearing. I'm going to get into the convent so I can have private speech with her, then I'll convey her information, make her argument, or whatever is required."

She leveled her severe brows at him. "The penalties for invading a religious house are rather harsh. Are you sure . . . ?"

"I'm not sure of anything, but this is my best judgment. And how, exactly, did you expect me to get her out without violating a religious house? Now," he said, ushering her out of the room, "I saw the cloister. Tell me as much about the rest of the convent as you can."

As they made their way out of the house and into Cheapside, she told him everything she knew.

"I can go in over the wall," he said, as they hurried along. "But noise might be a problem."

"I think you need to go in during chapel anyway so there'd be few people around." She glanced at the sky, judging the light. "You've missed prime. It will have to be terce, which is the time of the hearing."

"Christ's crown, that's too late." By the time they reached the lane behind the convent, they hadn't come up with a solution to that problem.

Raoul assessed the rough wooden wall. "Getting over that will be simple. I'll just have to hope that no one hears."

"Faint hope of that. Why don't I create a distraction?"

"What kind of distraction?" he asked. But by Christ's crown he loved the way she was his partner in this.

"If I turn up disheveled and incoherent, it will draw everyone's attention."

"And get you a whipping."

"And what will you get if you're caught invading a nunnery? Anyway, they probably won't punish me until I get my wits back. By then, I hope, we'll all be free."

So she, like Jehanne, was trying to save a man from trouble. There was no point in arguing about it here. "What will you tell them?"

"Nothing. I'll be completely mad." She twisted her mouth and rolled her eyes. "At least until after terce."

He had to laugh at the sight. *"Then* what will you tell them?"

"That the big city frightened my wits away? I hope by then it's all over."

Raoul shook his head, wishing she didn't sometimes seem so young. But he did need the distraction she could provide. "Very well. You escaped, thinking to contact Galeran and tell him of your predicament, but got lost and had to hide all night, terrified of beggars and bandits. Now you are desperate to return to the safety of the convent."

She looked around and stepped into a shadow between two houses, already unwinding her headcloth. She tore off the ribbons at the end of her already unraveling plaits and fingered them out. Raoul followed and gripped the shoulder of her kirtle to rip it a few inches so it sagged. He scooped up some dirt and rubbed it into the cloth and into her skin.

Proud that he'd not let any of his lewd thoughts show, he looked her over and nodded. "Ready?"

She smiled. "Ready."

"Brave girl." He kissed her lightly on the brow, then pushed her off down the lane toward the front of the convent.

In moments he heard the convent doorbell clang stridently. He counted to three, glanced around to be sure that no one was nearby, stepped back, then ran at the wall, leaping to grasp the top.

As soon as his fingers caught, he realized he had a problem. The wall was not very sturdy. For a moment it felt as if his pull might bring it down rather than him up. But it held, and he braced his hips against the top. A glance showed him nuns milling in the cloister gardens, and no one in the herb garden.

He swung over and dropped, ducking immediately into a corner behind a fragrant bush.

Wailing pinpointed Aline on the other side of the cloister, and a burst of exclamations and chatter implied a large gathering. Raoul hoped that soon the matter would be taken inside one of the buildings. It was going to be a little difficult to sneak close to Jehanne's cell with the whole convent gathered in the cloister garden.

Then he realized that they might bring Aline into the infirmary. Time to get out of here. He followed the first part of their plan, slipping into the infirmarian's workroom, through the thankfully unused infirmary itself, toward the convent's chapel.

There was no way to know what was beyond the solid door, but he'd be surprised if the altar were left completely unattended. The door would probably open into the side of the altar so that the sick could see the Mass. He could only hope it was far enough away from anyone keeping vigil there.

He took a deep breath, eased down the latch, and pulled it open a finger-length.

Two nuns knelt in prayer in front of the altar, but their heads were bowed and the door was slightly behind them and in shadow. Raoul didn't think they would notice him unless he made a noise. Thanking God that the door itself was silent, he opened it wide enough to slip through, closed it, then moved quickly down against the chapel wall to the main doors at the end.

This, however, was already farther than Aline's knowledge could guide him, and he hadn't seen the chapel door from the cloister. He might open it and be in full view of the community. He didn't think so, for even if they were still in the garden, they should be at the far side, but there was no guarantee.

Raoul shrugged. It had always been his way to make the best plan possible, then carry it through without further fretting. He carefully opened the door far enough to look.

Ah. God be praised. The chapel entrance was guarded by a deep porch set upon stone pillars. The space between the pillars provided excellent concealment from most directions. Raoul went through the door, again closing it neatly behind him, and moved between two pillars to consider his next move.

This was undoubtedly the tricky part.

Leaning out, he saw a cluster of black and white through the flowering bushes. That must be the nuns around Aline.

Why, by Saint Sever, didn't they take her inside somewhere?

He waited, counting slowly, but nothing changed. Oh, well, their attention seemed so focused on Aline, he'd have to take his chances.

The porch opened into the cloister walk, which went around all four sides of the garden. The walk itself was deep, roofed, and fronted by pillared arches so that in the sunlight it was deeply shadowed. With luck, even if one of the nuns saw him, they'd see just a shadowy figure and assume him to be one of the community.

Raoul walked normally, therefore, as he left the porch, turned right, and headed toward Jehanne's room. He wasn't actually intending to go to her door, since it was too close to the nuns and would be locked. He had his eye open for a passage through to the back of the rooms. He could talk to Jehanne through the small window.

Unfortunately, he didn't find any passageway at all.

It didn't seem right to curse in a religious house, but he did it anyway, silently. He couldn't go any farther, or he'd be too close to the chattering, exclaiming nuns. There didn't seem a lot of point in going back.

There had to be a way to other parts of the convent, but it must be through one of the many doors.

Which door?

He was trying to decide, when Jehanne took a hand. She suddenly started calling, "Someone! What is going on? Is that Aline? What's happened?"

Then she thumped on her door. Hastily moving back toward the bend of the cloister, Raoul judged her alarm to be genuine, and quite reasonable. All she would be able to hear would be her cousin's cries.

As Raoul watched, a figure emerged from the huddle. The mother superior stalked over to Jehanne's door, pulling a key out of a pouch on her belt. Opening the door, she snapped, "Compose yourself, Lady Jehanne. Your foolish cousin has returned, and appears unharmed though much distressed." She then slammed the door and marched back to her community. "Bring the girl into the chapter house. This is all most disorderly. A terrible disruption . . ."

But as her voice faded and the group flowed off into a building, a wild-haired, limp Aline in their midst, Raoul noticed that she really had been disrupted. She'd left the key in the lock. In moments the cloister was deserted and Raoul could slip down, turn the lock, and enter Jehanne's cell.

She was pacing, but she froze at his entrance, staring as if she couldn't believe her eyes.

Which was hardly surprising.

Then she gasped, "Oh, Sweet Mary be praised! It was all a ruse? Thank heavens." She was already heading for the door, but he grasped her shoulders to stop her.

She cried out.

He instantly let her go, watching as she panted, then controlled her breathing.

He didn't need to be told. "You've been beaten?"

She straightened as if nothing were the matter, and he thought she might refuse to answer. But then she grimaced. "Every three hours."

"Holy Father! By whose orders?"

"Bishop Flambard's."

It took him a moment to control his own feelings. "Why didn't you say anything? Galeran or I could have stopped this."

She was once more controlled and cool, however. Once more the Jehanne he had come to admire, and perhaps to fear.

"I didn't want it stopped."

"You take pleasure in pain?"

"Am I mad?"

"Why, then?" But he could guess.

"You know as well as I do that I deserve to be beaten. That the world will never be content until I am punished . . ."

"And this way Galeran will not be forced to do it," he completed. She was right, and even though his instincts protested her acting against her husband's wishes, he admired her for her courage.

He still couldn't help wishing she were a less militant

woman, though, and he didn't want to be around when Galeran heard about this.

"There's another advantage," she was saying, and she even smiled with satisfaction. "I don't think the king will be happy that the bishop has taken action before he has a chance to rule on the matter."

Raoul realized he was gaping, and closed his mouth. His mother and sisters were not weak or silly women, but he didn't think any of them would be willing to accept a beating every few hours for such a logical, political reason.

Yet again, though, she was right. She'd created a weapon they could use against Flambard.

"What were you intending to do?" he asked. "Burst in on the king and bare your back?"

She began to answer, but then stared at him. "What do you mean, 'intending'?" If she'd been a man, he'd have prepared to defend himself.

"I am not going to help you escape from here, Jehanne. It would not work in your favor with the king, believe me. However, I will take your words to him."

Even though she was weaponless, danger flickered in her eyes, but in the next moment he saw her consider his words and accept them, no matter how reluctantly. It was probably the reluctance that made her swing away to face the crucifix on the wall.

By the Cross, she was a woman in a million.

Thanks be. Many more like her and the world would shiver and fall.

"Do you have any idea how hard I find this?" she asked.

Raoul remembered sympathizing with her about having to stand and watch. Perhaps the key to understanding Jehanne was to put himself in her place. He'd hate to have to just wait for his fate, and that of the ones he loved, to be decided by others. He didn't know if he could meekly accept beating after beating in their cause, though.

He was a fighter, not a martyr, and at heart, he thought, so was she.

"I think I do understand," he said gently. "But if you want to help Galeran, you must stay here, hard though it will be." Then, however, he stopped his pious lecture. "Hell's cinders. That means another beating."

She turned back to face him. "That doesn't matter." Astonishingly, he could see she meant it. "What does matter is that the king give Donata to us, not Raymond. And that Galeran and Raymond not fight. I will do anything to achieve those ends."

Raoul raised his brows. "Do you not believe Galeran can win? Even if you think him the lesser warrior, do you not believe that God will decide right from wrong?"

"God probably has better things to do," she said testily, "but I'm sure Galeran has a fair chance of winning. I saw him fight you."

"So?"

"So Raymond does not deserve to die."

It was as if the earth had changed to quicksand beneath Raoul's feet. "Are you telling me your concern is for *him?*"

"Yes." She met his anger without flinching. In fact, with exasperation. "I love Galeran more than life itself, Raoul! But I cannot let an innocent man suffer to ease my way."

"Innocent?"

"What did he do, this dark villain? He loved me. Poor fool, he still does. His feelings are as much for Heywood as for myself, but it is love all the same. He hoped Galeran was dead. That might be uncharitable, but it is hardly an offense worthy of death. . . ."

"He committed adultery with you!"

Her color flared then, but she spoke calmly. "Have you never had sex with a willing married woman?" Before he could find a way to make 'yes' sound like 'no,' she went on. "Do you deserve to die for it?"

"If the husband had caught me at it, perhaps!"

She cocked her head slightly, looking almost amused. "So, Raoul, do you think you can take my words to the king and make my arguments persuasively?"

He muttered words that shouldn't be spoken in such a place, imagining himself standing before the king of England and his advisers, with Galeran by his side, and trying to make this case. By the Nails and Spear, he wished he were safe home in Guyenne.

But he could see what the cunning woman was up to.

"You are still not leaving here, Jehanne."

"You cannot make a case you don't believe in!" The tightening of her face showed that she'd hoped to scare him off the task. He admired her, but he'd like to throttle her too.

"I'll do my best. Now, let me see your back. I need to be able to swear to it."

She glared at him, but puffed out a defeated breath, disconcertingly like Aline for a moment. Then, wincing, she pulled off her embroidered tunic and turned. "I split the back of my kirtle so it would be easily seen."

He'd seen men flayed by a whip, and this wasn't so bad, but his jaw clenched at the sight of the network of swollen weals. It must be exquisitely tender to the touch, and yet she was willing to stay here to receive more strokes.

Irrationally, he again wanted to throttle her.

"How many strokes each time?" he asked, hearing the gruffness in his own voice.

"Ten." She turned back and her face paled as she tried to pull her tunic over her head.

He went to help her. "You can't take another ten."

The words were foolish and her look told him she thought so too. People could take the pain they had to. The only escape was death.

He rubbed a hand over his stubbly face. "When Galeran finds out I left you here . . ." He shook his head at the mere thought. "Come on. I'll get you out. Though I don't know how you're going to climb the wall—"

"No." She stepped away from his guiding hand. "You're correct about the king. Submission will carry more weight than intrusion. And think how my sufferings will cut my time in purgatory!" She threw it out as a joke, but her calm strength broke for a moment, causing her lips to tremble before she bit them. "Of your kindness, though, my friend, try to release me before sext."

He put out a hand to cradle her head, and drew her against his chest. She neither held him nor resisted, but the way she leaned for a moment told him much.

"It will soon be over," he said. "And I swear on my eternal soul to make sure that your sufferings are not in vain, that your cause is upheld. You have fought your fight and deserve victory. You will have your daughter, and Galeran, safe. And Raymond of Lowick will not die."

She pulled back at that, almost her usual self. "Or suffer in any significant way."

He wanted to throttle her again. There were any number of sufferings short of death. "Or suffer in any significant way," he agreed, adding with a sigh, "My life used to be simple once."

"I assume Aline has come to no great harm?"

It was not as irrelevant as it sounded, as they both knew.

"Yes. She was just creating a distraction. We can only hope your stern mother superior doesn't decide to punish her too. I must go."

"Thank you, Raoul. I will pray for you."

He kissed her hand. "And I will pray for you. God's strength be with you."

With that, Raoul peeped through the opening in the door. The cloister still appeared deserted, so he slipped out.

In fact, there was a sister walking at the far end near the chapel, but she didn't see him, and was soon out of view. Though he hated to do it, he locked the door again. As the lock clicked back into place, he heard the wail of an infant on the other side of the cloister.

He moved quickly away, retracing his route, suspecting that soon someone would be bringing Donata to her mother. He tried to imagine the course Jehanne had coolheadedly chosen for herself—feeding her baby every few hours, doubtless playing with Donata to summon baby smiles, then being beaten in between so that Galeran would not have to punish her.

And, in a way, so the man she had used would not suffer for her acts.

An extraordinary woman, but he was glad he wasn't married to her.

Since the coast seemed clear, Raoul went straight into the infirmary herb garden, fighting the temptation to go back to rescue Aline. What if she were even now being beaten for her escape?

He jumped up onto the roof of the infirmary, telling himself that a few strokes of the rod wouldn't do her any lasting harm. She'd doubtless had many such punishments in her life. He didn't think Aline was one to keep out of trouble all the time.

He ran lightly along the slope, wondering at himself. He'd never been one to turn squeamish over wounds and punishments. Life contained pain.

He wanted to guard Aline from all pain forevermore.

Foolishness.

But he seemed to be foolish these days.

He lay flat on the edge of the roof until a trio of gossiping women passed down the lane, then dropped down to the ground there. He brushed himself off and hurried toward Corser Street, wondering whether to tell Galeran about this after all.

He knew his friend would feel betrayed to have such matters hidden from him. On the other hand, to know about Jehanne's sufferings might muddy Galeran's thinking at the hearing. In fact, he might ignore the hearing in order to rescue his wife.

Logic said to keep Galeran in ignorance, but Raoul considered how he'd feel if the woman were Aline. By the time he reached Corser Street, Raoul was ready to tell Galeran all and let him decide how to handle it. Galeran, however, had already gone to Westminster, leaving a note asking Raoul to follow.

Raoul changed into a fresher and finer tunic, tormented now by the thought of Jehanne's next beating. It couldn't be very long to terce. He muttered curses to himself as he realized there was absolutely nothing he could do to stop it. If he told Galeran at Westminster, by the time any action was taken it would be over.

He had to try, though.

In a mood to pick a fight with someone, he set off for Westminster on foot, since speed was more important than show.

He hurried past the man without recognizing him, then swung back. "Lord FitzRoger!"

The king's champion turned and stepped away from the three men-at-arms who accompanied him on some errand. It was clear that he recognized Raoul but couldn't remember his name, which was hardly surprising when he must have met hundreds in the past weeks.

"Raoul de Jouray, companion of Galeran of Heywood."

"Ah, yes. The lord of Heywood's matter is to be settled shortly. Are you lost, sir?"

"No. I'm on my way to Westminster. I have a concern you might be able to assist me with, though, if you would be so kind."

"I am not engaged in anything urgent."

Raoul had acted on impulse, and now he was running over it in his mind, seeking hazards. He saw none, but that didn't mean there weren't any. He couldn't, however, do nothing and ever face Galeran again.

"The Lady Jehanne of Heywood, Lord Galeran's wife, is being held at St. Hilda's convent."

"So I understand."

"She is being punished there, and as far as I know, not by the king's command."

FitzRoger had been politely attentive, but now he was interested. "By whose command, then? Her husband's?"

"By the Bishop of Durham's."

As a warrior himself, Raoul recognized the stillness that came over FitzRoger. "Indeed? And what form does this punishment take?"

"Ten strokes of the rod at each hour of prayer. I think it should be stopped before terce."

Instead of hurrying off, FitzRoger hooked a thumb in his belt. "It could be said that the lady deserves to suffer for her sins."

"Is that not a matter for her husband and the king? It seems to me that the bishop exceeds his powers."

FitzRoger studied him for a moment, clearly considering all the implications. Raoul hoped he didn't ask just how he knew all this.

"I will at the least halt the discipline. Thank you for alerting me, Sieur Raoul." With that, he turned and headed off toward the convent at reasonable speed. Raoul hurried toward Westminster, hoping FitzRoger would be in time.

As he entered the area near Westminster Hall, he heard city bells announcing terce and tried to estimate whether there had been time enough or not.

Then he put it out of his mind. It was beyond further action. The important thing now was to decide how to fulfill his promise to Jehanne. How to make her suffering worthwhile.

As she waited for terce, Jehanne wondered at herself. Perhaps Raoul could have found a way to take her out of here, away from pain. Away from the degradation of pain. That's what she hated most—that her traitorous body would tremble and flinch, weep and cry out, when she wanted to be stoic.

But an attempt to take her with him might have jeopardized his own escape, and then he wouldn't have been able to take her words to the hearing. That was what really mattered. The hearing that would settle Donata's future, and perhaps that of Galeran and Raymond too.

And she did deserve punishment.

She kept telling herself that.

She just had not expected it to hurt so much.

Sister Martha, anxious sympathy in her eyes, brought Donata to be fed, and Jehanne had a little time of peace concentrating on her baby. Surely after the bishop had overstepped himself by ordering her beatings, the king would not support his ruling and tear her baby from her arms?

But what of the rest of it, she wondered, trying to smile for the baby even as worries whirled through her mind and pain stabbed with every movement. What if it came to swords? If Galeran died, she could not bear it. If Raymond died, though, she could never rid herself of the guilt.

He'd protested quite firmly when she'd gone to him, tearing off her clothes. Was it possible for a woman to rape a man, for she felt as if that was what she had done, even if he'd enjoyed it in the end.

She'd been mad with grief, of course, but did that excuse such sins?

Almost, when Sister Martha came to take Donata, and the mother superior came with her rod, she welcomed it.

Almost.

Jehanne's protesting body immediately began to tremble.

Nineteen

Two other nuns accompanied the mother superior, for they had found last time that her body would no longer remain still under the pain. The sisters gripped her arms and turned her, pressing her down to her knees.

"May the Lord forgive his wretched sinner."

Jehanne managed to keep her voice steady as she said, "Amen."

But at the first cut, she screamed and struggled to escape the agony.

Before the third stroke she heard voices. Her only thought was that somehow the interruption had stopped more pain.

A commanding male voice. Galeran? No.

The mother superior, protesting. Arguing.

Then the controlling hands of the two nuns left her arms. What was happening?

She could hardly hear for shaking, but thought she heard the king mentioned. Was she summoned to the hearing after all?

When she could, she pushed shakily to her feet and turned, still holding on to the prie-dieu for balance.

The mother superior stood by the door, tight-lipped and furious. "The king has sent to halt your penance until after the hearing, Lady Jehanne. I wonder how he discovered it. I will return, however, when it is proper to do so."

She stalked out, but the two other nuns remained. Jehanne realized why when a tall stranger entered. Dark-haired, about her own age, but with an aura of power worthy of the king himself.

"I am FitzRoger, servant to King Henry."

A great deal more than that, Jehanne thought, trying desperately to think straight. She must be ready for whatever twist of fortune was before her.

His clever eyes took her in from head to toe, seeing, she feared, more than she would wish. "Perhaps you should sit, Lady Jehanne."

She'd like to stand straight and dismiss the offer, but she fumbled back onto the plain bench, wishing it weren't so obvious that her legs were shaking.

"I've been whipped a time or two," he remarked. "The body objects even though we would rather it didn't. This was no part of the king's plan, my lady."

His no-nonsense approach steadied her. "I know that. I am told it is a judgment of the Bishop of Durham."

"Who may not have jurisdiction in these matters. However, if anyone thinks it is your husband's duty to punish you, it does seem to have been taken care of."

Jehanne was rather alarmed by his astute reading of the situation. She was not used to trying to handle people whose minds worked so like hers.

"I intend to report on this matter to the king," he said. "In order for my report to be complete, I would like to see your wounds."

"I have no objection. Sisters?"

The two nuns whispered together, then one said, "If he only looks . . ."

Alarmingly, Jehanne found she was unable to stand and had to ask the nuns to ease off her tunic. Raising her arms was almost impossible with the fresh welts, and she feared she would be sick or faint in the process. Eventually, however, it was off and he walked around to look.

He stayed there longer, surely, than it took to assess her

punishment. When he returned to stand in front of her, he said, "I think you should come to Westminster."

"Against the king's command?" It was what she had wanted, but, distressingly, now she felt too shaken and weary to fight directly for her cause.

"I have authority enough to remove you to another confinement closer to the king. He may wish to see for himself."

"I'll soon feel like a monster on display at the fair." But those were silly words, and she stood carefully.

FitzRoger had turned to discuss transport with the nuns. He soon turned back. "Can you ride? They have a cart, but horseback—or, rather, jennetback—might be more bearable."

"I trust in God to give me strength to do anything if I must."

"My philosophy exactly, my lady." And he gestured toward the open door.

It was astonishingly sweet to step into sunshine and smell the flowers. So sweet it almost weakened Jehanne to tears. But then she recollected her situation and turned to Fitz-Roger. "We must take my baby, the nurse, and my cousin Aline too."

It appeared he did have authority enough, for the party was soon assembled, and the mother superior appeared to argue only when she heard that they were taking her mount. FitzRoger stepped aside to have words with her, and the woman paled and stalked away.

"She meant well," said Jehanne when he returned to her side. "She thinks I deserve the punishment. And she was following the orders of a bishop."

"A singularly pernicious excuse." He shook his head at her. "It seems you are as forgiving as your husband."

"Oh, not at all."

Jehanne rode, with the rest of the party walking, for there was no speed in riding through the crowded streets. It hurt to ride, but then, it hurt to do anything but lie very still on her stomach, and when her breasts filled with milk, that wasn't particularly comfortable, either.

In fact, she did feel that she had perhaps suffered enough, and as they wended their way through the crowds to the king's hall, the suffocating burden of guilt she had borne for a year or more began to slide from her.

She took to praying, finding perhaps a touch of the sense of God that Galeran had. Christ had been whipped too, and since he had known his fate and embraced it, he, too, had accepted the pain for the greater good.

She grimaced. She could imagine what Galeran would say to that. Her thinking of herself as like the Son of God.

Instead, she addressed her prayers meekly, reverently, to Mary, Mother of God. But even then she couldn't help wondering if Mary had ever wanted to step in and turn her beloved Son from His painful course.

She really wasn't very good at meekness.

Despite that, the prayers and thoughts helped Jehanne handle the journey, but by the time she reached Westminster Hall she was almost faint and had to be helped into the building. Soon she was in a comfortable small room that contained a tented couch. She lay on it in relief, as much at being able to hide a tendency to tears as to ease her pain.

She didn't look, but sensed that FitzRoger left. Would he go straight to the king? Would he tell Galeran? She longed for Galeran but could imagine his anger at what she had accepted.

She could argue that she'd had no choice about the beatings, but when she sent Aline out to find help, she could have sent her to Galeran to put a stop to it.

She hadn't.

And he'd know why.

This separation from Galeran, spiritual more than physical, was a pain far deeper than her sore back.

She had never realized, when she'd sent him on crusade,

just how much she would miss him. With typical carelessness, she'd not considered how he was warp to the weft of her life, part of her every thought and action; how much she depended on him being there ready to discuss, argue, advise, object, comfort.

She'd felt almost half alive all the time he'd been gone, despite Gallot and the comfort of Aline's presence. Perhaps, she thought for the first time, her seduction of Raymond had not been out of grief and anger alone, but out of a loneliness made absolute by the loss of her child.

That loss brought tears to her eyes. Or perhaps they came from the loneliness, which still lingered because her sin stood between her and Galeran. And now her actions might make it worse.

Sweet Mary, but angry or not, she needed him here beside her . . .

Someone entered.

Jehanne turned her head sharply enough to hurt, but it wasn't Galeran. It wasn't anyone she knew. A monk.

He nodded. "I am Brother Christopher, my lady. I have a salve for your injuries, if you will permit . . ."

Jehanne nodded, and Aline came over to help uncover her back by the simple means of slitting the tunic neck to hem.

Jehanne heard Aline gasp, and wondered just how bad it was. "Is the skin broken?" she asked.

"Nay, Lady," said the monk, spreading the cloth a little wider. "Your clothes protected you from that. The damage is mostly bruising and swelling. Very painful, I'm sure, but it should cause no scars, and the risk of infection is small."

He began to spread something cool on her back. His first touch was painful, but soon the soothing effect took over. Jehanne sighed and relaxed. Vaguely, she remembered that Aline had been out all night, perhaps with Raoul, and that this should concern her. That the hearing was taking place close by and she should, perhaps, think about forcing her way in after all.

But her tormented mind had eased and refused to tangle itself again.

She slept.

Galeran had left early for Westminster, despite the fact that Raoul had not returned with further word of Aline. Despite the fact that the messenger he'd sent to Waltham to keep his father informed had not returned either.

He'd been driven. Driven by his concern about Jehanne and Donata. Driven by his hunger to be home again with all these things settled.

Driven, he knew, into leaving foolishly early as if that would have things settled sooner.

He did have some purpose, however. He hoped to have a word with the king's champion, FitzRoger. Galeran's travels had taught him that great men were temperamental and often let their foibles interfere with justice. Henry had enjoyed many liaisons, and acknowledged a number of bastards. How would that affect his view of Galeran's affairs? A talk with FitzRoger might tell him something useful.

FitzRoger was not in Westminster, however, so Galeran was left to pace a small room, waiting for the hour of the hearing.

Surely Henry's personal tastes would mean he thought little of adultery. That would lessen Jehanne's danger. Galeran was determined she come out of this without being punished in any way.

On the other hand, as Aline had pointed out, Henry had promised to restore law and order in England. Adultery and bastards were an offense to all men.

But surely, Galeran thought, circling the room as his mind was circling the problems, whatever the king's attitude to the law, he could not support the absurdity of taking a baby from its mother's breast and giving it to an unwed man to raise.

No, of course he couldn't.

Unless he was afraid to offend the Church. Flambard was a bishop, an eminent representative of the Church, no matter how little he deserved that honor.

Galeran knew, with bitter certainty, that Henry Beauclerk would do nothing that might jeopardize his long-sought prize, his hold on the Crown of England.

He turned and circled the other way. Were Lowick and Flambard already here? Were they together nearby, making plans? What plans? Galeran didn't see what new twist they could come up with, but he'd never underestimate the cunning of a man like Ranulph Flambard. And Flambard's ambitions could entangle the whole of Galeran's family.

He stopped, suddenly feeling surprisingly alone.

He'd grown up as part of a close-knit family, and once he married, there had been Jehanne who had soon become—as the Bible put it—his rib, his helpmeet, part of himself. He could hardly remember a time when she hadn't been by his side, ready to discuss, argue, advise, object, comfort. . . .

On crusade, he'd felt as if he had left part of himself behind, but he'd found Raoul and an unexpectedly deep friendship.

Now, however, he stood alone, most of his family back north, his father skulking at Waltham, and Raoul who knows where.

Vague thoughts of Christ in the Garden of Gethsemane flickered in his mind, but he laughed and shook them away. He was not abandoned and betrayed. He had just come here too early.

He heard the bells sound for terce and crossed himself, offering a prayer of his own. He was beginning to worry about Raoul's absence, however, and sent another prayer that nothing had happened to Aline. She was as innocent as Donata in all this, and should not suffer.

A moment later Raoul hurried in, surprisingly flustered and disheveled. There was no time to talk, however, as he was only a pace ahead of the page sent to lead them to the king's chamber. Raoul was of little practical help here, since he had no official status and didn't know English ways and customs, but Galeran was immensely pleased to no longer be alone.

The king awaited them in the same rich chamber in which they had been presented to him the previous day. On this occasion, however, Henry sat firmly on his throne, crown on his head. There were no courtiers or visitors here, though a number of people were present. Galeran tried to assess them all without taking his attention from the king, who was greeting him.

A monk at a high desk, ready to record the proceedings.

Two lords and a bishop. A couple of pages ready to run errands. Two armed guards.

The king had stopped speaking, so Galeran bowed again. "I thank you again, my liege, for your attention to this small matter."

"No matter is too small for my attention, Lord Galeran," said Henry, smiling like a wolf. "Have you news of your father?"

Galeran hoped his face was as expressionless as he wanted it to be. "No, sire. I am sure I would have heard if his condition had worsened, but I am concerned. As soon as the matter of the babe is settled, I intend to ride to Waltham Abbey."

Before the king could comment, the door opened to admit Flambard in full glory of gold-trimmed bishop's vestments, crook in hand. Behind him trailed Lowick, Brother Forthred, and a clerk. Brother Forthred looked at Galeran and smiled slightly, as if he scented revenge.

Galeran ignored that and studied Raymond of Lowick.

It was the first time he'd seen the man since leaving for the Holy Land, since the man had shared a bed with Jehanne. Lowick was still impressively handsome, damn him, but Galeran knew he wasn't worth the surge of rage in his gut, a rage that tried to pull his lips back from his teeth in a snarl.

He dragged his gaze away, fighting to calm his breathing. This was a place for law and reason, not vengeance. But part of him wanted to draw his sword and spray the elegant chamber with Raymond of Lowick's blood.

Raoul did have a purpose here after all. He'd stop such madness.

Galeran suddenly hoped it would come to a court battle, though. He wanted it. He needed it to drive away a deep pain that reason, understanding, and forgiveness did not seem to touch.

Flambard and Lowick were making their bows to the king.

Henry nodded to the two men, then called for extra benches to be placed in front of him. "This is not a formal legal matter, my friends. Sit at your ease as we try to settle it to the satisfaction of all."

Galeran and Raoul sat on one bench, Lowick and Flambard on the other, with the monks standing quietly behind. Galeran found it tempting to stare at his enemies and focused instead on the king.

"First," said Henry, "we make known to you our advisers in this. His lordship, the Bishop of London."

The elderly, sinewy man nodded.

"Henry Beaumont, Earl of Warwick."

Warwick was still a young man, but authority and strength stamped every line of his face and body.

"And Ralph Bassett, my legal adviser."

Bassett was surprisingly genial looking, with a scrubbed face. But Galeran had heard of him. He was a close companion of the king's and a blade-sharp student of the law.

"Does anyone object to these men hearing our discussion," Henry asked, "and advising me in this?"

No one did, though Galeran wished he knew more of the observers. The Bishop of London was supposed to be a worthy man. The Earl of Warwick, however, had been with Henry on the day his brother died, and might have had a hand in murder.

Galeran put aside such concerns as the king himself began to lay out the situation. "As we understand this case, my lords, while you, Lord Galeran, were away from England on the Enterprise of God, your wife bore a child to Raymond of Lowick. Does anyone here dispute that fact?"

Silence answered him.

"News, thankfully false, was brought to England of your death at Jerusalem, Lord Galeran, perhaps leading the Lady Jehanne and Sir Raymond to think themselves free to be intimate—"

Galeran almost objected, but he saw Raymond move and be restrained by the bishop. Very well. He, too, would wait and see just what plan they had.

"Upon your return, however," Henry continued, "their sin was clear to all. Raymond of Lowick confessed himself to the Bishop of Durham, and we assume the Lady Jehanne confessed herself to her priest and to you, her earthly lord."

This, it became clear, was a question requiring an answer.

"Yes, sire," said Galeran. He'd hoped to keep this hearing away from discussion of Jehanne's sin. Now he could only hope this wasn't heading straight toward the question of the suitable punishment for adultery.

It was.

"Sir Raymond," said the king, "received penance of the bishop—the penance which is contested here. What penance did the Lady Jehanne receive?"

Galeran tried an old device. "Sire, as soon as I heard of the bishop's wise judgment, I announced that my wife should perform the same penances, in prayer, in offerings to God's work, and in the raising of the child."

Henry nodded. "Thus leading to our dilemma. Unfortunately, as King Solomon found, a child cannot be divided between two contesting parties." Galeran thought they had passed over the treacherous spot, but then Henry added, "Did you not think it your duty, Lord Galeran, to impose some additional penalty upon your wife?"

"No, sire." Why did he feel as if he confessed a sin? Probably because of the disapproval emanating from all these men.

"And yet, I am told you struck her to the ground when first you met."

And who told you of that? "I did, sire. An action I regret. My wife's anguish and genuine repentance are punishment enough."

Flambard interjected at this point with a snide chuckle, "You are too fond, Lord Galeran. Too fond. It is easy enough for a woman to weep and wail. It does not serve good order for them to use that ability to avoid just punishment."

Galeran was hard pressed not to grin at the trap he was about to spring. "You think I should have beaten her, my lord bishop? But since my wife took on herself the penance imposed on Sir Raymond, would he not then have to be beaten too? In fact, it could be said that I owe him a blow. . . ."

Lowick erupted to his feet, hand on sword.

It was Flambard who snapped, "Sit down!" while glaring at Galeran. There was something more than just thwarted anger in his eyes, however. Why had this turn so worried the bishop? Did he not want the matter coming to violence?

Henry had his chin on his hand and was watching the reactions with great shrewdness. "We will leave the matter of the lady's just deserts to a later time. At issue here is the matter of the child, and the rights of the bishop to decide her placement. I am surprised, Lord Galeran, that you are so determined to keep a cuckoo in your nest."

There were any number of impassioned things Galeran could say, but he kept it practical. "The babe is at the breast, sire, and as all know, to deprive a child of its mother's milk is likely to harm it. I see no cause to injure an innocent. Since I wish to have my wife by my side, the babe must remain. And Donata, being a girl, will not threaten the interests of our future children."

"So you are willing to raise the child with the care and affection you would give to your own offspring, and arrange for her future well-being?"

"I am, sire."

Henry turned to the other bench. "Sir Raymond, I doubt you can do as well for your daughter."

"And yet she is my daughter, sire," said Raymond firmly.

"But you have no safe means to feed a baby. And if we were to give you the child when she is weaned, how are you to care for her then? You have no wife. You have no home."

"I will find a wife, sire. I will make a home."

The king raised his brows. " 'Tis not so easy, as I myself have found. I confess, I have daughters born out of wedlock, but I am content to leave them with their mothers for raising. Tell me, Sir Raymond, why do you want to burden yourself with a child?"

Under the direct question, Lowick's lips tightened. After a thwarted pause he said, "Because she's mine. I have the right."

It was laughably weak. What Lowick really wanted was Jehanne, and Galeran dead so he could claim Heywood, but of course he couldn't say that. Galeran noticed, however, that Flambard did not seem concerned by the hearing's progress.

That worried him.

The king leaned back in his chair and addressed his advisers. "My lords? Do you wish to question either party further, or do you have a recommendation for me?"

Galeran tried not to show his relief that the matter had come so easily to the end.

It was as well he hadn't, for the Bishop of London spoke. "Sire, we must consider the rights of the Church."

"Ah, yes," said the king. "You do well to remind me, my lord bishop."

It was clear to Galeran that Henry would rather not have been reminded, but it wasn't something the king could ignore. The Church had the right to judge in certain matters, and would not let that right be stolen.

Galeran felt his heart speed, though. This had always been what he feared most—the involvement of the Church as an institution. Flambard was a man, and a venal and unpopular one. The Church itself could not be ignored.

"Sire," said the Bishop of London, "this is an interesting case. The Bishop of Durham was within his rights to impose penance, and Lord Galeran is within his rights to lay penalty on his wife. When the two conflict, what is to be done?"

"If you don't know, my lord bishop," said Henry, "I certainly don't."

The bishop did not seem put out. "If there is no other solution, sire, I suggest that compensation be made. If Lord Galeran were to make an additional donation to some religious institution, that would balance the portion of the babe he has kept from Sir Raymond."

"The portion of the penance, you mean," pointed out the king. "I'd think Sir Raymond should pay to be relieved of that, despite his noble desire to rear his child."

"You are wise, sire," said the bishop with a dry smile. "Sir Raymond should therefore do some other penance. Since he is said to be a fine warrior, perhaps he should go as Lord Galeran did, to fight the infidel."

Henry almost smiled too, as he turned to Raymond. "What say you to that, sir? You must know that if this case were to be put formally before the law, both you and the lady could suffer severe penalties, including the loss of life itself."

It was so neat, even to getting Lowick out of the country, that Galeran wondered if it had all been arranged beforehand.

Lowick looked nothing so much as frustrated. "I would be honored to fight for Christ, sire, but I feel my first duty is to protect my child and her mother. . . ."

Flambard put a calming hand on Lowick's arm and used his jeweled and gilded crook to push himself to his feet. In his miter and vestments, he was an almost biblical figure. "Your pardon, sire, but there is an aspect to the situation that has not yet been raised."

Galeran shared a quick look with Raoul. He didn't know what was coming, but it was the surprise assault he'd been expecting all along.

"Yes, my lord bishop?" asked the king, who had also become suddenly watchful.

Flambard smiled—a beneficent smile worthy of a saint in a manuscript. "Your very reasonable assumption, sire— and that of my brother bishop—is that the intercourse between Raymond of Lowick and Jehanne of Heywood was unlawful. It was also my belief when I imposed penance, though I was merciful because of the circumstances. However, on further discussion with Sir Raymond, I discovered that he thought himself entitled to his actions, not only because he believed Lord Galeran to be dead, but because he believed himself to be the lawful husband of the Lady Jehanne."

"On what possible grounds?" Galeran demanded, but a sick fear coiled inside him. Could Jehanne have gone through a marriage ceremony with Lowick? He'd been a little surprised that she hadn't if she'd thought him dead, but if she had, surely she would have told him.

Flambard directed a triumphant smirk at him. "Prior betrothal, my lord."

"You lie!" Galeran was on his feet and almost had his hands around Flambard's throat before the guards and Raoul pulled him away.

"Sit, Lord Galeran," said the king with remarkable calm. "We will have truth here today, I assure you." As Raoul pushed Galeran back onto his bench, Henry turned to the bishop. "You have proof of this?"

Flambard snapped his fingers and Brother Forthred stepped forward to place a document in Lowick's hand. Lowick then knelt before the king to present it.

Galeran stared at the parchment as if it were a snake in the desert. Prior betrothal could invalidate his marriage. Could it be true? Cases cropped up now and then of forgotten or ignored childhood betrothals. . . .

His chief emotion, however, was pure rage. Would they try to tear away what he and Jehanne had made together, this bishop and his pawn? He'd kill them both first.

He forced himself to be calm. He needed sharp wits here, not a sharp sword. But the time for that would come.

He looked at Flambard, who seemed piously content.

He looked at Raymond of Lowick's back, seeking the unease that would reveal a lie. The man's proud posture told Galeran nothing.

The king unrolled the parchment and read down it quickly, then passed it to Ralph Bassett.

The Earl of Warwick, who'd looked rather bored to this point, leaned forward. "With your permission, sire . . . ?"

Henry nodded, and the earl addressed Raymond, who was still on one knee.

"Sir Raymond, if you were betrothed to the Lady Jehanne, why did you make no objection to her unlawful match with Lord Galeran?"

Lowick answered firmly. "I saw no point in it, my lord. Jehanne's father had changed his mind. I knew that if he'd wanted to, he could have found a way to negate the betrothal."

"But he didn't?" asked the earl.

"No, my lord."

Galeran studied Lowick's voice. He thought he detected the flatness of untruths, but it was hard to tell, and what he was saying was plausible. Galeran had been young at the time of his betrothal and marriage. If deceptions had taken place, he might have been unaware of them.

He couldn't believe, however, that no one was aware of the prior betrothal. His father, for example, would surely know. Damn Lord William for hiding in Waltham when he should be here.

"When the betrothal was drawn up," Lowick was saying, "Jehanne was too young for marriage and she still had two brothers living. When her brothers died, leaving her an heiress, her father wanted to wed her elsewhere."

"Why?" asked the earl. "Did he not consider you able to hold her properties?"

Galeran saw Lowick's neck turn red. He could almost feel sorry for the man except that he was lying. He was surely lying and his hesitation under this question was finally giving him away.

Glancing at Flambard, Galeran thought the bishop looked disgusted with his tool.

Lowick still had not answered the earl's question, and the king sternly commanded him to do so.

"He wanted her allied to a powerful family," Lowick said at last. "I have no such family."

"Then why," asked the earl, "did he feel you a suitable husband earlier?"

"I was like a son to him, my lord." Lowick's voice had steadied. "The betrothal was a way to bring me into the family."

"But one he did not want when she was his only child?" The earl leaned back, nodding.

It was so plausible that Galeran himself wondered if the story might be true. Old Fulk had a soft spot for Lowick and might well have decided to bring him into the family through marriage, perhaps intending to give the couple a small estate.

Still, it was incredible that a betrothal be kept secret. There were always witnesses. That was the *purpose* of witnesses.

Ralph Bassett and the Bishop of London had been scrutinizing the betrothal document, and now Bassett spoke up. "This appears to be a valid document, sire, but as always in these matters, it is the witnesses who matter. They must come forward to attest to the truth."

"Alas, sire," said Flambard. "I have had searches made and none of the witnesses still live."

Everyone's brows rose at that. When it came to witnesses to such documents, it was the more the merrier just to avoid this possibility.

Galeran almost sighed with relief. The document was a forgery with false witnesses chosen simply because they were dead. Now to prove it. "Who were these witnesses?"

Ralph Bassett read off names. The first were old Fulk and his sons, of course, all certainly dead. Next was Gregory the Seneschal, more recently dead.

"I knew that man," said Galeran. "He died only recently, and was witness to my own wedding. He would not have put his name to an illegal document."

Flambard interjected smoothly, "Even at the cost of losing his position, my lord?"

It was a pointless discussion, so Galeran listened to the other names. There were only eight.

"Sire," he said, allowing his astonishment to show, "my own betrothal document has over thirty names on it. Lord Fulk was a man of importance in the north and could have gathered as many or more to witness this document."

"An excellent point," said Warwick.

Flambard's eyes narrowed, but his smile stayed in place. "Perhaps, since Sir Raymond lacked family or connections, Lord Fulk thought it kinder not to overwhelm him. It was, after all, at the time an insignificant matter to do with a mere daughter."

"All the same," said Galeran, "there are notable omissions. Why, for example, were neither my father nor Hubert of Burstock at such a ceremony?"

The king nodded. "An excellent point. What a pity," he added with meaning, "that Lord William of Brome is not here today to speak to this matter."

Galeran wondered if his family's future was going to hinge on his father's allegiance after all.

The only thing to do was to take the step he both hated and thirsted for. He rose. "I am willing to put this matter to the test of the sword, sire. I challenge Raymond of Lowick to prove the right of his claim with his body."

Lowick rose immediately. "I accept!"

Twenty

The king frowned between them. "It would be to the death, sirs, with God as your judge." If there had been a planned end to this meeting, it was clear that they were now far from it and Henry was not pleased. He could not block a court battle, though. It was every man's right.

But at that moment a page came in to bow and murmur to the earl, who then leaned forward to speak to the king.

Henry's frown eased. "Sit, sirs, for the moment. It does not please me to lose good fighting men without need, and we might be able to cast light on this problem in other ways. William of Brome has arrived."

Even as Galeran turned to greet his father, he saw Flambard's face stiffen, and Lowick's sag with shock. Clearly neither of them had expected this.

What had they expected?

Probably that Galeran's death would be an accomplished fact before his father heard of any of this.

The door opened and Lord William entered in a statement of rich garments and jewels that could have been designed to counter Flambard's clerical magnificence. Three equally grand attendants paced behind him. Galeran was so accustomed to the hard-used cloth and leather his father wore at home that he almost laughed at this flamboyant display.

It served its purpose, though. It made his father's rank clear.

Lord William went directly but unhurriedly to kneel before the king, joined hands extended. A satisfied glint in his eye, Henry covered those hands with his own as he greeted him. It was a simplified version of the oath of fealty, but carried weight all the same.

"Lord William," said Henry, "we are delighted to see you in such good health."

"Aye, well," said Galeran's father as he rose, "I could perhaps have done with a day or two's more rest, sire, but I heard rumors that Raymond of Lowick was at Waltham asking about me and decided I'd better find out what he was up to." He glanced at Lowick and the bishop with a wicked twinkle in his eye. "Likely he got the impression I was sicker than I am. I think someone might have said I was at my last prayers, even."

"Indeed? We must not put your health and welfare at risk, my lord. Please sit." Henry ordered a chair brought forward, the only chair to be used other than the throne upon which he sat. It could just be concern for a possibly sick man, but the message was clear.

Support me, Lord William of Brome, and I will recognize you as one of my mightiest barons, leader of the north. And I will favor your family, today and on other days.

As soon as Lord William was settled, the king said, "You are come most opportunely, my lord, for you should be able to help us with a troubling matter. Sir Raymond of Lowick claims he was legally betrothed to the Lady Jehanne before her betrothal and marriage to your son, Galeran."

Lord William stared as if he'd been told the sun was made of cheese. "Rubbish, sire."

"He has a document that appears in all ways reliable. Unfortunately, the witnesses are all deceased."

"Of your kindness, sire, have the names of these witnesses read to me."

At the end of the short list, Lord William snorted. "Someone must have combed Northumbria for men of stature dead in the last ten years, sire. But we're a healthy lot up north, and that bunch were never gathered in one spot in their lives to the best of my knowledge. Certainly not at Heywood, where I would have known of it. What's more, there are a great many names that should be there for any such document to make sense. Such as mine."

"Perhaps Lord Fulk intended to keep the matter quiet," Flambard suggested rather desperately. "This document, which I accepted in good faith, casts doubt upon the right of Lord Galeran to child, wife, and castle, so it is not surprising that you would try to discredit it, Lord William. The only true test is by the sword."

Henry looked pensively at the players. "My lord bishop, I fail to see why you are so ardent in this cause."

Galeran could almost see Flambard controlling himself. "I merely wish to see right prevail, sire, as is my duty."

"Then perhaps instead of involving Lord Galeran, who has done no evil, and in fact is blessed by his service in the Holy Land, we should ask Raymond of Lowick to prove the truth of his claim by the test of hot iron."

Lowick was no coward, but he blanched at the thought of proving his lie by holding red hot iron in his hand, then seeing how badly he was burned. "I maintain my right to prove the truth by my sword, sire," he declared.

"Your majesty," said the bishop, "the most grievous sinner in all this, both by concealing her prior betrothal and entering an illegal union with Lord Galeran, and by later betraying those vows, not to mention the murder of her unwanted child—"

"By God . . . !" But Galeran was again stopped by Raoul before he could do the bishop bodily harm.

"Sit, Lord Galeran," snapped the king. "I have not heard previous mention here of murder."

"Because there was no murder," snarled Galeran, eye to eye with the bishop.

"How, then, did the child die?" Flambard turned smoothly to the king. "A healthy child, sire, of eight months, who went to bed one night and never woke. And the very night of his burial, the burial of her only child, Jehanne of Heywood joined with Sir Raymond in his bed. Willingly. It seems to me that the Lady Jehanne should be the one subjected to the ordeal of iron."

Galeran could feel the mood of the room change. Thus far, he'd succeeded in keeping Jehanne in the background, but now she was on trial, and in danger. She was that traitorous creature, the adulteress. But this was much worse. There could be mercy for an adulteress, and her husband was generally the final judge. There could be no mercy for a woman who killed her own child.

"The child who died was my son," he said, as calmly as he could. "If his death was suspect, do you not think I would have acted?"

"You know how the child died, my lord?" Flambard asked in false amazement.

"I know she would not have killed Gallot." Galeran turned to the king. "My wife loves children, sire, and desperately wanted a babe of her own. It was why I took the cross and went on the Enterprise of God. And God rewarded us with a child who was the more precious after being waited for so long. I can bring forward any number of witnesses to swear that my wife was a devoted mother, and grieved the loss of her child most deeply."

"I can swear to that," said Lord William. "She does not weep and wail as most women do, but to one who knows her, she was grievously hurt."

The Bishop of London spoke up. "The question is not did she grieve, but did she or did she not fornicate with this man on the day of her child's interment?"

Silence answered him until the king said to Lowick, "Well, sir? You are the one who can answer that question."

And Lowick said, "She did, sire."

He spoke reluctantly, though, and Galeran thought perhaps he, too, wanted to keep the danger away from Jehanne. It was a small mark in his favor.

"She had her reasons, sire," said Galeran, though he knew he was moving onto treacherous ground. Even if he could make sense of it here, he didn't want to mention Jehanne's war with God. "My wife has confessed all to me, telling me everything that went on at this time. Put most simply, she was driven mad. She thought I was dead, and when her son was torn from her as if by the hand of God, she lost her wits with grief. She sinned with Lowick but the once before coming to her senses, and I defy him to swear otherwise."

"Sir Raymond?" asked the king.

Lowick glanced once at Flambard, but then said, "It was just the once, sire, and yes, I do believe she was not in her right mind at the time. I tried to resist her, but proved too weak."

There was a stir, almost of amusement, at this picture, and Galeran felt a bit of the tension seep out of him. He could almost feel in charity with Lowick. He'd seen the danger to Jehanne and moved to lessen it.

In fact, he could have clasped him to his breast in brotherly love if it hadn't been for that forged betrothal document. But that was doubtless the work of Bishop Flambard.

Who had wanted Jehanne put to the ordeal.

All Galeran's anger focused on the bishop.

It was the Bishop of London who was speaking now, however, clearly concerned about murder. "What of the child's death, though? Perhaps the lady ran mad at the news of her husband's death and took the life of her child. A sad case, but not one that should go unpunished."

It was Lord William who addressed this issue. "Sire," he said, "it was an unusual death, but not totally unheard of. Generally people say that the mother overlaid the babe as they slept. Country people talk of spirits stealing the child in the night. My son was away, so I had certain inquiries made. There was no sign of physical damage other than some bruising where the child had lain after death. Nor was there sign of poison. It is hard to kill without leaving any sign. And," he added with meaning, "it is too easy for people to point the finger when there is any trace of suspicion."

Galeran stopped breathing. His father was raising the subject of William Rufus's death. He was as good as saying that if Jehanne was blamed for Gallot's death, Brome might join those who accused Henry of killing his brother.

He was threatening to support Robert of Normandy.

The king's eyes narrowed in the dangerous silence.

"Moreover," Lord William continued blandly, "I spoke with the infirmarian at Waltham Abbey on just this matter, it being of interest to me. . . ."

Galeran remembered to suck in a breath. Coming out of his shock, he noticed that FitzRoger had entered and was standing just behind the king's throne as if waiting to speak.

". . . Brother Garth agreed with me that such deaths do occur, with no reason being obvious. Generally the child is younger than Gallot, but all particulars of Gallot's death match cases he has known. I really think it must be put down to an act of God, that He in His wisdom decided to take the sweet child to His bosom."

"So be it," said the king shortly. "There seems no cause to look longer at such an insoluble mystery, and it is surely wrong to cast stones when there is no certainty of guilt. If anyone has sinned, God in His wisdom will act."

Henry looked at Lord William as he spoke, and it was almost as if he spoke of the suspicions about himself and his brother's death.

Speaking briskly, the king continued. "It seems to me, also, that there is grave doubt about this betrothal document. Grave enough doubt for me to dismiss it unless some evidence can be brought forward to support it. Since all the formal witnesses are dead, this will prove difficult." He smiled, though it didn't reach his eyes. "I'm sure you, my lord Bishop of Durham, took the document's validity on trust. But Raymond of Lowick must have known he was party to a deliberate deception."

At this swift change of focus, Lowick turned pale. He stood. "With all due respect, sire, I maintain the validity of that document, and claim the right to prove it in battle."

Henry looked nothing so much as exasperated, and Galeran suspected it was true that he saw such court battles as a waste of good fighting men. Galeran felt much the same way, and any desire he'd had to kill Lowick had drained away. The man had been used by Jehanne and duped by Flambard.

And he had spoken up to save Jehanne from harm.

FitzRoger stepped forward at this point to lean close to Henry and murmur in his ear. The king's expression changed again.

What now? Galeran wondered with a twist in his gut.

He wanted to leap up. Act. Do any crazy thing to end this sneaking through truth toward safety. Jehanne was probably safe from the worst punishment, and the Bishop of London had provided the compromise that would leave Donata with Galeran and Jehanne.

If their marriage could be preserved.

That marriage hung in the balance, however, if the king permitted an ordeal by sword. If Galeran died on Lowick's blade, God would have become substitute for all those dead witnesses and Jehanne would be Lowick's wife.

Galeran watched the king and his champion, wondering if they were arranging the details of a court battle. Then FitzRoger straightened and Henry's perceptive eyes scanned the people in front of him.

"Lord Galeran," he said, "would you not agree that an adulterous wife must be punished?"

Shocked by this turn, Galeran had to rearrange his mind before he could answer. "Sire, a lecherous one, perhaps. But not one briefly demented by grief."

"But as the Bishop of Durham says, repentance can be faked, as can madness, and it is often necessary to make a public example of sinners. What if I were to command you to whip your wife, to show the world that such infidelity is not to be tolerated?"

Galeran stared at the king, who had had so many lovers. Many married. Many of whom had borne him bastard children. As far as he knew, not one had been punished for her sin. "If it were your judgment, sire," he said slowly, "then I would have to obey."

He hoped Henry heard the message that by such a judgment he would lose a loyal subject. He hoped FitzRoger had passed on his veiled warning the other day.

Henry showed no reaction, and turned to Lowick. "Sir Raymond, by your account you could lay claim to the right to punish the Lady Jehanne for her seduction of you, to the peril of your immortal soul. Would you claim such a right?"

Lowick flushed. "Nay, sire! I have no wish to see Jehanne hurt in any way. When I left Heywood, I begged her to accompany me to a safe haven. I wanted to save her from just such a punishment. I have only ever wanted to protect her and my child."

And that, thought Galeran with surprise, was probably the truth, allowing for the fact that Lowick desperately wanted Heywood too.

Henry turned last to Flambard. "My lord bishop, what is your view of this?"

The bishop's eyes flickered uncertainly for a moment. "I gave judgment, my liege, and the Lady Jehanne deliberately evaded it."

"So you feel she deserves to be whipped for that evasion?"

Again Flambard's eyes searched the room as if seeking missing information. Galeran glanced at FitzRoger, wondering what news he had brought to start this new line of questions.

"Well, my lord bishop?" the king prompted.

"Yes, sire. Apart from her sin of adultery, the lady has demonstrated that she is willful and eaten by pride. She needs physical penance to help her see the error of her ways so that she may find salvation. If she could but be brought to submit herself to it."

Henry smiled. "But she has submitted to correction, and willingly. Hasn't she?"

"Willingly?" Flambard's alarmed query was drowned by Galeran's "What correction?"

His father threw out an arm to block him, and Raoul clamped a hand on his shoulder, so that with difficulty he was kept in his seat.

"Lord FitzRoger has something to report," said Henry.

The king's champion stepped forward. "By his majesty's orders, the Lady Jehanne, her cousin, her babe, and the babe's nurse were taken to St. Hilda's convent here in the city. Since the lady and her child were a source of contention, his majesty felt that they would be safer in custody there. In case the lady had any improper intentions, such as fleeing with her lover before judgment could be made, it was ordered that they all be kept in locked quarters until this hearing was over. That was the extent of the king's orders."

Galeran looked around the room again, seeking what lay beneath all this. He did remember that when he visited her, Jehanne was being kept apart.

Lowick looked puzzled.

Flambard was sweating.

"The mother superior of St. Hilda's is very strict," continued FitzRoger, "and a firm believer in physical chastisement to drive out sin. When she heard the full story of the Lady Jehanne's wrongdoing, and was told that the lady had refused to accept the penance laid on her by a bishop, she needed little encouragement to lay on the rod."

"Dear God . . ." Galeran whispered, again kept on his bench only by his father and Raoul.

"Steady, lad," murmured his father. "Steady."

"The lady has been beaten?" asked the king.

"The lady has been given ten strokes at each of the five canonical hours since she arrived at the convent. I intervened before the full measure could be delivered at terce today."

Galeran would not be restrained this time. He surged to his feet. "Who ordered this?"

"Why, Bishop Flambard, of course."

Galeran grabbed the front of the bishop's robe before anyone could stop him. "Then I think the *bishop* should meet my sword."

"Hold, Lord Galeran!" Henry's hand settled over Galeran's fist, which still gripped Flambard's silk robe. The king had left his throne.

"I believe I have a prior claim," said Henry softly, squeezing Galeran's hand with remarkable strength and in clear command. But it was the cold menace in the king's voice that made Galeran release his grip.

Menace directed not at him, but at the bishop.

"Mine is the power," said Henry softly. "Mine is the judgment. By what right, my lord bishop, do you overrule my orders?"

Flambard's now-pasty skin was running with sweat. It was not surprising. He was facing the man who had barehandedly tossed a man off the battlements of Rouen for opposing him.

"I did not overrule your orders, sire. But I have the right as a prince of the Church to impose penance for sin."

"What penance would you ordain, then, for the forgery of a betrothal document?"

Flambard actually stepped back until he bumped up against the bench. "If it is a forgery, sire, I had no part of it!"

"Did you not? I think careful inquiries in the north will reveal the truth." The king turned suddenly to Lowick. "Well, Sir Raymond? Speak the truth! Was there a prior betrothal?"

Raymond, equally white, dropped to his knees under the blast of the king's rage. "No, sire! There was talk of it. But Jehanne's brothers died before it was arranged."

"But you loved the lady and thought her yours by right?" Henry was speaking more calmly now. "You thought, perhaps, that you were betrothed in spirit . . . ?" The king was clearly offering Lowick escape if he had wit to take it.

He had.

He bowed his head. "Yes, sire. And when the Lady Jehanne bore me a child, I sought only to secure their safety with me. I most humbly beg your mercy."

Henry went so far as to raise Lowick with his own hands, smiling, though his color was still high. "And it was Bishop Flambard who devised the plan of pretending that the betrothal had really taken place?"

"Yes, sire."

"And it was he who provided the document?"

"Yes, sire."

Having obtained the testimony he needed, Henry turned from Lowick to look at Flambard. "What was the bishop's purpose, I wonder? Can we believe that he was so stirred by your lovelorn state, by the danger to your leman and her child, that he felt obliged to risk his position, his very life, to assist you?"

Again, stillness settled on the room, for they had come to the crux of it, and Flambard's terror was stamped on his face.

"Well, Sir Raymond?" asked the king almost sweetly, never taking his eyes off Flambard. "Tell us what explanation the bishop gave for helping you try to gain control of Heywood Castle."

Lowick stared around, and Galeran felt genuinely sorry

for him. He was teetering on the edge of treasonous matters, and knew it.

"Sire, the bishop resented the power of William of Brome and his family. He thought that if he had a supporter in Heywood, he could wield greater power in the north."

"With a Church principality that stretched from coast to coast, he was concerned about one small castle?"

"Sir William opposed him, sire."

"But did the bishop show such interest in your affairs from the very beginning? When you first went to him after Lord Galeran returned home, what was his demeanor?"

Lowick frowned over that. "He listened to my petitions for help, sire, but—"

"But did little. When did that change?"

Lowick was now sweating like the bishop, but he answered clearly, "After news of your brother's death, sire."

"Ah," said the king, moving away a few steps. "After his greatest supporter was gone, and he faced my patronage. Or lack of it. Total control of Northumbria would be a useful weapon, wouldn't it? But to be used in whose cause?"

Flambard had regained some control, and was ready to argue for his life. "I merely sought proper order in the north, sire. It was why your brother appointed me there."

"Was it? But then why did your interest in Sir Raymond's case grow after my brother's tragic death?"

"I merely took time to consider his case, sire. As you have seen here today, it is not a simple one."

"And I suppose the forged document was merely an attempt to simplify it. As was," added the king, "the attempt on Lord Galeran's life."

Flambard licked his lips. "Attempt . . . ?"

"Lord FitzRoger took a man of yours into custody this morning, my lord bishop. He has already been most informative. The crossbow is a devilish weapon. Even the Pope agrees that it should only be used against the heathen."

In the midst of a deadly silence, Henry turned and resumed his throne, looking ominously content.

Lowick turned on the bishop. *"You?* You were behind that attack?"

"Ranulph Flambard," said Henry, overriding Lowick, "I find you to be under suspicion of attempted murder, of forgery, and of a great overstepping of your clerical authority."

"With all due respect, sire," stated Flambard, his glance flickering between Henry and the Bishop of London, "you have no jurisdiction over a prince of the Church."

"Have I not?" Henry turned slightly, "My lord Bishop of London, perhaps you wish me to see to the secure custody of this dubious churchman while full inquiry is made into these matters."

Flambard was universally disliked, and the bishop almost smiled. "The Church would be grateful for your assistance, sire."

"Then I consign him to the Tower until such time as the truth is known." Before Flambard could form any argument, the king continued. "And it seems to me that the Bishop of Durham is willful and eaten by pride. Perhaps he needs penance to help him see the error of his ways so that he may find salvation."

"A plain diet of bread and water might be salutary, sire," said the Bishop of London.

"Indeed," murmured Henry. "And yet, just a short time ago the bishop himself advocated physical penance to break the sin of pride. . . ."

"Ah." An almost gleeful light shone in the elderly bishop's eyes. "Ten strokes at each canonical hour, sire?"

"How wise. How judicious." Henry glanced at FitzRoger. "See to it, my friend."

"With pleasure, sire." And FitzRoger supervised the removal of the protesting cleric.

"You'll regret this!" Flambard screamed as the guards

forced him toward the door. "You'll find you need me, as your brother did!"

Henry merely smiled. "Go peacefully, Flambard, or I'll double the strokes."

In the moments it took for the bishop and his servants to be cleared from the room, Galeran considered the possibility that all of this—barring a few surprises thrown into the pot—had been planned. Henry perhaps knew Flambard could be useful to him, but only as a humble, broken servant, not as a man with power enough to challenge the Crown. Henry perhaps had seized an excuse to break him.

Henry Beauclerk was an interesting man, but Galeran hoped to live out his life far from his eagle eye.

When the door cut off the bishop's threats and pleas, the king turned his attention to those who were left—Galeran, Raoul, Lord William, and Lowick. The recording clerk, Warwick, and the Bishop of London were now only observers.

"Sire," said Galeran. "I must go to my wife—"

"In a moment, my lord. I assure you she is safe, and resting under the best possible care." He turned to Lowick. "Now, Sir Raymond . . ."

To Galeran's surprise, Raoul, not Lowick, stepped forward to sink to one knee before the king. "If I might be permitted to speak, your majesty."

"Sir? I did not think you had any part in this."

Typically, Raoul grinned up at Henry. "I wish I didn't, sire, but the Lady Jehanne asked me to speak for her here."

"The Lady Jehanne, if you will note it"—and there was a warning edge in the words—"is no longer in any jeopardy. Most of her guilt has been explained away, and if she deserved any punishment, she has received it."

"But she is concerned for Raymond of Lowick, sire."

His words caused the thunderous silence of astonishment, broken only when Galeran hissed in a breath. At this point . . . At this point was he to be betrayed?

"The lady has no deep feelings for Sir Raymond," Raoul said, as if unaware of the consternation he had caused. "But she holds herself responsible for his problems, sire, since it was her action during her brief time of madness that led him astray. She pleads for mercy on his behalf, and asks that her husband not be burdened with his death."

"Ah. She has some concern for her husband, then?" asked Henry caustically.

"The greatest concern, sire," said Raoul calmly. "If she considers Sir Raymond largely blameless, think how she regards her wronged husband. Her wish is only to make all right for him, and not to place upon him the need to injure others, as she knows he dislikes to do."

"Including taking a whip to her," said Henry. "A most intriguing woman, though—*mirabile dictu*—I find myself in some sympathy with Flambard. It is not a woman's place to act in this way to affect the affairs of men."

Seeing at last what had been going on, Galeran was running over choice things he longed to say to Jehanne. But first he had to handle this. He went to kneel at Raoul's side. "Sire, I ask your pardon for my wife if she has offended you by her actions. I suggest it is the depth of her repentance that makes her behave in this way."

"She's normally a meek, well-behaved woman, is she?"

From the tone, Henry doubted this greatly, and Galeran decided it was wisest just to give a man-to-man shrug.

Henry laughed. "Women can be a thorn in a man's side, particularly the sharp ones. But they're worth every jab. Stand up, my friends, you have done your part. So," Henry asked Galeran, "do you support your wife's petition for clemency?"

Galeran looked at Lowick, regretting, just a little, the battle that would not happen.

"I forgave my wife, sire, and I do not think Sir Raymond is any the more to blame for the adultery than she. For his other sins, however, I would ask that you follow the guidance of the Bishop of London and send him to fight for Christ. He has great warlike talents that should be put to the service of God."

And by God's grace, thought Galeran, I need never see him again.

The king turned to Lowick. "What think you, Sir Raymond?"

Lowick, however, looked troubled rather than relieved. "I would accept such a merciful judgment with gratitude, sire, as long as I have Lord Galeran's word that he will not punish the Lady Jehanne further, or in any way harm my child."

A tightening around Henry's mouth told Galeran that he was losing patience, so he intervened. "Raymond, would I hurt an innocent child, or Jehanne, whom I love?"

Lowick frowned as if seeking truth, and Galeran realized that the man was sincere. He truly feared for the safety of Jehanne and Donata. "It is not easy for any man to accept an unfaithful wife, or a child not his own. You hit her, I heard tell."

Galeran had often wondered what evil that blow would bring, no matter how excused. Now he knew. It had, perhaps, caused all these problems by fueling Lowick's fears.

"It was the first time I'd raised my hand to her, Raymond, since we were children, and I will never do so again. I swear it here, on my hope of eternal life."

Lowick's handsome face was set in lines of ferocious thought. "And Donata?"

"Is already as a daughter to me."

After yet more frowning contemplation, Lowick nodded. "Then I truly beg your pardon for the harm I tried to do you, Galeran." He turned and knelt again before the king. "I see now, sire, that I let myself be led into wrong through my unlawful love, through my natural feelings for my child. And," he added resolutely, "through my ambitious greed for land. If your mercy still stands, sire, I will happily fight for Christ."

"So be it," said Henry impatiently, and waved him out of the room.

The king then sat on his throne, taking off his crown and placing it on a table by his side. "That man is just the type of noble fool who wreaks havoc without any bad intent at all. Are you content now, Lord Galeran?"

"Completely, sire, if I have my wife and her child safe, and can return home."

Henry raised a brow. "I detect a little something in your voice, my lord. Perhaps you are tempted to beat your wife after all for this business. She had no choice but to be whipped."

"Had she not, sire?" The king was right. Relief was beginning to make room for sharp irritation. "The reason Raoul de Jouray became involved is that my wife's cousin escaped from the convent, seeking his help. But my wife sent no message about her punishment, for she knew I would put a stop to it. If I do not want to beat my wife, I do not want her beaten."

Henry snapped his fingers, and a page hurried forward with a goblet of wine. "I heard of it all from Lord FitzRoger. As you doubtless guess, your wife accepted her punishment to prevent you from having to deliver it—which I might well have ordered despite your fierce stare. Order must be preserved. As it is, we can let it be known that she has been suitably chastised. There is no need to explain the circumstances."

Galeran could find nothing civil to say to this.

"Apparently," continued Henry, "she also accepted the punishment because she saw that in ordering it, Flambard was overstepping himself. A clever and resolute lady."

"Yes, sire."

"Whose neck you would dearly like to wring. That is up to you." The king turned abruptly to Lord William. "I have served your family today, my lord. I hope you will serve mine."

Lord William must also suspect that the king had served mainly himself, finally finding a way to confine Flambard with the blessing of the Church, and tie William of Brome to his cause. But he bowed. "You have my oath, my liege."

Henry could doubtless hear the reservations behind it, but it was good enough to bind a man like the Lord of Brome. "Then you and yours will have my favor always. And you do not need to fear Flambard or any Bishop of Durham again. I intend to break the power of that bishopric once and for all."

Henry sipped his wine, glancing at Galeran. Suddenly he laughed, showing his strong white teeth. "Whether to kiss her or throttle her, you are itching to see to your wife, are you not? Go, my lord. This lad will take you to her. But don't murder her here, please. And serve me well in the north."

Twenty-one

She was here? Galeran had counted on the journey to the convent, or to Hugo's house, to sort out his curdled feelings and prepare to meet Jehanne kindly. He had only to follow the page through three rooms and into a fourth, however, before he was with her.

But she was sleeping.

She sprawled somewhat awkwardly on her side, her back toward him. Her clothing had been slit and spread apart, probably so a greenish salve could be applied. He hoped the cream soothed her, but it did little to hide the swelling of abused flesh, crossed red and black by the rod.

Anger fled, except rage at those who had done this to her. He wished he could lay the rod to Flambard himself.

But then anger at Jehanne snapped back, hilt to blade with fierce pride at her courage. The first beating would not have been so bad, nor even the second. But she had continued to accept them knowing, especially when she sent Aline out, that by a word she could put a stop to it.

And all for him.

The small room was plain—perhaps a place for a senior servant of the king to catch some sleep without leaving Westminster. Aside from the narrow curtained bed, the only furniture was a table with a bowl and ewer.

Galeran leaned against a wall as he worked through his feelings.

She should have trusted him to bring them all home safe.

This was Jehanne, though. Just as she had always been. If he wanted a meek wife who would never try to take a hand in the management of their affairs, then he had been poorly used by fortune.

He had not been poorly used by fortune.

He could imagine no other wife. What other woman was as beautiful, as intelligent, as courageous, as resolute, as generous . . .

He was growing hard with desire, but it looked as if they had a good stretch of chastity ahead of them while she healed. It was as well he'd practiced the discipline.

Quietly, so as not to wake her, he opened another door and found Aline, Winifred, and the baby. He placed a finger on his lips before Aline could cry her surprise.

When he'd closed the door, she asked, "Is everything all right?"

"Yes. Jehanne is safe, the baby remains with us, and Flambard is in the Tower."

"Praise God! But what of Lowick?"

"By heaven's gates!" he exploded. "Why is everyone so concerned with that man's fate? What it is to be handsome!"

"Handsome?" Aline scoffed. "He's as handsome as my father's best bull. It's just that he's at heart an honorable fool. He needs protecting."

Galeran burst out laughing. It had been so long since he'd laughed that way that it felt as if his face were cracking. He collapsed down on a bench, weak with it. "Poor Raymond. A bull!" But then he controlled himself. "What of Raoul, then? Are you going to protect him too?"

Color rushed into her face. "He's no fool. He can protect himself. Like you."

"But Jehanne thought she had to protect me from fighting Raymond."

Aline put her hands on her hips. "Are you going to turn silly over that? She loves you, so she wants to protect you. What choice does she have? What choice does anyone have in these things? We want to protect the ones we love. It's as natural as breathing."

He smiled at her ferocity. "Is it? No one seems to have told men that it works both ways."

"Perhaps it's just that men never listen."

"Perhaps it is. So, Aline, do you want to protect Raoul?"

She stared at him, startled. "I don't know."

"Perhaps," he said, "you just aren't listening to yourself." Galeran went over to the blanket in the corner upon which the baby slept, her tiny body rising and falling with each deep breath. Would she grow up to be like her mother and aunt, fierce as a wolf-mother in protecting her cubs?

Or in protecting her mate.

"How long since she fed?" he asked.

"Since before we left the convent. She'll wake soon."

He felt able, therefore, to gather Donata into his two hands and bring her close to his chest. His nose told him the cloths were wet again, but it didn't bother him. He settled her in the crook of his arm and tested the softness of her skin with a finger, wincing as his roughness brushed against petal smoothness. "You are as my own, little one," he said softly. "I have sworn it."

With a gummy yawn, the baby awoke, opening big blue eyes to look fixedly at him. But her mouth immediately started working.

"Food, food, and nothing but food, eh?" he said with a laugh. "A fine sense of the priorities. Very well. Let your Aunt Aline change you, and I'll take you to your mother."

Then I'll have an excuse to wake her.

I need her awake.

I need her.

The child made no complaint as she was unwrapped, cleaned, and changed, but continued to stare toward Galeran as if she knew how central he was to her world.

Would she ever know the mayhem her existence had caused?

He would do his best to make sure she never did.

When Donata was fresh, he carried her in to Jehanne. Sitting gently on the end of the bed with the baby in one arm, he shook one of Jehanne's stocking feet. "Wake up, sleepyhead."

She stirred slowly, almost reluctantly. Then pain and reality hit her, and she hissed. Fixed in an awkward position, she stared at him, blinking. "Galeran? Where . . . ? What . . . ? Oh, Donata."

"Yes, she needs feeding." He put the baby down, then helped Jehanne move to sit on the edge of the bed. Surely any movement must hurt, but she showed no sign of pain except a sharp out breath when it was over.

Clearly feeling abandoned, Donata squawked.

"Patience, little one." Galeran gave her a finger to hold on to as he asked, "How will you manage?"

"I'll be all right. Just give her to me."

But as he picked up the baby and placed her carefully in Jehanne's lap, Jehanne eyed him anxiously, almost fearfully. He knew she had many questions, but the baby would not wait, and was already beginning to cry in genuine distress, nuzzling at the cloth over the breast.

Jehanne murmured to her as she raised her tunic. In moments the only sound was the contented suckling of the babe. Jehanne looked at him in a direct way that was close to her usual manner. "Is everything all right, then?"

"Why do you assume that?"

"You look . . . relaxed. Happy?"

It wasn't fair to tease her. He let himself smile. "Everything's all right. And yes, I feel relaxed, and close to being happy."

She closed her eyes briefly. "Thank heavens!" But then she asked, "Raymond?"

Galeran burst out laughing. "The honorable bull? He's hale and hearty and off to gore the Infidel."

"Bull?" she queried, but then smiled. "That was well done. He'll like that."

"He seems content now that he's sure I won't knock you into walls when I'm in a bad mood, or raise Donata in the kitchens."

At that, she looked down and changed her hold on the baby slightly, but he guessed it was mostly to take time to think. When she looked up again, she asked, "So, what problem remains?"

"None."

"Yes, there is something."

Now didn't seem the time. He'd thought perhaps it need never be spoken of, that they could just go home and finally pretend that none of it had happened.

Except for a child who wasn't his, and the grave of a child who was.

One could never go back. One could only ever make today good.

But there was one problem he could talk of. "Do you think me an honorable fool? To be protected?"

She understood immediately. "Oh, Galeran, in these matters men and women are not much different. Could you stand by and see me walk into a bog without trying to prevent it?"

"No. But I have always let you walk your own path, trusting you to watch where your feet step. You might do as much for me."

"And I misstepped, and fell into the bog! What's worse, I dragged both you and Raymond in with me. It was for me to get us all out."

"Not this way!"

At his sharp voice, Donata startled and came off the breast. Jehanne's milk kept flowing and there was a moment of chaos as she caught the stream on her gown while settling the baby again.

More quietly, he said, "I was handling everything. I could have stopped your beating if you'd sent me word."

"But I did sin, Galeran. In the adultery, but more so in defying God." She looked up. "I needed to be punished."

"So be it," he said bitterly. "We'll send you back for more."

"No, thank you." She didn't react to his anger. In fact, she was smiling, and looking into her eyes, he realized a startling truth.

"You are at peace."

"Yes. Bishop Flambard did not intend to do me good, but he did. The time apart, time and peace to pray, cleansed me, even of my grief for Gallot and the bitterness I still felt about that. I learned about myself, and the punishment helped in some way. I found I couldn't control my body's weak reaction to pain, but I could control my mind. It made me stronger. Cleaner. I am at peace with myself and God, and ready to start again without wounds or shadows. Can we?"

"I would feel blessed to have it so." He moved closer, resting against her, frustrated that he couldn't crush her to him as he wished. For this was a new Jehanne. Not the resentful girl, or the exciting young woman. Not the desperate would-be mother, or the wounded sinner.

Out of the crucible had emerged the best of all of them, and a woman he loved even more than before.

He could not hold her but, as she switched the baby to the new, full breast, he told her about his own trials and self-knowledge. About Jerusalem. About the massacre and the blood flowing through the streets. And about his attempt to save the children, even though he knew it was suicidal.

"Raoul stopped me, but I fought him, even though I knew I was abandoning you and Gallot. It was a wrong decision, but even now I know I would do it again. He had to knock me out to save me, and for days I wandered in my mind. I think in that wandering I learned more of myself. It gave me time to come to terms with my place in God's world, with God's purpose for me."

He smiled at her. "I know for a while Raoul was afraid I really had gone mad, but I was just growing accustomed to what was new about me."

"I wondered. You were always a good man, a strong man, but it runs deeper now. It frightened me because I didn't think such goodness could still love me. I feared the strength would be turned against me. I understand better now. The stronger, the better, the better we can love."

She reached out her hand and he wove his dark, callused fingers through her smoother, paler ones. They meshed perfectly.

"Thanks be to God," he said.

Aline watched Galeran carry Donata to Jehanne, and knew it was over. The adventure was over.

That meant other things might be over too.

Like an assault on her castle.

She searched the warren of anterooms until she found Raoul, chatting to FitzRoger and some other men. They looked at her strangely—a woman invading men's affairs—but Raoul just spoke briefly to FitzRoger and stepped apart with her.

"What's happened?" she asked him.

He looked around and steered her behind a curtain. She expected a room, but it was hardly that. More a space with a small window looking out into the crowd of hawkers, gawkers, and entertainers. The king had clearly started another day of receiving his people.

"I suppose I shouldn't have interrupted you," she said.

"Why not? I presume Galeran is too absorbed in Jehanne to give long, coherent explanations." So he related the whole affair, and Aline took it in. But for some reason a large part of her unruly mind was more interested in his height, his breadth, his golden skin, and his very special smiles.

Perhaps it was obvious. When he'd finished, he said, "But you didn't really want to hear all that."

Aline snapped her wits out of heating longings. "Didn't I?"

"I hope not." He stepped forward. She retreated.

In such a tiny space, a two-step retreat had her up against a wall with nowhere else to go.

"I think you were as desperate to see me as I was to see you." He reached to coil a hand around the side of her neck. "As desperate to touch." He leaned forward, his other arm braced on the wall. "As desperate to kiss."

She didn't admit it, but she didn't resist, either.

His kiss was as sweet as her dreams remembered, but it wasn't just a matter of lips on lips. Though he didn't press against her as he had that time in Waltham, it was as if the spirit of him, or his essence, pulsed out to surround her, engulf her, melt her into a need so strong that she wrapped her arms around him and enthusiastically kissed him back.

Slowly, with tiny parting kisses, he pulled out of her arms.

"Until a while ago," Aline complained, "I'd never kissed anyone. And now I can't seem to do without!"

He gently smoothed her brows. "Don't frown so. I promise to keep you well supplied."

"Only if I'm with you."

"I think that would be a requirement, yes."

"But you don't want to live in Northumbria. . . ." She wished she didn't have to say these things, but there was a problem here, and it wouldn't melt under kisses, not even those of Raoul de Jouray.

He stopped teasing and turned serious. "Aline, it's a wife's place to live in her husband's house."

"But yours is so far away!"

He considered her soberly, but then smiled. A mild smile,

but still enough that she was glad she had the wall at her back to support her. "It has all come upon you suddenly," he said. "It's less than a month since we met. Perhaps you aren't even sure yet that you don't want the religious life."

There was a question there, and she answered it. "No, I'm not entirely sure."

But it was a lie. She knew now that she could never settle peacefully to the chaste and tranquil religious life.

"Go back home with Galeran, then, and consider these things. I'll come again next summer to hear your decision."

"Next year! You addict me to kisses, you wretch, then tell me to wait a year?"

He raised his brows in astonishment. "What else?" But a glint of humor in his eyes suggested that he understood her all too well. As he always had. Perhaps that was what irritated her most about him.

Aline pushed away from the wall and away from him. "I think you just want an excuse to sail away and forget me. You like to travel, not stay at home. You fall into bed with every willing woman who crosses your path. You know every brothel in every town. You doubtless have wives scattered all around the world—"

With warrior swiftness, he seized her, covering her mouth with his hand. "You don't have to drive me away with silly words, Aline. Just tell me to go."

When he uncovered her mouth, she wailed, "I don't know!" and burst into tears on his chest.

There were no seats in the plain room, so he just settled on the floor with her in his lap until she'd cried herself out.

"I don't know what's wrong with me," she sniffed, deeply mortified, but relishing being in his strong arms all the same.

He held her even closer, in a comforting embrace, not a lustful one. "I must have been mad to press you for an answer at such a time, love. Put it down to rash ardency."

She ventured a look up. "Are you? Ardent."

He moved his hips and she felt his ardency quite clearly.

"Mere lust," she muttered, hot-cheeked. "Do you really want to marry me, Raoul?"

"Yes."

"Why?" And she looked fully at him, needing the answer.

"Because," he said simply, "I've never met a woman who affects me quite as you do. I've been fond of many, I admit it, and even fancied myself in love a time or two. But I've never felt this way before. It's as if part of me would be lost if I leave you behind."

Aline stared at him, seeking a way to doubt him. It was a weighty burden to bear, being so important to another person. Of course he was as important to her. If he sailed away, she feared she'd be half alive for the rest of her days.

He rubbed his knuckles against her cheek. "I can wait, little one, until you know how you feel."

"I know how I feel," she grumbled. "I feel wretched! And lustful," she admitted. One of his beautifully muscled arms stretched in front of her, and she ran her hand along it, feeling the power and heat. "I really do feel lustful." She wriggled slightly to settle even closer to his body.

He gripped her hips to still them, but grinned. "That's a promising start."

"Hah!" She made herself stop playing with his arm and looked him in the eye. "Half the women you meet lust after you, Raoul de Jouray, and they don't love you."

"Only half?"

She thumped his chest and scrambled to her feet. He followed at his leisure, dusting off his clothes.

That gave her a moment to study him, which did nothing to cool her longings. Perhaps she was going to have to send him away, to never see him again, to never . . .

"If we made love," she suggested, cheeks heating, "then I'd know if it was just lust or not."

He raised a brow. "If we made love, my luscious grape, you'd be addicted for life."

"Oh, you . . . you . . . prideful cock!" Over his laughter, she demanded, "Is that enough, though, for the rest of our lives? To want to make love?"

He gave it careful thought. "If it is making love, yes. If it's just lust, no."

"How do we tell the difference without trying? Maybe I wouldn't like it at all—lust or love. Some women don't. Then I'd know I was supposed to be in the convent. . . ."

She was trying to find logical arguments, but the truth was that she was terrified that she would never know his body as she wanted to. Never see him naked again. Never lie skin to skin . . .

She knew her face must be cherry-red.

"You'd like it," he said with quiet confidence. "My years of practice have to be worth something. But beg as you will, Aline, I have no intention of making love to you until we are sanctified by God."

At the word *beg* she hit out. "So, you're going to wait in celibacy until I make up my mind?"

And thus came, impulsively, to the heart of her problem. She would rather lose him for all time than share him with other women.

And the wretch didn't instantly promise to be faithful.

He thought about it.

Aline turned and fled the room.

When Galeran emerged from Jehanne's room to arrange to get his party back to Hugo's house, he found Raoul already had the matter in hand. "The king's stables have provided extra horses. Your father has his own."

Galeran eyed his friend, detecting something close to ill humor in him, but now was hardly the time to ask about it. He wanted Jehanne safely back at Hugo's house before he even thought about other matters. He'd rather have her safely back at Heywood, but since people couldn't fly, and she couldn't travel, that was out of the question.

Jehanne wore Aline's tunic over her ruined clothes, and when she walked out and mounted the mother superior's jennet with the help of a mounting block, no one would have thought she was in great pain. But Galeran could tell the effort it was to preserve her pride in that way.

He smiled with fierce joy at her courage.

Being a large body of riders, they pushed easily through the crowds and out into the streets, but then had to fight their way slowly against the human tide all the way to Corser Street.

Hugo and Mary were delighted to play host to the mighty William of Brome, but their house was now even more crowded than before. Since their hosts also wanted an account of all their adventures—as well as details about the king's looks, his clothes and apartments, not to mention the wines he drank!—it was evening before Galeran had a chance to speak privately to Raoul.

In the meantime, however, he hadn't missed the fact that Aline also looked tense. Galeran feared his obsession with Jehanne's problems had allowed these two to be foolish. In the end, he invited his friend out into the street, where they weren't alone, but had some privacy amid the uncaring passersby.

"Is something the matter?" Galeran asked.

"Why do you ask?"

"Raoul, don't spar with me. What's happened between you and Aline?"

Raoul gave a sharp, humorless laugh. "Absolutely nothing. Which is probably the problem."

Galeran leaned back against a hogshead that was waiting to be rolled into the warehouse. "You can hardly have expected Aline to be a candidate for a pleasure bout."

A startling anger flashed through Raoul's eyes. "Do you think so little of me?"

Galeran raised a hand. "Pax, friend. But what do you want, and what is the problem?"

It seemed as if Raoul had some trouble putting the words together, but then he said, "I want Aline as my wife. The trouble is that she has again said no."

"Really?" Galeran might have been obsessed with his own affairs in recent weeks, but he didn't think he'd been mistaken in the bright sparks dancing between Raoul and Aline. "You did make it clear what you were offering, didn't you?"

"Ha! Entirely clear. It was the fair lady herself who proposed an unblessed romp. She wanted to test the blade before she purchased it."

Galeran was hard pressed not to chuckle. "You must have unsettled her mightily, then. A few weeks ago she never would have suggested such a thing."

"I've deliberately unsettled her, thinking she'd fall neatly into my arms like a plum loosened on the branch. But no. The women of your wife's family do nothing in the normal way."

"One becomes accustomed. And there are compensations."

Raoul paced restlessly in front of the vintner's house, the passersby keeping well out of the way of such a tall and frowning warrior. "I would be delighted to become accustomed, but how? I offered her marriage, and she wanted me to live in Northumbria. You know that's impossible."

"You'd shiver to death."

Raoul sent him a scathing glance. "More to the point, I have property and responsibility elsewhere. I offered to give her a year to make up her mind—and that stretched my nobility and restraint to its limit—and she proposed a test of the wares!"

"Perhaps that is the best idea."

"Test the wares?"

"Give her time."

"I don't dare." Raoul looked down the street, though Galeran suspected that he wasn't seeing much. "I daren't risk returning to find she's taken her nun's vows. Or married another now that I've whetted her appetite."

"She wouldn't do that."

"Women are fiendishly unpredictable. I've broken down her walls. I can't leave her now that she's vulnerable."

Before Galeran could ask an explanation of that, Raoul looked him in the eye and said, "I won't lose her, Galeran. I'll abduct her if necessary."

"I'd have to stop you."

"I'd try to make sure you didn't have the chance." But, his stance said silently, if it comes to blood, so be it.

Was this whole tangled affair going to end at sword's point after all? Not if Galeran could help it. He hadn't come through the war to lose all in a minor skirmish of the aftermath. "Why did she refuse you?"

"Some nonsense about my fidelity, and about traveling abroad."

"Hardly nonsense. Fidelity has not been your way to date. And would you rather have a wife who'd throw her common sense to the wind at the first touch of desire?"

Raoul grinned. "Sometimes, yes."

Galeran shared the smile. "Indeed. But it's no easy matter for some people to leave their home to live in a strange land. A girl like Aline, even if she had planned to marry, never planned to do such a thing. She would have married a man from a nearby estate."

"There's no choice in it, though. I've enjoyed traveling, but I've always intended to settle on my land in the Guyenne."

"Perhaps Aline would not care for the Guyenne."

"A person would have to be mad not to love the Guyenne."

"If people loved only the most pleasing corners of God's earth, we'd be in a sorry state. My friend, I think you have wooed and won Aline's heart, but you will not woo her out of her common sense. You'll have convince her head that she will be safe and happy in this strange soil, far from her family and friends, alone in times of trouble."

"She will not be alone. . . ."

"You must convince her of that."

Raoul exclaimed, "Christ's crown, if only I were a better liar!"

"What?"

Suddenly rueful, Raoul said, "She asked me if I would be faithful to her while she made up her mind."

"You said no?" Galeran could hardly believe it.

"I didn't say anything. I was trying to be honest, Galeran! I was giving it careful thought. I haven't been celibate for a year since I first had a woman, and I had no intention of making a promise I could not keep. She didn't wait to hear."

"Can you make that vow now?"

Almost as if in pain, Raoul said, "If it's her price, yes."

Galeran shook his head, pushing off the cask. "It's not that simple. She has to trust you with her life. Almost literally. I suggest you put your mind to convincing her, for I assure you, she's not leaving England unless she goes willingly."

Jehanne, propped up on cushions so she could lie on her front without pressing on her sensitive breasts, listened to Aline relate her adventures during her escape without actually mentioning Raoul de Jouray except in passing.

"You spent the night together in a bed?" Jehanne asked. It was a deduction, since Aline hadn't actually said as much.

"I slept!" Aline snapped.

"I'm sure you did."

"He didn't do anything . . . Well, almost nothing . . . He's amazingly restrained."

Jehanne worked at keeping a straight face. "You sound almost disappointed."

"Of course I'm not." Aline paced backward and forward,

skirts swishing. "It's nice to know he can sometimes keep his weapon in its sheath."

"He seems to have acted competently in keeping you safe and getting into the convent. And I understand he spoke for me before the king."

Aline stopped. "I never said he wasn't competent."

"True. So, what holds you back from him?"

"Holds me back?" Aline asked with spurious puzzlement.

"If I'm any judge at all, the man loves you and wants to marry you. And yet you do not have the look of a happy couple."

"Would you marry half a world away?" Aline challenged.

"I'd follow Galeran beyond the ends of the earth, to heaven or hell itself."

"Yes, well . . . Would you have done that when you'd scarce known him a month?"

Jehanne laughed. "No, you have me there. But we were very young." Yet Aline was young, Jehanne thought. It was easy to forget that she was only eighteen and had lived, until recently, a protected life. "Perhaps it is wiser to wait."

"Wait! But what's the point in waiting? If he comes back in a year, will I know him any better?"

"You may know your heart better. It's been an intense time and he's tempting enough. But sometimes the fiery interest fades down to cinders with a little time and distance. Once, you know," she added with a grimace, "I thought Raymond of Lowick stood only one rung below God."

Aline laughed at that. "But there's no comparison between Raymond and Raoul." She picked up the salve pot, looking at it as if she'd never seen it before. "You're probably right, though, that Raoul's interest in me will fade with a little time and distance. I suppose I'd be doing him a kindness to send him away."

"Aline, I was talking about you! Raoul is older, and a great deal more experienced. I doubt he'll change as easily."

"If he loves me at all . . ."

"Would a man like that want to marry unless he loved? I presume he did ask for your hand in marriage."

"Oh, yes." Aline gave in. She put down the pot and recounted the whole of her conversation with Raoul.

Jehanne groaned at the end. "But you know, cousin, when a man like that makes such a snarl of it, it is a sign of something."

By the next day, Jehanne could sit up, and even move around a little without too much pain. As she worked her way along the narrow corridor to the hall at one end of the building, however, she took uncharitable satisfaction from the notion that Bishop Flambard had received a full cycle of the rod. Perhaps Galeran could find the grace to forgive the man, but she couldn't. It wasn't the beating she held against him, but the harm he had tried to do to her family.

When she found Galeran in the hall, she said as much.

"You overestimate my charity," he said, as he helped her to a bench near an open window. "I hope he's in agony, and that there will be worse for him in the future."

They smiled with the easy understanding once taken for granted, now deeply appreciated.

"About Raoul . . ." she said.

". . . and Aline," he completed with a humorous grimace.

"What are we to do?"

"Turning matchmaker?"

"Why not? Marriage is a wonderful institution."

Again, their smiles danced together, and they spoke silently of other things entirely.

"I suppose Raoul didn't handle things well," said Galeran.

"An understatement! But Aline is sensible to have reservations, no matter what honeyed words he tempts her with."

"His word is true," said Galeran sternly. "That was the problem. He won't make a vow he cannot keep."

She reserved comment on that. "Is there any hope for them, then?"

"We'll have to see. But I have one thought I'd like your verdict on."

"Yes?"

"I don't think Hubert of Burstock will be best pleased to have his only daughter married off without his leave. We'll have to take them back home to be wed."

"Oh, poor Raoul! Back to the harsh north."

"And we're moving toward autumn. We'd better provide him with furs."

And they laughed together at simple human foibles.

Twenty-two

When the first gift came, Aline was sitting in the room she shared with Jehanne, Winifred, and the baby. Hiding, really. She didn't want to see Raoul. She didn't like the amused look in everyone else's eyes. This situation was not the slightest bit funny.

A servant entered carrying a prettily carved wooden box just the size of the palm of her hand. When she opened the domed lid, she found an exquisite sprig of blossoms. For a moment she thought it was real, but when she touched a leaf she found it was metal colored green, and the blossoms were carved out of ivory. Accompanying it was a message, so beautifully written that he must have hired a scribe: *As beautiful as the almond blossom.*

The only thing she'd seen similar to this was the rose Jehanne owned, the one with the petals that kept falling off. This was a finer piece, though. Had he just found it, or had he stood over a craftsman all day and night as it was created to his order?

It was a marvel, but sadly, it didn't change anything. She knew he was devoted to her now, but she had seen devoted couples grow apart. Sometimes love dies entirely, and in such times friends and family are the only comfort and protection. She knew, too, that a bride far from all she knows is in a perilous position.

She could not help but go show the pretty ornament to Jehanne, however. She found her cousin in the hall with

Galeran, laughing as they had in the old days. For a moment she felt a bitter stab of jealousy, for if she could not have Raoul, there would be no other to laugh with like that.

"How lovely." Jehanne touched a blossom with one careful finger, then smiled up at Galeran.

"Indeed," said Galeran. "Take care of it, Aline. Such treasures can be broken." Though he addressed Aline, his eyes never left his wife's.

"And mended," Jehanne murmured.

Aline overrode their byplay. "I won't be swayed by gifts."

"Of course not," said Jehanne, turning to her. "But you might consider what they say of the man."

"That he's not penny-pinched?"

"No bad thing in a husband, surely."

Suddenly thoughtful, Aline put her gift in a safe place and went off in search of Lord William. At least she could try to sort out practical matters. She found him in the storeroom discussing wine storage with Hugo, and eventually managed to get him away for a deep and detailed discussion about dower property. Having handled that, she moved on to ways of protecting a woman in a foreign land.

He rubbed his bristly chin, eyes twinkling. "I'd been thinking along the same lines, my dear. In fact, Raoul reminded me that Hugo is a relative of his. That there are many links between Guyenne and England. Letters pass between Bordeaux and London regularly. And we did discuss establishing a trade link to Stockton."

"Reminded you recently?"

"Just this morning."

Aline returned to her hiding place in the sleeping chamber to take out the ivory almond blossom and ponder. Had Raoul raised the subject of links and letters on purpose? If there were letters, she would not feel so cut off from home, and if there were regular trade to a port near her home, it would be even better.

More importantly, as Jehanne had pointed out, she had to

think what all this said of the man. Perhaps he was not just trying to turn her head with pretty gifts, but trying to deal with her reasonable fears.

Hope beginning to stir, Aline ventured out to help Mary in her kitchen, where she was supervising the stewing of rabbits for the midday meal. Aline managed to bring the talk around to France and Guyenne. She soon established that Hugo himself traveled to Bordeaux once a year, and that he had interests in three ships that regularly visited that port.

Guyenne was suddenly not quite so far or strange a place.

When everyone gathered for the midday meal, however, she could not bring herself to look at Raoul, never mind smile at him. She suspected she was almost won over, but she still had a few doubts, and it wouldn't be right or fair to imply otherwise.

And anyway, she admitted to herself, she wanted to see what he would do next.

What he did was leave.

The next day, Raoul de Jouray was gone, with no word as to his whereabouts.

Aline felt a frantic urge to run into the streets searching for him, but there was no point. He'd taken his horses and his two men. Perhaps he'd decided he couldn't marry a woman not willing to trust him mindlessly, and sailed back to France.

He'd left most of his clothes, though. Surely he must be coming back.

Lips quivering, Aline told herself that if he'd left, he'd merely proved her right. He didn't truly desire her and was incapable of constancy. The thought gave her no comfort at all, but now she refused to hide.

If he came back, he would not find that she'd been pining.

Jehanne watched Aline set violently precise stitches in a gown edging, and murmured to Galeran, "Where has he gone?"

Galeran had Donata lying on his lap, clutching his two fingers. "I don't know."

"Is he coming back?"

"He didn't say."

"If he doesn't, someone should seek him out and kill him."

Galeran just grinned. "Then it'll have to be you, love. I'm for home and peace."

Two days later Aline—still militantly acting as normal—was crossing the courtyard to the smokehouse to choose smoked fish for Mary, when she was captured and swung into the dim granary.

Held tight with her back to a rock-hard body, she knew who it was by instinct before logic told her, and by instinct her body heated.

But if the wretched man thought terrifying her like that would sway her . . .

Strange, bulbous objects appeared before her eyes.

A second later, focusing, she realized they were grapes, held in his hand. She'd never actually seen a bunch of grapes, but Hugo had some carved into a lintel, and had been happy to tell her of them.

"Not from Guyenne, alas," he whispered into her ear. "But there are vineyards in some parts of this benighted country."

"They look like gooseberries."

He chuckled. "And would taste like them, I fear. They need quite a few weeks more to be at their best, and then they would taste nothing like the grapes of Guyenne." Somehow, without letting her go, he nuzzled around to kiss the corner of her mouth. "For the grapes of Guyenne are plump, sweet, and juicy, just like you."

Though she knew she shouldn't, she turned her head a

little so her lips were more accessible to him. She was struggling not to cry with relief.

He hadn't gone.

He hadn't given up the siege before she had a chance to surrender. She'd known for days that she wanted to surrender, but if he planned to woo her some more, she certainly wasn't going to object.

"Thank you for the flower," she murmured, her mouth moving against his.

"Is this kitchen love, then? Just gratitude?"

She thought of protesting the word *love,* but then let it lie. It was true. "I'm trying to see beyond the gift."

She turned just a little farther, so her lips were almost entirely available to him.

He completed the alignment and kissed her quickly, but openmouthed. "And what do you see, my Jimena?"

His use of that name set her heart fluttering. "A man who seems to want me very much indeed. I'm not sure why."

His brows rose. "Do you doubt that you are worthy of love?"

"No."

"Then why question it?"

Because I worry that whatever draws me to you might fade, and then where would I be?

Abandoned, in the vineyards of Guyenne.

After a moment, she found the courage to tell him her fears.

He leaned back a little to study her. "Aline, Aline! Why would you think such a thing? How can your nature, your self, your spirit, ever fade? These, above all, are what I love."

She couldn't think what to say, because she didn't entirely believe him. Oh, she believed he spoke the truth as he saw it, but was it the truth of his heart?

He let go of her, placing the bunch of grapes in her

hands, and opened the pouch at his belt to extract a vial. "Water," he said. "There is no sierra in England to hold the snows of winter, but I found a place where the water rises pure and cool from the chalky downs." He took out the stopper and tasted some. "It is very like. Taste, Aline. It is as pure as my love for you."

She let him put the vial to her lips and tip it so a little pure water ran onto her tongue. "It is good," she said, licking a trace from her lips, realizing that he had searched southern England for these items for her. Like El Cid undertaking quests to win his Jimena.

"And," he said, looking into her eyes, "if you want a year to think about this, I will be faithful to you for that year. Even though it'll probably ruin me for life."

She bit her lips, fighting a giggle that she knew would be like a flag of surrender.

"So," he asked, and something in his eyes told her he wasn't fooled. "What else do you want, my lady fair? The pelt of a white bear? Sugar crystals from the East? Rubies from Asia . . . ?"

Aline looked down and plucked a green grape off the bunch, lifting it to her lips to taste it. Then she spat it out. "It's *worse* than gooseberries!"

"Aline . . ."

"But just unripe, you said. In time it will be sweet. I was unripe, Raoul. Even a few days ago I was still green and sour. I think I'm growing riper and sweeter by the day. . . ."

"Aline," he said in a different tone entirely, reaching for her.

But she raised a hand. "You asked what I wanted."

"Yes?" Suddenly he was wary. And worried. That worry made her want to cry, for Raoul de Jouray was never worried. But they'd be tears of happiness.

"I want a part of the income from my dower property here in England to be placed, for my use alone, with a certain Ingelram, an English wine merchant in Bordeaux."

His brows rose, but he nodded. "I agree. Anything else?"

"Two maids from Brome or Heywood among my women, if they will come."

"Of course. You must choose your women as you wish. Anything else?"

"Well," she said, "if you *insist* on finding me sugar crystals from the East . . ."

He pulled her into his arms, a fierce flare of joy in his eyes. "You are sweet enough already." After a crushing silence he said, almost hesitantly, "That was a yes?"

Tears did spring to her eyes as she nodded.

He pushed her back to look at her, and the joy in his face made her cry some more.

"An excellently negotiated surrender, little castle." He wiped tears from her cheeks. "Christ's crown, but you'll fit right into my family. Did I ever tell you you remind me very much of my mother?"

His kiss this time was thorough, and under the heady knowledge that they were to be married, that she would soon lie skin to skin and more with this man, passion bubbled up in Aline like water from a cracked rock.

But when the kiss ended, she had to break the news that Galeran insisted that they go home to get Hubert's consent.

"Yet more time in the north?" he groaned, but he was smiling as if he'd never stop, and had her tight against his body as if he'd never let go. "I'll perish."

"Perhaps I should find you the pelt of a white bear." She ran her hand over his chest, wishing she could touch his skin.

"Or cuddle up to me at night . . . no," he added. "That would be fatal."

"Fatal?" She ran her fingers up to his neck, where at least there was skin to be touched. "People don't die of a little self-restraint, you know."

He captured her hand and kissed her fingertips. "Witch. Some of us know what we're missing."

"Some of us are more practiced in self-restraint, you mean," she retorted, snatching her hand free with a grin. Before he could pursue the matter, she pulled him out of the granary, eager to find Galeran and Jehanne and share the news.

He went willingly enough, but murmured, "Throwing challenges from the walls again, my green cadet?"

Warned by those words, Aline wasn't totally surprised when Raoul appeared in her room that night.

She shared a bed with Jehanne, while Winifred slept on a pallet on the floor by the baby's crib. Raoul had woken her with gentle hand and quiet voice, and now gestured to her to go with him. Driven by curiosity and a simmering excitement, she put her hand in his to be pulled to her feet.

But standing there in her shift, she mouthed, "What do you think you're doing?"

"Taking up your challenge." He gestured toward the door.

Aline knew she shouldn't go, but as always, she couldn't resist his challenges. She did glance back at Jehanne, the notoriously light sleeper, and thought she saw a smile.

So much for chaperones and guardians!

An excitement was building, almost stealing Aline's breath, but for the moment she was intrigued by practicalities. How would he find a private corner in this crowded house?

This upper floor contained the hall and three linked rooms leading off it. The women's chamber she'd shared with Jehanne lay farthest from the hall. The door led into the men's chamber full of Lord William's snores, and where Raoul and Galeran had pallets on the floor. Beyond that they entered the solar, where Hugo, Mary, and two daughters slept in a big curtained bed, their personal servants sprawled around the floor.

Picking her way through the room, Aline heard rain. He couldn't be taking her outside.

The hall would be jammed with servants.

Quite a challenge, even for an experienced warrior.

He led her to the corner between the hall and the solar, where stairs ran down to the lower floor. But the lower floor, she knew, was used by the vintnery servants and the men-at-arms.

The stairs were wooden, and a straight flight turned at a flat landing. He stopped there under a narrow window and slid down to sit, taking her with him, tucked cozily against his side.

"Very clever," she whispered, knowing she was about to be soundly defeated by a master. She could hardly wait.

"Elementary scouting." He kissed her gently on the cheek, almost as her father might, or as she might nuzzle against Donata.

And yet the feelings were different, and the excitement within her became a shiver.

He rubbed her arms gently, as if she had shivered from cold, speaking to her in a voice so soft, she felt she picked up words from his breath on her skin rather than from sound in her ear.

He spoke of his arrival at Heywood and his first sight of her, of the progression of his feelings from curiosity to interest, from admiration to obsession, from obsession to love. It was a devastating assault, melting any lingering resistance into aching tenderness for him, for her beloved.

And all the time his hands worshipped her without ever doing anything that could be considered improper at all.

Had he stolen her from her bed to talk and cuddle?

And how could cuddling be so unsettling?

Restlessly, she shifted so she was closer, so her left hand could touch his chest, stroke him as he was stroking her, learn him through touch in the dimness. Such a mighty chest, covered only by a light linen tunic. Such broad shoulders so well layered with muscle. Such a hard belly. She suspected that she could bounce on his belly and he'd hardly notice.

He shifted too, moving his leg over hers. So she explored the hard, well-trained muscle of his thigh through the cloth. At the hem, however, she encountered naked flesh, roughened by hair. In her mind she could see golden hair on golden skin. She hesitated only a moment before sliding her hand under the cloth, her mouth suddenly dry, her heartbeats clear to her, every one, even though she didn't dare explore higher.

"I've wanted to feel your hand on me like that, Aline," he murmured, shifting a little so his hand found the edge of her shift, and her naked thigh. She felt calluses as he worked up to cup her buttock.

Aline sucked in a breath and swallowed. "I thought even the tortures of the damned wouldn't make you dishonor me."

His tormenting hand did not move. "We are to be married. There is no dishonor in this. But even so, I will not make love to you tonight."

"Oh." She hoped she didn't sound disappointed. "What will we do, then?" His hand had moved to the small of her back and circled there. She could have purred.

"Just test your defenses, my green cadet, and show you a little of what you're missing." Breath warm against her neck, he whispered, "Your defenses are totally inadequate, you know. See the army now, massed around you, pennants flying, blades glinting in the sun. Hear the drums of your defeat."

He must mean her thundering heart. "I'm not sure about this," she said.

"Do you fear surrender to your rightful lord?"

"I fear being discovered here like this with you."

He chuckled. "No one is likely to find us unless you cry out."

"Why would I do that?"

"Remember Dame Helswith's house?"

She stared at his shadowy face. "Are you going to hurt me, then . . . ?"

"I will do my best never to hurt you, Aline. But it is possible to scream with pleasure."

Before she could express her skepticism, he covered her mouth in a powerful, conquering kiss that reminded her strongly of Waltham. Just from curiosity, she felt for his scabbard, and found it empty.

He chuckled, but didn't stop kissing the wits out of her.

A part of Aline—the well-bred, well-trained almost-nun—urged that she struggle and scream just to prove that she was a good woman. The sensible part said she could struggle and scream if it got to the point where she really wanted to.

Scream the alarm, that is. She didn't believe she could ever be brought to scream with pleasure when it would bring people out to catch her at this.

She settled to learning this business of kissing, mouths open, tongues engaged. When his hand found her breast, it enhanced the pleasure of his hot mouth and she kissed him even more enthusiastically, running her fingers into his hair to hold him close to her.

He disengaged and moved her a little. That's when she realized she'd scrambled on top of him like a child climbing a rock. If she was trying to appear to be a reluctant conquest, she was failing miserably.

He cupped her breast, raising it so his mouth could play with her through the fine linen cloth. From stroking, her fingers in his hair turned to clutching. "What are you doing now?" But she kept it quiet.

He raised his head long enough to ask, "Don't you like it?" Since his hand still pleasured her other breast, Aline managed only an inarticulate noise.

He seemed to interpret it correctly, and returned to his labors.

The sensations were quite extraordinary. Rather like a high fever in the nicest possible way. Still, Aline thought smugly, she was not even tempted to scream.

Then he slid her shift off her shoulders and down so his mouth found her naked flesh, just as his hand found the place between her thighs that was even more sensitive than her breast. Aline did almost let out a squeak of astonishment, but managed to control it.

It wasn't that she was surprised to be sensitive there. She'd heard talk of the pleasure to be found by rubbing between the legs. She'd tried it, though, and it hadn't seemed exciting enough to sin for. Clearly, she thought, clutching at his sleeve, she'd been doing something wrong.

For an assault on a castle, his stroking hand was remarkably slow and gentle. . . . Except inside her, where something hot flared.

"Mining," she murmured.

He raised his head from her breast. "Yes, I'm yours."

"No. Yes. I mean, mining. You're mining me. Undermining my walls."

He laughed softly. "I've been undermining you for weeks, little castle. Burrowing under your walls. Placing tinder there ready. Tonight I'm putting torch to tinder so that heat will crack your bastions, and you'll be defenseless before me."

"I think I already am. . . ."

"Shall I stop, then?" She heard by the laughter in his soft voice that he knew the answer.

"No, but . . ."

"Shhhhhh," he said, his lips fluttering against hers. "Just remember to be very quiet. You don't want your overlord to ride to your rescue at this point, do you?"

Then, returning to the pleasuring of her breasts, he used his thigh to spread her legs wider and stroked more firmly so she had to clutch on to him for fear of falling. Which was ridiculous, when they were already on a solid surface.

Then, at the peak of a stroke, he sucked hard on her

breast and slid his finger into her so that a jolt shot right between the two points.

"Ah!" She managed to swallow it, but only just.

"Bite me if you want," he whispered, circling gently again.

So Aline filled her mouth with the cloth and muscle of his shoulder, wondering if perhaps she should scream for her overlord after all.

Raoul's big hand summoned the fire that would destroy her, and like an encircling army, his thigh between hers would not let her evade it. She almost felt as if she were fighting for her life as she stiffened, hands gripping him, teeth clenched in him.

But she wasn't fighting to escape, even though he was destroying her. The inarticulate sounds she was choking against his shoulder were not cries for help.

Then the tinder caught, the wood burned bright, and her walls shuddered, cracked, and fell.

Through them she saw light.

No. Light was too weak a term.

Through the broken walls, she saw heaven. A momentary glimpse of the infinite wonder of heaven.

His hand. His slow and gentle hand held her suspended there until she thought she'd faint, but then, part sorrowing, part relieved, she felt the wonder fade, felt herself float back down to the wooden landing like a tuft of thistledown on a very still day.

He moved to hold her in his arms, smoothing down her shift, then continuing to stroke her gently in a way that made her never want to part from him at all.

"I don't think I screamed," she said at last.

"Can you be sure?"

"No one's raised the alarm."

"True. I'm not sure I'm not scarred for life, though." But she could hear a smile in it.

She touched a damp patch on his tunic where her mouth

had been. Underneath, she felt the indentations left by the teeth. "Oh, dear."

"A warrior expects a little pain in so conclusively conquering a castle. Are you now my vassal?"

She didn't answer that, but instead said, "Perhaps, in time, I can learn to undermine *your* walls."

He laughed softly, laying his head against hers. "I'm already rubble, love, but I look forward to your attempts at further destruction."

She stroked him, and that was sweet, to be able to cherish him as he had cherished her. "I can see now why you were reluctant to promise to do without that pleasure for a whole year." There was a question in it, and she blushed to hear it. She was begging for more.

He looked up at her. "I won't deprive you. Once we are married."

"Once . . . !" She'd almost spoken at normal volume and returned to murmuring. "You mean, you won't . . . ? Until we are married?"

"Self-restraint, remember?" he teased.

"Oh, you! But it *is* good for the soul."

"Our souls are going to be very healthy, then." He gathered her into his arms and she cuddled there, giving thanks for finding this one man in the huge world. It was terrifying to think that they might never have met, and frightening to part with him, even for the few remaining hours of the night.

Perhaps he felt the same, for in the end it was she who pulled away, stood, and led them both back to her sleeping chamber.

"Good night," she whispered, wanting to say so much more but not quite comfortable with the words as yet.

He, of course, was more at ease. "Sleep well, beloved. And when you dream, dream of me."

* * *

In the next days, Aline decided that a strong, resolute man could be a pain in the neck. Or in other places. Tease him as she might, Raoul would give her no more than a sisterly kiss, and generally, he avoided her. Aline went through the days in heated frustration, though that could be attributed to the fact that southern England was baking under a heat wave.

For distraction, she threw herself into work. When she wasn't preparing for the journey home, she was pestering Hugo and his friends for any and all knowledge of Guyenne, its people, its agriculture, and its trade.

From being fearful of the adventure, she now couldn't wait to marry and sail to a new land with her husband. The marrying was the important part, however. Why did they have to go north to be wed?

When her father rode into Hugo's yard, therefore, she threw herself into his arms with ecstatic delight.

"Hey, hey!" said Lord Hubert, staring at her. "What's up, chicken?"

Aline was suddenly tongue-tied, and it was Galeran who said, "She's hot to marry Raoul de Jouray."

Aline went brick-red and wailed, "Galeran!"

But Galeran just grinned. "It's the truth. You two are probably responsible for this heat wave. It'll be a relief to the south of England to get you calmed down a bit."

Lord Hubert scratched his head as he was led into the house. "I thought you wanted the church, chicken."

"I've changed my mind, Father. He has land," she said quickly, getting to the important part.

"Has he? Well, that's something."

It was soon clear that Lord Hubert had decided he, too, should come to pay homage to Henry. He listened carefully to his daughter's adventures—a somewhat edited account—then took Raoul aside for a long talk.

Aline was left suddenly fearful. She'd never considered that her father might refuse the match, but now she wasn't sure. He clearly felt all the qualms she first had, and he wasn't at all swayed by charming smiles and broad shoulders.

Raoul came out of the room and just raised his brows. "He wants to speak to you, Aline."

"What does he say?"

"Go and talk to him."

Raoul was being infuriatingly uncommunicative, even by expression. Aline went in, rubbing damp palms on her skirts. "Yes, Father?"

Lord Hubert just looked at her. "Do you want him?"

"Oh, yes."

"Do you trust him?"

"Yes."

He shrugged. "So do I, though he might just be a fine trickster. You've always had a head on your shoulders, though, lass, so if you're sure, I'll not stand in your way."

Aline ran into her father's arms. "Thank you! He is honorable, and I do love him."

Her father patted her shoulder. "And you're like your mother, God rest her. Sensible and warmhearted at the same time. He wants to marry you here and now, chicken, but I'll make him wait if you'd rather."

Aline blushed. "Oh, no."

He chuckled. "Aye. I judge he'll serve you well in bed at least. We can get the contract drawn up today, since I gather you've already settled most of it, and you can be married tomorrow if you want."

"Tomorrow?"

"Don't say you're going to change your mind now!"

Aline leaped to her feet, "No! Oh, no. But what should I wear?" She ran out to find Jehanne.

She wore her best red tunic and a girdle set with a ruby. Raoul had given it to her that morning, along with a chance to escape.

"It's not so long since we met, love, and not so long since you had doubts. I will wait if you want."

She looked down at the lovely gift. "I don't want. I know my mind. If you have doubts . . ."

He raised her chin. "None at all." And she saw in his eyes the same devotion and hot need that burned in her.

"Then we'll have no more nonsense, please."

They walked to nearby St. Stephen's Church to take their vows at the door, accompanied by as many friends and connections as possible, future witnesses to their words. They were considerably startled, however, when a trumpet blast cleared the way for the king, crown on head, surrounded by nobles and guards.

With a mighty crowd now gathered around them, Henry declared, "I heard rumor of this event and thought I'd best witness it myself. We don't want more uncertain marriages in the family, do we, Sir William?"

Hugo and Mary looked as if they would faint with excitement, and the crowd was like a swarm of buzzing bees, but Aline could think only that the king's presence might slow things down.

The ceremony went off smoothly, however, and soon they were returning to Corser Street in a much more magnificent procession.

"Is the king coming back?" she whispered to Raoul.

"Looks like it." He gave her a rueful smile. "Many hours before we can be alone, love. Remember, self-denial is good for the soul."

"My soul's so healthy, it glows!"

"Ah, is that the light in your eyes?"

And she laughed up into his shining eyes, deciding it didn't matter if the king was here. She was married to Raoul. She could wait.

Showing sensitivity, Henry didn't stay at Hugo's house longer than it took to toast the couple, speak to the most important people, and place a large order for wine. Then he rode away, leaving family and friends to relax and celebrate. Hugo, however, was still in a daze and planning to rename the gate into his yard King's Gate.

They still couldn't, with decency, rush off to be alone, though. Aline tried to talk coherently as she sipped wine and nibbled cakes, but all she really wanted to do was eat her husband. He, however, didn't seem impatient at all. He even found an instrument and entertained. He did sing the song about almond blossoms, though, smiling into her eyes.

Most of the women were dabbing their eyes when he'd finished.

When the vesper bells sounded evening, Aline could at last hurry to the corner room that would be theirs alone tonight. Laughing women followed to help her prepare. Their jokes were as suggestive as the men's, and Aline was pink with blushes when she was ready, gowned only in her hair.

Raoul came in then, clad only in a cloak, which he discarded.

Certainly his short hair provided no cover, but then, who'd want to obscure his magnificent physique?

He smiled at her, unselfconscious even though he was already coming erect and both men and women were making scandalous jokes and appreciative comments all around them. For the second time in her life, she stared at his private parts, knowing she was turning a deeper and deeper red, but not caring a jot.

"Go away," he said to their companions, drawing her into the protection of his arms.

She was dimly aware of laughter and a closing door, then only of silence.

Silence, and Raoul, and her own growing lust.

"Nervous?" he asked.

She looked up at his darkened eyes. "Not at all. I warned you I was unnaturally stimulated by men's naked bodics."

He laughed. "I don't see anything unnatural about it,

love. But it's perhaps as well that you're about to surrender to a suzerain able to satisfy your needs."

"I'm holding you to that promise." Her hands were already wandering over him hungrily.

"And I'm suddenly terrified. . . ." And perhaps it was true. She noted with delight that his hands trembled as they slid around her neck to lift her hair high, then let it drift down again around her. "You do remind me of a juicy grape."

"Plump?"

"I adore plump. And sweet. And juicy. Touch me more, love. I hunger for your touch."

She pressed closer, hot skin to hot skin, soft curves to hard muscle, exploring his chest, his flanks, his back, with her greedy hands and lips.

As his hands and lips wandered her in turn, smoothing, squeezing, exploring, and raising her desire to even higher heat.

His erection pressed hard against her, and he was surely desperate, so she moved back a little to touch it. "Isn't it time for the conquering warrior to enter the captured citadel?"

Despite the need she could sense in him, he gently moved her hand. "Impatient to surrender, are you? Tush-tush. There is a proper procedure for these things, you know." He swung her into his arms. "For example, I need to be cautious. How can I be sure you have truly surrendered? That you don't have an ambush planned?"

"Ambush? I'm completely weaponless!"

He laughed at that, swinging her around. "Your armory is astonishing, love. Your hair, your eyes, your cheeks, your lips, your breasts . . . Ah," he said, looking lovingly at her breasts, "indeed, those could bring a strong man to his knees." And he lowered his head to suck at each nipple in turn, making her clutch at him.

"It seems to me," she gasped, "that they are my weakest point. They surrender instantly!"

"Point. Yes." And with a wicked grin he applied himself once more, drawing each nipple up high, and driving Aline down into a swirling, fevered pit.

Then he laid her on the bed. When she opened dazed eyes, he was beside her. "But not your weakest point," he said, and slid his hand between her thighs.

"Oh."

"Oh, indeed. I did think you'd have remembered this, love."

She remembered, indeed she did, and so did her body. It began to respond almost immediately, and she spread her thighs without any urging. "Come in to me. Now. I want you in me."

"Soon, love, soon. In good time and proper order. I must make sure first that your defenses are completely disarmed. . . ." He kissed her lips, her neck, her shoulders, sucked on her earlobes, and on both breasts, until she could hardly tell where the pleasure disarming her body came from.

In the midst of impending chaos, Aline had a flash of clarity—that someday very soon she would learn more of these matters and drive him to disintegration just as he so easily did to her. Indeed, she *was* planning an ambush, but she didn't think he'd mind too much.

For the moment it was sweet to surrender without fear to the undoubted touch of a master. His hand gentled as the moment came, drawing it out for her, then his lips sealed hers to catch her cries. Still joined at the mouth, he moved over her.

"Now," he said against her lips, "now you are ready, little castle."

He began to enter her.

The first sensation was exquisite relief to her yearning

flesh, but then came a pain and she couldn't help but stiffen against it.

"Dig your nails in, love. Make me feel it too."

Then he sealed her lips again and broke through her maidenhead in one stroke. Aline shouted into his mouth, and she dug her nails in as hard as she could. It was partly natural reaction, but she also had his words in mind. It seemed only fair that men share the pain.

After a moment he released her lips and grinned. "As bad as that, eh?" He moved slightly within her. "Does that hurt?"

She marveled at his control, for she could see the same tense desire in him as both lingered and gathered in her. "It's nothing. Go on. Please. Go on."

"You are a pearl among women," he whispered, and began to relax his control, moving more strongly, then almost violently, in and out.

It did hurt, and in places other than her torn membrane, but it was wonderful, too, both in her burning body, and in what she saw of him. She grasped his shoulders and raised her legs to lock them around him in an act of sheer, crude possession.

He grimaced as he disintegrated, choking out her name. She trembled, loving every moment of his surrender to her powers.

Collapsing onto his side, he gathered her into his arms, nuzzling at her neck as she cherished his sweaty chest with her hand.

"I think I'm finally conquered," she murmured. "Isn't it lovely?"

"That's because you ambushed me after all. I'm your prisoner for all time."

"Of course." She ran a hand smugly down over his wonderful body. "Isn't that the way it's supposed to be?"

He rolled onto his back, pulling her on top of him so

her breasts were ready to flickering tongue. "I do hope so. I'm a very contented slave. Now, give me your commands. What do you wish me to do, O mistress mine?"

Twenty-three

Galeran approached Heywood this time at a more lei-
surely pace, though his mind was once more full of lovemaking. Tonight, in their new bed, he and Jehanne could
make love as they had not done since his return, but with
Jehanne by his side there was nothing to race to.

They'd lingered in London to see Aline and Raoul sail
off to their new home. There had certainly been nothing
muted about the new couple's happiness, and he hoped it
lasted them all life long.

When Jehanne was healed, they'd begun the slow journey
north again, stopping at various places to visit relatives and
cement alliances.

There'd been sleeping quarters along the way that were
suitable for lovemaking, but he and Jehanne had agreed to
wait. It was like waiting for a wedding, a new start. They'd
start afresh in Heywood, where he had always pictured her.

And now there was Heywood, rising before him as it had
during his dreams in the Holy Land. His home. Home of
all he valued in the world.

Lord William and his men had split off at Brome, and
Hubert's party had separated in Hey Hamlet. Galeran rode
up to Heywood with Jehanne by his side, and no army sat
before his walls. This time, at his approach, the great gates
opened to welcome the lord home, and his people cheered
and smiled.

Jehanne rode beside him, and deliberately, he carried Donata. There was no need to make announcements about what had happened in London, for the story would spread on its own. Everyone would know that Jehanne had suffered for her sin, and been forgiven.

He still wished that had not occurred, but he knew it would make everything easier.

All was restored.

Wasn't it?

Something in his heart denied it.

He dismounted and, Jehanne at his side, entered his keep, where Jehanne took Donata away to be tended by the women. The dogs ran forward, and he greeted them, then took ale to rinse away the dust of the journey.

It could not rinse away a lingering bitter taste.

Jehanne returned to his side, once more the comfortable, efficient lady of her domain, the wife he had longed for through those arid years. Galeran looked around the hall, thinking that perhaps, in a way, everything was the better for their adventures, the more precious for almost having been lost.

And yet . . .

While she spoke to a servant about some minor problem, he wandered into the solar to look at the big new bed. This was what he'd fought for, wasn't it? His peaceful home, his beloved wife, his marriage bed. Idly he picked up an ornament, the ivory rose.

The petal fell off.

Then it hit him like the blow of an ax.

His son.

His son was dead.

Sharp pain made him look at his hand. More white petals were shattered, now touched with red. His blood. Jerusalem.

But the void that engulfed him was not Jerusalem. It was his lost child. His son was nothing. He had no memories— no picture in his mind of a smile, no sounds of a babbling voice. No smell. No feel . . .

For him, Gallot did not exist.

No wonder he'd cut off all who'd tried to speak of the child. No wonder he'd wanted to kill Lowick. It was not so much for the adultery. It was for this. For knowing the son he did not.

He heard Jehanne calling him, but he slipped away, down to kneel in the graveyard by the small stone.

But there was nothing there except a name, nothing in his heart but an emptiness growing larger by the moment, threatening to swallow all the hard-won joy.

A whisper of cloth and a hint of perfume warned him of Jehanne, but he didn't want her here at this moment. She had what he had not.

She had a child in her mind to remember.

Sinking to her knees beside him, she held out a roll of parchment. Courtesy made him take it, though he had no idea what it could be and even less interest. To take it, he had to put down the broken rose. He heard her gasp at the sight of the broken, bloodstained petals, but at this moment he couldn't care that she'd be saddened.

He laid the pieces on the grave beside the bush that bore real roses. Jehanne had real roses. She had memories. He just had shattered ivory.

Because it would be cruel to reject whatever she was offering, he hid his bitterness, untied the ribbon, and un-curled the sheets. A number of sheets with a long knotted string in the middle.

He couldn't help thinking that she'd been extremely wasteful with parchment, but then he read the first words.

On Saint Stephen's Day, in the Blessed Year of Our Lord, 1099, was born at Heywood Castle in Northumbria, Galeran, son of Galeran and Jehanne, his wife, lord and lady of this demesne . . .

He looked at her, seeing tears glimmering in her anxious eyes. "I had the scribe write it. I knew you were missing so much, and I wanted it for you, even though I never suspected . . ."

Heart pounding, he read on.

His length on the day of his birth is to the first knot in the string. All the women say he is a good length and will be a tall man. He breathed quickly and well and moved his bowels on the first day, and though the substance was unpleasant, the wise women say it is good.

Galeran looked a question at her.

"Brother Cyril thought it improper of me to record such things. But it is a strange matter they pass at first. Like something from the bottom of a pond, but sticky."

Galeran counted the sheets. Five of them. "Is it all here?"

"Everything I could think to relate. The bad as well as the good. Like the three nights he kept us all up when he was teething. Like the way he would bounce in time to a drum . . ." Her eyes were still searching his anxiously. "I didn't give it to you sooner because I wasn't sure . . ."

"No. You were right. I wasn't ready. But now . . ." He had no words for what was in his heart. "Now . . . I thank you . . ." Suddenly unable to speak, he gathered her into his arms. "Thank you. Oh, God, thank you."

She held him tight, stroking him. "In a way," she whispered, "I, too, never mourned him properly. It all whirled out of control so fast. . . . If you will, perhaps we can read through this together. And weep together."

He nodded his head against her shoulder, parchment crushed tight in his hand, and prayed that his son—now surely an angel in heaven—intercede for them. Surely they deserved happiness, and the gift to be of benefit to the world. And perhaps, if God was truly good, one day another child, theirs to enjoy in peace and harmony.

Later that night, after tears and laughter, with a picture of his son filling his heart, Galeran made love to his wife. Not as he had dreamed of on the way home from Jerusalem, in a healing blast of released need. Not as they had done since, trying to cobble the tattered fragments of their love together as best they could. But in wonder at each other, that what had been so good could become, through the crucible, a richer, deeper treasure.

Epilogue

Jouray, Guyenne, September 1103

Aline went out of the fortified house that was her home, searching for Raoul, who was somewhere in the fields checking on the grape harvest. She carried little Hubert on her hip, though at just over a year, he was wriggling to get down.

"In a little while, love. I want to find your father and tell him the news."

She hurried down a path edged by flowering bushes. The number and richness of fruits and flowers here still astonished her. There were times when she longed for her bleaker homeland, but not so many. And even if she were homesick, she would never want to be anywhere but near Raoul. She just hoped peace continued so he'd never have to travel far from her.

A silly thought for the wife of a warrior, and one she did not trouble him with except to scold when he injured himself practicing.

As he had just the other day.

She'd deliberately bound his arm so tight, he could hardly move it. He'd grumbled about that, but made it an excuse to lie passively beneath her last night while she inflicted her every whim upon him.

Thinking about it, she chuckled, and Hubert chuckled too.

"Papa!" Hubert called, pointing.

The child had inherited his father's long sight, for there indeed sat Raoul on his horse, overseeing the workers, who were gathering the plump, juicy grapes into baskets.

Some of the previous night's whims had to do with plump, juicy grapes. She did enjoy harvest time. . . .

Aline dragged her mind off such thoughts, or she'd be wanting to seduce her husband in the fields. Again. She'd done that more than once, and would have done it today if it weren't for the child.

Raoul heard his son and waved. In moments he cantered over to them. "Trouble?"

"The very opposite!" Aline waved the letter. "Jehanne was safe delivered of a son three weeks ago."

He swung off his horse and took his son in his arms. "That is good news. Read it to me."

Dearest cousin,

I send you the best and happiest news, that we were blessed with a healthy son on St. Giles's Day. The labor went easily and he was born with the dawn. We have called him Henry, for the king had something to do with our happiness, and his favor could be useful one day. He is not very like Gallot, being dark-haired and -eyed as far as we can tell.

Donata loves her little brother, and calls him Henny. Of course, she wants to hold him all the time, but she is too little yet to do so without supervision. She is bright and mischievous, and everyone says she is just like me at that age. I will have to teach her to think before she acts.

All is peaceful here, God be praised, since the failure of Duke Robert's invasion, and King Henry has established firm law throughout the land. This spring his queen gave birth to their first child, so, God willing, England can look forward to peace and prosperity.

I hope that soon you will travel with one of Raoul's family's ships to Stockton and visit us up here in the bleak north, for I long to see you again, and your child.

Your devoted cousin,
Jehanne of Heywood

Hubert was increasingly restless, so Raoul put him down to explore. "God truly does seem to have smiled upon his people. There were times, you know, when I doubted Galeran and Jehanne would find their way again."

"But they had trust." Aline stepped over to wrap her arm around her husband's waist. "With trust, anything is possible. Have I told you I trust you?"

He kissed her. "Every day, in every way. As I trust you." A wicked twinkle entered his eye, warning and exciting her. "In fact, I might trust you enough to let you tie me up."

"Tie you up!" She stared at him, growing hot at the thought. "Er . . . is that a hint?"

"Perhaps. Or perhaps it's a warning. Since you trust me. Why don't you go back to the house and plan your strategy while I sit and contemplate sweet, plump, juicy grapes?"

Aline watched him ride away, even more tempted to ravish him in the fields, then picked up her son and hurried home, making plans, and very much looking forward to the coming night.

Author's Note

First: What's true and what's not?

The historical facts in this novel are as accurate as I could make them. However, I couldn't find any information about what happened in London in the early days of the reign of Henry I, so I made it up!

Ranulph Flambard was a real person, however, and as far as I was able, realistically portrayed here. He rose from obscurity in the service of William the Conqueror, hitting the highest point of his career under William's son, William II (Rufus). Contemporary accounts of him are confusing, with some writers crediting him with charm and cleverness, and others with unmitigated evil. He surely was extremely clever, and probably needed charm to stay on the right side of the kings. It seems clear he was entirely without scruples, and avariciously ambitious.

Under William Rufus, Flambard ended up virtually running the country and being extremely unpopular. There does seem to have been an attempt to kill him by capturing him and taking him out to sea. It's difficult to imagine how he avoided death, but as the story goes he talked his way out of a ship full of pirates and armed enemies, so perhaps he did have a great deal of charm and cleverness!

There's no record of when Flambard became a priest, but in 1099 Rufus made him Bishop of Durham. Though Canterbury, York, and London were the bishoprics of greatest religious importance, Durham held the most land—most of the north of England, in fact. Flambard was now a powerful baron. How infuriated he must have been when his royal patron so carelessly got killed only a year later.

Henry Beauclerk, who, as I say in the book, wanted the Crown of England almost from the day of his birth, was quick to dissociate himself from his brother's most unpopular creation. He imprisoned Flambard in the Tower. Though contemporaries record the joy at this act, no one states the reason for the imprisonment, so in my story I've provided Henry with the excuse he must have needed. There's no indication in history that the bishop was beaten or harmed in any way.

In late 1100 or early 1101, Flambard apparently got his guards drunk at a banquet, then escaped from the Tower by climbing down a rope smuggled in to him in a wine cask. (At times it's difficult not to admire Ranulph's style!) He fled to Normandy, to Henry's brother, Duke Robert, who promptly gave him great power, and Ranulph organized Robert's attempt to invade and seize the Crown of England.

That attempt failed, however, and Ranulph began to woo Henry, soon achieving a pardon. Within a few years he was back in England, restored to his bishopric in Durham, and doubtless finding ways to squeeze money for the king. True to his promise in the book, however, Henry had broken the great power of the diocese of Durham, so it wasn't the prize it once was. Also, Henry was himself a shrewd and able administrator with his own hand-picked "household" of legal and financial experts, so Ranulph Flambard never regained the kind of power he had held under William Rufus. Flambard died in 1128.

A note about literacy, since it's a subject I sometimes get letters about. This is a hotly debated topic, but I side with those who believe that many nobles in the Middle Ages could read after a fashion, women more than men. It was considered a suitable skill for women, but a potentially weakening one for fighting men.

Writing, however, is a physical skill requiring a lot of practice to do well. Add the technical difficulties of writing on parchment or vellum with fragile pens and homemade inks, and it is reasonable to believe that people would use scribes just as executives used to use typists.

Now, on to time.

Before clocks—and clocks as we know them are hundreds of years in the future—most people did not reckon time in hours and minutes. They went by the sun and the church bells, and most churches and religious houses were going by the sun anyway by using sundials.

Early sundials made no allowance for the seasonal change in the sun's position and angle. This wasn't stupidity; it was because time was only needed to reflect the reality of people's lives, and lives changed in harmony with the seasons.

So, in fact, time was flexible.

Theoretically, the day was divided into eight equal portions marked by specific prayers. Matins was midnight, lauds was three A.M., etc. In winter, when nights were long, the time periods—read from sundials—meant that prime (meaning *first* in Latin, or daybreak) would be about eight A.M. and vespers (meaning *evening*) at about four P.M.

But in summer, when nights were short and days long, prime would be about four A.M. and vespers at around nine P.M. (And incidentally, in religious houses matins and lauds were usually said—i.e., prayed—together, so that people did get at least four hours of uninterrupted sleep.)

These time divisions, marked by prayer and bells, provided the rhythm for medieval life. They are called the canonical hours, and are as follows, with their approximate modern equivalent:

  prime—six A.M.
  terce—nine A.M.
  sext—noon
  none—three P.M.
  vespers—six P.M.
  compline—nine P.M.
  matins—midnight
  lauds—three A.M.

You'll see that they counted the day hours from one (prime) through to nine (none) with vespers signaling the end of most workdays. More logical really than our system, which has the day starting when nearly everyone is fast asleep!

Did you spot him? Those of you who have read my previous books will have recognized FitzRoger, the king's champion. He is the hero of an earlier book, *Dark Champion,* though that book actually takes place after this one.

The Normans in England not forty years after the Conquest were a small, tight-knit community.

I enjoy hearing from readers, and send out an occasional newsletter or other mailing. Please write to: Jo Beverley, c/o Alice Orr Agency, 305 Madison Ave. #1166, New York, NY 10165. An SASE is appreciated to help with the cost of a reply. Or you can contact me on the Internet at ab439@freenet.carleton.ca or as Jo.B on GEnie.

My books to date. Please note that not all are available new, and that they rarely turn up used. You should be able to order some through your favorite bookseller, however, and I've marked them with a star.

Traditional Regencies:

*Lord Wraybourne's Betrothed; The Stanforth Secrets; The Stolen Bride; *Emily and the Dark Angel; *The Fortune Hunter; *Deirdre and Don Juan

The Company of Rogues Regencies:
*An Arranged Marriage; An Unwilling Bride; Christmas Angel; *Forbidden; *Dangerous Joy*
The Mallorens (Georgian):
*My Lady Notorious; *Tempting Fortune*
Medievals:
*Lord of My Heart; *Dark Champion*

WATCH FOR THESE HOT ROMANCES
NEXT MONTH

PROMISE ME   (0-8217-5336-3, $4.99)
by Elaine Kane
Deidre Ramsey, new Countess of Ramshead, is the lonely mistress of
a barren ancestral estate. The tender promises of seductive Jared
Montgomery, Marquess of Jersey and society's most eligible bachelor,
are most tempting. But then Deidre learns the truth—Jared has secretly
wanted Ramshead all along. Dare she trust he covets her as well?

GENTLE HEARTS   (0-8217-5337-1, $4.99)
by Clara Wimberly
As the Civil War raged, Lida Rinehart was content in her simple Amish
world. But when her brother dies helping a slave escape to freedom,
she struggles to carry on his mission with the help of John Sexton. An
outsider to her people's ways and a threat to all she believes, John awak-
ens Lida's desire and demands what she is forbidden to give: her love.

NO PLACE FOR A LADY   (0-8217-5334-7, $4.99)
by Vivian Vaughan
Spoiling for reform, suffragette Maddie Sinclair hasn't counted on the
complication of sinfully handsome Tyler Grant having a mission of his
own. The six-foot-tall hunk has secretly sworn revenge against Maddie's
brother, and she fits perfectly into his scheme. Falling in love could
prove disastrous, as warring passions heat up for a showdown that could
set one incendiary town and two blazing hearts—on fire.

HEARTS VICTORIOUS   (0-8217-5335-5, $4.99)
by Marian Edwards
Bethany of North Umberland is the beloved mistress of Renwyg castle
until she is suddenly stripped of power and imprisoned, slave to Norman
conqueror Royce de Bellemare. Determined to outwit her captor, she
soon finds that when it comes to her seductive enemy, passion has no
allegiance.

*Available wherever paperbacks are sold, or order direct from the
Publisher. Send cover price plus 50¢ per copy for mailing and handling to Penguin USA, P.O. Box 999, c/o Dept. 17109, Bergen-
field, NJ 07621. Residents of New York and Tennessee must
include sales tax. DO NOT SEND CASH.*